A Very Merry Detour

A Very Merry Detour

A Novel

COURT BEHR

THE DIAL PRESS
NEW YORK

The Dial Press
An imprint of Random House
A division of Penguin Random House LLC
1745 Broadway, New York, NY 10019
randomhousebooks.com
penguinrandomhouse.com

A Dial Press Trade Paperback Original

ISBN 978-0-593-97902-0
Ebook ISBN 978-0-593-97903-7

Printed in the United States of America

1st Printing

BOOK TEAM: Production editor: Michelle Daniel • Managing editor: Leah Sims • Production manager: Meghan O'Leary • Copy editor: Faren Bachelis • Proofreaders: Debbie Anderson, Dawn Davis, Alicia Hyman, Taylor McGowan, Taylor Teague

ADOBE STOCK ART: Lala (Winter/Christmas ornaments)

Book design by Sara Bereta

The authorized representative in the EU for product safety and compliance is Penguin Random House Ireland, Morrison Chambers, 32 Nassau Street, Dublin D02 YH68, Ireland.
https://eu-contact.penguin.ie

For my darling

A Very Merry Detour

Chapter One

Seven Days Until Christmas

If someone had asked Alaina where she would be a week before Christmas, she would've said snuggled up with her boyfriend on the couch, watching a rom-com, drinking eggnog, and enjoying the holidays for the first time in a decade.

She would not have said stuck in a snowbank in the middle of god-knows-where, Utah, after swerving to avoid what she definitely thought was a deer on the pitch-black road.

And yet, there she was, just after midnight, her beat-up Toyota half swallowed by snow. Reversing had only spun her tires deeper, and the drift on her right was piled so high she couldn't see out the passenger window. She'd tried a quick expedition outside, the cold cutting through her hoodie the second she'd opened her door and stepped into the dark. Her headlights were useless, smothered by the drift she'd plowed into, casting only a faint, murky glow. With no shovel and zero plan, she'd managed maybe three minutes of clawing at the snow with her bare hands before retreating, fingers numb and stinging.

Normally she'd call Cole. Not an option anymore. And with

her phone reading SOS instead of even one bar of service, she was truly on her own.

What had that Instagram reel said to do in this exact scenario? Leave the car running? Or turn it off in case the tailpipe got blocked?

Shit, shit, shit. Alaina put her head down on the steering wheel.

This was so stupid. She was out here chasing a guy who didn't even know if he wanted her, armed with a half-baked plan to prove they were a perfect match, and now she was going to die alone in her car.

A sharp knock rattled her window.

Alaina's head shot up, her whole body going rigid. Slowly, she turned. Headlights lit the road, barely visible through the heavy snow. A person stood in their glow, face obscured by a thick black scarf and fur-lined hat pulled tight. Just a silhouette.

This was it. She was going to be taken out by an ax murderer during a blizzard in the middle of nowhere. Classic.

Then the stranger raised a gloved hand, and because she was apparently incapable of self-preservation, Alaina waved back. Although, what kind of killer waved at their victim before chopping them into bite-sized pieces? A friendly wave had to be a good sign.

The hand motioned for Alaina to get out. She hesitated, then glanced around the inside of her car. Not much worth taking. She grabbed her phone and stared at the lock screen. It was a photo of her and Cole at the carnival, her curly brown hair windswept and wild at the top of the Ferris wheel. She looked like a mess, but Cole looked like a model, so it became her phone background anyway.

Alaina tucked the phone, along with her keys, into the pocket of her still-damp hoodie. Bracing herself, she swung the door open. An ambush of cold slapped her in the face.

"Holy shit." She laughed, because what else was there to do? She'd been in her apartment in San Francisco ten hours ago. Now she was about to follow a stranger through a snowstorm. Possibly to her doom.

"Come on." The voice was soft, almost lost in the wind. Definitely a woman. Maybe British? Or Australian? "Before you freeze to death."

Alaina followed her, boots crunching through snow, toward the other vehicle. She hadn't even heard it pull up. Snow seeped into her Converses with each step, drenching her socks and chilling her to the core. She hugged herself tightly and pushed forward, barely able to see past her own eyelashes.

The woman led her to the passenger door of a pickup truck. She yanked the handle, and a fierce gust of wind flung the door open, slamming it straight into Alaina's shoulder.

"Fuck!" She staggered back, nearly slipping, then felt a firm hand on her back, steadying her. Even hunched against the wind, the woman stood a few inches taller than Alaina. Then again, at five foot two, Alaina found most people did.

"Careful," the stranger said. With surprising strength, she ushered Alaina up and into the cab, then closed the door behind her.

Alaina looked at her car, stranded ten feet from the road and rapidly disappearing under snow. A deep chill ran through her, and not just because she was practically a human Popsicle. If this was how she felt after a few trapped minutes, she would've been frozen solid by morning.

She pried her hands from her armpits and held them up to the warm air streaming through the vents. Her fingers throbbed as feeling crept back in. The driver's door opened, bringing another burst of frigid cold. Alaina swore under her breath.

The stranger climbed in, peeling back the furry hat to reveal dark brown hair tied into a neat bun. The scarf came off next, finally revealing the face underneath.

The woman looked to be in her late twenties, maybe thirty. Serious expression. Sharp jaw. Freckles dusted her cheekbones like someone had painted them on with a fine brush. Her eyes were warm brown, ringed with gold, like melted honey. Why were Alaina's muddy eyes so boring, when eyes as fascinating as these existed?

It took Alaina a moment to realize she was being spoken to.

"Huh?" She blinked.

The woman's mouth pulled tight. Her first flicker of emotion. "What were you thinking?" she said. "You would've been buried in an hour if I hadn't driven by. Did you not see the news?"

"I—I didn't know there was going to be a storm." Alaina's teeth clacked as she spoke. "I'm not from around here."

"Clearly. No one from around here would be out in this weather."

"*You're* out in this weather."

The woman's brow creased. She turned to the road, shook her head, and wordlessly adjusted the vents toward Alaina. Warm air blasted her face. Her lashes started to thaw, her body giving a grateful shiver.

"Thanks, by the way." Grumpy or not, the woman had rescued her. "You totally saved my ass."

"Language," the woman snapped.

Alaina's eyebrows shot up. "You're kidding." One look at her face and—nope, not kidding. Okay then. Alaina raised her hands. "Sorry."

The woman reached for the gearshift.

"Wait!" Alaina lurched forward.

"What?" The word shot out, sharp as a cat's claw.

"We can't just leave Bertha here."

Alaina's eyes darted to the snowbank, where the Corolla's trunk still peeked out. She'd christened the car the day she handed a wad of cash to a chain-smoking, heavily perfumed woman in a Ralphs parking lot years ago. Since then, Bertha had faithfully carried her through thick and thin; she couldn't just abandon her now.

"Who is—"

"My car. Don't you have, like, a shovel or something?"

The stranger's eyebrows knitted together. "The snow's coming down faster than we could ever dig out."

"Can't we call for help?"

"And make someone else come out in this mess?" Her voice was flat, unyielding. "It's too dangerous."

"But—*ugh*. Fine."

With that, the woman eased the truck onto the road. Alaina twisted in her seat, watching Bertha shrink in the rearview until she disappeared entirely. She made a silent vow to return as soon as this blizzard let up.

She slumped back, fingers instinctively reaching to fidget with the golden chain around her neck. Her eyes drifted across the truck's interior—an older model, with a simple dashboard. No bells, no whistles. Nothing like Cole's tricked-out pickup. The seats were worn leather, comfortable and soft.

Not a single wrapper on the floor. No crumpled receipts or empty bottles. Spotless.

A prickle of shame crept up Alaina's spine. This woman had just seen the inside of her own car, which was nowhere near as tidy. She wasn't sure why she cared—she had much bigger problems than whether or not this stranger thought she was a slob.

"Where are we going?" Alaina asked.

"There's a hotel not far from here." The woman kept her eyes on the road as the truck rolled forward. "Figure you'd rather sleep somewhere that's not a tin box in a snow squall."

"I definitely would." Just the thought of heat and a bed loosened the knot in her shoulders. "I'm Alaina, by the way. Or Lani, to my friends—and rescuers."

Silence. The woman drummed her fingers against the steering wheel as the truck crawled forward. With enough caffeine, a sloth could've beaten their pace, but at least they wouldn't spin out into another ditch.

"Nice to meet you too," Alaina muttered. Gratitude aside, she did wish her knight in shining armor were slightly more . . . well, charming.

"Alaina," the woman repeated, her now-clearly British accent stretching the vowels into something softer.

At least she was nice to listen to.

"Yes?"

The woman blinked, like she hadn't realized she'd spoken aloud. "What are you doing out here?"

Chasing the love of her life. The answer sat ready on the tip of her tongue, but it was too pathetic to say out loud, even if it was true. The thought of Cole had her insides contorting into shapes so twisted a balloon artist might as well have taken up residence in her stomach.

"I'm . . . on a road trip. An adventure. Seeing the sights."

"That sounds dangerous."

"It's not." Alaina huffed, sliding down in her seat. "I can fend for myself."

The woman didn't respond, but Alaina saw her eyebrows rise.

"Right, okay," she said, wincing. "But, like, *besides* this, I would've been totally fine."

The woman regarded her briefly before shifting her eyes back to the road, skillfully navigating a curve despite the ice-slick pavement.

Alaina rolled her eyes. All she wanted now was a hot shower. Maybe a Swiss Miss packet with the tiny marshmallows.

"How far is this hotel?"

"Just up ahead."

They fell into silence. A few minutes later, warm light glowed through the falling snow. It was a hotel—the Mountainview Inn, judging by the sign illuminated in the headlights. The log exterior looked rustic. Quaint. Someplace she definitely wouldn't mind staying the night.

The truck came to a stop at the front entrance. The woman turned to her and frowned. Again.

"You didn't bring anything warmer?"

"No." Alaina crossed her arms, in both defiance and an attempt to keep warm. The oversized USC hoodie was Cole's, one of many she might have to give back if this whole plan blew up in her face. She'd planned on staying in her car most of the drive from San Francisco to New York. "I didn't exactly know I'd be stranded in a blizzard."

There was a pause, then a sigh. "Here."

Something heavy landed on Alaina's head. Feeling around, she realized it was the woman's trapper hat. It was warm and soft, and smelled of citrus and cinnamon. Her mood lifted instantly.

"You know," Alaina said, adjusting it, "I've always wanted one of these. Very . . . lumberjack chic."

The woman gave her a strange look, as if trying to decide whether Alaina was serious or maybe suffering from some sort of hypothermia-induced delirium. Then she exited the truck, closed her door, and walked toward the entrance without a word.

Alaina scrambled out after her.

The inn was straight out of one of those holiday rom-coms Alaina guiltlessly binged each December. Twinkling lights, a towering Christmas tree in the corner, garland looped artfully above a crackling woodstove. It smelled like pine and firewood and maybe fresh cookies if she was being optimistic. They probably had a top-tier continental breakfast.

"Priscilla!" called a smiling woman behind the front desk.

Priscilla. The name fit her. Proper and elegant.

"Callie," Priscilla said, smiling for the first time since Alaina had met her. Warmth filled her voice.

Callie came around the counter and hugged her. Hugged. Priscilla. Not a quick one-arm pat—this was a full-on long embrace. Alaina hesitated near the doorway.

"It's good to see you. It's been a while." Priscilla was still smiling as she pulled back.

Callie raised her eyebrows. "A while? It's been weeks! We tried calling."

"I've been busy—"

"And texting."

"Yes, well." Priscilla cleared her throat, glancing back at Alaina.

Callie seemed to notice they weren't alone for the first time. "Oh! Who's this?"

"This is Alaina." The warmth vanished from Priscilla's tone like someone had hit a switch.

Alaina stepped forward, and Callie offered her hand. "I'm Callie. It's so nice to meet you!"

Now this was someone Alaina could feel comfortable

around. Deep green eyes, bushy red hair, a sweet smile—a smile that morphed into a gasp when her warm hand wrapped around Alaina's freezing fingers.

"My goodness!" Callie covered Alaina's hand with both of hers. "You're freezing!"

"She was caught in the storm." Priscilla nodded toward the snow still piling up outside. "Car's stuck out on Brooks Canyon. She needs a place to stay."

Alaina had to hide her surprise that Priscilla hadn't taken the opportunity to mention, for the millionth time in their twenty-minute acquaintance, how incredibly stupid it was of Alaina to be out in this weather.

"I'm so sorry." Callie's eyes softened, full of genuine regret. She gave Alaina's still-cold hands a gentle squeeze. "We're all booked up."

"What? Here?" Alaina couldn't keep the disbelief out of her voice, the vision of a cozy night in the lodge slipping through her fingers. They were in the middle of Nowheresville, Utah. How could they not have any vacancies?

Priscilla's lips pressed into a line. As if reading Alaina's mind, she said, "It's a ski town. We get a lot of tourists this time of year." She locked eyes with Callie, desperation evident in her gaze. "Callie, please. You have to have something."

Callie shook her head. "You know if I did it'd be yours, Sil. I'm sorry."

Sil. The nickname shot a crack through Priscilla's cool, polished veneer. It made her seem . . . human.

Alaina didn't have long to marvel before panic set in. Her car was stuck in a snowbank, she was in the middle of god-knows-where, and she had no place to spend the night. Add all that to the fact that her heart was hanging on by a string, and Alaina was having a very bad time.

"All right." Priscilla sighed before leveling Alaina with a long, hard stare. "I guess you're going to have to stay with me."

For a moment, Alaina could only blink in response, her mouth falling open in surprise. "With you?"

"Yes." Priscilla's eyebrow arched, a silent, challenging lift. "Unless you have a better offer?"

Alaina blinked again, then gave a quick shake of her head. "No, definitely not, but . . . are you sure? I feel like you've already done too much for me, and—"

"I'm sure," Priscilla said, cutting her off. "See you later, Callie. Stop by the shop soon, won't you?"

"Only if you promise to actually answer your phone sometime," Callie shot back. "But yes, of course. I'll come by later this week to get a present for Lauren."

Chapter Two

The truck rumbled back onto the road, headlights cutting through the snow as Priscilla steered them carefully forward. The cab was warm enough, but Alaina's nerves wouldn't settle. It wasn't that she wasn't grateful. Being rescued from a snowbank and offered a place to sleep made her top-ten list of things to appreciate. It was the rescuer herself who unsettled her. Priscilla's quiet, steady presence made Alaina painfully aware of her own chaos—damp hair dripping into her hood, her still-chattering teeth, the way her hands wouldn't stop fidgeting in her lap. Priscilla's composure should have been reassuring, but instead it left Alaina feeling like a drowned rat sitting next to a marble statue with cheekbones sharp enough to cut.

Maybe knowing literally anything about her host would help. "So . . ." Alaina's fingers drummed against her thigh. "Have you lived here a long time?"

"Almost ten years," Priscilla said without looking away from the road.

That was it. No explanation, no follow-up.

Fine. Alaina loved a challenge. "Where are you from?"

"A lot of places." Alaina nearly rolled her eyes. Nonanswer of the century. Priscilla must have realized it wasn't satisfactory, at least, because she added, "I moved around a lot as a kid."

Alaina looked at Priscilla, watching the way her fingers tensed around the steering wheel. She knew that feeling—the inability to claim one place as *home.* At least that was one thing she could relate to about Priscilla.

"How . . . mysterious," Alaina said. Priscilla glanced over, and Alaina flashed one of her go-to smiles, the kind that usually chipped away at even the iciest exteriors. "Is there a *Mr.* Tall, Dark, and Mysterious in the picture?"

Something flickered across Priscilla's face. It was gone before Alaina could pin it down.

"No."

Alaina's smile wilted. She sank deeper into her seat. Was she making a fool of herself by trying to get this woman to warm up to her? Probably. But that didn't mean she would stop. She needed a distraction from everything going wrong in her life, and unraveling a mystifying stranger seemed like just the thing to lift her mood.

"Where do you live?"

"Not far. Another ten minutes with this snow, probably." Her eyes cut sideways. "You're shaking."

Priscilla slowed to a stop right in the middle of the road. Not that there was much road to speak of, the pavement completely hidden under snow. She activated her hazards and twisted around, rummaging behind her seat, then turned back with a heavy blanket that she dropped into Alaina's lap.

Alaina's fingers traced the herringbone pattern, the wool's softness surprising her. "Wow. This is gorgeous."

Her hands were trembling too much to unfold it, so Priscilla reached over and did it for her.

"How long were you out there? You're freezing." She tucked the blanket around Alaina's shoulders. "You should have said something sooner."

Alaina scoffed, curling into the warmth. "You're the one who's been hiding this beauty this whole time."

Priscilla frowned but kept adjusting the blanket. "Yes, well, I travel prepared. Unlike some people."

Alaina should have been offended, but she saw the perfect opportunity. "Ice burn. Get it? Like nice burn, but—"

"I get it." Priscilla's voice was dry as she put her hands back on the wheel.

Alaina didn't say anything else for the rest of the drive. She figured Priscilla would just tell her to conserve her energy or something equally joyless. Instead, she stayed quiet, letting herself relax, swaddled in wool and silence.

Alaina didn't even register that they'd stopped until Priscilla turned the key in the ignition, killing the engine.

"This is it," Priscilla said. She was watching Alaina with narrowed eyes. "You all right? Can you feel your toes?"

Alaina gave them an experimental wiggle. "All good."

Without warning, Priscilla started shrugging out of her coat. "Here, you'll need this. No use in warming you up just to have you freeze again."

Alaina shook her head. "I already have your hat. You need it more than me."

Priscilla's eyes hardened. "I definitely do not."

Alaina's stomach did an involuntary flip. Had she missed something? Had her lips gone blue without her realizing?

Priscilla stepped out into the snow, vanishing for a moment before reappearing on Alaina's side of the car. She opened the door and extended an arm, guiding her out of the truck with ease. The strength in her grip was surprisingly solid.

"Which way?" Alaina shouted over the wind.

No answer. Priscilla hunched her shoulders and trudged forward through the snow. She led Alaina around a brick building toward a glass storefront. It didn't look like the sort of place someone would live, but Alaina was too cold to care. Shelter was shelter.

She ducked her head, shielding her face from the icy snowfall. A lock clicked, and she followed Priscilla inside.

Tall wooden shelves filled with books lined the walls of a sizable room, complete with old-fashioned rolling ladders. Shorter shelves split the space into winding aisles. A worn armchair waited by the front window, bathed in the faint glow of a streetlamp.

Alaina's mouth dropped open. "This is a bookstore."

Priscilla shot her a look. "What gave it away?"

Her tone was sharp, but Alaina barely registered it. Wonder overrode everything else.

"You live in a *bookstore*?"

"I live *above* a bookstore," Priscilla said. "My bookstore. I own this place."

The store had a classic, charming feel, like it had been here for decades. She could easily picture customers browsing the shelves and stopping to pull out a title that caught their eye. She could also picture Priscilla behind the counter at the other end of the store, greeting patrons and recommending books they'd never even heard of but would probably love.

"Wow." Alaina stepped farther inside, the old hardwood floors creaking a welcome beneath her feet. "It's beautiful."

Something soft flickered in Priscilla's expression. She tilted her head toward the back of the store. "Come on. You can look around in the morning if you'd like. You must be tired."

Alaina nodded, following her through the maze of shelves.

Her body sagged with exhaustion, feet dragging. At last they reached a spiral staircase behind the counter.

The stairs might as well have been Mount Everest. She gripped the railing, hauling her half-frozen limbs up the narrow steps after Priscilla, trying not to look like a total mess. Priscilla, cool as ever, reached the top and stopped at a door, fingers sorting through a ring of keys she'd unclipped from her belt loops. The lock clicked open and they walked inside.

Alaina had expected something minimalist. Sleek. Cold. But the apartment was cluttered in a cozy, lived-in way. The room they were standing in was large, a kitchen in one corner, a dining table buried in books in another, and a living room area with an old, floral-patterned couch near the entrance, a large lamp on a side table lighting the space with a warm glow. The wall to her right had two doors—one, Alaina assumed, was a bedroom, and the other, Alaina hoped, was a bathroom. The idea of hot running water sent a sudden burst of energy through her.

"Do you have somewhere I could freshen up?"

Without a word, Priscilla pointed toward the first door.

In the bathroom, Alaina caught sight of herself in the mirror and nearly screamed.

Frizzy hair swept in all directions by the wind. Skin chapped from the cold. Eyes bloodshot and swollen.

She looked like she'd been through a blender. A very cold, vindictive blender.

She raked her fingers through her hair, resisting the urge to rifle through the drawers for a hair tie. Instead, she cupped warm water in her hands and splashed her face until she felt vaguely human again.

When she was done, she still looked like hell. Just slightly less frozen.

It wasn't like Priscilla would care. Still, something about

being this much of a mess in front of someone so composed made her cheeks burn redder than they already were from the cold.

"Come on, Lani," she muttered to herself. "It's a night on a stranger's couch, not a *Vogue* photo shoot."

She took a breath and opened the door.

Priscilla was waiting in the kitchen. When the door to the bathroom creaked open, Priscilla's eyes found Alaina's immediately.

"Feeling better?"

"Much."

"Good."

Priscilla pushed off the counter, taking a hesitant step toward her. When was the last time she'd had a stranger in her space? Judging by Priscilla's rigid posture, Alaina guessed never.

Priscilla cleared her throat. "Do you want something warm to drink? Decaf? Tea?"

Alaina tilted her head as she considered her options. "Do you have any hot cocoa?"

An inscrutable expression flickered across Priscilla's face.

"Or tea," she said hurriedly. "Tea is good too." She could have guessed Priscilla wouldn't have hot chocolate. Priscilla struck her as the kind of person who was meticulously stingy about her sugar intake.

Alaina shuffled the short distance from the bathroom to the couch, legs barely holding her up. It wasn't a bed, but it beat a night out in the cold. She sank into the cushions with a quiet groan, let her eyes slip shut, and listened. Cabinet doors opening. Water running. The low hum of a kettle starting to boil. The soft, domestic rhythm of someone else's home.

She must've dozed off, because the next thing she heard was: "Here you are."

Her eyes blinked open. Priscilla stood before her holding two mugs, one crowned with an indecent amount of whipped cream.

"Oh my god, yes." Alaina took the mug meant for her, its heat soaking into her fingers. Her eyes fluttered closed again at the feeling, and a sigh escaped her lips. "Thank you. This is everything I've ever wanted."

When she opened her eyes, Priscilla was watching her with a neutral expression. Then—just for a second—a half smile tugged at her lips. Small. Tentative.

Alaina made herself a promise then and there that by the time she left here tomorrow, she was going to earn an honest-to-god grin from this woman.

Priscilla raised her own mug to her lips. "You seem like the sort of person who would like whipped cream."

Alaina narrowed her eyes. "What's that supposed to mean?"

"Nothing."

Sure, okay. She considered asking why Priscilla had whipped cream in her fridge if she thought it was beneath her, but bit her tongue. Instead, she leaned back into the couch and switched tactics.

"So, now that we're *warming up* to each other . . ."

Alaina waggled her eyebrows, holding up her steaming mug for emphasis. Priscilla's shoulders tensed, her eyes narrowing. But there it was again, the slight curl at the edge of her mouth.

". . . you should tell me about yourself."

She took a big sip of cocoa, warmth pooling in her chest, radiating outward.

"There's not much to say." Priscilla looked down, fingers tracing the rim of her mug. "What do you want to know?"

"Anything. Everything." Alaina leaned forward, her elbows on her knees. "We're stuck together, at least for tonight. We should be friends."

"Friends," Priscilla repeated, like the word tasted strange.

"Surely you've heard of those?" Alaina said, her chin lifting slightly.

She *had*. Alaina had seen the proof with her own eyes—how easily Priscilla accepted Callie's hug and good-natured ribbing. Callie liked Priscilla enough to miss her.

"I suppose I have," Priscilla said, as if she were contemplating the stock market and not interpersonal relationships. "Should I start braiding the friendship bracelets now, or . . . ?"

A laugh burst out of Alaina, then melted into a yawn midbreath.

Priscilla stood, placing her mug on the coffee table—on a coaster, naturally. "You should get some rest. We'll figure out what to do with your car—"

"Bertha," Alaina said.

"—with Bertha in the morning."

Alaina felt tempted to persuade Priscilla to stay up a little longer. Another hour and she might get a laugh, maybe even a full smile. But then another yawn clawed its way out of her, and she gave in.

"Sleep does sound pretty good right about now."

Priscilla left her for a moment, going into the other room and emerging with a pillow, flannel sheets, and a fuzzy blanket she set on top of the couch. She also had a pair of pajamas that she offered to Alaina. "You can change in the bathroom."

Was Priscilla afraid she might just strip down right there in the living room? Alaina was so tired the idea wasn't entirely unappealing, but she took the pajamas and retreated to the privacy of the bathroom without another word, locking the door before taking off her soggy clothes.

Alaina pulled on the pajamas, feeling the weight of the day lift just a bit. Priscilla's clothes were large on her, which wasn't surprising given their height difference. It just made them all the more cozy. When she came out, Priscilla was tucking sheets under the couch cushions. Alaina watched, amused. She would've just thrown the blanket down and collapsed face-first. But Priscilla's methodical approach was . . . well, sweet. In her own tightly wound, emotionally repressed way.

"There." Priscilla slipped the final corner into place and straightened. "Do you need anything else?"

Alaina reached down, running her fingers along the soft fleece blanket Priscilla had laid out for her. "This is perfect, thanks."

Priscilla stepped back. "Good night."

Alaina gave her a nod and a small smile. "Night."

She stood until Priscilla shut her bedroom door behind her, but didn't climb into the makeshift bed right away. Instead, she wandered around the apartment, her curiosity getting the better of her despite her exhaustion.

The space was small enough to explore in a matter of minutes, but Alaina took her time. On one wall was a set of photos. Alaina recognized Callie from the inn standing with a few other people. There were several pictures of this group through the years. In one photo, a younger Priscilla was wedged between Callie and a dark-haired guy, her head thrown back midlaugh, caught in a moment of real, unfiltered joy. Alaina stepped closer, trying to reconcile that version of Priscilla with the closed-off woman who'd rescued her from the snow.

Another photo in the same frame showed the trio drenched from rain, or perhaps from an ill-advised jump into the lake in the background, grinning despite their soaking-wet clothes.

Then, in the center, an outlier.

This photo was older, frayed around the edges with a smoothed-out crease in one corner. What caught Alaina's eye wasn't just the tiny Priscilla in a tutu, but the woman holding her. Same jawline. Same eyes. Her smile was gentle but distant, with the exact restrained softness Alaina had seen flicker across Priscilla's face earlier tonight.

A dull ache tugged at her ribs.

She thought back to high school, to her first role in the spring musical. She'd had three whole lines, and she practiced in the bathroom mirror until they were perfect. She remembered peeking through the curtains at all the faces, parents with camcorders poised, ready to capture every syllable.

Her aunt had said she would come. But Alaina's cousin Shauna had a playoff game that went into overtime that same night, and priorities were priorities.

The worst part had come after, in the lobby. All her classmates' parents wrapped them in congratulatory hugs while she stood there alone, pretending to check her phone. She hated the pity in their eyes when they realized no one was there for her.

She hadn't auditioned for anything again until college, when her roommate practically dragged her into the theater. It was easier there, where no one knew her. She wasn't the girl with the dead mom. She could just be Alaina.

She shook off the memory and forced her attention back to her self-guided tour of Priscilla's life. There were a few other telling details around the apartment. The shelves in the corner were lined with books, each title facing the same direction, the edges of their spines arranged in a perfectly straight line. No dishes sat in the sink aside from the mugs they'd just used, and Alaina made a mental note that she should take care of those in the morning. It was the least she could do.

Priscilla's life was neat, tidy.

Alaina was probably the messiest thing she'd let in for a long, long time.

A crucifix hung above the entryway, catching Alaina off guard. She stared at it for a second, blinking slowly. Was that why Priscilla had snapped at her for swearing earlier? She couldn't remember the last time she'd met someone her age who was actively religious. Then again, Priscilla didn't exactly scream "typical millennial." She seemed like the type who had always been a little out of step with the rest of the world.

Alaina's curiosity was finally losing its fight against her exhaustion. She sank into the couch like her bones had been waiting all day for this exact moment.

When she pulled out her phone, she groaned.

Two percent battery.

"Seriously? Is today National Kick Alaina While She's Down Day?" she muttered, eyeing the outlets in Priscilla's apartment for a stray charger. No such luck.

Notifications flooded the screen. More than a dozen texts from Nico, her roommate and arguably her only real friend these days. She'd missed the messages thanks to the blackout of service and the automatic do-not-disturb mode that kicked on whenever she was in a moving car.

10:30 p.m.: this lo mein you left in the fridge is still good right?

10:42: heated it up, it's delishhhh

11:01: can't believe you left me here to eat leftover chinese alone to chase after a dumb boy

11:57: um alaina?

11:57: why does your find my say you've been stopped on some side road in utah for twenty minutes?

11:58: ok maybe you just lost service

11:59: i'll try to remain calm

12:02 a.m.: there better be a hotel there that isn't showing up on google

12:04: just looked on street view and there DEF isn't a holiday inn there

12:06: oh good, you're moving!!

12:15: you okay???

12:18: lani???????

12:22: ALAINA DAVIS ANSWER ME!!

12:32: you better be ok. i do NOT want to have to give an interview to some true crime podcaster about how your smile lit up every room

12:33: i mean, it does, but still

1:04: seriously babe, i'm getting worried. call me when you get a chance.

Guilt twisted in her stomach. She hadn't meant to worry Nico. Her battery dropped to 1 percent.

She tapped out a message quickly.

1:14 a.m.: Oh my god hi!! Sorry!! My phone is like seconds from dying but I'm okay. I did have a little... well, a tiiiiny crash, but I was rescued by a very kind stranger and now I'm staying on her couch until we can get my car out of the snowbank in the morning. I'll call you tomorrow <3

She stared at the message for a beat before sending it. "Very kind" might have been pushing it when it came to Priscilla. Puzzling? Absolutely. Vaguely terrifying? At times. But she had rescued her. She'd offered a blanket, a couch, and hot chocolate.

That counted as kind, right?

With her phone on its last breath, she opened her thread with Cole. His last message was from three days ago.

Be there in five.

Alaina had been all set for a comfy night in until he showed up at her door and dashed every dream she'd had of spending her holiday with someone who was in love with her. He hadn't even come inside to do it. Just stood in the doorway of her San Francisco apartment, face devoid of its usual dimpled smile when the door swung open in front of him.

She'd tried to play it off with a grin of her own. "Baby! You're just in time. Our dasher just picked up our pizza." She'd ordered his favorite—the greasy kind piled high with just about every topping you could imagine—plus a side of garlic knots.

He'd winced. Actually winced. Her stomach dropped, landing somewhere near the ridiculous Christmas welcome mat at Cole's feet: a cartoon reindeer tangled in Christmas lights.

"What's wrong?"

Cole shifted his weight, eyes darting past her shoulder. "I don't know, Lani. I've been thinking . . ." His voice trailed off, and then he met her gaze. "I'm just not sure we fit, you know?"

Her heart stuttered to a stop. No. She didn't know. Not at all. Cole was the Harry to her Sally, the Noah to her Allie, and suddenly, he was morphing into the one that got away right in front of her.

"What?" she whispered. "What do you mean?"

"I think I need to be with someone more my speed. More spontaneous, you know?"

Her mouth fell open. "Spon—wait, is this because of New York?"

When he'd sprung the idea of a last-minute trip on her the day before, she hadn't told him *he* couldn't go. She wasn't that type of girlfriend. It was his dream to be an influencer, and getting a sponsored trip to New York was a big deal, even if it was to promote some stupid energy drink called PowerPunch.

But she had a job, responsibilities, and a whole vision for their first Christmas as a real couple that didn't include a hotel room three time zones away. She'd picked out the perfect playlist, planned a whole dinner that would take her and her limited culinary skills hours to cook. She even had a backup plan in case she burned everything: a Chinese food place a few blocks away that she'd already called to make sure was open on Christmas. Nico would be home for the first time in years to celebrate with their girlfriend—they usually went to visit their family for the holidays—and the four of them were supposed to have Christmas dinner together.

She'd thought maybe if she said she wanted to stay, he'd want that too. He'd said he'd think about it.

Apparently, he had.

"It's just—" He'd paused, taking a deep breath. "I think we need a break."

And that was it. She'd nodded, throat locked tight around all the things she wanted to say. Then she'd cried for two days straight. Through meals, *Love Actually,* and Nico's desperate attempts to distract her with every form of junk food known to man.

The second night, somewhere around 2 A.M., a single thought broke through the noise.

What would Mom do?

And suddenly it was obvious. Her mother—lover of classic rom-coms, firm believer in true love even after her own had crumbled—would've packed a bag and gone after him. Always.

"You don't give up on love," she'd told Alaina one night. Alaina had been maybe ten, sunk deep into the couch beside her after a movie. *Notting Hill*? *Sleepless in Seattle*? They all blurred together now.

"I don't get it," Alaina had said as the credits rolled. "Why do they always go through all that trouble? It seems like so much work."

Her mom had smiled. "Because love is always worth the trouble. Even when it breaks your heart. You don't give up on love. Not ever."

It was one of her clearest memories of her mom—one she held on to tightly now.

So Alaina had packed her car, promised Nico she'd be back after Christmas, and set off cross-country to chase after love. Now, staring at a dead screen, stranded in Utah, she wondered if love knew she was still on her way.

Chapter Three

Alaina awoke to the aroma of brewing coffee. Her back screamed as she sat up, and a groan escaped her before she could stop it. She blinked hard, trying to shake off sleep.

At the stove stood Priscilla, her back to Alaina, something sizzling in the pan. She wasn't in pajamas, instead wearing a black sweater and dark-wash jeans, her hair twisted into that same no-nonsense bun from the night before.

How long had she been awake? And how had she made it through a full morning routine without making a single sound?

Alaina opened her mouth to say good morning—then stopped.

A pair of yellow eyes stared back at her from the coffee table.

"Jesus!" Her hand flattened against her chest, trying to force her heart back into place.

Priscilla glanced over her shoulder. "I see you've met Lola."

"Like . . . the showgirl?"

"I'm not entirely sure. You'd have to ask Callie. She's the one who named her."

Lola—showgirl or not—was a petite brown tabby with a white chest and a tail that curled into a perfect question mark. Her unblinking eyes sent anxiety crawling up Alaina's neck. Had Lola been watching her all night?

"I didn't realize you had a cat."

"She was hiding in the closet when we got in last night. She can be a little reserved."

Like mother, like—well, cat.

Priscilla looked over her shoulder again. "I hope you're not allergic."

Alaina tested a breath through her nose. No stuffiness. "I'm not. Or at least, I don't think I am. I've never really been around a cat before."

"After a night on that couch, you'd definitely know if you were. She sleeps there most of the day."

Alaina leaned forward, stretching out a hand. A whisker twitched, and Alaina paused. Lola looked like an owl tracking its prey.

"Is she friendly?"

"On occasion."

Alaina retracted her hand. She didn't speak cat, but she was pretty sure Lola did not want Alaina on her couch anymore.

She swung her legs off the sofa, toes flexing against the carpet. At least she hadn't gotten frostbite. Cautiously, she navigated around Lola, feeling her watchful eyes on her all the way over to the kitchen.

"What time is it?" Alaina asked, voice still rough with sleep.

"Nearly ten." Priscilla whisked something in a bowl. "You're quite the sound sleeper."

"My phone died." Alaina ran a hand through her tangled hair. "No alarm."

Without looking up, Priscilla reached for a kitchen drawer and pulled it open. "There should be a charger in there."

Alaina spotted the charger and reached for it like a lifeline.

"There's a free plug near the table," Priscilla said before Alaina could even ask.

Between the towering stacks of books piled high on the small round table, Alaina squeezed against the wall to reach the outlet. She placed her phone on top of the precarious pile as she waited for the Apple logo to appear. Finally, her lock screen flickered to life—Cole's face staring up at her from behind the glass.

The lump in her throat threatened to choke her as she typed in her passcode, opened their thread, and—

Nothing. Nada. Zilch.

He still hadn't texted. Her only notification was Nico adding a heart reaction to her message from last night. She'd have to call them as soon as she had a minute alone.

Alaina heaved a sigh, turning back toward the kitchen. The lack of messages stung, but the smell of breakfast—sautéing onions and peppers, from what Alaina could tell—was already lifting her spirits.

Priscilla glanced over at her as she approached. "I hope you like eggs."

"I like everything."

Her stomach growled with theatrical timing.

"There's coffee." Priscilla nodded toward the full carafe at the end of the counter. "Unless you'd prefer more hot chocolate?"

Alaina shook her head. "Coffee sounds perfect. Do you have creamer?"

Cole used to tease her about her coffee—something about drinking a mug of creamer with a splash of coffee in it. An exaggeration, but barely. She preferred drinks that could double as dessert.

A look of disgust rippled across Priscilla's face. "No."

Alaina blamed her lack of caffeination for the undignified huff that left her lips. "Seriously?"

Of course this woman would be a black coffee kind of person.

"Yes, seriously. I don't know how you drink that stuff. It's essentially pure palm oil."

Alaina had no idea what that meant and didn't care. Creamer made any coffee drinkable, even in the worst of circumstances. Coffee mate had seen her through too many brunch shifts to be slandered now.

"I can't speak for everyone, but *I* drink it because it's delicious. But—fine, whatever. You have milk and sugar, right?"

Priscilla nodded toward a cabinet in the corner. "Sugar is in there. Milk is—"

"I can figure that one out myself, thanks," Alaina said, a little too sharp. She grimaced. That tone belonged to a bratty teenager, not a grown woman who hadn't had her coffee yet.

She pulled the milk from the fridge and doctored her cup, trying to be subtle about the generous spoonfuls of sugar she stirred in to make up for the lack of . . . palm oil, was it? Behind her, she could hear the soft clink of ceramic as Priscilla plated their food.

Priscilla cleared space on the table, moving a pile of books to the floor. Were they for the bookstore, or part of Priscilla's personal collection? The question dissolved when Priscilla set a plate in front of her—a golden omelet and whole wheat toast. Alaina wasted no time before digging in.

Across the table, Priscilla watched intently as Alaina took her first bite, which was immediately followed by a second. She hadn't realized how hungry she was. The eggs were delicious, and the grainy bread surprised her. It was nutty and satisfying, and not nearly as strange as she'd expected.

She couldn't remember her last homemade meal; she and Nico lived off staff discounts during their shifts at the restaurant they both worked at, and Uber Eats when they were at home. Ordering in every other night wasn't exactly a financially sound decision. Maybe she could make it a New Year's resolution to fix that.

But home-cooked had never been her default setting. After her mom died when she was fifteen, Alaina had moved in with her aunt and uncle—well, technically Doreen was her second cousin, once removed, or something like that. For months, Alaina spent family dinners hiding in her bedroom. No matter what they would make, it just made her miss her mom's cooking. She'd wait for everyone to go to sleep, sneak downstairs, and microwave whatever she could scavenge—usually a Hot Pocket or Lean Cuisine.

Alaina savored her next bite with a hum. "This is *so* good."

The edges of Priscilla's mouth curled into a small smile. Not the grin Alaina was waiting for—they weren't there quite yet—but Alaina would count it as progress.

"I'm glad." Priscilla cut her toast with precise movements, placing a piece of omelet on top of it. After she swallowed, she dabbed at her mouth with a napkin. "I contacted a friend of mine who is a mechanic. I told him where your car was, and he's going to try to tow it out this morning."

Alaina swallowed before she spoke, unusually conscious of her manners in front of Priscilla.

"That's so nice. Thank you."

She was surprised. She hadn't expected any of this—the rescue, the breakfast, the willingness to help. And definitely not from someone she'd been half convinced was an ax murderer. She felt a sting of guilt for assuming the worst, for judging Priscilla so harshly last night for her grumpiness. Her fingers fidgeted with the napkin in front of her.

A flush crept onto her cheeks. "Listen, I'm sorry about all this. You've been more than accommodating, and I haven't even really thanked you."

Priscilla shook her head. "Any decent person would have—"

"Maybe," Alaina said. "But you actually did. Don't downplay that."

Priscilla looked briefly caught off guard, then gave a small nod, clearing her throat. "Well, I am sorry if I seemed standoffish yesterday."

"Nah. I mean, it's not like you were actively hostile." She was ready to move on if Priscilla was, which, judging by the breakfast and coffee, seemed like a very distinct possibility. "Which is good enough for me."

"It can be frustrating living here." Priscilla sighed, shaking her head. "People put themselves in danger all the time and don't even realize it."

It hadn't occurred to Alaina that Priscilla's attitude the night before might've been born out of concern for her rather than pure annoyance. "I definitely didn't think ahead," she said. "I have . . . kind of a lot going on."

As she spoke, she raised a hand to trace the contours of her necklace's blue gem, a moonstone set in a gold prong that Cole had gotten her for her twenty-fifth birthday in May. Her birthstone was emerald, but still, it was the thought that mattered. She hadn't taken it off since.

"I'm sorry," Priscilla said. "I hadn't even considered that you were out there for a good reason."

"I wouldn't say a good reason." Alaina picked up her fork,

pushing a bit of egg around her plate. "Let's just say I am . . . trying to fix some problems."

Problems like the love of her life asking for a "break." The word still sat like lead in her stomach. She wasn't a football game—he couldn't just call a time-out on loving her. It made no sense.

She glanced up to see something pass over Priscilla's face—understanding, maybe. "Right."

"I'm glad you're the one who found me. I mean, a badass bookstore owner rescues me from certain death?"

Priscilla shrugged. "Not certain. Just likely."

"Either way, thank you." Alaina smiled, and a thrill ran through her when Priscilla returned it, even though it didn't linger. "Why are you being so nice to me?"

"I thought I was being 'not actively hostile.' That's a far cry from 'nice.'"

"Yeah, well, for some people, that's as good as it gets."

A small flash of hurt struck across Priscilla's features, and Alaina immediately wanted to take the words back.

"Not that I'm saying—that's not the case for you. You're genuinely, actually nice. Really. A saint."

"A saint?"

The memory of the crucifix near the door gave Alaina pause. "Sorry, is that, like, sacrilegious or something?"

Priscilla's gaze held hers, and Alaina had to fight the urge to look away under the weight of her dark eyes. "No," Priscilla said.

"God's not gonna smite us? We won't be smittened?" The word felt wrong the moment it left her mouth, but Priscilla's smile reappeared. Alaina wouldn't have taken it back even if God himself came down to give her the chance.

"Smote, and no." Priscilla tucked her smile back into its hiding place, though evidence of it lingered in her eyes. "I think we'll be okay."

❄

When Priscilla offered a shower before they left, Alaina accepted eagerly. The cold from last night still hadn't left her bones.

Warm water went a long way toward making her feel human again. As it washed over her, she planned the day ahead. Good breakfast? Check. Decent cup of coffee? Done. Now she could get back on track. She'd be on her way to Cole in no time.

It wasn't until she stepped out of the shower that she realized two things:

First, the pajamas she'd borrowed from Priscilla lay in a soaked heap under her feet—she'd stepped onto them instead of the bath mat.

Second, she didn't have any clean clothes.

Her suitcase was still in her car.

Alaina poked her head out of the bathroom door, wrapped in a towel that was noticeably not up to the task of preserving her modesty. The edges barely met, forcing her to clutch it closed. She didn't understand why anyone would buy a towel that wasn't big enough to wrap around their body twice. For her, it was bath sheets or bust.

"Um, Priscilla?"

No response. The living room was empty.

Stepping out of the bathroom, Alaina knocked on Priscilla's bedroom door with an embarrassed grimace.

"Sorry, I was just—" Priscilla opened the door, then paused, jaw going slack. Her gaze drifted from Alaina's damp hair to her bare shoulders before she tore it away, cheeks flushing pink. "Oh, um—something . . . uh, wrong with the shower?"

"No, it was perfect. Just wondering if I could borrow clothes until I get back to my car?" Alaina's grip tightened around her towel. She felt bad making Priscilla uncomfortable by showing up mostly naked at her bedroom door. "I did remember to pack a suitcase—before you say anything—but we couldn't exactly get to my trunk in all that snow."

Priscilla's eyes remained trained just over Alaina's shoulder. "Right. Of course."

"Thanks. And don't worry—I'm not usually this much of a hot mess." Alaina paused. "Wait, that sounds like I'm calling myself hot. Which I wasn't. I meant disaster. Hot disaster? No, that's worse—"

A smile formed on Priscilla's face as her eyes met Alaina's. "I'll find you something to wear."

Chapter Four

Priscilla's pajamas had been comfortably large, as all pajamas should be.

Priscilla's clothes were a different story. Alaina felt like a child playing dress-up. She was no stranger to an oversized fit, but Priscilla's clothes seemed to be men's, cut for her broad frame. The pants dragged well past Alaina's feet, and the sweater hung off her shoulders, sleeves swallowing her hands to her fingertips.

Priscilla waited in the kitchen. She looked up, her eyes widening as Alaina approached.

"I know, I know. I look ridiculous." Alaina held up an arm as proof.

Priscilla gave a barely there shake of her head. "No. You look . . . fine."

"If you say so."

The thick knitted wool of the loaned sweater was incredibly warm, but Priscilla still pressed a jacket and hat into Alaina's hands before opening the apartment door. After last night,

Alaina didn't argue. Her threshold for freezing had been permanently recalibrated.

Lola zipped past with a happy chirp, making Alaina jump back. "Is that . . . okay?"

Priscilla nodded. "She has full run of the place."

A cat in a bookstore. Could anything be more charming?

At the top of the stairs, Alaina paused. From here, the store unfolded below them, warm light streaming through tall windows. The armchair by the window wasn't the only one; little reading nooks were tucked all around, each one cozier than the last. She could picture herself here so easily—another mug of hot cocoa, snow drifting outside, a book in her lap—

No. No daydreams. She had a plan to get back to, and it certainly didn't involve sitting on her butt when she could be on her way to Cole, no matter how comfortable the chair or decadent the cocoa.

When they reached the bottom of the stairs, Priscilla held up a finger. "Wait here a moment." She slipped behind the counter.

Alaina took in the shop up close. As charming as the bookstore was, something felt missing as she walked through the shelves.

Books, antique reading lamps, a store cat. Why did she feel like this Hallmark movie–worthy bookshop lacked something essential? Then it hit her.

"Hey, Priscilla?" she called toward the counter. "Why don't you have any Christmas decorations up?"

"I don't celebrate."

Alaina jumped. She hadn't heard her approach, but Priscilla now stood next to her, a rugged leather bag slung over her shoulder. It looked like something Indiana Jones might carry if he traded hunting ancient artifacts for tracking down first editions. The bag suited Priscilla better than any purse ever would.

Priscilla's hands fiddled in front of her for a moment before she said softly, "Bad memories."

Yikes. Alaina had had her own fair share of those.

The first Christmas after her mom died, her aunt and uncle had tried to create some holiday magic, but it was just a few months after her mom's accident. Alaina turned down every invitation to help decorate, to bake cookies, to watch movies—even with her cousin Shauna, who'd been her childhood best friend before Alaina and her parents moved when her dad got a job in New Mexico. They'd been inseparable as little kids, but by the time Alaina moved back to Colorado as a teenager, parentless while Shauna's life was still intact, the distance between them was too wide to bridge. Shauna felt like a stranger, their shared childhood a lifetime ago.

Alaina had spent that Christmas alone in her room, watching cheesy Hallmark films. Her family mistook her silence for apathy, not realizing it was grief, too heavy to explain. The next year, they didn't ask her to join the festivities, and she didn't offer.

She'd been watching Christmas from the sidelines ever since.

She promised herself that, someday, she'd find her way back to that holiday magic. She'd hoped this year, with Cole, would be it. Her first real Christmas in a decade. One that might finally feel like home again.

And then it all imploded.

"Sorry," Alaina said. She'd assumed the answer would be something religious—maybe Priscilla thought the commercialization of the holiday was, like, a diss on Jesus or something. She hadn't meant to touch a nerve. "We don't have to talk about it."

"Good." Priscilla gave a firm nod. "Let's go see about your car, shall we?"

"We shall," Alaina replied in a faux-British accent, hoping it didn't sound like she was teasing. She just really liked the way Priscilla talked. It sounded sophisticated. "Lead the way."

Outside, the storm had passed, leaving the town wrapped in a blanket of snow. Priscilla navigated her truck out of the unplowed lot behind the bookstore and onto the street. Road crews had clearly worked through the night, though a layer of packed snow still covered the pavement.

As they passed beneath a decorative arch stretching over the street, Alaina caught the words painted across it: WELCOME TO BROOKS in bold letters, with SMALL TOWN, BIG HEART in script underneath.

They retraced last night's route, but now, with daylight and clear skies, it felt like stepping into a new world.

Brooks was small, but picture-perfect. The bookstore was just one of many shops lining the street. Snow had collected on the canvas awnings that dotted the storefronts, creating delicate white slopes. Most of the buildings were only a few stories tall, with retail spaces on the bottom floor and what Alaina assumed were apartments above, just like Priscilla's. Alaina spotted the warm glow of what had to be a café, judging by the large coffee cup on its sign. Across the street, an ornate clock tower stretched toward the crisp morning sky.

"Wow," Alaina breathed, taking in the winter wonderland. "Your town looks like it jumped straight out of a Christmas movie."

Priscilla didn't respond, but when Alaina glanced over, she caught the remnants of a smile.

Beyond downtown, the landscape morphed from storefronts to snow-covered houses. Craftsman homes and cabins sat back from the road, smoke curling from their chimneys.

As they pulled up to the mechanic's shop on the outskirts of town, the morning sun caught the freshly fallen snowflakes, making them shimmer like a blanket of diamonds.

"Grant?" Priscilla called out once they entered the garage.

"Back here," a voice responded.

They walked through to the back room, where Alaina was greeted by the sight of Bertha, her beloved car, no longer entombed in snow. A man stood near the propped-open hood.

Grant was tall. Skyscraper tall. Like "probably getting asked to grab something from the top shelf by little old ladies every time he shopped" kind of tall. A tattoo peeked out from underneath his sleeve, color contrasting against his dark skin. His head was shaved smooth, reflecting the overhead fluorescent lights. It gave him a polished, military look—a general commanding his personal army of nuts, bolts, and spark plugs.

He glanced up at them as they approached. "Priscilla." His voice had a rich timbre, deep and resonant, like a radio deejay. "Who's this?"

He took Alaina in with a calm, calculating look. She was unsure whether she would pass his apparent inspection or be declared a total write-off.

"This is Alaina," Priscilla said. "And *that* is Alaina's car."

"Nice to meet you," Alaina said with a smile. "You must be the mechanic."

"Grant." He wiped his hands on a rag and extended one, his handshake as firm as his stare. "So you're the girl Sil rescued, huh?"

There it was again—Sil. Another person close enough to use Priscilla's nickname. Now that Alaina thought about it, she was pretty sure Grant had been in a few of the photos hanging in the apartment.

Priscilla cut in. "I did not say I rescued her," and Alaina laughed.

"That's me, and she totally did. A regular white knight. I'm honestly not sure how I'll ever repay her."

Priscilla smiled, and Alaina realized she had lost count of how many of those she'd won so far. She grinned back until Grant cleared his throat.

"Sounds about right. Anyway, I just got started here. It's gonna be a while."

Priscilla nodded. "How long do you think you'll need?"

"No way to know right now, but I'll give you a call. Hey, while you're not chained to the shop, why don't you stop in to the diner? Ned would love to see you."

Alaina remembered what Callie had said last night—that it'd been a while since she'd seen Priscilla. And here was Grant, echoing the same sentiment. Did Priscilla work too much? Alaina could picture it easily: Priscilla buried in books and paperwork, rarely surfacing for meals or social calls.

Priscilla hesitated, proving Alaina's theory right almost immediately. "I haven't had the opportunity to return his calls. Do you think he'll be mad?"

"At you? Never. I'll let him know you're going to stop by."

Downtown bustled with life, even more charming now that the sidewalks were full. The first block they drove down gleamed with upscale storefronts—a boutique with cashmere sweaters, an art gallery showcasing mountain landscapes, a wine shop with bottles that probably cost more than Alaina's monthly grocery budget.

But when Priscilla turned onto Main Street, everything shifted.

Here stood the heart of Brooks: a barbershop with a classic red-and-white pole, a brick post office, a hardware store whose window display looked like it hadn't changed in decades, complete with a model train running through a miniature evergreen forest. Each building was adorned with white lights, wreaths, and garlands. It was the perfect little Christmas village.

Priscilla parked, and they got out to take a stroll. The explosion of holiday cheer should have made Alaina happy. This was just the kind of Christmas joy she'd been chasing, trying to get back the years she'd squashed those feelings down. She almost whipped out her phone for a photo, then stopped herself. Who would she even send it to? Nico was at work, and she doubted a badly taken photo of Christmas lights on a telephone pole would impress Cole.

Her heart thumped painfully at the thought. God, she missed him. Wished he were here, his hand clasped in hers. Cole always loved to be touching her—not in a gross or clingy way, but like he couldn't get enough. His hand at the small of her back. Kisses pressed to her temple. Fingers laced through hers. Grounding. Safe.

Nico used to joke that they were magnets, ever since finding them curled together on the couch after their first date nearly a year ago. It hadn't been planned—she'd met him at work one lunch shift, and they'd spent practically every second of the next twenty-four hours together, inseparable from the start. Their second date was only three days later, both of them too excited to see each other to wait.

Cole had been her first real boyfriend in years. She'd tried dating, of course, but the spark always fizzled fast. She'd been ghosted more times than she could remember.

But Cole put effort into their dates—picnics at golden hour, late-night drives to stargazing spots outside of the city. Sure, their outings had been featured heavily on his Instagram stories and had to have whatever audio was trending on TikTok. The lighting had to be perfect. He'd pull over mid-drive to capture her posed against sunsets or city lights. But she hadn't minded. The way he wanted her, proudly showing her off, had felt intoxicating. His interest in her never wavered. Until, suddenly, it did.

She should have just said yes when he'd asked her to come with him to New York. She could be there with him now. Together. Happy.

Instead, she was here, marooned in a snow-covered small town.

At least it was beautiful.

"This is, like, ridiculously pretty." Alaina took a few quick steps to keep up with Priscilla's long-legged pace.

"It is. Would you like to grab a bite to eat?" Priscilla asked. "I need to drop something off at the diner and say hello to Ned."

It had been just over an hour since breakfast, but Alaina nodded anyway. She never turned down comfort food.

"Always. But I feel bad taking up so much of your time. You must have other things to do besides babysit me."

"There's no need." Priscilla waved a hand. "I have an employee. He'll be able to handle things on his own for at least a few hours. Sunday mornings are typically slow, and I have some deliveries to make while I'm out anyway." She patted the leather bag where it sat against her hip. "Though we should try to stop back in to the bookstore at some point to check in on Clark."

They turned the corner and stopped in front of another brick building. This one had a sign that read PATTY's in red brush script.

A bell rang as they stepped inside. Alaina hoped her eyes didn't go too comically wide at what waited for them.

A classic jukebox near the entrance played a jazzy rendition of "Jingle Bell Rock," its chrome body reflecting the bulbous vintage Christmas lights flashing green and red around the room. A large group decked out in snowsuits congregated at the tinsel-wrapped counter, laughing loudly over the clatter of plates and silverware. Along the windows, faux snow clung to the glass. The specials board proudly displayed their pancake flavors of the month—eggnog and gingerbread, because what else could they *possibly* be this time of year—and a snowman clutching a syrup bottle.

"Wow," Alaina whispered. This place was incredible. It had so much more personality than the hokey, fake neighborhood vibes of the chain where she and Nico worked back in San Francisco.

Behind the antique register stood a distinguished older woman, her short hair a rich shade of black peppered with strands of gray. She didn't smile, but her eyes warmed when they landed on Priscilla.

"Long time, no see, kid."

"Hello, ma'am." Priscilla sounded formal, even for her. "Sorry—you know how busy the Christmas season gets."

"You don't have to explain yourself to me, hon." Her eyes flicked over to Alaina, giving her a once-over before returning to Priscilla. "Your booth is free."

As they slid into a booth at the far end of the diner, Alaina leaned in, glancing back toward the register. "She seemed . . . friendly."

"That's just how she is." Priscilla sat across from Alaina. "When she's not being friendly, you'll know it."

"You know her well, then?"

"I do." Priscilla nodded, teeth sinking into her lip. "Patty took me under her wing when I first arrived in Brooks."

Alaina itched to ask more—what had brought her here, what made her stay—but didn't want to press too hard. Priscilla was finally opening up. Better to not spook her.

But then, Priscilla kept going.

"I wasn't quite sure what I was doing yet, and I may have never figured it out if it weren't for her. She saw that I never missed a meal."

Before Alaina could respond, Patty arrived with two oversized menus. She placed them down and turned to Priscilla, hand on her hip. "You know, it's been quite a while since you've brought someone here. How did the two of you meet?"

Priscilla glanced over at Alaina. "It's kind of a long story."

"Priscilla saved my ass from a snowbank last night, and we've been inseparable ever since," Alaina said. Patty's lips twitched downward at her choice of words.

Seriously? Did everyone around here have a problem with cursing? Maybe she really was stuck in a Christmas movie. Did that mean her life was rated PG now?

"By which I mean," she said, "she can't seem to get rid of me, because I have literally nowhere else to go until Grant finishes fixing up my car."

Patty didn't look impressed. "Quite the storm to be out driving in."

Alaina's face warmed. Sure, driving in a snowstorm hadn't been her smartest move, but did this woman have to make her feel like a reckless teenager?

"Before I forget . . ." Priscilla said, rescuing Alaina from Patty's scrutiny. She reached into her bag, pulling out a brown paper package tied with neat twine. Alaina could picture Priscilla carefully creasing the edges, tongue caught between her teeth in concentration. Maybe the town's resident Scrooge had a softer side for Christmas than she let on.

She handed it to Patty. "I managed to track down that signed Le Carré for Tom."

Patty's entire demeanor changed as she took the wrapped book, clutching it to her chest. "You didn't! He's going to absolutely love this. You're a miracle worker, Priscilla."

The bell above the door chimed as a group of snow-dusted tourists poured in. Patty glanced over her shoulder. "Well, duty calls. Your food is on the house—enjoy your date, dears."

By the time Alaina's brain caught up to what Patty had actually said, the woman had already bustled away to greet the new customers.

Enjoy their *date*? Her brain tripped over the word, but Priscilla didn't seem to even notice, her eyes fixed on the laminated pages as if her life depended on finding the dish with the highest protein-to-calorie ratio.

Priscilla flipped the menu over to look at the lunch options, lips pursed. "Maybe I'll have the avocado toast."

But Alaina couldn't brush off what Patty had said.

"She said our 'date.' Did she think we're . . . together?"

"Did she say that?" Alaina caught the slight hesitation, the way Priscilla's fingers tightened on the menu. She was deflecting, but why? Her eyes glanced up from the menu to find Alaina's. "Does that make you uncomfortable?"

"What? No, of course not." Alaina shook her head, a small laugh escaping her lips. She wasn't gay, but if she were, she could do worse. A lot worse. "If anything, I'm flattered. I mean, look at you."

The instant the words slipped out, she could almost feel her foot lodging itself in her mouth.

Priscilla's eyebrows rose, and for the first time since they'd met, she looked caught off guard. Alaina wondered why. Priscilla was clearly attractive. She must be used to getting hit on.

Then again, from what Alaina could tell, Priscilla was pretty religious. Maybe she didn't like the idea of them being mistaken for a couple.

Alaina was on the verge of blurting out an apology when she was saved by the bell. Or, rather, the bell-like voice of the waiter.

"Morning, Sil!" he called out as he approached their table. He had a bright, inviting smile, his hair a bundle of lively curls thrown into a messy ponytail. Alaina recognized him immediately—the man from the lake photo, grinning next to Priscilla and Callie. He set down two mugs of steaming coffee with a flourish. They were mismatched, one with the words WORLD'S BEST GRANDPA and one with a comic of a cartoon dog.

"Patty figured you'd want these."

"Thank you. She knows me well." Priscilla raised one of the mugs—WORLD'S BEST GRANDPA—and sipped from it like it was a shield. Her gaze stayed fixed on the coffee, but a flush lingered on her cheeks.

The waiter turned to look at Alaina, smile not dimming a single watt. "And who is this?"

"This is Alaina, the girl whose car Grant is fixing right now."

Alaina's eyes found the man's name tag. Ned. Right. Grant had mentioned him.

"Lani, please." She held out her hand to shake his, like Grant had done earlier. Ned accepted it with a warm smile.

"Nice to meet you, Miss Lani." His voice had a melodic cadence, sweet and soft. Ned was far friendlier than Grant, but his gaze was just as discerning as he took her in. "You're the one keeping Priscilla busy?"

"Wow, word travels fast, huh?" Alaina said.

Ned shrugged. "Not much else happening in Brooks. And anyone who can pry Priscilla away from her shop is someone I want to get to know. I feel like I should be presenting you with a medal or something."

There it was again—pry away. It was confusing. Priscilla had seemed so willing to help Alaina out all morning. But then again, she *had* mentioned making deliveries. Maybe this wasn't a day off so much as it was a slight detour from her usual routine. Either way, Alaina was grateful Priscilla was making time for her.

"Anytime!" Alaina said, then caught herself. "Well, not anytime, since I *do* only have one car to crash into a snowbank during a blizzard, but—" She gave a sheepish wave. "Happy to help."

Ned laughed, and Alaina brightened at the sound. At least one person around here found her even slightly charming.

"Can I get you anything while you look over the menu?"

Alaina didn't need to look. She already knew what she wanted.

"A slice of cherry pie, please."

If anything could right all the wrongs in her world right now, it would be the bliss of syrupy cherries with streusel crumbled on top. She might not have Cole, but at least she had sugar. No one could take that away from her.

Priscilla gaped at her. "It's barely noon."

"Exactly," Alaina said, as if Priscilla had just proved her point. "Can I get a scoop of vanilla ice cream on the side?"

"You got it," Ned said. "Patty's pies are legendary."

Ned jotted down her order on an actual pad. No glitchy, frustrating tablets like the ones at her restaurant that seemed designed specifically to make her shifts even more stressful. There was something refreshing and straightforward about ink on paper, a simplicity she could definitely use more of in her life right now.

Ned looked over at Priscilla. "Sil? The usual?"

She paused, then handed her menu over. "Apple pie. Hold the ice cream, though."

Alaina's mouth dropped open in a surprised grin. "Wow. I never thought I'd see the day."

Priscilla arched an eyebrow. "You've known me for less than twenty-four hours."

"And I'm already a great influence!" Alaina beamed.

Her phone buzzed on the table, and Alaina scooped it up.

Please be Cole, please be Cole, please be—

A message from Nico was waiting for her instead.

Nico 12:04 p.m.: you good???

Shit. She'd meant to call them when she'd woken up, but the morning had gotten away from her.

Alaina 12:04: Sorry!! dealing with all the car stuff, but I'll call you once I'm back on the road <3
Nico 12:05: you'd better! i want to hear your voice so i know you're not an impostor with lani's phone
Nico 12:05: quick, what's something only lani would know

"Something wrong?" Priscilla asked.

"No! No, it's just my best friend. They want to make sure I'm okay."

To Nico, she wrote back: I think there's still kombucha on top of the cabinets from the time you tried to make it at home.

A thumbs-down popped up seconds later.

When their plates arrived, Alaina eagerly dove in. Priscilla hesitated, scooping up the tiniest bite on her fork.

Her face contorted as she swallowed. "Ugh, that's sweet."

"Sweet *and* delicious." This was no frozen Sara Lee pie—this masterpiece was clearly made with love. "But if you don't like yours, I'll take it."

Priscilla pushed it across the table, eyeing Alaina warily. "Your arteries are doomed."

"Live fast, die young, right?"

The next hour passed in a blur of coffee refills and carefully curated anecdotes, the kind designed to make you seem interesting without baring your soul. Alaina had perfected this art at work—telling stories that were funny enough to earn the occasional quiet snort of laughter, but sanitized of anything too personal. She started with Nico's disaster of a kombucha experiment, then moved to the time she'd photobombed a wedding, finishing with a classic:

"—and that's why I'm banned from three different Whole Foods."

Priscilla hid a smile behind her mug. "Only three?"

When their mugs ran dry yet again, Priscilla checked her watch and frowned. "I really thought we would have heard from Grant by now."

Alaina shrugged, masking her nerves. "Better he takes his time with Bertha." She toyed with her mug. "You still have deliveries, don't you? I can come along. Unless you'd rather do them solo, which is totally cool."

"I suppose someone should keep you from getting banned from any local establishments," Priscilla said, reaching for her leather bag. "Besides, I surprisingly don't mind the company."

Alaina grinned, but quickly faltered when Priscilla stood up to walk away. "Wait—surprisingly?"

Ned was perched on a stool behind the register, fingers tapping away on his phone with a smile on his face.

"Hey, Ned," Priscilla said, stopping in front of him. "We're headed out."

"It was really good to see you, Sil." He pushed off the counter and stepped forward, wrapping Priscilla in a tight hug. "You'll be there Sunday?"

Sunday—aka Christmas.

Priscilla avoided his eyes. "I'll let you know."

Alaina didn't miss the way Ned deflated for a beat before he turned to Alaina, holding out his arms.

"It was so very nice to meet you, Lani."

Alaina stepped into the embrace. When she pulled away, she immediately missed the warmth. She'd really needed that hug after the roller coaster of the past twelve hours.

"Hope everything works out with your car," he called out as they exited.

Once they were back outside, Alaina turned to Priscilla, feeling nosy once more. "So . . . do you always spend Christmas with Ned? He seems really sweet."

And very handsome. She tried to picture Priscilla and Ned together. The height difference would be cute, at the very least.

"Not exactly," Priscilla said. "Every year, the town gets together just after sunset on Christmas Day to light the tree in the square. Ned was part of the decorating committee this year. I don't typically attend, but he has it in his head I should be there."

"Wait—the town gets together on Christmas *Day*?"

Priscilla shrugged. "It's a small town. People like each other here."

"No kidding. Hey, is it weird to live in, like, Christmas Town, USA, when you don't like to celebrate?"

Something in Priscilla's rigid posture reminded Alaina of a coiled spring, of all the times she herself had needed someone to back off instead of prying deeper. Of lunch periods spent dodging questions about parents who never showed up for career day, of well-meaning teachers who couldn't understand why she never wanted to talk about her life outside of school.

Priscilla nodded. "It can be trying, yes."

As they walked, Alaina nudged her shoulder against Priscilla's. "I think it's really nice you have people who care about you enough to want to celebrate with you, though."

It was what Alaina had always wanted for herself.

"On that," Priscilla said, "we can agree."

After lunch, Priscilla led Alaina through the rest of her deliveries. They stopped at the hardware store, where the owner's face lit up when Priscilla handed him a wrapped package, and then the post office, where the clerk practically bounced with excitement when Priscilla walked in.

"You're like Santa," Alaina observed as they walked back to the truck. "Except you deliver books instead of toys."

"Santa brought me books as a child," Priscilla said. "But yes, I suppose."

They continued through Brooks, weaving through the downtown streets. Priscilla pointed out the library, the elementary school, a small park where summer concerts were held. It was all aggressively quaint.

By the time Grant called, Alaina had nearly forgotten why she was here. Nearly. But pulling up to the garage brought her crashing back to reality.

"Tell me the good news!" Alaina sang as she sauntered into Grant's shop, hoping her optimism would have some effect. Manifestation and all that.

Grant was leaning over the hood of Alaina's car, his hands

dirty with a dark liquid. The whole scene was ominous, but Alaina was determined to keep a positive outlook—until Grant looked up and winced.

"No can do. You'll need a new bumper, and your alignment is messed up. But that's the least of your problems. You busted the oil pan—it's cracked."

The oil pan? Whatever that was, it was clearly not good news.

"The oil pan cracked?" Priscilla sounded incredulous. "But that snowbank was fresh powder."

Grant shrugged. "Must've hit something hiding underneath the snow. It'll take me a few days to fix, at least. Maybe longer, depending on how messed up deliveries are from the storm."

"A few days?" Alaina's heart plunged to somewhere near her stomach lining. "You can't be serious."

"Don't shoot the messenger. Besides, I'm not the one who plowed your car into a snowbank."

"Yeah, that was all me. Fuck."

"It's all right, Alaina." Priscilla reached over, settling a hand on Alaina's shoulder. "Grant's the best. He'll have it—Bertha—fixed in no time. Right, Grant?"

"Right," Grant drawled in a way that was less than encouraging. "In the meantime, I guess you'll have to stick around. At least you have Sil here for company."

Alaina's shoulders slumped under Priscilla's hand, the weight of the situation pinning her down. Not only would this completely derail her plans, but she also couldn't help the freight train of guilt that ran through her at the idea of overstaying her welcome. "If she doesn't kick me out by then."

"You can stay as long as you need to," Priscilla said. She nodded toward Bertha. "We should grab your suitcase before Grant gets to work. You'll feel much better once you're in your own clothes."

Alaina did her best to smile, but the gnawing feeling in her stomach sank its teeth in deeper.

The drive back to the bookstore became a battleground for Alaina's racing thoughts. She had a plan, and spending days trapped in Utah wasn't part of it, no matter how enchanting the snowy streets were or how welcoming its residents seemed. Would she even make it out before Christmas? It was a week from today. How long could a car repair take? She tried not to picture Cole gallivanting around New York without her, but the image was as persistent as a pop-up ad.

She wanted to talk to Nico about it, but they were currently working one of the many shifts Alaina had bailed on when she hit the road. When Alaina hatched her plan to win Cole back, only one obstacle had stood in her way: work. Nico's offer to cover for her had meant everything. They'd never come out and said they disliked Cole, but Alaina could tell that their enthusiasm was lacking, to say the least. Their willingness to help anyway spoke volumes.

"Something wrong?" Priscilla asked, voice filled with unexpected concern. When Alaina only offered a half-hearted shrug, she tried again. "You look like someone stole your puppy."

"Just thinking." Alaina's fingers fidgeted with her shirt hem as she calculated how many days she could be delayed and still make it to New York by Christmas. She pulled out her phone and punched Times Square into her GPS. Thirty-two hours away by car, and that wasn't taking into account breaks to eat, use the bathroom, and sleep. Even if she cut back the number of hours of sleep she got to six—and she was easily an eight-hours-a-night kind of girl—the situation would look bleak if it took Grant more than four days to fix up Bertha.

She dropped her phone into her lap and threw her head back against the headrest, groaning. "I'll never make it to New York in time."

"New York?" Priscilla's eyebrows lifted. "What's waiting for you in New York?"

"My boyfriend. Well—my not-boyfriend. We're on a break." Alaina let out a hollow laugh. "He said I wasn't 'adventurous' enough. Then he left for this last-minute gig he got in Manhattan, and I decided the best thing I could do was drive cross-country and show up on Christmas to prove him wrong—because that's totally what a person in control of their life would do."

"And now you're here."

"And now I'm here."

Priscilla considered Alaina's words. "You know, there are plenty of adventurous things to do around Brooks. You could make the most of being stuck here, cross a few items off your bucket list."

"Yeah? Like what?"

"You could . . . chop down your own Christmas tree. Go wild skating out on the lake. Skiing, or snowboarding, if you'd prefer. Hike up the mountain and camp under the stars."

Alaina brightened. "That sounds amazing." Cole would've loved to do any of those things. She could prove she could keep up with his lifestyle, pass the time until she could go to New York, and win him back. Surely one of her cards had room for a plane ticket out of Utah if her car wasn't ready in time. She'd take a red-eye on Christmas Eve if she had to.

Birds, meet stone. Sorry there's just one; you'll have to share.

There was only one thing that could make this plan even better.

"You should be my tour guide."

They stopped at a red light, and Priscilla looked over, arching an eyebrow. "Should I?"

"Please? It'll be so much fun! You can show me what you love about Brooks, and take some time off from the store. Maybe it would prove to your friends you're not, like, a workaholic or whatever."

To be fair to Priscilla's friends, Alaina was pretty certain Priscilla *was* way too addicted to work. Or at least, she had been until Alaina turned up. Maybe Alaina was already having an effect on her new friend.

The seconds ticked by, Priscilla's fingers drumming against the steering wheel. Alaina was convinced she'd stuck her foot in her mouth again when Priscilla nodded. "It would be nice to get them to stop worrying about me."

"Plus, I'll need someone to take pictures to show to my—um, Cole."

"Pictures?"

"Skiing, camping, and—wild skating? What even is that?" Alaina twisted in her seat, hands clasped in a dramatic plea. "Everything you just said sounds way better than whatever pit stops I'd make on a road trip. Please?"

Priscilla's mouth pulled sideways. She did that a lot, it seemed. It was kind of endearing.

"I can see if Clark wants to pick up a few more hours. And maybe you can help out around the store while you're here. It gets busy this time of year, and it's just us. If I'm going to ask him to cover while we're gone, I'd like to at least make sure he feels supported while we're there."

"Deal." Alaina stuck out her hand. "And I can keep crashing on your couch?"

"Until a spot opens up at Callie's, sure," Priscilla said as she shook Alaina's hand.

Alaina glanced down. Priscilla's grip was firm but warm—just like her. After a moment, Priscilla let go and eased off the brake as the light turned green.

"Speaking of, I should probably text Callie back. She sent me a message this morning asking about you."

"That's really sweet."

"She wanted to know if I had strangled you yet."

"Oh." Alaina blinked. "That's not something you do, right? Strangle people? I just think I have a right to know, if I'm going to be staying with you and all."

"I suppose you'll just have to wait and see."

"Wait, Priscilla, seriously—"

"No, Alaina."

Chapter Five

The bell above the door announced their entrance to the bookstore, its chime all but drowned out by the din of customers inside. A blond man—Clark, Alaina guessed—rang up shoppers one by one, the line snaking through the aisles. Relief washed over his face when he spotted Priscilla.

"Wow. That's a lot of customers for just one guy," Alaina said, pausing in the doorway with her suitcase.

"It's not usually this busy on Sundays." Priscilla frowned, surveying the chaos. "Holidays get unpredictable."

"Put me to work," Alaina said. They'd just struck a deal, after all.

"Oh, you don't have to—"

"C'mon." Alaina nudged Priscilla's shoulder. "I promise, I'm great with people. How can I help?"

Priscilla's lips pursed in thought. "Could you handle the online pickups? They're all prepaid. Just take the name, find the order in the back—they're labeled—and bring it out."

"Easy peasy. Let me just run up and get changed first." She would feel a lot more capable of dealing with the public when she was wearing clothes that fit.

Upstairs, Alaina tossed her suitcase onto the couch and tugged at the zipper until it gave way. Inside was a mishmash of styles, at best. Packing in a rush at 4 A.M. hadn't exactly lent itself to thoughtful wardrobe planning. Other than the dress she'd brought to wear when she saw Cole, the contents were a jumbled assortment of skirts and shirts, and her favorite worn-in jeans.

She pulled out a green sweater that looked respectable enough, grabbed the jeans, and slipped into the bathroom.

She dressed quickly, securing her curls in a low ponytail with one of the scrunchies she'd unearthed. A glance in the mirror confirmed she looked how she already felt: much, much better. Not that she didn't look cute in Priscilla's clothes—oversized could be a look—but she felt more herself in her own style. With a grin, she hooked in a pair of dangly earrings, a final touch of flair before heading back downstairs.

The crowd hadn't slowed much in the ten minutes that she'd been gone. Clark was still behind the register, and Priscilla was walking through the stacks with a pile of books in her arms. She paused when she saw Alaina, watching her come down the stairs.

"You look . . ." She paused, thinking it over. "Different."

Alaina hesitated at the last step. "Good different?"

Priscilla blinked, then nodded and cleared her throat, her eyes darting away. "Come with me."

In the storeroom, a table overflowed with wrapped books, each tagged with the name of the customer and the titles in the order. The level of organization was no surprise, but Alaina's eyes did widen at the sheer volume.

Priscilla glanced over at her, wearing a guilty look. "Sorry there's so many. Online orders have skyrocketed since Clark set up our website last year."

"Don't worry, boss." Alaina cracked her knuckles. "I've got this."

Back at the counter, she cupped her hands around her mouth and called, "Anyone here for an online order, form a line against that wall."

She pointed across the room. A third of the customers peeled away from the register. Clark exhaled audibly.

"New employee?" she heard him ask Priscilla as she walked away.

Alaina handled pickup after pickup for an array of customers—tourists, locals, every variety of small-town reader. A professorial man in glasses had ordered a thriller. A ski instructor snagged three bestsellers for her lodge book club. A mom in lululemon came next.

"My kids would lose it if this place ever closed," she said as Alaina brought out her stack of middle-grade books. "I mean, sure, Amazon's cheaper, but have you seen the kids' reading nook Priscilla set up? Last weekend the boys spent hours in those beanbag chairs."

Alaina smiled. Connecting like this was a breath of fresh air compared to her usual job, where a quick thank-you from a dude-bro in a jersey after she dropped off his order of atomic wings was too much to ask for.

Next in line was an elegant older woman with perfectly styled silver hair, holding a printout between manicured fingers. "I believe I have a book to pick up, dear—for Eleanor Park."

Alaina scanned the slip, then grinned. "*Passion in Paris,* huh? Sounds . . . spicy."

"At my age, a bit of spice is exactly what the doctor ordered." Eleanor's eyes twinkled. "Keeps the heart young."

Alaina ducked into the storeroom to find Eleanor's book.

When she returned, Eleanor was leaning against the counter, a wistful smile softening her features.

"It's good to see this place so busy," Eleanor said, tucking the book into her purse. "I had my doubts it would survive after Mr. Peterson threw in the towel. The store was empty for a few years. Thank goodness Miss Kane swooped in when she did. Every small town needs a bookstore."

Miss Kane? Alaina frowned, then her eyes widened.

Priscilla Kane.

Her gaze drifted to Priscilla, who was now behind the counter, sliding a stack of books into a brown paper bag for a customer. The woman who'd rescued her had also saved this entire store? The plot, as they said, thickened.

By late afternoon, the rush faded into a gentle lull. As pickup orders slowed, Alaina busied herself straightening shelves, but her thoughts spun. Priscilla was full of contradictions: a recluse who ran the town's most beloved gathering spot, a Brit who'd chosen America's Christmas capital as her home despite not celebrating the holiday, someone who kept her friends at arm's length yet inspired such genuine affection from people she barely knew.

If Alaina was going to be stuck here, she might as well start unraveling some of these mysteries.

Scanning the store for Priscilla, Alaina saw only the blond man, Clark, standing behind the counter. She was about to go over and introduce herself properly when Priscilla's accented voice drifted out from one of the aisles.

". . . and if he's interested in American history, this one is a great place to start." Alaina followed the sound and spotted Priscilla speaking with a middle-aged man. "It's an incredibly detailed military history of the first two years of the American

Revolution. Americans think of George Washington as this incredible commander—and he was, in the end—but this showcases just how hard of a start he had at the beginning of the war. It's part one of a series, so if he likes it, there will be much more to come."

The man lit up. "Perfect! He's going to love this. You've definitely secured my spot as the favorite uncle this Christmas."

When he left, Alaina stepped forward. "Didn't know I was in the presence of a history buff."

Priscilla looked up at the sound of Alaina's voice. "It's my job to know these things," she said. "But my dad was a history professor at Oxford. Dinner conversations were always a bit academic. I suppose I picked up more than I realized."

There was something about the way Priscilla's mind worked that made Alaina want to lean closer and pay attention to every word. She was brilliant, the kind of smart that usually made Alaina's mouth snap shut, afraid of sounding stupid. But with Priscilla, her mouth seemed to have other plans, words tumbling out before she could stop them.

She cleared her throat. "The online pickups seem to have died down. What's next?"

Priscilla surveyed the thinning crowd. "I think we've got it covered. Why don't you go relax upstairs?"

Alaina was still wiped from last night, and as charming as most were, the customers had drained her social battery. Some rest sounded pretty good right about now.

"Are you sure?"

"Positive." Priscilla nodded. "I know you had a long day yesterday. Thank you for your help."

"No problem. If you need me, I'll be crashed out on the couch."

Priscilla made her way behind the register to join Clark, and Alaina trudged upstairs. She flopped onto the couch, sinking into the cushions, phone in hand.

Her thumb swiped until she reached Cole's Instagram profile. No new posts. Not even a story. That was unusual for him. Cole treated his Instagram like a full-time job—stories several times a day, feed posts with captions he'd fine-tune for an hour, all in the name of "gaming the algorithm." He'd tried to explain his posting strategy to her once, something about engagement rates and optimal timing, while Alaina nodded along. At first, Cole had found her cluelessness about social media cute. Now she wondered if it had been another way she didn't quite measure up.

Cole would have turned this whole detour into content gold by now with a reel about embracing life's surprises set to a Taylor Swift song. Meanwhile, she posted three times a year and had never even shared anything to her stories.

With a groan, she tossed her phone aside and grabbed the remote. If there was a God, Priscilla would have cable. When the television clicked to life, she was happy to see the dopey face of Joey Tribbiani staring back at her. A *Friends* marathon was exactly what she needed right now. It was the comfort food of television—cheesy and predictable, offering zero intellectual sustenance but undeniably satisfying.

Alaina sank deeper into the couch, letting the nostalgia wash over her. If her life were a *Friends* episode, it'd probably be titled "The One Where Alaina's Plans Go Awry" or, more accurately, "The One Where Alaina Has No Clue What She's Doing."

The theme song was playing in the fourth episode in a row when her phone buzzed from beneath a throw pillow.

Nico 6:28 p.m.: bro

Shit. She'd meant to call Nico hours ago.

Alaina hit the off button on the remote and the call button at the same time.

"About damn time," Nico answered. "Why aren't you on the road?"

Alaina looked around the room. "How do you know I'm not?"

"You shared your location with me in case you got kidnapped, remember?" Nico paused. "You *haven't* been kidnapped, right?"

"You already asked me to prove I haven't."

"No, I asked you to prove you weren't being impersonated. Who's to say you're not being held hostage?" Concern bled through Nico's sarcasm. "I can't really see any other reason you're camped out in Utah."

"Besides Bertha being out of commission? Here." Rolling her eyes, Alaina pressed the FaceTime button and waited until Nico appeared on her screen. A bit of tension she hadn't realized she was still carrying in her shoulders relaxed at the sight of them.

"See?" The camera spun as she panned the room. "No kidnappers."

"Good." Nico's eyes narrowed. "But where the fuck are you? That doesn't look like a hotel."

"It's an apartment." Alaina sank back into the couch. "Long story."

She recapped the last eighteen hours—the storm, the snowbank, the rescue, the grim car prognosis.

"So, this woman pulled you out of the snow and she's now gallantly allowing you to stay on her couch while her friend fixes your car? She's basically Prince Charming. Is she hot?"

"Nico!" Heat flooded Alaina's cheeks, and her eyes darted to the door. What if Priscilla heard? The last thing she needed was to make Priscilla uncomfortable right after she'd agreed to let Alaina stay. "No! I mean—that's beside the point."

"Is it? Because it kind of sounds like *the* point."

She and Nico had clicked as soon as she walked into their freshman dorm room on move-in day. They'd been standing in the middle of the room, hands on their hips as they surveyed the gay and trans pride flags they'd hung on the wall. When Alaina entered, they'd raised their eyebrows, as if asking, *Is this going to be a problem?*

It wasn't. In fact, Nico's ability to be themself—an agender force of nature with an unabashed love for women—was something Alaina had always admired about her best friend.

"Maybe it's 'the point' to you."

"Yes. And I am always right." Nico grinned, but it quickly turned into a yawn. "Sorry, long day."

Guilt tugged at her. Of course Nico was tired—they'd worked their usual Saturday night shift last night and picked up Alaina's Sunday brunch shift today. "Thank you again for covering for me this week."

"No worries, babe. You know I can use the money, anyway—engagement rings are expensive."

"Please. You could propose with a Ring Pop and Josie would say yes."

Nico and Josie had gotten together during their last year of college and hadn't hit a bump in the road even once. The night after Cole left, Nico had told Alaina she was still more than welcome to spend Christmas with them, but being a third wheel postbreakup sounded about as fun as dental surgery with no anesthesia.

The next morning, she'd woken up with a plan. By afternoon, she was on the road.

Nico snorted. "Yeah, probably. Still, I want to get her something nice, you know? She loves jewelry, and I found this really cool independent shop where—oh shit, I think she's here. Baby?"

A muffled voice answered in the background.

"Tell Jo I say hi," Alaina said.

Nico's eyes flicked back to the screen. "Will do. I'll send you the link. Love you."

They hung up before she could say it back.

Alaina stared at the black screen for a moment, then grabbed the remote. *Friends* flickered to life—Monica was freaking out about something, naturally. The familiar dialogue washed over her as she settled deeper into the cushions.

Two minutes later, her phone buzzed.

She glanced down, expecting Nico.

Unknown number 6:56 p.m.: Alaina?

Her heart kicked into overdrive. Cole? It wasn't his usual number. Could he have lost his phone?

Alaina 6:56: Who is this?

The reply took three minutes, and she spent all of them staring at her screen.

Unknown number 6:59: It's Shauna. Can we talk?

Alaina's heart tripped over itself. She hadn't spoken to Shauna, her aunt, or her uncle since her college graduation three years ago, and that had been the first time she'd seen them since she left their house at eighteen.

Her aunt and uncle had tried to form a connection with her, especially at first. But they weren't people Alaina had grown up with. Her mom had lost touch with most of her family after she followed Alaina's dad from Colorado to New Mexico when

Alaina was only four—before he broke her heart and left them both behind. By the time she was back in Colorado after her mom died, her relationship with Aunt Doreen and Uncle Craig was flimsy at best. And Alaina hadn't made it easy. She never yelled or acted out. She just . . . shut down. Eventually, her aunt and uncle had stopped trying to close the gap.

It was the same story with Shauna. As children, they'd been best friends. But at fifteen, they couldn't have been more different. Shauna was an all-state athlete, effortlessly cool and popular. She'd tried to include Alaina, but Alaina had just felt like the sad girl with the dead mom. She'd busied herself with school, earning a full ride to study business at the University of San Francisco. Once she left, she never looked back, spending summers and holidays alone in the apartment she and Nico rented.

Every year, Nico offered to bring her home to Washington for Christmas, fold her into their family, like it was easy. Every year, Alaina stayed behind, hoping her own family might call. They never did. They'd turned her bedroom into a home gym the minute she left for school.

It wasn't until Nico came along that Alaina had remembered how it felt to let someone see her.

The door to the apartment creaked open, jerking her back to the present.

"I closed up for the night," Priscilla called as she stepped inside, Lola trailing behind her.

Alaina straightened, scrambling to pull herself together.

"Did you get up to anything interesting while I was gone?"

"I—no, just . . ." Alaina's fingers twisted in her lap. "TV, mostly."

Priscilla paused, eyebrows lifting, a flicker of concern passing over her face before she smoothed it away. "You must be hungry. I'm afraid I don't have anything to prepare for dinner.

Would Chinese be okay? I know a place with the most amazing bean and mushroom stir-fry."

Alaina's stomach answered for her, letting out an impressive growl. She looked at the clock—it was already after seven. She hadn't eaten since that slice of pie at the diner. And now, as the edges of Shauna's text message began to fade into something less sharp, a new, more immediate crisis presented itself: avoiding a dinner composed entirely of vegetables.

Finally, something she felt equipped to handle.

Chapter Six

Six Days Until Christmas

"I made a list!"

Alaina waved a piece of paper in the air as she skipped into the kitchen the next morning. Priscilla was back in front of the stove. After considerable pleading from Alaina, Priscilla had caved to making pancakes, despite noting their total lack of nutritional value.

Priscilla looked at Alaina over her shoulder. "Did you check it twice?"

"I thought you didn't do Christmas. Anyway, no, it's a list of the stuff I want to do to win Cole back."

"Let's see it."

Alaina handed over the paper, suddenly aware of how messy her handwriting looked. Priscilla scanned it, her gaze moving back and forth like a typewriter carriage. "'*Chop down a tree, ice skating, learn to ski, camp under . . .*'" She looked up. "Alaina, these are just all the things I suggested."

"They sounded like good ideas." Alaina shrugged, heat creeping up her neck. "Plus, I added one of my own."

Priscilla's eyes darted down to the last line, and she read

aloud, "*'A grand romantic gesture.'*" Her brow creased, her nose scrunching along with it. "Do you think he'd like that sort of thing?"

"I mean, yeah. I think if you do a good enough job, anyone would. Who wouldn't want to be on the receiving end of the caroling scene in *Love Actually*? Or the speech in *When Harry Met Sally*?"

Priscilla shook her head. "I wouldn't. Those moments aren't really about love, they're just . . . Hollywood's way of trying to sell a fantasy."

Alaina chewed on her bottom lip, self-doubt beginning to simmer. Was Priscilla right? Maybe she *was* chasing a fantasy, setting herself up for disappointment with expectations pulled straight from a movie screen.

But still.

Her mom had raised her on a steady diet of Meg Ryan and Julia Roberts, of rain-soaked kisses and airport dashes. Even when her own love story hadn't worked out, her mom never stopped believing the next one might.

You don't give up on love.

Alaina had taken that to heart. She wanted the swoop, the spark, the speech that made the world tilt. She'd been on enough dead-end dates with guys who barely looked up from their phones to know that what she wanted wasn't easy to find.

Cole had made her feel like the leading lady. Like she was worth showing off.

That was the kind of love she was chasing. The kind she couldn't lose.

She plucked the list from Priscilla's hands. "If someone's willing to stand in the rain to profess their love for me, I say let it pour."

Priscilla shot her a sidelong look.

"Look, it's not really about the gesture, it's about taking the risk. It's about showing up. About saying, 'Even if this makes me look ridiculous, even if I fail—I still want you to know I tried.' That's love to me. Not just the grand part. The brave part."

Priscilla paused, mid–pancake flip, the spatula hovering. "I've never thought about it like that."

"Well, have you ever been in love?"

Her eyes lingered on Alaina a beat too long before she turned back to the stove and laid the pancake down. Batter hissed as it hit the griddle.

"I thought I was. Once."

"And you didn't want to . . . I don't know, do anything crazy to prove it?"

Priscilla exhaled slowly. "It was ages ago. I was a kid."

"A kid in *love.* That's the dangerous part. Being young is one thing, but love? Love makes you do irrational things no matter how old you are."

Alaina was the perfect example of that.

"Maybe," Priscilla said, flipping the last pancake in the pan.

The word sounded too heavy. Time for a change of subject.

"So," Alaina said brightly. "This whole chop-down-your-own-tree thing—do we just, like, wander into the woods until we find The One?"

Priscilla's lips twitched. She was definitely fighting a smile. "No."

Alaina bit her lower lip, cheeks warming.

"There are farms for that sort of thing," Priscilla said gently. "If that's what you want to do."

She plated the final pancake and brought the wobbly stack to the table.

"I do! I just don't exactly have somewhere to put one," Alaina said. "And since you don't celebrate . . ."

Priscilla tilted her head, thinking. "We could put it in the store window. It could do with some seasonal charm."

"Really?" Alaina's eyes lit up. "You'd do that?"

"Sure. Most of the people in town right now are here for the holiday. It might draw them in, drum up some business."

Maybe this holiday season wouldn't be so bleak after all.

❄

After pancakes, they bundled up to hunt for a Christmas tree. This time, Alaina donned her own clothes, using Cole's now-dry hoodie as a base layer, a sweater on top, and the jeans. Priscilla insisted she borrow a coat, a beanie, and a pair of boots as well. She had to wear two pairs of thick socks to make the boots stay on her feet comfortably.

Downstairs, Clark was behind the counter, tall and easygoing, his grin widening when Priscilla waved him over.

"Well, if it isn't our newest employee," he drawled. "Thanks for the help yesterday."

His Southern lilt made the words sound warmer. With his straw-blond hair, square jaw, and red flannel, he looked like he'd wandered off the set of one of Alaina's favorite Christmas rom-coms.

Alaina smiled. "It was my pleasure."

"Clark, Alaina's staying with me for a few days. Why don't you show her around the store while I make a few quick phone calls?"

"Sure thing, boss."

Clark led her through the stacks, pointing out the sections while Alaina trailed behind. The floor creaked beneath their feet, muffled by faded rugs that stretched between the aisles.

"Classic literature is one of our biggest sellers—Sil's quite proud of that," Clark said, gesturing to the right. "Though she keeps wanting to expand the history section. Says it's criminal to have Austen but not a decent biography of her."

Alaina nodded like she knew what he meant, but she was too focused on how his voice softened when he said Priscilla's nickname.

"How long have you known Priscilla?"

Clark leaned against a shelf, a soft smile playing across his undeniably handsome face. "Two years, just about."

"What's she like to work for?"

Clark thought for a moment. "She's tough, but fair. Makes me dust every shelf weekly, especially the ones nobody touches. But she also lets me take home any damaged books instead of tossing them. And I'm glad you're getting her to take some time off."

Alaina looked over at Priscilla, who was behind the counter with a phone pressed between her shoulder and her ear. "Does she work too much?"

Clark lowered his voice. "Way too much. Stays late. Skips breaks. Says she doesn't mind, but . . ." He paused. "The holidays are hard for her. Something with her family."

What was it Priscilla had said? *Bad memories.*

"Well, we're going to go get a Christmas tree today. Maybe that'll help her get in the holiday spirit."

His eyebrows shot up. "Well, I'll be. I never thought I'd see the day."

"I happen to be very convincing."

Though truthfully, she hadn't had to do much convincing at all. Priscilla had offered. Maybe she wasn't as opposed to taking time off as everyone seemed to think.

"I don't doubt that one bit." Clark gave her a crooked smile.

Alaina was opening her mouth to ask how long he'd been in

Brooks—his accent definitely wasn't like anyone else's she'd met around here—when the bell above the door chimed, and Clark's eyes caught on the woman who had just walked in.

"Duty calls." Yeah, this man was definitely all Southern charm. If he had a hat, he'd probably tip it toward her as he went to greet the customer. Instead, he winked. "Nice talking to you, Alaina."

"You too!"

She glanced toward the counter. Priscilla was still on the phone, worry creasing her brow. Whatever the call was about, it didn't look like something she should interrupt. Instead, she made her way over to the teen section, settling in on one of those beanbag chairs the mother had mentioned yesterday. She had just gotten comfortable when her pocket buzzed.

Alaina let out a groan. The beanbag had swallowed her whole, making even simple movements difficult—like trying to pull her phone from her back pocket. Thankfully, she was hidden by tall shelves, out of sight from both Priscilla and Clark. After a series of contortions that nearly sent her rolling onto the floor, she finally managed to free the device.

But once her phone was in her hand, she hesitated.

What if it was Shauna? Then, a more hopeful thought—what if it was Cole?

Nope. It was Nico.

They'd sent a photo of the restaurant, empty except for two tables.

Nico 11:15 a.m.: tip money is rolling in without you. think i can retire by lunch?

Alaina snorted, then typed out another over-the-top thank-you for covering her shifts. When Nico asked what she was doing today, Alaina laid out the full new plan—a list of adventures that she would use to impress Cole into giving her another shot.

Nico's reply came fast. They didn't say much about Cole—they never did—but told her they were glad she was having fun.

"Alaina?" She heard Priscilla's voice from somewhere near the front of the store and scrambled to get up. There was no way she was going to let Priscilla, of all people, witness her ungraceful exodus from this damn chair.

"Alaina?" Priscilla called again.

"Over here!" she said, rocking forward with as much momentum as she could muster. She'd just managed to right herself and smooth down her shirt when Priscilla appeared between the shelves, wearing an apologetic look.

"Sorry that took so long. I had to track down a missing shipment that contained a few special orders."

"Oh no—are they Christmas presents? Did you find them?"

Something in Priscilla's face shifted at Alaina's concern. She nodded. "They ended up at another indie in Park City. They'll be here tomorrow."

"Look at you, making sure everyone gets their gifts on time. Regular Priscilla Claus over here."

The joke slipped out before she could second-guess it. But instead of brushing it off, Priscilla smiled slightly before she cleared her throat. "Ready to go chop ourselves a tree?"

"Let's do this."

❄

The bookstore was quieter than it was yesterday, which made it easier for Clark to wave off Priscilla's guilt about leaving him alone to man the fort. Still, she insisted on buying him lunch from the sandwich shop next door before they left.

A half hour later, they pulled into Brooks's cut-your-own Christmas tree farm. Alaina shivered at the brutal cold as she rounded the truck.

Her eyes widened when Priscilla reached into the truck bed.

"Do you expect me to use that?" Alaina asked, staring at the alarmingly large ax in Priscilla's hands. Maybe chopping a tree was a little ambitious for her first adventure. Maybe she should start with something smaller—like, say, eating spicy food or jaywalking—but Priscilla just smiled and started toward the red barn at the entrance before Alaina could say anything.

"Wait up!" she shouted, trudging after her through the snow.

A teenager in a puffy jacket offered them a much more reasonable handsaw when they came in, but Priscilla turned it down. He gave them a list of rules—cut low, shake off any excess snow, and please stay within marked areas—but Alaina barely heard him, too overwhelmed by her mix of nerves and excitement.

Then they were outside again, moving through the rows of evergreens. Alaina lagged behind, grateful for Priscilla's borrowed boots even if they were a size too big. They were still better than her bright yellow Converses, which remained tragically soggy from her first night's snow trek.

The quiet here was different from San Francisco's fog-muffled mornings. The blanket of snow seemed to catch and hold every sound except for the distant squeals of children and the occasional shout of "This one!"

Past the neat rows of Fraser firs and blue spruces, the Wasatch Mountains rose against the sky, their jagged edges lit with early afternoon sun. It looked like something on a postcard.

Alaina turned in a circle, taking in the endless rows of perfect trees. "God, it's so beautiful out here."

"The trees?" Priscilla sounded amused.

"Well, yeah, but—the snow too. There's so much of it, completely untouched."

"You act like you've never seen snow before."

"We don't get much snow in San Francisco, you know," she said with a chuckle. "But I actually grew up in Colorado. I loved the snow as a kid."

It was one of the things she'd missed most when they moved. She'd been so young that Colorado was more of a feeling than a memory, just cold air and white mountains and a house full of people she couldn't quite picture anymore. Alaina's mom had walked away from all of it for an older man her family didn't approve of.

A year later, he left them both for a woman he'd met at work.

Her mom had been barely older then than Alaina was now, all alone with a five-year-old in a state where she knew no one. Too proud or maybe too ashamed to crawl back to the family whose advice she'd ignored. In New Mexico, it was just the two of them. They bounced from town to town, chasing cheaper rent. Making friends was difficult, but Alaina didn't mind. Her mom had always been enough.

"Snow is rather pretty," Priscilla said. "We didn't get much in Oxford—flurries here and there, but rarely anything that would accumulate like this. I've gotten used to it since moving here."

Alaina's boots crunched over the frozen path. Her fingers tightened into fists inside her gloves.

"There was this book my mom used to read to me when I was really young. I don't remember the name, just that it was about the snow, and this little boy who tried to keep some of it in his pockets." She laughed, but it broke halfway through, her eyes stinging. "I remember my mom saying I tried to do that too."

"That's very sweet," Priscilla said gently. Alaina wondered if

Priscilla could hear the tears in her voice. Thankfully, her next question was pointed in a different direction. "If you love the snow, why did you leave Colorado?"

"Family stuff," Alaina said quickly, eyes on the path ahead. No way was she steering the topic into what she liked to call the Dead Mom Ditch. Nothing killed a conversation faster. She searched for a detour. "Have you done this before? Cut down your own Christmas tree?"

To her surprise, Priscilla nodded. "Yes. It was something my family used to do every year when I was younger. How about you?"

"Nope. I'm a tree-chopping virgin."

Priscilla shot her a look.

"Like, I've never chopped a tree before, not that I'm—"

"I understood you perfectly," Priscilla said, her voice clipped, and Alaina burst out laughing.

"So, how tall can we go? Ten feet? Twelve?"

The tip of Priscilla's nose was turning pink in the cold, and it scrunched as she looked at Alaina in disbelief. "Do you truly think the ceilings in the store are twelve feet tall?"

"Um, maybe?"

"Fascinating." Priscilla was making fun of her, but the word still sent a spark of joy through Alaina at the idea that someone as cool as Priscilla might find her interesting. "If it's going in the window, I think we should aim for something closer to five feet."

"That's so short! Even I'm taller than that."

"Are you?"

"You're, like, an inch taller than me, Sil." Alaina tested out the nickname she'd heard everyone else use on her. If Priscilla noticed, she didn't react.

"Four, at least, and they make a big difference."

"Low blow," Alaina muttered, then grinned. "Get it? Because I'm so tiny?"

Priscilla shook her head, sighing. "I've never met someone who enjoyed puns quite as much as you do."

"You say that like it's a bad thing. Admit it. You love them."

"Maybe," Priscilla said. "But I have a reputation to maintain."

Alaina raised an eyebrow. "Oh yeah? And what reputation is that?"

"Does tall, dark, and mysterious ring a bell?"

She looked quickly away from Priscilla's smirk. Her cheeks went red-hot. Had she really said that to Priscilla within minutes of meeting her? God, she was corny.

Priscilla stopped and pointed toward a squat, round tree dusted in snow. "That one should do nicely."

Alaina followed her gaze and nearly squealed. "Oh my god, it's so cute."

"It is," Priscilla said, much calmer than Alaina. But when Alaina looked over at her, she caught something rare: a full, genuine smile, teeth and all. Not the polite, barely there version she'd come to expect.

"We should name it."

Priscilla looked puzzled. "You want to name a tree?"

Alaina circled the tree, studying his stubby branches. Then she clapped her gloved hands. "Humphrey! He's just a little guy, but he means business. Humphrey has gravitas. You can tell by the way he holds himself."

She said it with as much seriousness as she could muster.

"Humphrey," Priscilla repeated. Then she handed the ax to Alaina. "You know, they say you should never name something before you kill it."

Alaina raised an eyebrow. "Speaking from experience?"

"If you're going to keep insisting I'm a murderer, you should probably find somewhere else to stay."

"You're the one with an ax just lying around, Sil," Alaina said. "It's not that far-fetched. But no, I like to live on the edge."

Then, with a grin, she swung the ax at Humphrey's trunk—

—and missed completely.

The blade whooshed past the trunk and dragged her off balance, feet skidding in the snow. Before she could face-plant, strong hands caught her shoulders and steadied her. The ax slipped from her grip and landed in the snow with a muted thud.

"I don't know what I was thinking," Priscilla muttered behind her, hands falling away. "Give me that."

"Wait!" Alaina pivoted to step between Priscilla and the ax, bringing them face-to-face, closer than she'd expected. Priscilla froze midreach. "You—um, you have to take a picture of me with it first."

"Right." Priscilla took a step back, but kept her hand out. "Give me your phone then."

Alaina fished out her phone, wincing as her lock screen lit up with the photo of her and Cole on a Ferris wheel, her face squished against his, the giant teddy bear he'd won her tucked between them. Her eyes had lit up the second she'd spotted it hanging from the top of the carnival booth, and he wouldn't walk away from the definitely rigged ring-toss game until he'd won it.

Countless quarters later, it was hers.

They looked so happy together at the time, but . . . maybe she had been wrong.

Maybe she was the only one who had been happy.

She pushed the thought away and handed over the phone. "Here."

Alaina trudged a few steps through the snow, retrieved the

ax, and positioned herself in front of Humphrey again—this time with a little more respect for the ax's weight.

Priscilla tugged off her gloves and tucked them under her arm, frowning as she looked down at the phone. She pressed a few too many buttons to just be pulling up the camera app. "I don't—I don't know how to use these stupid things."

"A . . . phone?"

"Smartphones," Priscilla grumbled. "Before you say anything, I do have one. They're just . . . perplexing."

"No wonder no one can get in touch with you."

It was meant as a joke, but the second it left her mouth, she regretted it. The way Priscilla pulled back, like she'd been stung—yeah, that hadn't landed right.

"Sorry, I meant . . . here, let me." Alaina took the phone back and opened the camera app. "Just point and press that little white button in the—"

"I know how to take a picture, Alaina." Priscilla's voice had cooled, the earlier warmth gone.

"Right, of course, sorry." Alaina turned back to Humphrey and struck a pose, ax over her shoulder, chin out. "How's this?"

Priscilla shook her head. "You look like you're modeling. I thought you wanted to look adventurous."

"I do!"

"Then—here." Priscilla tucked the phone into her pocket and stepped behind Alaina. Her arms came around her, reaching for the ax, and Alaina leaned back into the contact without thinking. Priscilla paused, but then adjusted Alaina's grip, lifting the ax slightly while Alaina's hands stayed fixed to the handle.

"Stand like this. Legs apart—good."

Alaina's breath caught. She nearly cracked a joke—something light and vaguely suggestive—but for once, she held back.

"One hand up here." Priscilla's voice was low, close to Alaina's ear. Warm. When she stepped back, the cold air rushed in to fill the space she'd left behind.

Alaina shivered at the loss of contact. She blinked, a little thrown by her own reaction. Not even a full week had passed since Cole walked out and she was already this touch-starved?

Focus, Alaina. Her grip tightened until her knuckles were probably white beneath her gloves. "Okay. What now?"

Priscilla circled back around to the other side of the tree, framing the shot. "Stand a little closer to the tree. Don't—don't look at *me,* you don't want it to seem posed, right?"

Alaina nodded. "Just tell me when to swing."

"I think we've already established that isn't going to work. This is just for the photo."

Right, okay. Act like she was about to fell a tree—she could do that. Alaina looked at the tree like it was an enemy she was about to cut down on the battlefield.

"Less rage. This is meant to be a fun activity. Wholesome, even." Some of the frost finally melted from Priscilla's voice, her light, teasing tone from earlier returning.

Alaina changed tactics, plastering on a grin as she held the ax like a pro baseball player. She felt confident, cool, like she could take on the world—or at least like she could take on a five-foot-tall tree. If only her arms would stop trembling from holding up what felt like the world's heaviest ax.

She was convinced she was selling it until Priscilla lowered the phone a few inches to peer at Alaina over the purple case. "Alaina, are you taking this seriously?"

Alaina dropped the grin with a sigh. "It doesn't have to be perfect! Just take a bunch and I'll pick out the right one."

"Not perfect," Priscilla mumbled. "Sure."

The phone rose again. Alaina turned back to the tree, repositioned the ax, and went for her most convincing faux swing.

"I'm getting pretty good at this!" Alaina faked another chop.

Priscilla took a deep breath, then said, "One might even say you're doing . . . *tree*-mendously."

Alaina let out a startled bark of laughter. "Oh no. I've ruined you."

They ran through a few more shots—some exaggerated, some completely unhinged. Alaina leaned into the ridiculousness of it, buoyed by Priscilla's dry commentary and the crisp bite of the air on her cheeks.

"Let's see what we're working with." Alaina bounded over, rising up on her toes to peek at the screen as Priscilla swiped through the photos.

"There." Priscilla paused. "That's definitely the one."

In the photo, Alaina stood midswing, legs planted wide, one hand high on the ax handle, the other gripping low. Her posture was strong, but her face was caught midlaughter at something Priscilla had said—her eyes bright, mouth open, teeth showing. The sunlight hit her just right, turning the loose strands around her beanie into a halo of soft brown.

Her face was turned slightly toward where Priscilla stood. Against the backdrop of the snow-dusted pines and winter sky, she looked like she was the star of a Brooks-based Hallmark movie about a city girl finding her holiday spirit in the midst of an unexpected adventure.

"Oh wow," she breathed. The realization hit her like a snowball to the chest: she actually *liked* a photo of herself. This was unprecedented. In Cole's carefully constructed Instagram feed, she always looked like someone trying very hard to look like they weren't trying at all, her smile a little too wide and unconvincing, no matter how many photos Cole snapped of her. He would call her beautiful. She just couldn't see it.

But this wasn't curated or filtered to perfection. This was

her—ridiculous and a little flushed and genuinely, unexpectedly happy. And Priscilla had captured it.

"Is it okay?" Priscilla's voice was uncertain. "We could take a few more if you want."

Alaina shook her head, looking up to smile at Priscilla. "It's perfect."

"I thought you didn't want perfect," Priscilla said, teasing.

"Well, apparently 'perfect' is kind of your thing, so . . ."

"That's true," Priscilla said, earning another laugh from Alaina. "No, not that I'm always perfect. I just . . . hold myself to a certain standard."

Alaina lifted the ax. "Does that standard include making chopping down this tree look easy?"

"As a matter of fact, it does."

When Priscilla stepped forward to take the ax, Alaina's arms gave out with relief. But Priscilla didn't seem to mind the weight—her hands settled on the handle, lifting it easily. Which was . . . impressive? Intimidating? Whatever it was, Alaina couldn't look away.

From her safe distance on the other side of Humphrey, Alaina watched as Priscilla stepped up to the tree. The first swing landed with a satisfying thud. Then another. And another. Each stroke was precise. Alaina found herself holding her breath, just watching each effortless swing.

With a final, echoing crack, Humphrey toppled onto the snow-blanketed ground with a muffled thud.

Priscilla turned, brushing a loose strand of hair from her eyes with the back of her hand, cheeks flushed from exertion or the cold.

"See?" she said. "Easy."

Alaina blinked. Her brain had momentarily gone quiet. "Yeah," she breathed, eyes still locked on to Priscilla. "Easy."

Priscilla stooped to secure the branches of the tree, binding them tightly with a length of twine she'd brought along. Afterward, she straightened, brushing the snow off her gloves.

"Ready?" she asked. Alaina nodded, and the two of them got into position on either side of the tree, each grabbing a large, sturdy branch to drag it back to the truck.

Halfway there, Priscilla spoke.

"About what you said earlier, how my friends aren't able to get in touch with me . . ."

A flash of guilt burned hot across Alaina's face despite the cold. "I'm sorry, I didn't mean—"

"You were right."

That wasn't the problem; Alaina knew she was right. Pretty much everyone in Brooks had said some version of *I miss you* to Priscilla. Still, it wasn't okay for Alaina to just throw that in Priscilla's face. Her mouth had a bad habit of racing ahead of her brain.

"Okay. So I'm right. Do you want to talk about it?"

Priscilla huffed, a cloud of steam rushing out from her lips. "I don't want you to think they're bad people, or that I'm avoiding them. They're basically my family."

"So . . . what's the problem?"

"Sometimes I think they're . . . too kind? They want things for me I don't even know how to begin to imagine for myself."

Alaina let that thought settle for a moment. She was glad Priscilla had that kind of friendship in her life, people who showed up for her. She had Nico—thank god—and they too had become family by choice, not by default.

Still, she also knew that when people expected things from you—even good things—it was terrifying to think about letting them down.

Alaina adjusted her grip on Humphrey's branch, the bark

rough against her gloves. "Those things they want for you, whatever they are—I'm sure you deserve them. It can just be hard to see our own worth sometimes."

"Yes, well, they definitely see things in me that I do not," Priscilla said. "You know, Alaina, you're a lot wiser than you seem."

"Thank y— Wait, what's that supposed to mean? I don't seem wise?"

"Well, I did find you an inch from death—"

"What happened to Miss 'I did not say I rescued her'?" Alaina parroted in an awful accent.

"—trapped under a mountain of snow."

"It was inches. Okay, maybe a foot or two—"

"Completely unprepared in every way imaginable—"

"That's not true! I had . . ." Alaina searched desperately for an answer. "My phone?"

Priscilla's smile took over her face as she shook her head.

Alaina stopped walking, staring at her. "Wait. Are you fucking with me right now?"

"Language, Alaina," Priscilla said. "But yes."

"Huh." Alaina grinned. "Awesome."

Chapter Seven

On the way back from the tree farm, they stopped for a late lunch at a café, then went back to the bookstore. They left the tree in the alley that led to the parking lot Priscilla had shepherded her through that first night. Alaina hadn't noticed it then, but above the store hung a hand-painted sign that read BROOKS BOOKS in gold lettering against a green backdrop.

Priscilla stopped in front of the window, where newly released books were showcased on the other side of the glass. "I'll start clearing off the display."

"I can help," Alaina said. "I mean, I don't know where anything goes, but I've got two hands. You could put them to good use."

Priscilla paused to think this over, then nodded. "Right. Come on then."

She held the door open for Alaina, the bell above it chiming as they entered. After yesterday's holiday rush, the quiet felt almost jarring. Only a few customers browsed the shelves, probably locals savvy enough to avoid the weekend crowds days before Christmas.

Immediately, Priscilla began shifting books and knickknacks from the window display, and Alaina jumped in to help.

"What should I do with these?" she asked, clutching a stack of hardcovers that came up to her chin. She tried to channel the effortless confidence Priscilla had when swinging that ax earlier, but her arms wobbled under the weight. Without a word, Priscilla removed a few books from the top to steady her.

"Place them on the counter for now," Priscilla said, nodding toward the back of the store. "Clark will handle the shelving."

In no time at all, they had cleared the front window, and Alaina stood back to imagine what it would look like when the tree took center stage. Even bare, Humphrey would transform this part of the bookstore into something magical—though she worried he might look a little lonely without lights and ornaments to keep him company.

Priscilla joined her, seeming to read Alaina's mind. "We're in need of some decorations."

"We could go to Target?" Alaina said. "They might have some stuff left." This close to the holiday it would probably be slim pickings, but it would be better than nothing.

Priscilla shook her head. "The nearest one is almost an hour away."

Right. Small-town charm, meet small-town inconvenience.

Alaina twisted her mouth to the side as she thought, then grinned. "Or—hear me out—what if we invited your friends over for a tree-trimming party? Everyone could bring a few ornaments, like a decorations potluck. Besides, I think they'd really like to see you."

Was it the understatement of the year? Maybe. But she didn't want to put too much pressure on Priscilla. She'd already done so much for Alaina by letting her stay and agreeing to help her with The List. She was dangerously close to crossing the line of

Priscilla's grinch-esque comfort zone. One more little nudge and Alaina could be back out in the cold.

Thankfully, Priscilla didn't seem all that bothered, nodding as she pulled out her phone. "Ned may have leftover decorations from the tree in the town square." She glanced up. "You wouldn't mind all the chaos? My friends can be a bit . . . enthusiastic."

"Chaos is my brand," Alaina said, as if her entire existence in the state of Utah wasn't evidence enough. The girl who'd driven across two states chasing love was probably not in a position to judge anyone else's enthusiasm levels.

Priscilla nodded again, though it was unclear whether she was agreeing with the plan or just the general assessment of Alaina. "Then—yes, that sounds quite nice, actually."

Alaina's eyes jumped over Priscilla's shoulder to Clark, who was standing behind the counter.

A mischievous smile tugged at her lips. "What about Clark?"

Priscilla didn't look up from her phone. "What about him?"

He'd spoken fondly of Priscilla earlier. He was objectively attractive. And Priscilla was . . . lonely. It wasn't a stretch. In a holiday rom-com, he'd be the obvious match. The sensible, bookish boss and the charming employee with a heart of gold.

"You could invite him too."

Priscilla frowned. "I doubt he'd like to stay after hours at work."

"Can't hurt to ask."

Priscilla glanced up. "If you want, you ask. He's more likely to say yes to you."

"What? Why? He doesn't even know me."

"Yes, but you're . . ." She waved a vague hand at Alaina. "You."

Alaina snorted. "Okay then. You invite everyone else, I'll take Clark."

"Deal."

Alaina stuck out her hand, and Priscilla stared at it for a moment before reaching forward and shaking it. Priscilla's hands were larger than hers, which made sense, given their height difference. Alaina, struck by the warmth radiating from Priscilla's palm, let the touch linger.

Priscilla pulled her hand away, reaching up to tuck a loose strand of hair that had fallen from her bun behind her ear. She cleared her throat, then stepped back. "I'm going to call Ned."

Alaina strolled over to the counter.

Clark looked up and smiled. "We meet again. Mission success, I take it?"

"It was," Alaina said with a grin. "We're going to decorate in here tonight, if you'd like to stick around. Priscilla is inviting some friends over."

His brows lifted, visibly surprised. "Really? I'd love to, but I've got dinner plans with my mom. She's visiting."

Something in her chest pinched. She ignored it. "Mama's boy. That's adorable."

Priscilla came up beside her, catching the tail end of their conversation.

"They're in." Priscilla looked over at Clark. "You?"

He shook his head. "Another time, though."

Alaina smiled. "I'll hold you to that."

Alaina went upstairs to shower, needing to wash off all the real sweat from the faux effort of chopping down Humphrey. She got dressed for a cozy night in, putting on a long, flowing skirt, layering a turtleneck with a short-sleeved blouse over it.

By the time she made it back downstairs, Priscilla had disappeared between the bookshelves to restock. Alaina didn't want to distract her, so she claimed a snug corner of the store, sinking into the embrace of an old, plush armchair. It was much more her speed than the beanbag, and 100 percent less likely to throw her back out when she got up. She'd grabbed a paperback from the romance display, figuring if she was stuck inside a Hallmark movie, she might as well do her research.

Somehow she got hooked. Fully, embarrassingly hooked.

For the first time in, okay, years—unless you counted skimming Cole's coffee-table books on "aesthetic living" and habit stacking—she was completely invested. Lucy Bennett, a relentlessly chipper TV producer, was trying to turn the failing Pine Ridge Lodge into the set of her network's newest Christmas dating show: *25 Days of Dating,* complete with holiday-themed challenges, heart-shaped hot tubs, and a lot of scripted snowball fights. But naturally, the lodge owner's brooding son, Ethan, hated the idea—and Lucy.

While they were snowed in at Ethan's remote cabin, Lucy spotted a photograph on the mantel of a woman in a wedding dress, caught midlaugh. Cue the twist: Ethan, the man who seemed to hate love, had been married. His story was tragic. Young, in love, and widowed after one perfect year. The lodge was more than a business to him. It was the place where he shared his last moments with his wife. And turning it into the set of a dating show felt like a betrayal.

Ethan was telling Lucy that some loves you only get once in a lifetime, when—

"Thought you might be hungry. Clark picked up—oh. Are you okay?"

Alaina jumped, hastily wiping at her eyes. Of course Ethan would rather lose the lodge than taint their sanctuary.

She sniffled. "God, yeah, sorry I'm a mess. This book is just so good, have you read it? It's about—oh my god, are those tacos?"

"Yes, they are, and no, I haven't." Priscilla's expression was carefully neutral, but Alaina caught the slight arch of her eyebrow. "Would you like some tissues?"

"Just the tacos, thanks."

Alaina waited until Priscilla disappeared into the stacks again before diving back in, desperate to know if Lucy could convince Ethan that second chances at love were worth the risk. The rest of the afternoon slipped away as she followed their glacially slow progress toward healing, Ethan accepting that honoring the memory of his wife, Emma, didn't mean staying frozen in grief; Lucy realizing that real love couldn't be manufactured, but it could be found in unexpected places.

As she lifted her gaze from the final pages, a jolt of surprise shot through her—it was already dark outside, the Christmas lights once more brightening the street. It felt like it had only been a few minutes since she'd cracked open the cover, yet somehow, Clark was already flipping the sign on the door.

"See y'all tomorrow," he called, the bell above the door chiming his farewell.

With a theatrical sigh, Alaina reluctantly got up and meandered over to where Priscilla was counting the day's earnings at the register. She lingered for a moment, observing in silence, not wanting to break Priscilla's concentration. The rhythmic shuffle of paper passing through nimble fingers filled the quiet space around them.

Once the last bill was securely stowed away, Alaina leaned over the counter. "So, what's the plan now?"

"Now . . . I'm going upstairs to change, while you wait for our guests. Think you can handle it?"

"I think I can manage to not burn the place down in the next ten minutes. No promises, though."

Priscilla disappeared upstairs, and Alaina wandered the aisles, fingertips brushing over spines. The bookstore felt different with no one else around—like it belonged to her, just for a moment. How did Priscilla decide what to stock? Had she read most of them? Alaina couldn't remember the last time she'd picked up a book for fun before today.

After a few minutes, the bell above the door rang out, and—after jumping almost a full foot in the air—Alaina peered around the shelf to see who it was.

"Alaina!" Callie's voice called. She stepped inside, setting a giant tote on the floor and opening her arms. Alaina didn't hesitate, stepping right into the hug.

"Call me Lani, please," she said, giving Callie a tight squeeze before she pulled back. Normally, that nickname was reserved for people who'd known her more than forty-eight hours, but Callie had the vibe of someone you trusted immediately.

"Lani it is. I hear we have you to thank for Priscilla finally inviting us over."

"She took almost no convincing," Alaina said. "It's good to see you again. Hopefully I look a little less disheveled this time."

Callie gave her a once-over, then grinned. "Love the skirt."

"Thanks! I packed in such a hurry I'm honestly surprised I managed to grab anything that matches."

At that, Callie's eyebrows quirked, a question forming in her eyes. The bell above the door rang again, and both of them turned to see who'd arrived.

"Alaina. Nice to see you again." Grant gave her a nod and a tight-lipped smile before turning to Callie.

He dropped a bag beside her tote and opened his arms. Callie had to rise onto her toes to hug him as they exchanged hellos.

"How's the inn?" Grant asked once they'd separated.

"Fully booked. I held an ornament decorating class for a few of the families staying for the holidays. Glitter everywhere. I'm pretty sure I'll be finding sparkles in weird places until Valentine's Day."

"Sounds festive."

"And the garage?" Callie asked. "That weird noise Lauren's Jeep is making came back. That's still covered under your friendship warranty, right?"

"Tell her if she'd stop hitting every pothole in Brooks, maybe her suspension would last longer than six months." Grant's delivery was bone-dry, but there was warmth beneath it. In a way, he reminded Alaina of Priscilla. She could see how they would make good friends.

"You can tell her yourself—she'll be here in a few."

Callie and Grant fell into an easy rhythm, tossing jokes and names back and forth. Alaina couldn't keep up. She hovered at the edge, smiling when they did, nodding like she was following along.

It felt familiar. Too familiar. Like the nights she'd spent with Cole at networking events, pretending to be fascinated by the rim of her wineglass while conversations flowed around her. Like family parties after her mom died, where she'd drifted through rooms of people who didn't know her.

That same weight settled now, low and familiar. She was so deep in it she almost didn't notice the silence.

She looked up. They were both watching her.

Her stomach flipped. "Sorry, what?"

"Grant was just saying you'll be with us a few days," Callie said.

"Oh, right." Alaina shook her head, trying to clear it. She remembered her calculation. Three more days to hit the road, or else she'd miss Christmas with Cole. "I mean—hopefully not too long. What are we looking at?"

His shrug was less than encouraging. "I ordered the part."

"When will it get here?"

"No way to tell."

"There's no tracking number?" Alaina asked.

Grant raised an eyebrow. "Do I look like Amazon to you? Look, you'll probably be here until Christmas, at least."

Until *Christmas*? Her heart plummeted. Shit. There went plan A. But there was still plan B: fly to New York. She just had to find a flight she could afford.

"Sil!" Callie called, and Alaina was glad for a reason to turn away from Grant's unimpressed stare.

Alaina looked up toward the apartment steps—and blinked. Then blinked again.

Gone were Priscilla's usual practical layers and perfect bun—instead, Priscilla was descending the spiral staircase in a gray Henley with the sleeves rolled up, showing off her notably muscular forearms. Her dark hair was tied back in a loose, low ponytail, softening her sharp features in a way that made something in Alaina's chest trip over itself.

She'd never seen Priscilla look so . . . relaxed? Normal? Though "normal" seemed like the wrong word for someone who could make a basic long-sleeved shirt look like it belonged in a magazine—even if that magazine was less *Elle* and more L.L.Bean.

"Grant, Callie—glad you could make it," Priscilla said as she crossed the floor, boots clicking against the hardwood.

"Are you kidding? Glad you finally invited us," Grant said, hugging her with one arm. "And for Christmas decorating? What's gotten into you?"

"That would be me," Alaina said, raising a hand. Grant

arched an eyebrow at her, and Alaina flushed, realizing how that sounded. "I mean, uh—she's been—we're—"

Priscilla came to her rescue. "Alaina is a big fan of Christmas."

A big fan in theory, Alaina thought. In practice, Christmas cheer had been elusive for nearly half her life. But this was going to be her year. It had to be.

Grant looked around the store. "So where's this tree? I brought a garland."

Priscilla motioned for the door, and the two of them headed off to retrieve it.

As soon as they were gone, Callie leaned against a shelf and gave Alaina a knowing smile. "So . . . you two seem to have warmed up to each other."

It was true. Their dynamic had definitely shifted since Callie saw them that first night.

"Definitely. I am so lucky she was the one who found me in that snowbank."

"I think she was lucky to find you too," Callie said gently.

Alaina dropped her gaze, warmth creeping into her cheeks. Before she could stumble through a response, she caught sight of a small brown blur as it rushed past her.

"Lola!" Callie gasped.

The cat made a beeline straight for Callie. Much to Alaina's surprise, Lola bumped her head against Callie's shins, a purr vibrating through the room. Callie scooped her up in her arms and scratched her plump cheek with a finger.

"Who's a good baby?"

Lola looked like she was in heaven.

Alaina stared, stunned. "Wow, she really likes you. What's your secret?"

"I found her as a kitten. She was out in the cold, the tiniest little thing. I'm horribly allergic so I couldn't keep her myself." As if to prove it, Callie's nose twitched as she sniffled.

"So you asked Priscilla to take her in?"

"She volunteered, actually. She'd never had a cat before, but this one won her heart. God, watching her with this little baby kitten that couldn't have weighed more than two pounds was . . . well, it was adorable. And now she's just the sweetest little girl, isn't she?"

Alaina looked at the cat warily.

The bell chimed again, and Alaina looked up, expecting Priscilla and Grant. Instead, a woman walked in wearing a black peacoat lightly dusted with snow, her sleek blond bob framing ice-blue eyes and sharply arched brows.

"Oh good!" Callie brightened. "Lauren's here!"

The woman strode toward them, using the distance to take in Alaina from top to bottom. If her goal was to intimidate her, it was working.

But when she reached Callie, her expression melted into something almost warm—just for a moment—as she squeezed Callie's arm. Then it snapped back to arctic as she turned to Alaina.

"You must be our stranded tourist."

"Yes! Yeah, that's, uh—that's me. And you must be Lauren."

Lauren's face didn't change as she nodded.

Alaina rushed to fill the silence. "And what do you do?"

What role would Lauren be assigned in the holiday movie that was Brooks? She could see her being a local politician, or maybe the town's lawyer. Something that made the cool, cutting vibe make perfect sense.

"I run the inn with Callie."

Or . . . that.

Priscilla and Grant reappeared, the tree trailing behind them, its thick body snagging on the doorframe. Alaina's eyes flicked their way, watching as they brought Humphrey over to the window.

"So Priscilla found you—where, in a snowbank?"

Alaina tried to ignore the judgmental tone as she turned back to Lauren. "Yes! And she's been an absolute lifesaver, letting me crash at her place," she said. "I can't believe I ended up stranded in Utah."

One of Lauren's perfectly plucked eyebrows arched upward. "What's wrong with Utah?"

Alaina wanted to sink into the floor. "Nothing! Nothing, it's beautiful. I'm loving it so far, actually. Very cool. Everyone's . . . nice?"

"Hm." Lauren gave her another once-over. "And where are you from, Alaina?"

And how soon can you go back there?

"Colorado, originally, but I moved around a bit as a kid and ended up in California." The explanation was well rehearsed, one she'd given a hundred times. "And, well, I've been there ever since. Until now, that is."

"California? So where were you headed?"

"Stop interrogating her, Lauren," Priscilla called, not even looking up from where she and Grant were adjusting the tree in its stand.

Alaina exhaled, grateful. Because, yeah, it really did feel like an interrogation, like she might slip up and say the wrong thing at any second. Everything about Lauren—from her pristinely pressed peacoat to her perfect posture—screamed "pragmatist." The type of person who'd see Alaina's quest to prove herself to Cole not as a grand romantic gesture but as a restraining order waiting to happen. Even imagining trying to explain The List to someone who probably color-coded her calendar made Alaina want to crawl under the counter in embarrassment. She rarely had a plan—The List was honestly impressive for her, and even that was incomplete.

God, she really, really needed to work on that. What was she going to say to Cole?

Callie rescued her with a change of subject. "Jeez. Did the two of you really chop that down yourselves?" she asked, looking over at the tree.

"Yes! Well, Sil did. I mostly just watched."

Alaina's eyes flitted over to Priscilla, her memory rewinding to Priscilla swinging the ax in the snow.

When she managed to tear her gaze off Priscilla, she noticed Lauren was watching her again. "So, Alaina . . . how long are you staying?"

It was a fair question. One Alaina had been asking herself. But coming from Lauren, it landed differently—like a subtle nudge toward the door. Her stomach dipped. She hoped she hadn't flinched, but judging by how quickly Callie jumped in, maybe she had.

"You heard Sil, Lauren," Callie said. "Besides, Alaina can stay in Brooks as long as she'd like!"

Alaina wasn't sure how Callie and Lauren could run a business together. Callie seemed like the type to leave chocolates on the guests' pillows, Lauren more like she'd be watching the minute hand on the clock to make sure the guests checked out by exactly 11 A.M. Total opposites. And yet, at Callie's words, Lauren backed down, offering Alaina a thin smile. "Of course. Any friend of Priscilla's is a friend of ours."

Polite, but not exactly warm.

"Yeah, same, totally," Alaina said, nodding too fast.

Her nerves had officially taken the wheel.

It didn't matter that Callie clearly liked her, or that Ned and Clark had taken to her right away. Even Grant's gruffness seemed manageable in the face of Lauren, who made Alaina feel like she was tracking snow all over a freshly mopped floor.

She couldn't figure out why Lauren's opinion mattered to her. It wasn't like she'd be sticking around once her car was fixed. Maybe it was because for the first time since arriving in Brooks, she felt like she was back in Cole's world, where everyone else seemed to know the rules to some game she'd never heard of. Or maybe she just wanted to prove she could fit into this cozy life Priscilla had built, even just for a few days.

Her gaze drifted across the store. Priscilla was kneeling by the tree, tightening something at the base while Grant supervised. As if on cue, she glanced back and met Alaina's eyes.

Was she checking on her? The tension in Alaina's chest eased a little.

Alaina jerked a thumb toward Priscilla and Grant. "I'm going to see if they need a hand with Humphrey."

"Humphrey?" Lauren repeated, bewildered.

Humphrey stood tall in the front window, already looking like he belonged. Grant threw Alaina a tight-lipped smile that felt like it might as well have been a grin after her conversation with Lauren.

"How's it going over here?" Alaina asked, crouching beside Priscilla.

"Good." Priscilla turned the knob on the tree stand one last time, then leaned back on her heels, looking up at her. "We'll be ready to decorate in no time."

Alaina lowered her voice. "You're doing okay?"

"So far," Priscilla said. "You?"

Despite the vibe she got from Lauren, Alaina nodded. "Yeah. Your friends are nice. This is going to be fun."

The door opened again, and in walked the server from Patty's diner. Ned had changed out of his powder-blue uniform shirt and apron and was instead wearing a cozy-looking knit sweater, his curls falling loose around his shoulders. His arms were loaded with plastic bags, several hanging off each arm. He made a beeline straight for Grant.

"Hey, gorgeous." Ned stood on his toes to kiss Grant on the lips.

Alaina grinned as she connected the glaringly obvious dots. "Wait, you guys are together?" Her heart warmed at the thought. "That's so cute!"

Grant rolled his eyes but didn't hide his smile as he took the bags from Ned.

Ned beamed at her. "Alaina! It's nice to see you again."

"You too." Alaina rose to her feet, and Priscilla followed. "That pie was amazing."

"I'll pass it on to Patty! She'll be happy to hear it."

Alaina couldn't quite picture the woman from the diner being happy to hear anything, especially not anything to do with Alaina, but she wasn't going to argue. Maybe Patty was a secret softie. Priscilla had mentioned how kind the older woman had been to her when she first arrived in Brooks.

"Grant told me your car's out of commission. Hope Sil here doesn't drive you nuts." With a wink, Ned nudged Priscilla in the arm. "Has she tried to make you eat cottage cheese yet?"

"It's a great source of protein—" Priscilla said, but Alaina cut her off.

"No, and she absolutely will not be doing that. My body may be a temple, but this temple demands a sugary sacrifice." Alaina shook her head, laughing. "Speaking of—this kind of feels like a perfect occasion for some festive drinks."

Ned held up a plastic bag. "Great minds think alike! I brought eggnog."

Alaina squealed. "Perfect! Sil, tell me you have rum."

"I do." Priscilla sounded resigned. "I'll go get it."

"I'll help you carry the cups!" Ned followed her toward the stairs.

Alaina watched them go for a beat, then turned to find Grant's eyes on her. He gave her a small almost-smile. Maybe he was warming up.

"How're you liking Brooks?" Grant asked.

"Honestly? When I found out I was stuck here, I panicked. But . . ." Alaina found herself smiling. "There's something about this place, and it's not just how it looks like a Christmas movie. People here actually care about each other. Like you guys, all showing up to decorate this tree? And Priscilla . . ." She trailed off, looking down at her feet.

She couldn't quite think of how to describe Priscilla. Had it really been less than forty-eight hours since they'd met? It felt like so much longer.

"Sil likes you," Grant said. "Don't fuck that up."

Alaina's head snapped up. The abrupt shift in conversation left her momentarily speechless. "I like her too," she said finally. "And I won't."

"Good." Grant nodded at the stairs, where Ned and Priscilla were descending. Ned held up the bottle of rum like a trophy, and Grant started toward him.

Alaina shook off the seriousness of the moment and let out a whoop. "Let's get our nog on!"

Priscilla stopped midway down the stairs to look at Alaina, expression unamused. "I'm going to regret this, aren't I?"

They all gathered at the counter, where Priscilla lined up tumblers and Ned poured with a generous hand. They raised their glasses in a toast, then took a sip. The spiced rum hit first, smooth and warm, followed by creamy eggnog. Alaina closed her eyes, humming in satisfaction as she swallowed.

"Wow, that's—what kind of rum is this?"

"Ron Zacapa," Priscilla said, a little sheepish. Alaina didn't recognize the name but clocked the way Grant raised his eyebrows. "It's probably a bit much for eggnog, but it's all I had on hand."

"I'm not complaining." Grant took a swig.

Alaina grinned. "Me either."

Soon they were back in front of the tree, Grant and Ned stringing warm yellow lights through the branches. They glowed soft and golden, casting a halo around Humphrey.

"Let's see what everyone brought!" Callie clapped her hands together before reaching into her oversized tote. She pulled out strings of cranberries and popcorn, and a few handmade ornaments—reindeer faces made out of Popsicle sticks, complete with a red pom-pom nose. "Lauren and I made these with some of the kids staying at the lodge. Cute, right?"

"Adorable," Grant said, though it looked like it might have pained him to admit it.

Lauren produced a set of six angels that looked like they were carved out of crystal. She held one up and it caught the light perfectly. They looked a little ridiculous beside the googly-eyed reindeer, but Alaina kind of loved that.

Ned's contribution was a collection of mismatched ornaments. "We have people drop off unused ornaments at the diner to put onto the community tree," he said as he held up a ceramic snowman family. "You're lucky—we actually ran out of space this year. Plenty of leftovers."

Even Grant had something to offer: a box of carved wooden ornaments. Alaina picked up a pine cone with perfectly whittled details.

"My grandfather taught me woodworking," he said with a shrug, suddenly shy.

Alaina gaped. "You *made* these?"

"You know you all didn't have to—" Priscilla said, but Grant interrupted her.

"We wanted to. Now, would someone get some music going in here?"

Alaina pulled her phone out. "Dibs on the playlist!"

"The speaker is behind the counter," Priscilla said. "Come on."

Alaina followed Priscilla toward the register, a bounce in her step. She'd been working on the perfect Christmas playlist for weeks before Cole left.

A sharp pang hit her chest. But before it could stick, Priscilla pressed the power button on the sound system.

"What do you have on there?" Priscilla leaned over her shoulder to peer at her phone, and the hairs on the back of Alaina's neck stood at the almost-contact.

"Just the best Christmas mix ever."

The Bluetooth finally connected, and she opened her music app. She forced Cole out of her head and a smile onto her face as she hit play. Tonight wasn't about The List. Or proving anything. Tonight was for Priscilla and her friends. No moping.

Ariana Grande's "Santa Tell Me" blasted through the speakers, and a cheer went up from the other side of the room. Ned shimmied toward a reluctant Grant, throwing a string of garland around his neck as he pulled him in for a kiss. Alaina looked away from the private moment, repeating *no moping* in her head over and over again. Just because the guy she loved had left her didn't mean she had to be jealous of other people's happiness.

Priscilla tilted her head, drawing Alaina's attention back to her. "I prefer classical."

Alaina rolled her eyes, a smile taking over her face. "Of course you do. That's why I'm in charge."

Brooks Books was even more magical when decked out in Christmas cheer. Ned had boxes upon boxes of leftover decorations that took several trips out to his car to retrieve.

Alaina paused to snap a photo of the tree. Between the lights and layers of mismatched ornaments, it looked borderline ridiculous—but also perfect. As she lowered her phone, a warm ache stirred in her chest. Her mom would've loved this. She could still picture her, tangled in strings of lights, humming off-key as she transformed their cramped apartments into something enchanted.

This may not have been the Christmas she'd dreamed of spending with Cole, but there was something about this unplanned, unconventional, unexpectedly lovely version that felt like its own kind of magic.

Priscilla picked a piece of tinsel off her sleeve. "This stuff gets everywhere."

Callie stood on a ladder, draping some garland over the top of one of the shelves. "It's part of the fun, Sil." She hopped down, and Lauren pressed a kiss to Callie's temple, making Alaina do a double take.

Wait—Callie and Lauren were *together*? She thought back to all the moments between Callie and Lauren, how Callie had mentioned getting Lauren a present from the bookstore, how she'd lit up as soon as Lauren arrived that evening.

Okay, yeah. It made sense. Opposites did attract, after all.

So Ned and Grant were together, and Callie and Lauren

were together. She thought *what are the odds,* then caught herself. Nico always joked that queer people had a sixth sense—like echolocation, but for spotting other queer people across a crowded room. Maybe in a small town it wasn't strange at all that they'd found each other.

Her gaze slid to Priscilla. *Huh.*

Suddenly, Patty assuming they were on a date made a lot more sense. She made a quick mental note: Priscilla probably wasn't straight. Not that it mattered. It didn't. Obviously.

She looked away quickly, catching Lauren whispering something to Callie that made her burst into giggles and swat her shoulder. Alaina blinked. Apparently, the woman did have a sense of humor. Maybe she just saved it for Callie.

Surrounded by so much affection, something twisted tight in Alaina's chest.

She blinked it away and reached to hang another ornament—one of Grant's wooden reindeer—on a lower branch.

"You've got an eye for this." Priscilla was beside her again. "Are you having a good time?"

Alaina nodded. "Absolutely." And that was the truth—despite the feelings about dead mothers and boyfriends on a break, this was Christmas joy, pure and simple. "You?"

Priscilla's eyes found hers, and she smiled. "I am. Thank you."

"I think we should take a picture," Ned said. "God knows when this is going to happen again. We might have to invite Alaina back next year."

The idea of being invited back—of being wanted here—sent a thrill through her.

"I'm down!" Alaina grinned.

"Fine, one picture." Priscilla looked around. "Where's Callie?"

"Be right there!" Callie popped around a corner a second later. "Just adding a few finishing touches."

They propped up Callie's phone on a shelf. She hit the timer, then jogged back to stand next to Lauren. At the last second, Priscilla's arm wrapped around Alaina's waist, pulling her in close. The unexpected touch sent a ripple of warmth through Alaina's chest.

The picture was adorable, Lauren and Callie bracketing one side, Grant and Ned on the other. In the middle, in front of the tree, Priscilla stood smiling, Alaina beaming up at her.

"Can you send this to me?" Alaina asked Callie. Callie nodded and handed over her phone for Alaina to type in her number.

Another hour later, Alaina leaned against the counter, watching Callie and Grant hang a wreath Grant had brought for the door. The lights were twinkling on the tree, gently glowing against the dark backdrop of the street outside. The rum was warm in her stomach, and her eyes stung with hot tears.

It was just too beautiful. How had she gone from shivering on the side of the road to this in only a few days?

"Alaina?" Priscilla appeared, like an answer to her question. Her eyes scanned Alaina's face, concern tugging at her eyebrows, and—great, apparently one of those tears had made it all the way down her cheek. "Are you all right?"

Alaina sniffled, dabbing at her face with her sweater. "Yeah. I'm fine. I swear. Just"—she gave a small, embarrassed laugh—"happy tears."

"Okay." Priscilla didn't sound convinced. "Are you sure?"

Alaina gave her a tepid smile. "After my mom died, I couldn't—I didn't want to celebrate without her. And this year, I thought, you know, it's been ten years. Maybe I was ready to try again." She paused. "And somehow, I ended up here, doing all this. And it's . . . perfect."

When she glanced up, Priscilla was watching her with a strange expression.

Oh no. Had she really just dropped the dead-mom bomb in the middle of what was supposed to be a fun-filled, cheerful night? A flush crept up her neck. "God, sorry," she mumbled, brushing her hair back. "Alcohol turns me into an oversharer."

Priscilla's hand landed gently on her shoulder. "You don't have to apologize."

Something settled in her chest. She'd never told anyone what she'd just told Priscilla, never laid her grief so plainly at anyone's feet. Not even Nico, and definitely not Cole. Saying it out loud felt like tempting fate. What if she wasn't able to summon the Christmas magic she'd been hoping to channel through her mom's memory? She didn't want to put that on anyone.

Yet here she was, spilling it to Priscilla.

"I'm really glad we could give you a little Christmas cheer," Priscilla said, dropping her hand and moving so they were standing side by side. "And I'm sorry I've been such a grinch about it."

Alaina raised her eyebrows, her mouth falling open into a smile. "A grinch? Was that a movie reference?"

"It was a book first," Priscilla said.

Alaina grinned. Priscilla dipped her head, but not fast enough to hide her smile. They stood there in the hush between songs, neither of them rushing to fill it.

"You don't have to apologize either, by the way," Alaina said, leaning so her shoulder nudged Priscilla's. "For not liking Christmas. I get it. You've got your own stuff."

Priscilla looked up, a hint of vulnerability in her eyes. "I do.

But I have to admit, this was nice. Maybe it's time for some new memories."

The way the warm light hit Priscilla's cheekbones, the closeness between them, the way the room had quieted—it all made Alaina feel slightly unsteady. The rum buzzed under her skin, and everything around her seemed sharper and softer at once.

"Well," Alaina said, offering a crooked smile, "if you ever need help making those new memories, you know where to find me."

She meant it as a joke. Like, obviously Priscilla knew where to find her, since she was staying on Priscilla's couch.

But at her words, Priscilla's gaze dipped, barely, for the briefest second, to Alaina's mouth. Alaina's breath caught.

She looked away, brushing it off. It wasn't the first time a couple of drinks had made her feel this way around a woman. A little flustered. A little drawn in. And usually, by morning, it passed—like a spark that flared and faded before it could mean anything.

"Hey, you two!" It was Callie, waving them over. "It's time to put on the star. Sil?"

Priscilla walked over to take the star from Callie. She looked at it for a moment, then held it out to Alaina. "Here, you should do it. You're the reason we're all here tonight."

"Me? No, it's your tree, I can't—"

"Afraid you won't be able to reach?"

Alaina snorted. "Okay, first of all, fuck you. Second of all, fine."

She took the star from Priscilla's hands, enjoying the warm glow of it against her skin. Stepping up onto the window display, she stretched to place it at the top of the tree.

When she looked down, Priscilla had her phone raised, snapping a photo. "For your collection," she said when Alaina raised an eyebrow.

It wasn't like she was doing something daring or adventurous enough to impress Cole, but Alaina appreciated having the moment captured nonetheless. It was one she would want to remember for a long, long time.

❄

"Today was pleasant," Priscilla said. Everyone else had left, and they were upstairs on the couch, Lola curled up on Priscilla's lap.

"Be less enthusiastic about it, I dare you."

Priscilla cracked a smile. "It was a perfectly acceptable way to spend an evening."

"That's more like it." Alaina leaned back into the couch. "Your friends are kind of amazing, actually. The way they all just showed up, bringing pieces of their lives to make this happen. It felt special."

"They are. And it was."

Alaina paused to think of just how to phrase her next thought with the subtlety it deserved.

"They're also all gay."

Nope, that wasn't it.

She watched as Priscilla continued stroking Lola, her gaze fixed on the cat, her expression indecipherable. Had she overstepped? God, she wasn't trying to dig. She just wanted to learn everything she could about Priscilla in the few days she had to spend with her.

Priscilla exhaled an uneven breath. "That tends to happen, when one is gay themself."

There it was. It seemed Alaina's gaydar was finally getting better.

She nodded. "Yeah, I know."

Priscilla's eyes snapped up to Alaina's. "You do?"

"Oh, not that I'm—I mean, I'm not. Not gay. Or—um, anyway, the point is my best friend is queer, and I've seen their friend group, so I understand how it works. Not that all gay people are the same, I mean, just—"

"Alaina," Priscilla said. "Breathe."

"I'm breathing!" she said, but the high-pitched wheeze in her voice said otherwise. "I guess I was just trying to say that I'm glad you found your people, even in a town as small as Brooks."

That earned her a soft smile. "I'm glad I found them too."

"Lauren's pretty scary, though."

Priscilla huffed out a laugh. "She's all bark. Unless—did she say something to you?"

"It was more of a vibe."

"They're . . . protective of me." It sounded like Priscilla might be puzzling this out as she spoke. "Not that you're—they mean well, is all."

"It's cool. It's nice, actually, that they look out for you. I wish I had that. My social circle's more of a dot," Alaina said, trying to make a joke out of it. It didn't really land. "I mean, there's Nico. But everyone else was sort of . . . borrowed from Cole's life."

Although, now that Alaina thought about it, even Nico had started to seem distant. There'd been too many rain checks, too many missed calls on both sides. Nico was spending most of their free time with Josie, and she'd been busy weaving herself into Cole's world, where no one really bothered to get to know her.

"And Nico is your best friend?"

"Yeah." She pulled her knees in closer, hugging herself. "But we haven't had as much time to spend together lately."

"That happens sometimes," Priscilla said. "Lives change. People get busy."

"They do. But with best friends, it shouldn't matter."

Was she trying to convince Priscilla or herself? When she got Cole back, she'd do better. Be better. Stop treating her friendship with Nico like a houseplant she occasionally remembered to water.

"No matter how long it's been, things just fall back into place, right?" Alaina asked.

"Yes." There was a sadness in Priscilla's voice that felt all too familiar to Alaina. Could she reach out and hold her hand, do anything to comfort her? Were they there yet? Probably not.

She settled for saying, "I'm glad you have them."

"I am too. My family wasn't exactly . . . accepting." The admission seemed to cost Priscilla, each word measured and heavy. She paused, gathering a breath as if to fortify herself against the memories. "Growing up in a very religious household, coming out . . . It was as if I had betrayed them. They didn't outright disown me, not at first. But their disappointment was clear—they demanded I never do anything to embarrass them."

"Fuck that."

Maybe that was a little strong, especially around the woman who didn't like curse words. But she had never heard anything more absurd than Priscilla being an embarrassment, and she was still maybe just a little tipsy.

Priscilla didn't admonish her for her language this time, at least.

"It felt like I was letting them down by being a lesbian."

"I don't understand. Who could ever be embarrassed by you? I've known you for two days and you're already, like, the coolest person I've ever met."

Priscilla smiled a little at this, but it didn't reach her eyes. "I did my best to follow their rules, but . . . a year later, I fell in love for the first time."

Alaina thought of her middle-school boyfriend Devon, her own first heartbreak. How she'd poured every ounce of herself into that relationship. For Valentine's Day, she'd spent hours writing him a hundred love notes, tucking them in every corner of his life: his locker, backpack, even amid his socks. In hindsight, it was an avalanche of affection after just a month of dating, but hey—she'd seen the movies. She knew love was supposed to be intense, and she wanted so badly to get it right.

He'd dumped her a week later. Her mom—and *Bridget Jones's Diary*—had been there to help her get over him.

Priscilla, the definition of poised and proper, infatuated with someone to that degree? It was hard to imagine.

"What was she like?"

"Funny. Ambitious. A little too snarky for her own good. She convinced me that my parents were wrong for holding me back, and wanted me to confront them, so . . . I did."

Alaina frowned. "Were you ready for that?"

"No." Bitterness dripped from that single syllable, and Alaina's heart broke for Priscilla. "But I was terrified of disappointing her. And when my parents didn't take it well, things . . . fell apart. They didn't kick me out, exactly, but I couldn't stay. The tension was unbearable. I moved in with her, but—" Priscilla stopped to let out a shaky breath. "That didn't work out either. Then I was on my own."

Alaina couldn't stop herself from reaching for Priscilla's hand. She watched as Priscilla's eyes fell to the touch, and was relieved when Priscilla squeezed back a second later.

"How old were you?"

"Eighteen." It came out as a whisper. "I didn't know what I was going to do with my life, so . . . I picked a spot on a map. Threw a dart at it, actually. And that brought me here, to Brooks. I had dual citizenship because my mother was born in the States, and a fair amount of money in a trust fund my grandmother left me. She loved books, so when I saw this place for sale, I just knew. She would've loved it here."

Alaina couldn't imagine Priscilla doing anything so impulsive. She must've been really desperate for a fresh start—or completely out of options.

"I'm glad this is where your dart landed," Alaina said. "Otherwise, I'd probably still be stuck in the snow."

"I'm glad too." Priscilla smiled again, and this time the warmth of it reached her eyes. "I like my life here. My friends, the store. It was a terrible thing to go through, but it got me to where I am. I wouldn't take any of it back."

Alaina studied Priscilla's face, trying to reconcile the woman who clearly treasured these friendships with the one who'd needed convincing to invite them over. There was a story there, but Alaina wasn't sure she had the right to ask quite yet.

She nodded instead. She knew what it was like to be young and lost, searching for a place to belong. She was still holding out hope that one day she'd find her home too.

Sitting there, her body still buzzing pleasantly from the rum, Alaina had a feeling she was moving in the right direction.

Chapter Eight

FIVE DAYS UNTIL CHRISTMAS

The noon sun caught the glistening snow as they wound their way out of downtown Brooks. While Priscilla drove, Alaina smoothed out the crumpled piece of paper against her lap, studying it.

1. Chop down a Christmas tree
2. Go ice skating on a lake
3. Learn to ski
4. Hike a mountain
5. Camp under the stars
6. Win Cole's heart with a grand romantic gesture—big movie moment? TBD!!!

She drew a thick, satisfying line through the first item. One down. In a few hours, she'd cross off number two. They'd only needed to wait for Clark to start his shift, and just like that, they were off to the lake Priscilla had said was perfect for skating this time of year.

Alaina had never been on the ice before. She had no idea

what to expect. Did you buy skates? Rent them? Was there some kind of learner's permit required before letting amateurs loose on a frozen lake?

Her pen drifted down to the last item. Writing "TBD" yesterday morning had felt reasonable, even optimistic. Now, though, determining the "to be determined" was considerably more stressful than the movies implied.

What could she even say to Cole in New York? The perfect words were supposed to come easily, weren't they? Yet after days of thinking, nothing. She needed the end-of-the-movie monologue—the kind the guy gives the girl after running through the airport, except this time she'd be the one doing the dramatic confession. But every time she pictured herself standing in front of Cole, she was as speechless as she'd been the night he left.

The weight of the moment pressed heavily on her chest, forcing out a sigh. Inspiration needed to strike, and soon.

"We're here." Priscilla threw the truck into park, pulling Alaina from her thoughts. Straightening, Alaina glanced out the window at a store with a giant sign that read FRANKLIN'S SNOW SPORTS SUPPLY.

"Wow." Alaina hopped out of the truck and slammed the door before walking around to the front of the cab, where Priscilla waited. "This place is a lot bigger than I expected."

Priscilla shrugged. "Like I said, we get a lot of tourists. Come on."

Inside, the store was unmistakably Brooks—a converted barn with exposed wooden beams and worn floors that creaked beneath their shoes. Near the entrance, a coffee station offered free local roasts, while a bulletin board overflowed with trail updates and community notices. An older man in a flannel shirt greeted them from behind a workbench where he was waxing skis, calling out to Priscilla by name and pointing them toward the ice skates.

As they moved through the aisles, Alaina slowed by a towering wall of snowboards and skis. They were enormous—bigger than on TV—with designs ranging from peaceful mountain scenes to eye-searing neon.

Had Priscilla said she skied or snowboarded? Either way, Alaina bet she looked badass doing it. Just the thought of strapping herself to one of those things made her palms sweat.

Baby steps. Skating first. That was just walking, but on blades. How hard could it be?

When they reached the skate section, Priscilla stopped at a bench. "Sit down and take your shoes off while I find you a pair."

Alaina plopped down with a grin. "Yes, ma'am."

Priscilla rolled her eyes, but a small smile teased at her lips. "What's your size?"

Alaina told her—seven, unless the shoe was particularly narrow, then seven and a half—and Priscilla was off. Shoeless, Alaina wiggled her toes along to the Christmas music humming through the speakers. She half expected Priscilla to reappear instantly with whatever pair she grabbed first, but a couple of songs went by and still no Priscilla. Probably comparing ankle support and blade sharpness. The thought made Alaina smile.

She pulled out her phone and opened Instagram, pressing the plus beside her profile picture. She loaded her favorite shots from yesterday: pretending—somewhat convincingly—to cut down the tree, then Humphrey, fully decked out.

A few seconds later, her phone buzzed in her hands. It was a message from Nico.

Nico 11:37 a.m.: who thought it was a good idea to give you an ax?

Alaina 11:37: I'll have you know I was very responsible and only almost cut off one limb

She swiped back to her messages. Below Nico's was the unknown number—well, not so unknown anymore, she supposed.

Shauna, left on read. What was Alaina supposed to say? It had been years. What could her cousin want?

"Here you go."

Alaina looked up at Priscilla's voice—and blinked at what she held in her hands. These were not scuffed beige rentals destined for the feet of clumsy first-timers. Instead, in front of her were a pair of classic white figure skates.

"Are those for me?"

"If they fit." Priscilla crouched, holding them out like an offering. "Let's see."

Alaina eagerly took the skates from Priscilla and slipped her feet into them. Priscilla pressed her fingers to the toe of the skate. "Feel good?"

They felt as good as they looked—amazing. She couldn't stop staring at them.

"They're beautiful."

Priscilla began to lace the skates, tightening them around Alaina's ankles, the sides pulling together to provide stable, comforting support. When she was done, Priscilla stood, taking a step back to offer Alaina her hand. "Take a few steps to see how they fit."

Her knees wobbled as she stood on the thin blades for the first time, clinging to Priscilla to make sure she wouldn't fall.

She took a few tentative steps on the carpeted floor, trying to get used to the weight of the skates on her feet.

Priscilla watched, glancing between the skates and Alaina's face. "Do your ankles feel supported?"

"Yeah."

"Not too tight?"

"They're perfect, Sil." Her grin bubbled up again—giddy, unfiltered—and she was delighted when Priscilla smiled back at her.

"Good. Wait here just a moment."

Priscilla walked off, leaving Alaina to gape at the skates. She ran her thumb along the white leather, watching light bounce off the blades. It brought back a memory so clear and sudden it startled her—a sharp contrast to the fuzzy edges of most memories of her mother.

She'd been curled up against her mother's side on their living room sofa, watching the Winter Olympics on television. Skaters spun effortlessly across the ice, mesmerizing her. She remembered the softness of her mother's sweater, the warmth of her smile when Alaina looked up at her.

"Can we go ice skating?" she'd asked. "I want to learn to do that."

Her mother had laughed. "Of course. One day we'll go together and I'll teach you."

Had her mother actually known how to ice skate? Probably. She'd grown up in Colorado and loved all things winter. Who could she even ask? Would Doreen know?

Alaina eased the skates back into their box, tucking the memory away with them, and wrestled her Converses on. By the time she was done tying her shoes, Priscilla was back, hands in her coat pockets, a small curve to her mouth as she watched Alaina.

"Ready?" Priscilla nodded toward the exit.

"Oh, let me just pay for—"

"It's been taken care of."

That wasn't computing. "Huh?"

"I took care of it," Priscilla said. "We're good to go."

"What?"

Heat rose in Alaina's chest, emotion swelling too quickly. Oh god, she wasn't going to cry in front of Priscilla again, was she? Twice in twenty-four hours would just be plain embarrassing.

"Priscilla, no, I—I can't let you do that. Let me pay you back, please?"

Priscilla shrugged. "It's not a big deal. Franklin owed me a favor, and I already have everything I could ever need from here. They're yours."

"Like—to keep?"

Priscilla nodded, and Alaina's body moved before her brain caught up, arms looping around Priscilla's shoulders. "Thank you."

Priscilla stiffened briefly before her arms folded around Alaina—one at her waist, the other along her upper back.

They held there for a few seconds before Priscilla stepped away, her gaze on the ground, her cheeks a light pink. She cleared her throat. "You're welcome." She pivoted toward the exit.

Alaina lingered, pulse skittering.

Damn, Priscilla gave good hugs. She was going to need more of those.

❄

They stood at the edge of what Priscilla had called "the locals' lake," hidden about twenty minutes from town at the end of a winding mountain road. The scene before them was breathtaking—a wide expanse of black ice peeking through patches of snow, perfectly reflecting the mountains that rose up around them. The afternoon sun turned everything blindingly white, and Alaina had to squint to see the other skaters: a couple holding hands as they moved in lazy circles in the distance, and a mother teaching her kids to skate near the shore.

"Is this a good time to mention that I've never been skating before?"

Priscilla shot her a disbelieving smile. "You're joking."

Alaina shook her head. "Nope."

The smile fell, leaving only the disbelief. "That might have been an important detail to mention a little earlier."

"I'm sure I'll get the hang of it in no time. How hard can it be?" Alaina took a tentative step toward the ice. It was more difficult to walk in skates here than it had been on the nice, flat carpet in the store. Go figure.

Priscilla's mouth twisted skeptically. "Then let's do this."

"Like walking—with *style.*" Alaina pushed onto the ice. Exactly four seconds later she ate her words, nearly tumbling as her balance wavered. "Oh shit!" Priscilla lunged to catch her, but Alaina steadied herself at the last moment, thrusting out a hand. "No, wait, I've got this."

"If you say so."

Alaina pressed forward, determined to prove herself, gliding ahead with every ounce of confidence she could fake. And for a moment, it worked.

"Look, Ma, no hands!" She held her arms wide, grinning—until the grin slipped, replaced by panic as she wobbled and crashed to the ice.

Priscilla was beside her in an instant. "Alaina! Are you okay?"

"My ass broke my fall, don't worry." Alaina took the hand

Priscilla offered, hauling herself upright. "God, ice is hard, did you know that?"

"I'm sure He does."

"Ha." Alaina shook her head. "Now she's got jokes."

She staggered away from Priscilla like a toddling penguin, then took off—sort of. The ability to control her direction and speed remained elusive, but at least she was moving.

Well, for about a minute, anyway, before she nose-dived onto the ice, knees and palms protesting loudly. "Damn it!"

Priscilla appeared beside her, annoyingly graceful. "Still don't want my help?" Her eyebrow quirked in a challenge.

Alaina playfully swatted Priscilla's hand away and shoved herself up again. "I'm getting the hang of it, I swear."

She was not getting the hang of it.

First, her left skate betrayed her, the toe pick catching the ice and almost sending her into a face-plant. Next, a failed turn sent her down, her hip connecting with the ice in a painful smack. The fall after that plopped her on her butt, legs comically splayed. Priscilla swooped in, coming to an effortless stop between Alaina's feet.

"That's it. I'm not having you break your tailbone because you're too proud to let me teach you." Priscilla held out a hand, and Alaina accepted the help to her feet, yet again.

Snow clung to Alaina's coat, and Priscilla casually brushed it away. "It's okay, we can take it slow." Priscilla's hands found hers, steadying them between their bodies.

"That's what she—"

Priscilla cut her off. "Just hang on to me, all right?"

Before Alaina knew it, they were moving again. Priscilla bent slightly to match Alaina's height, eyes focused, pulling Alaina into a rhythm.

"Bend your knees, but keep your center of gravity . . ." Priscilla adjusted Alaina's posture. "There. Now, mirror my feet. Push and slide. You're not walking, you're gliding."

Alaina tried to emulate Priscilla's movements, but mostly she was just being towed along by Priscilla's firm grip on her arms.

"How'd you learn to skate backward?"

"I've been skating since I was a little girl." Priscilla smoothly steered them around in a graceful curve, turning back the way they came. "Ice skating, ballet, piano lessons—my parents signed me up for all the so-called 'proper' activities."

"So you're—what, a princess?"

Priscilla chuckled. "Not quite. But I was put in lessons practically as soon as I could walk. It's second nature by now."

Alaina's heartbeat quickened along with their pace; the sensation of flying across the ice was thrilling and terrifying all at once.

"You're getting the hang of this." Priscilla's smile was warm and proud.

Her own grin bloomed as she let out a shaky breath. "I am?"

"Definitely. But I'm going to need to let go of you to take a picture," Priscilla said. "I'll get you up to speed, then all you need to do is stay upright while I snap a quick shot."

Alaina raised an eyebrow at her. "You make it sound so easy."

"It will be, just don't fall." Priscilla wore a cheeky grin, not bothering to hide her amusement.

Alaina's mouth dropped open indignantly. "Fuck you!"

In response, Priscilla let go, leaving Alaina suddenly unsupported, arms pinwheeling as she fought for balance.

"Wait! Okay, okay, I take it back."

"Good." Priscilla's hands found hers again, stabilizing her. "Ready?"

Priscilla slowly withdrew, and somehow, Alaina didn't immediately fall flat on her face.

Priscilla's supportive comments were almost as reassuring as her grip had been. "Glide. That's it," she said, putting enough distance between them to frame a good shot.

"Am I doing it right? Do I look like I'm skating?" Alaina tried to keep pace, fumbling without Priscilla directly in front of her to mimic.

"You *are* skating, so yes."

Well, that was reassuring. "Do I look cool?"

Priscilla lowered the phone, smirking playfully. "More like terrified, but with the right filter, it might pass as exhilaration."

Alaina focused on Priscilla's feet, copying her rhythm. Her hands hovered uncertainly in front of her, grasping at invisible support. She sucked in a deep breath and extended her arms wide, savoring the rush of cold wind against her fingers. Tipping her head back, she smiled into the thrill of the moment.

Priscilla's delight came through her voice. "There you are."

Right on cue, Alaina tilted a bit too far back. Balance thrown, she flailed, trying desperately to recover—but gravity won.

Except, before the painful collision she was anticipating could unfold, strong arms circled her waist. Her skates skidded uselessly, but she didn't hit the ground. She hung suspended in a graceful dip, arms instinctively looping around Priscilla's shoulders for support. Relief flooded through her. She couldn't handle another fall.

Panting, Alaina clung to Priscilla, both of them frozen in place.

"That was close," Alaina finally breathed. "Are you okay?"

"Am I—you're the one who nearly fell." Priscilla gently eased Alaina upright, but her hands lingered at her waist.

"It was fun." Alaina sounded breathless. Why was she so breathless? She hadn't even fallen, but her heart was racing anyway. "Plus, I knew you'd catch me."

Priscilla chuckled. "I almost didn't."

"Hand me that." Alaina reached for the phone, flipped to the front camera, and stretched her arm out for a selfie. Priscilla began ducking out of the frame, but Alaina caught her hand, pulling it back around her waist. "Stay."

"This isn't an adventurous action shot," Priscilla said in protest. "How is this meant to impress your boyfriend?"

"It's not," Alaina responded. "This is for me. Now smile."

They stayed on the ice until dusk, watching the sun sink behind the mountains, painting the sky in shades of pink and orange. When they finally stopped at the lake's edge, their breath came in clouds of steam. Now that they weren't gliding across the ice, a shiver crept up Alaina's spine, every tremor sending a burst of pain through her, souvenirs from her numerous encounters with the ground.

"You're freezing." Priscilla rubbed Alaina's arms to warm her.

Alaina tried to steady her shivers, wanting to milk just a few more precious moments on the ice, but her body betrayed her. "I'm f-fine," she said through clattering teeth.

"Come on." Priscilla took her hand firmly. "Let's head back to the truck."

They made their way to a nearby bench where they'd changed into their ice skates, Alaina's muscles protesting every step across the snowy ground. Changing from skates back into shoes was a struggle, her frozen fingers clumsy and stiff. Once ready, they gathered their things and trudged up the incline toward the parked truck.

Alaina leaned against the rear bumper, catching her breath,

and tilted her head back to admire the sky. "Wow," she murmured. "This might be the most beautiful sunset I've ever seen."

"Then we should stay and enjoy it." Priscilla opened the door to the truck, reached into the back, and pulled out the wool blanket that had saved Alaina from freezing to death the night they met. She lowered the tailgate, nodding toward the bed. "Hop in."

They settled against the cab, the blanket large enough to sit on with some left over to swaddle their legs if they sat pressed together. Alaina snuggled in closer than was strictly necessary, savoring the warmth.

She pulled out her phone to capture the melting sherbet clouds hovering over the mountains, but the screen lit up to reveal Cole's smiling face instead. Seeing him startled her—it wasn't painful, exactly, just jarring. Like tripping over something familiar in a place it didn't belong.

Priscilla glanced at the screen. "That's Cole?"

Alaina nodded. "That's him."

"He looks . . . nice. You can tell me about him. I mean—if you'd like."

Alaina tapped the screen again, making the photo light up once more. It was a good picture of him—dark hair swept back, the corners of his brown eyes crinkled in a grin—but it didn't make her smile anymore.

Now it just made her sad.

"We met at work," Alaina said. "I was waiting tables, and he came in with a bunch of friends. They were loud and obnoxious, but Cole was different. He didn't try to flirt with me, or make any inappropriate jokes like guys his age normally do after a few too many beers. After they paid, the rest of his friends left, but he stayed behind and asked me out for coffee."

"He asked you out at work?" Priscilla didn't sound impressed.

"It wasn't like that."

"What was it like?"

She'd been hit on at work more times than she could count. Usually it came with a wink she didn't ask for, or a hand lingering too long when giving her the check. She'd learned to smile politely, decline gently, and steel herself for the inevitable meager tip. But Cole hadn't played that game. When she brought the check, he was the only one who thanked her. Genuinely. As he looked up at her with those gorgeous soft brown eyes, she'd felt like he was actually seeing her as a person.

He'd waited until his friends were gone, then apologized for their behavior.

"Don't worry about it," she'd told him, determined not to let a bunch of drunk boys ruin her day.

"Let me make it up to you," he'd said. "Do you like coffee?"

When she said yes, his dimples had appeared, and he told her there was a place just down the street.

Alaina shrugged. Priscilla probably didn't want to hear all of that. "I could've said no, but I didn't want to."

"That's . . . nice."

It didn't sound like Priscilla thought it was very nice at all. Alaina switched gears. "He's a really good boyfriend. He's always bringing me on these amazing dates, things I never would've thought to try on my own. An indoor trampoline park, a food truck tour—he even found a drive-in theater showing a *Scream* marathon on Halloween. And this one time, we went to a farmers' market and we had to do this cooking challenge with the stuff we bought for his TikTok. You can only imagine how badly I lost at that."

"TikTok?" It sounded like Priscilla was hearing the word for the first time.

"It's a social media platform where you—"

"I know what TikTok is, Alaina, I was just surprised you have one."

"I don't—well, I do, but mostly just for scrolling. Cole is the one who has, like, a hundred thousand followers. He wants to be an influencer. Go around the world and post it all on Instagram, that sort of thing."

"That's . . . a job?"

"Kinda." Alaina shrugged. She let the phone fall back into her lap, Cole's photo fading to black. "He's starting to get some brand deals. That's why he's in New York. He's promo-ing some energy drink for New Year's. He called it step one toward achieving his dream of being a full-time influencer."

Priscilla's eyes found hers, softened by the sunset into a rich, molten honey. At this distance, Alaina could spot tiny brown specks around her irises, like the bits of vanilla bean in an ice cream sundae.

Priscilla's gaze was gentle, searching. "And what about you? What do you want?"

The question pulled Alaina up short.

What *did* she want? When was the last time anyone had asked her that? When was the last time she'd asked herself?

She'd graduated college with a business degree she had no real plan for, taken a job at the same restaurant as Nico mostly because they could put in a good word for her. Her life had felt like one long holding pattern since—until she met Cole.

"Is it bad if I say that what I want is him? Cole is the only person who has ever made me feel wanted, you know?" Alaina laughed bitterly. "God, that sounds so sad, considering the fact that he left me."

"It doesn't." Priscilla reached for her hand, giving it a reassuring squeeze.

"I just want someone to stand by me," Alaina said. "Someone who won't bail."

She still hoped—despite everything—that Cole could be that someone.

Alaina nudged Priscilla's shoulder. "What about you? What does your dream girl look like?"

Priscilla let out a laugh on a breath. Her expression was unreadable, complicated by something Alaina couldn't quite decipher. Whatever it was, Priscilla quickly shook it off. "Nothing. I don't think there is someone out there for me."

"That can't be true. There's someone out there for everyone."

Priscilla shrugged. "Not for me."

"Priscilla—"

"No. I've made peace with it. I prefer it, actually. I like my life here too much. Bringing someone else into it would just complicate things. It's not worth the risk."

Alaina studied her—the woman who'd taken her in, fed her, made her laugh when she hadn't expected it. Priscilla might claim she enjoyed solitude, but Alaina had watched her closely these past few days. She saw loneliness, the subtle yearning for connection that Priscilla stubbornly kept at arm's length.

Maybe Alaina wasn't exactly an expert on love—her own track record wasn't winning any prizes—but she certainly didn't think it was something you wrote off entirely.

You don't give up on love.

Alaina squeezed Priscilla's hand. "Maybe someone could be worth it, one day. How would you ever know if you close yourself off to the opportunity?"

Priscilla withdrew abruptly, sharp enough that Alaina wondered if she'd crossed an invisible line. "I don't *need* someone to love me, Alaina."

She might as well have poured a bucket of ice water over Alaina's head. Priscilla's tone made Alaina feel small, like wanting to be loved was some childish, foolish thing.

"So you—what, don't believe in love?"

Priscilla kept her eyes downcast as she shook her head. "Not for me. But I hope you find what you're looking for. With Cole, or with someone else. You deserve someone by your side."

So do you, Alaina wanted to say. But she bit it back. If Priscilla didn't want to hear it, what was the point? Instead, she folded her hands in her lap and let the quiet stretch between them, thick as fog.

Chapter Nine

Alaina collapsed onto the couch. "I think I might be dying."

She felt like she'd run a marathon without training. Knees throbbing, feet cramped, palms raw—and worst of all, her butt hurt every time she moved it, which apparently was all the damn time. Walking, sitting, standing. Ouch, ouch, ouch.

From the kitchen, Priscilla shot her down without even glancing her way. "You're not dying."

"How do you know?" Alaina groaned, letting her eyes fall shut as she tilted her head against the cushion. "I could be fatally bruised. I'm pretty sure I've seen that on an episode of *Grey's*."

She couldn't see Priscilla's face, but she could swear she heard her stifle a laugh.

"What hurts?" At least Priscilla was kind enough to pretend to care.

"Everything." The day had been amazing, but nobody warned her that ice was about as forgiving as concrete. Would she even be able to walk tomorrow? The couch dipped as Priscilla sat next to her. "My ass, most of all."

"Language." But Priscilla's voice lacked any of its usual fire. Instead, it sounded suspiciously like—

"Are you . . . are you laughing at my pain? My broken ass?"

"No."

Priscilla might deny it, but the smile in her voice was unmistakable.

"Good. That would be really mean."

"It would be, wouldn't it?"

This time, Priscilla didn't even try to hide her giggle. Alaina delighted in it. A *giggle.* Alaina laughed too, despite her body protesting every breath. The tension after their earlier conversation had lingered all the way home, prickly and uncomfortable, and she was relieved to break free of it—even at her own expense.

"Fine, you can laugh at me. I'm pathetic."

"Just a little." Priscilla's voice was soft, warm, and Alaina's heart puddled in her chest at the sound. She opened her eyes, surprised to see Priscilla holding out a mug practically overflowing with whipped cream.

Alaina snatched it eagerly, sighing in relief as the warmth seeped into her fingers. "Oh my god, I take it back. You're an angel."

Priscilla tilted her head. "Do you tell that to everyone who gives you hot chocolate?"

"What can I say? I'm easy."

Priscilla's eyes widened, and she cleared her throat quickly, suddenly very interested in looking anywhere but at Alaina. "Did you have fun today? Besides breaking your . . . butt?"

Alaina snorted into her drink. "Yes. Me and my butt had a great time."

"It's 'my butt and I,'" Priscilla said, looking far too pleased with herself when Alaina rolled her eyes. "Good. I'm glad."

Alaina set her mug aside, reaching into her pocket and pulling out The List. She unfolded it carefully, smoothing out the wrinkles with her thumb.

"Can I borrow a pen?" she asked. Priscilla went to the kitchen to get one, and with a small, satisfied smile, Alaina drew a line through "Go ice skating on a lake." She folded the paper and slipped it away again.

One step closer to getting Cole back.

Priscilla hesitated at the edge of the couch. "Would you like to go to bed? It's been a long day."

"What?! No! The night's still young. It's only . . ." Alaina glanced at the clock. "Eight. We should do something!"

Priscilla raised an eyebrow at her. "Like what?"

"Watch a movie, maybe?" Alaina gasped. "A Christmas movie!"

"Absolutely not." Priscilla's tone was resolute, but Alaina already knew how easily she could soften her.

"Oh, come on—you've already bent your grinch rule once, and it turned out great! You had fun last night."

Priscilla sighed. "I did."

"So?" Alaina put on her best puppy dog eyes. "Just one movie. I'll pick a good one. I've seen, like, every Christmas movie there is."

"Fine." Priscilla didn't look convinced, but she handed the remote to Alaina. "But if it's terrible, I'm turning it off."

"Deal."

As Priscilla headed to the kitchen to make popcorn, Alaina scrolled through the streaming app, dismissing movie after movie—too corny, too sappy, too sad—until she found the perfect one.

"*The Holiday*! It's a classic."

Returning with a popcorn bowl, Priscilla settled beside her. She gave Alaina a tired look. "I don't know, Alaina. I don't really enjoy romantic comedies."

"It's not *just* a rom-com. It's about two women completely changing their lives on a whim! And Jude Law looks *so* cute in—wait, wrong angle," Alaina said, remembering her very gay audience. "The whole movie is basically about how sometimes the best things happen when your plans get completely derailed. Sound familiar?"

Priscilla hummed, clearly unimpressed.

"And Kate Winslet is in it." Alaina was not above shameless pandering. "She's pretty, right?"

She didn't know exactly what Priscilla's type was, but honestly—whose type wasn't Kate Winslet?

A thoughtful beat passed. "She's very pretty."

"I'm taking that as a yes!" Before Priscilla could reconsider, Alaina pressed play and the opening credits rolled. The soft orchestral music began, and Priscilla huffed, already less than impressed.

"Give it a chance," Alaina said, brightening when Jack Black appeared on the screen. "I *love* him."

"That guy?" Priscilla sounded doubtful.

"Trust me. He's adorable. Now be quiet and watch!"

Five minutes in, they'd both settled deeper into the couch, though Alaina struggled to keep quiet. "Do British people really say that? 'Happy Christmas'?"

"Yes, Alaina."

When Cameron Diaz hurled a shoe at her ex, Priscilla shook her head disapprovingly. "She needs to work on her aim."

"Sh!" Alaina threw a piece of popcorn at her, earning an impressive eye roll.

When Jude Law finally appeared onscreen, Alaina sighed dreamily. "God, he's gorgeous. And that accent."

Priscilla had moved slightly toward the middle of the couch to reach the popcorn. She turned, brows furrowed in confusion. "What about it?"

"British accents are hot, Priscilla. Come on, you have to know that."

Priscilla didn't answer.

By midway through the movie, Priscilla had migrated from her rigid perch at the far end of the couch to sitting close enough that their shoulders almost touched. She looked comfortable—feet tucked under her, head resting on her hand. Completely absorbed.

Alaina barely glanced at the screen. She didn't need to; she could quote *The Holiday* in her sleep. Besides, watching Priscilla surrender to the slow, inevitable pull of a good rom-com? Way more interesting.

At least it was—until *that* scene started. Kate Winslet's voice filled the room, soft and aching, talking about the kind of love that leaves you hollow. Was this how she sounded when she talked about Cole? Clinging to the hope that if she just said or did the right thing, he would take her back?

She sat frozen, barely breathing. Onscreen, Iris's heartbreak turned to something else. A flicker of hope, a promise of healing. Alaina felt something crack open inside herself.

Exhaustion swept through her all at once. Her head dropped softly onto Priscilla's shoulder. When Priscilla tensed beneath her, Alaina almost pulled away, an apology forming on her lips—but then Priscilla relaxed, gently resting her cheek against Alaina's hair.

Something thick lodged in Alaina's throat, and she blinked rapidly. She'd seen this scene dozens of times, but now, watching someone slowly rebuild herself somewhere new—surrounded by unexpected love—she finally understood it.

Iris's words washed over her as she drifted off to sleep.

"Alaina." A gentle hand shook her awake. "Alaina?"

"M'up," Alaina mumbled, stretching and wincing at a pinched muscle in her shoulder. "I'm up. What did I miss?"

"The end. They all lived happily ever after." Priscilla offered her half a smile. "But you already knew that. Come on. You're not sleeping out here tonight, you're in too much pain. I'll take the couch."

"Nope. Nuh-uh." Alaina shook her head, suddenly wide awake. "I'm not kicking you out of your bed."

Priscilla had already done too much for her—no way was Alaina going to allow her to give up her bed, even for just a night. She wasn't even *that* sore, though the bruises did seem to be getting worse by the hour.

Priscilla folded her arms. "And I'm not letting you sleep on the couch."

"Well, then." Alaina crossed her arms back at her. "It seems we have reached an impasse."

They stared at each other for what felt like an eternity until Priscilla broke, rolling her eyes. "This is absurd. We can't both sleep on the couch, Alaina."

"True . . ." Alaina trailed off, then brightened when an idea occurred to her. "But we could both sleep in the bed. I'm assuming you don't have a twin-sized mattress in there."

"No."

"No to the twin size, or no to sleeping together?"

Alaina's eyes widened. Foot, meet mouth—again.

If Priscilla noticed Alaina's accidental innuendo, she didn't show it. She shook her head. "You don't need to—I'll be just fine out here, really."

"And so will I." Alaina shook her head firmly. "You've already done way too much for me. Seriously."

"Fine." Priscilla took a deep breath, then nodded, as if reassuring herself. "We can share the bed."

"I call big spoon." She watched Priscilla's face contort for a second before adding, "Just kidding."

Alaina hobbled to the bathroom, trying not to wince with every step, then dug through her bag for pajamas. Her limbs protested loudly as she pulled on the soft fabric. Finally, she shuffled back to Priscilla's bedroom door, giving it a soft knock.

The door creaked open.

Priscilla stood in the doorway in a loose, faded shirt that slipped just enough off her shoulder to reveal a glimpse of collarbone. Her dark hair, usually neatly styled, was pulled into a messy ponytail, strands escaping to frame her face, softening her features.

"What?" Priscilla asked.

"Huh?"

"You're staring."

Shit. Priscilla was right—Alaina had been so caught off guard by the change in Priscilla that her mouth had even dropped open a little. *Say something, Alaina.*

"Your shirt, um—you've been to Banff?"

She'd never even heard of Banff before this moment. Had zero clue what it even was, besides it being hilariously named. The shirt had mountains on it, so—nature?

"No," Priscilla said. "But Callie's family is from Alberta, and she brought me this when she came back from a visit a few years ago. She said I would've loved it there—the camping, the mountains. It's all the sort of thing she hates, but she got close enough to go to the gift shop." Priscilla tugged self-consciously at the oversized shirt. "The shirt is too large, but it's comfortable."

Was Priscilla . . . rambling?

"It's adorable, is what it is."

Priscilla avoided her gaze, stepping aside so Alaina could enter. Alaina moved slowly, taking in the room—the hardwood floors softened by a faded rug, an armchair nestled near a table stacked high with more books, the soft amber glow from a lamp casting cozy shadows across the walls. The queen-sized bed was piled high with a thick quilt of warm creams and forest greens, perfectly matching the wallpaper with climbing leaves behind it.

"Dibs on the inside," Alaina said quickly, hoping to avoid another debate.

As Alaina brushed past her toward the bed, she couldn't shake the sudden weird tension humming between them. Sharing Priscilla's mattress shouldn't feel this strange. They'd practically cuddled in the back of Priscilla's truck, and during the movie she'd literally fallen asleep on Priscilla's shoulder. But somehow, crawling into the same bed felt different—more charged, more personal. Maybe because it was Priscilla's bed, with Priscilla's sheets, smelling faintly of Priscilla's shampoo.

Alaina settled against the wall, sinking into the mattress with an embarrassingly grateful sigh as her bruised muscles finally relaxed. It was hard to resist spreading out like a starfish, but she curled herself smaller instead, determined not to crowd Priscilla. The mattress dipped as Priscilla climbed into bed.

Alaina risked a glance sideways. Priscilla lay stiffly on her back near the opposite edge, an unnecessarily large gap stretched between them. Alaina almost laughed. This was ridiculous. Why the sudden cautious distance? Was it because Priscilla was a lesbian? Did she worry Alaina might feel weird about that?

"Comfortable?" Priscilla asked. She sounded genuinely concerned, like Alaina might actually find the couch's lumps more inviting than her memory foam mattress.

"Very," Alaina answered truthfully. "Thank you for letting me stay in here."

"You're welcome."

There was another long, quiet pause before Alaina heard Priscilla shift slightly, rolling toward her. She turned her head, surprised to find Priscilla closer than she'd expected, face gentle in the dim glow filtering in from outside. She'd taken down her ponytail. Dark hair fell loose around her shoulders, softening the usually neat lines of her face.

She looked so different like this. Less composed. Alaina had the absurd thought of reaching out to brush her hair away, to see if it was as silky as it looked, but stopped herself.

Priscilla's gaze was unreadable, thoughtful, almost careful. What was she thinking? Why did the silence suddenly feel so heavy? Priscilla's lips parted, and she took a deep breath like she was about to say something, then stopped herself. Before Alaina could question it, Priscilla rolled onto her back again, reaching over to switch off the lamp.

"Good night," she murmured as the room went black.

"Night," Alaina whispered, eyes wide in the dark. Her body ached with exhaustion, but her mind wouldn't quiet. She stayed flat on her back, eyes trained on the dark ceiling, counting slow, deliberate breaths. One, two, three, four.

What had Priscilla almost said? Something was there, caught behind her lips. Alaina could still feel her—the rhythm of Priscilla's breathing, the slow shift of the covers with each inhale, the faint warmth of her body. The scent of her shampoo drifted over—soft, citrusy, something deeper underneath. Alaina had used the same bottle in the shower, but it didn't smell like this on her. Was it bergamot? Cinnamon? It was dark and warm and a little spicy. She wanted to lean in, just a little. Inhale it deeper. Try to identify exactly what she found so comforting about it. Would that be weird?

God, of course it would be weird. *She* was being weird. It was just that the last person she had shared a bed with was Cole. She was just missing him. She was tired and touch-starved and lonely, hyper-focusing on any kind of human connection.

She needed to focus on something—*anything*—else.

She pictured the moment she'd see Cole again: snow flurrying around them in slow motion. He'd turn, their eyes would meet, and she'd go to him, wrap her fingers around his coat lapels and say . . .

What?

"Cole, I've changed." Too cliché, too simple.

"I know this seems crazy, but just hear me out—" Way too defensive.

"Cole, I love you and I know we're meant to be together because . . ."

Because what? She knew in her heart they belonged together the same way she knew ice cream was necessary for human survival and pineapple had no business being on pizza—undeniable facts of her world. Things she believed without explanation.

But how could she make him feel it too? Maybe if she live streamed the whole thing. He'd probably love that.

"Alaina?" Priscilla's voice cut through the dark, startling Alaina out of her imagined reunion with Cole. Despite being nearly a whisper, it felt loud in the quiet room.

"Yeah?"

"Can I ask you a question?"

"Shoot."

There was a long moment of silence. Had Priscilla fallen asleep? Alaina almost considered poking her to check when she spoke again. "What you said back at the lake—that there's someone out there for everyone. What makes you so sure?"

Alaina's answer wasn't immediate. Not because she didn't know, but because it was buried deep, folded into old memories.

"My mom used to say love was the one thing that made life worth all the mess," she said eventually. "Like, no matter how bad things got, there'd be someone out there who saw you—all of you—and chose you anyway."

She hadn't always believed it herself. Not after losing her mom. Not after the stretch of years that followed, when she felt more like she was passing through other people's lives than belonging in any of them. But somehow that stubborn hope had lingered in her heart, refusing to fade completely.

When she met Cole, she had thought holding on to hope had finally paid off.

"I guess I believe because she believed," Alaina said. "And because I want to live in a world where love like that is real. Does that make sense?"

There was another pause before Priscilla spoke. "It does."

The silence swallowed their conversation again. Alaina stared at the ceiling, the memory of that moment in the truck still sitting heavy in her chest—Priscilla's voice, cool and certain, saying she didn't need love. Like Alaina was being immature for still wanting it.

She needed to know if Priscilla meant that.

"Do you think it's stupid?" Alaina turned to face Priscilla as she whispered. Her chest felt painfully tight. "That I want to be loved?"

"What?" Priscilla shifted. Alaina's eyes had adjusted enough to make out the dip in her brow. "Of course not."

The tightness in Alaina's chest eased slightly, but she couldn't quite let it go yet. "It's just—earlier, when you said you didn't need love . . . I worried you thought it was silly. Or naïve."

Priscilla let out a soft breath. "That wasn't about you. I didn't mean it like that."

"Okay."

She watched as Priscilla let her gaze drift toward the ceiling again, clearly wrestling with her thoughts.

"I think it's hard for me to want something that has done nothing but hurt me in the past."

The words landed with a thud in Alaina's chest. She knew that kind of ache. Devon. Cole. The people who'd loved her until they didn't. Even her own family had lost interest.

And then there was Priscilla—who'd had someone drag her out of the closet and leave her exposed and alone. Who'd been let down by the people who were supposed to protect her. Who'd hidden away in this small town with her books and her cat.

"I get that." And she did. The feeling of wanting something that kept slipping through your fingers—Alaina understood how that felt better than Priscilla could ever know. "But for me, that makes me want it even more. Does that make me a masochist?"

"No." Priscilla shook her head, her eyes finding Alaina's in the dark. A beat passed between them. "I think it makes you incredibly brave."

Chapter Ten

Four Days Until Christmas

"Yes!" Alaina yelled from the couch.

Priscilla's eyes darted up from her book. She sat at the dining room table, coffee steaming beside her, eyebrows raised as Alaina tapped away on her phone. "What?"

"I found a flight to New York. It's at three o'clock on Christmas Day, but hey—beggars can't be choosers, right?"

She'd set up alerts on her phone, hoping for a price drop, and somehow managed to snag a ticket that wasn't five hundred dollars. Sure, the purchase left her with exactly six dollars of available credit, but she could fix that later with a couple of double shifts. It would all be worth it. The flight meant she could make it in time to spend the remainder of Cole's vacation with him. And New Year's Eve was romantic too. The ball dropping, champagne at midnight. She and Cole could toast the New Year, then come back together to pick up her car and start fresh.

All she had to do was win his heart back. Piece of cake.

But Priscilla's expression changed, hard to read, almost wary.

"Right." She returned her gaze to her book and flipped the page.

Alaina's stomach twisted. She should have asked before booking the flight. Christmas was still days away, and here she was, assuming she could crash in Priscilla's space indefinitely. Had Priscilla only said she could stay to be polite?

Before she could spiral too far into embarrassment, Priscilla's gaze lifted back to her. "Clark has the day off so I need to be at the store all day. You're free to stay, but I thought you might enjoy exploring the town a bit."

"Getting sick of me?" Alaina asked, not at all insecure about it.

Priscilla shook her head, her mouth softening into a faint, amused smile. "Surprisingly, no."

That morning, Alaina had woken up to an empty bed. It wasn't really a shock—Priscilla had woken up earlier than Alaina every day since she'd started staying here. But still, when she emerged from the bedroom to see Priscilla, relaxed with her nose in a book, it had felt less like she was intruding and more like she belonged.

Alaina rose and walked over to the table, stopping beside Priscilla. "Whatcha reading?"

"*Les Fleurs du Mal.*" Priscilla lowered the book to meet Alaina's gaze. "It's a collection of poems by Charles Baudelaire."

Alaina moved to peek over her shoulder, then paused. "Is this in French?"

"Yes?" Priscilla sounded baffled by Alaina's surprise, but Alaina couldn't contain her admiration.

"Holy shit, Sil." She laughed, then held up her hands. "I know, I know. Language."

❄

Twenty minutes later, Priscilla's footsteps faded down the stairs to the bookstore, leaving Alaina alone in the apartment. Well, almost alone. She plopped down on the couch, giving a sidelong glance to Lola, who was perched gracefully on the coffee table.

"Looks like it's just you and me, girl." All she got in response was that unblinking feline stare—simultaneously curious and judgmental. "All right, Miss Lola," Alaina muttered. "Staring contest it is."

They locked eyes. Alaina's internal monologue raced: *Do cats blink? Is she judging my outfit? Maybe I should've worn the other sweater.* But Lola's stare was unwavering, her eyes as inscrutable as shiny marbles. Every once in a while, her tail would twitch, as if she were mocking Alaina's feeble attempts at maintaining eye contact.

After several intense minutes, Lola blinked, slow and deliberate, then gave a little chirp, stretched languidly, and padded away into the bedroom.

Alaina rubbed her dry eyes. "That's the last time I challenge a cat to a staring contest."

She reached for her phone and searched "how to make a cat like you." The results surprised her—apparently, that slow blink hadn't been Lola admitting defeat, but instead was a sign of trust. And here Alaina had been trying to win a dominance contest. No wonder Lola kept avoiding her.

She scrolled through article after article: don't make direct eye contact, let them come to you, respect their space. Everything she hadn't been doing, and yet, for some reason, Lola had blinked at her. She'd made the first move, in terms of cat diplomacy. Maybe some part of her recognized a kindred spirit in Alaina—another stray taken in by Priscilla.

Comforted, Alaina opened her camera roll, found the best

shots from yesterday—one of her skating, one of the sunset over the mountains—and posted them to her story. Then she checked yesterday's post. It had plenty of views, but none of them had been Cole.

Her brow furrowed as she flicked through the stories that appeared after her own. Still no Cole. But he never missed a daily post—it was part of his brand, his commitment to "authentic lifestyle content" or whatever he called it. Before he left for New York, he'd always pulled her into his shots: their morning coffee routine, weekend hikes, dinners, and late-night drives. Girls commented how lucky she was, and she'd always agreed.

But today? Nothing.

She pulled up his profile, heart jumping at his smiling face—but sure enough, there was nothing new on his page. She'd expected at least one staged shot from Times Square, some behind-the-scenes glimpse of the PowerPunch campaign. Maybe something she could overanalyze, searching for signs he missed her. But there was no content at all, nothing to dissect.

"Huh."

That wasn't like Cole. PowerPunch was his biggest sponsorship yet, his gateway into becoming a serious influencer. So where was all the promo—the carefully casual selfies, the branded stories?

Where are you? she wondered.

Maybe he wasn't in New York. Maybe he'd changed his mind. Maybe—God, maybe—he'd flown back to San Francisco to find her, only to show up at her apartment when she wasn't there.

She shook her head. No. If he couldn't reach her, he would've called. Nico would've let her know if he'd shown up, no matter how they felt about him.

Still, that tiny, glittering shard of hope burrowed in deeper.

She tapped back to the home screen, then zeroed in on Josh, Cole's friend. They had gone on several double dates with him and his girlfriend, Renee, over the last year. If Cole was with anyone in San Fran, it might be him. But no, the only thing Josh had posted was a birthday wish for Renee.

Alaina's thumbs hovered over the keyboard before opening Renee's profile and tapping into her DMs.

Hey girl!!! she wrote, then erased two of the exclamation points. No need to sound like an overeager puppy. Happy birthday!

The message showed as delivered—then seen. A second later, a reply popped up:

thank u!

"Not giving me much to work with," Alaina mumbled aloud. She typed again:

Alaina: Hope you're celebrating with something amazing!

Did that sound too desperate for a response? Maybe. Too late.

Renee: yesss josh got us reservations at state bird
Alaina: That's incredible! Last time I was there was actually with Cole—

No, no, no. She backspaced frantically. Too forced.

That place is incredible. The pancakes changed my life!

Renee: i know!!! it was such a nice surprise

Three minutes passed as Alaina stared at her screen, trying to think of a natural segue. Nothing came. Screw it.

Alaina: Have you heard from Cole lately? His socials have been pretty quiet.

The second she hit send, she regretted it. She watched the dots come and go—Renee typing, then stopping, then typing again. Like someone trying to soften a blow.

Renee: listen, lani, i really like you, but josh is cole's best friend and i just don't think we can be talking to his ex about him, you know?

"Ex." The word knocked the breath out of her. That wasn't right. They were on a break, figuring things out, not broken up. What had Cole told his friends? Her vision of Cole showing up at her apartment door, telling her he'd made a mistake, that New York meant nothing without her, melted like a snowman in the rain.

Totally get it, she replied, blinking hard against the sting behind her eyes. Have a great birthday. :)

She tossed her phone aside like it burned, then pinched the bridge of her nose. The tears came anyway.

She'd driven across the country chasing a fantasy. And what did she have to show for it? A shrinking credit limit. A knot in the pit of her stomach. A one-way nonrefundable ticket to heartbreak.

Maybe she was brave, like Priscilla had said last night.

Or maybe—and more likely—she was just a fool.

After she showered and got dressed, Alaina plodded down the stairs. The bookstore was nearly empty save for a few customers between the shelves. She'd expected more of a crowd this close to the holiday, but maybe people had finished their shopping.

Priscilla looked up from where she stood alone at the counter. "Headed out?"

Alaina hesitated. She didn't like the idea of leaving Priscilla here all alone, even without a crowd. What if there was another rush?

"Do you need help? I could unpack books, or help with the pickup orders, or—"

Priscilla shook her head. "It's been quite slow. That happens sometimes on nice days. Most people are out on the mountain. You should go out, enjoy Brooks."

"But I—" The words stuck.

Saying *I don't want to be alone* out loud sounded way too needy.

"Alaina." There was a firm kindness in Priscilla's voice. "Go. Enjoy yourself."

The thought of wandering around the unfamiliar town made Alaina's nerves spike, but staying behind meant stewing in her thoughts, replaying Renee's message in her mind, scrolling Cole's empty socials.

"If you're sure."

Her boots left soft impressions in the snow as she moved down the street, her steps heavy and slow. The holiday lights, twinkling in vibrant hues, hung overhead, but their magic barely touched her mood. She passed shop windows without really seeing them, her thoughts still knotted up from earlier. Eventually, she pulled herself into the present, forcing her eyes to scan the displays with purpose.

If she was staying until Christmas Day, she needed to find a Christmas gift for Priscilla.

Nothing big, just a token to say thank you for taking her in. For not making her feel like a burden, even when she probably was.

But nothing felt right. A leather-bound journal caught her eye, but it felt too obvious for someone who literally owned a bookstore. A rainbow hand-knit scarf was gorgeous—soft, vibrant, a little whimsical—but she couldn't picture Priscilla wearing anything that colorful. She lingered in a cozy cheese shop longer than expected, briefly considering a basket of high-end jams. But it felt too generic. Too safe. She didn't even know if Priscilla liked marmalade, though the free sample nearly convinced her to buy a jar for herself.

The truth was, she wanted something that would get her one of those rare, genuine smiles—the kind she'd been determined to earn since that first night.

Walking through Brooks without Priscilla beside her made everything feel different. Bigger. Less familiar. It turned out Priscilla wasn't just her guide to the town. She'd been her anchor. And now, without her, even the most festive windows felt a little bit colder.

With the sun climbing higher and her stomach starting to grumble, Alaina changed course. Time to find food. A twinge of regret pinched her—she should've asked Priscilla for a recommendation. Why did she always do this? Just . . . leave, unprepared?

Lost in this thought, she slowed as a familiar sight caught her eye—Patty's diner.

She pushed open the door and barely made it two steps before someone called her name. Turning, she spotted Clark tucked into a small booth across from an older woman. Both their faces lit up at the sight of her, and Clark gave a friendly wave, motioning her over. Alaina summoned a smile and headed their way.

"Wow, this really is a small town, huh?"

Clark grinned. "Sure is. Ma, this is Alaina." The family resemblance was unmistakable—that hay-blond hair, those emerald eyes. "She's a friend of Priscilla's."

"Nice to meet you, Clark's mom," Alaina said, offering her hand.

The woman's handshake was confident, just firm enough—not the kind that crushed your fingers, but the kind that said she'd seen some things and didn't rattle easy. Priscilla had that handshake. So did Lauren and Callie. Alaina made a mental note: she needed to figure out how to bottle that kind of energy.

"Monica," she said with a drawl, heavier than Clark's. "And you too. Why don't you join us? We've haven't ordered."

Honestly, eating alone hadn't sounded great—she'd already spent most of the day stuck in her own head, ping-ponging between thoughts of Cole calling her his ex and Priscilla's words from last night echoing in her memory, only to land back on Cole. A little human interaction might help.

She pulled up a chair and plopped down in it. "Thank you!"

"How are you liking the town?" Clark asked.

God, she didn't really feel like engaging in small talk right now. But she needed a distraction. "It's really cute. Lots of great people, present company included." Alaina leaned forward on her elbows. "People aren't friendly like this where I'm from."

"That is one nice thing about this place." Monica wore a fond smile as she looked around the restaurant. "It's quaint."

"Mom here is a city girl. 'Quaint' is her polite way of calling it dull. But she braves the boredom for me."

They exchanged a wry glance, and Alaina couldn't help but smile.

"So," Clark said, turning back to her. "Alaina, I've been meaning to ask—how long have you and Priscilla known each other? I don't think she's ever had someone visit her before."

"Oh, we—" Alaina paused. Clark looked genuinely pleased, like he was happy Priscilla had someone in her life. Someone from her past, someone who cared enough to visit for the holidays. Would it embarrass Priscilla if he knew the truth? That Alaina was a stranger who didn't have anywhere else to go?

She gave a small shrug. "Well, you know. It feels like forever."

Not a lie.

"And you?" she asked, shifting the spotlight. "How long have you lived here?"

Clark launched into the story of how he'd ended up in Brooks—how a snowboarding trip three years ago had turned into something bigger. He'd fallen in love with the mountains, the quiet pace, the crisp air. That kind of clarity, that sudden pull toward a new life, was the kind of romantic notion she usually only found in movies.

Alaina leaned in, caught up in his words—how he'd left behind everything familiar just because something in his gut told him he'd found home.

He'd bounced between jobs for a while, but it was Priscilla's store that finally stuck. Sure, he missed home sometimes, but his mom visited every Christmas.

"And he makes it down to Dallas every Mother's Day," Monica said.

Monica was magnetic. She was a powerhouse lawyer from the city, handling billion-dollar contracts for oil tycoons and tech moguls. But Monica just shrugged off Alaina's wide-eyed reaction with a smile, like negotiating deals that could reshape the Texas economy was just another day at the office. For Monica, she supposed, it was.

"I love my work. Married to it, if you ask my ex-husband." She sent a glance toward Clark, catching him mid–eye roll. "But I always make it a point to be here, with Clark, on Christmas. The holidays are for family, after all."

Alaina's heart clenched.

"Patty!" Clark called, waving his hand.

The name alone made Alaina sit up straighter, instinctively tucking her hair behind her ear as a strange nervous flutter moved through her.

"Our friend Alaina decided to join us. Alaina, this is—"

"We've met." Patty looked at Alaina with a tight smile. "Still staying with Priscilla?"

Automatically, Alaina replied, "Yes, ma'am."

"Good." Patty's eyes crinkled, her smile warming and relaxing subtly at the edges. There it was—a hint of the warmth and comfort that Priscilla must've found in Patty. "You seem like a good pair."

Alaina's mind flew back to the other day, when Patty had assumed she and Priscilla were a couple.

"Thanks. Priscilla's the best."

Another misunderstanding she hadn't corrected. Another tiny lie she let live. She sat with the guilt while Clark and Monica ordered, until Patty looked back at her.

"What'll it be, hon?"

Alaina's eyes raced over the menu. She wasn't in the mood for lunch, and eggs felt uninspired. She was on the verge of ordering a slice of pie again before another delicacy caught her eye.

"I make those myself—good choice." Patty winked as she collected the menus. "That'll be right out."

With Patty gone, Clark turned his attention back to Alaina. "So, Alaina. Where are you from?"

"San Francisco." She decided to skip the backstory this time.

"What's it like there? I've never been."

"Well . . ." She wasn't quite sure where to start. How could she possibly sum up an entire city? "It's home. For the past seven years anyway."

Clark tilted his head. "And you like it there?"

"Sure," Alaina said. "What's not to like?"

"A lot of things."

"Clark," Monica said with a soft, knowing warning in her voice.

Alaina chuckled, raising an eyebrow. "I thought you'd never been."

"I haven't. But I've been to plenty of cities. After a while, they all blur together. No one looks at you. No one talks to you. But here? You're not just another face in the crowd. People actually see you."

Alaina nodded, but her throat felt tight. Maybe that was the part that scared her the most about a place like Brooks.

"But doesn't that ever get . . . stifling? Like everyone's in your business all the time?"

The idea of being seen sounded nice in theory, but what about the messier stuff? What if she had a bad hair day, or needed to buy a family-sized tub of chocolate ice cream just for herself? Or worse—what if someone witnessed her parallel parking?

It seemed like all of Brooks had known about her crash within hours. Surely she would find even more ways to embarrass herself if she stuck around much longer.

Clark shrugged. "Sometimes. I kinda like it that way, though.

In a big city, you might live next to someone for years and never know their name."

Alaina's mind went to her own apartment, her floor of identical doors and all the faces she vaguely recognized but didn't truly know. The man who nodded every morning while retrieving his paper. The woman who once helped her carry groceries up four flights when the elevator broke. They were kind, sure—but she hadn't seen that woman since. For all she knew, she'd moved months ago.

"Here?" Clark gestured subtly toward a man in a red flannel at the counter. "That's Joe. Runs the hardware store down the street. Helped me fix a leak in my house last winter and refused to charge me. And when I came down with the flu, Patty showed up with enough chicken soup to feed an army."

Alaina nodded slowly. She remembered when Priscilla had said that when she moved to Brooks, Patty had made sure she always had a warm meal.

"Point is—in Brooks, if you fall, there's a whole town ready to pick you up. It's a community, and every day I'm reminded I'm part of something bigger than myself." He paused, chuckling. "And, well, the traffic's better here too."

"Yes, that's all lovely. But some of us prefer to live somewhere you can get takeout after eight," Monica said. "I'm sure there are plenty of things Alaina likes about living in the city."

That was true. She loved foggy mornings in Golden Gate Park. The coffee cart near the dahlia garden. The hole-in-the-wall dim sum place in Richmond where she and Nico would stuff themselves with pork buns for under twenty bucks. The way the city lit up at sunset, all pink and gold reflecting off the bay.

She glanced at Clark again. He spoke about this town with such clarity. Like he knew in his bones that he belonged here.

Did she feel that way about San Francisco?

"People here look out for each other," Clark said, eyes still on Alaina. "There's just a comfort in that, you know?"

For a moment, she pictured a life here, waking up to Brooks's soft, lazy murmurs instead of the city's nonstop noise. The idea made her heart race, but she couldn't quite tell if it was from excitement or fear. What would it feel like to really belong somewhere?

"Here we are." Alaina looked up to see Patty balancing several plates on her arms. A club sandwich for Monica, a burger for Clark, and—

"Holy shit."

The cinnamon roll in front of her was nearly the size of her head, coated in a molten glaze that dripped down the sides.

Patty didn't even flinch at the language. Instead, she chuckled. "Enjoy."

Alaina pulled the plate closer, and the smell of the cinnamon roll rose up, warm and comforting. A bright, clear memory hit her. A sunny kitchen, standing on her tiptoes to see the counter where her mother had placed a tray of fresh-baked cinnamon rolls. Sunday mornings, sticky fingers, laughter echoing off the walls of their tiny apartment. She hadn't thought about those days in years. But the memory didn't hurt. Not this time.

Instead, it warmed her—bright and golden, like the sun through the kitchen window all those years ago. She took a bite, let the sweetness melt across her tongue, and let out a soft sound of delight.

When Alaina glanced up, Clark and Monica were observing her with amused smiles.

"What?" she asked once she'd chewed and swallowed. She was a lady, after all.

Clark chuckled, shaking his head. "Nothing."

When they'd finished, Monica insisted on paying. "It's my pleasure. Any friend of Clark's is a friend of mine."

Obediently, Alaina put her wallet away. Why wouldn't anyone let her pay for a single thing in this town? She wasn't exactly made of money, especially not after buying her plane ticket, so she wouldn't complain. But still, it felt odd accepting this much generosity.

Alaina followed Clark and Monica out onto the sidewalk, her hands tucked into her jacket pockets. "What are you guys doing with the rest of your day?"

Monica smiled over at her son. "We're baking Christmas cookies. One of our little yuletide traditions."

She reached out to ruffle his hair, but he dodged her hand expertly.

"What kind?"

"Gingerbread, sugar cookies—all sorts. I'll bring you some tomorrow if you'd like," Clark said.

"Oh, I don't know. I don't really have much of a sweet tooth," Alaina said, beaming when they laughed. "Please. I would love that."

They said their goodbyes, and Alaina turned down the block, her boots crunching through the snow. She hadn't gotten far when someone called her name. She turned to find Clark jogging after her, cheeks flushed from the cold.

Had she forgotten something? She checked her pockets, but her phone was tucked securely in the front, her wallet in the back.

Clark came to a stop in front of her, breath visible in short puffs. "Hope this doesn't come off as forward." He flashed a sheepish grin. "But I was wondering if you might like to grab dinner sometime. Just us two."

A dimple appeared through his stubble as he smiled. He really did look like he'd stepped out of a Hallmark movie. And for a second, she considered saying yes. Why not? Clark was handsome, funny, sweet. It could be fun.

Wait. Why was she even considering this? She had a boyfriend. Or—did she? Maybe she was the last person to realize she was single. Was what Renee had said a misunderstanding? Was The List pointless? Was Cole even still in New York?

The silence stretched between them, Clark's hopeful expression slowly shifting to concern.

"I'm sorry, I—" she said, but he shook his head.

"No, no—no excuses necessary. I just didn't want to not take the chance." His smile returned, a few watts dimmer. He really was a sweet guy. "Catch you tomorrow, Alaina."

As he turned back, a flicker of guilt tugged at her, but she knew she'd made the right call. Besides, she had a feeling those Christmas cookies would help ease the sting.

A lightbulb went off in her head at the thought, stopping her suddenly on the snowy sidewalk. She knew exactly how she wanted to spend the rest of her day.

An hour later, Alaina slipped into the bookstore with several plastic bags hanging from her arms. She spotted Priscilla at the counter, engaged with a customer, and swiftly veered behind a nearby shelf. Her heart drummed—timing was everything if she wanted to sneak upstairs without Priscilla seeing her. This had to be a surprise.

She crept through the stacks, tiptoeing quietly between the shelves, avoiding the creaky floorboards, and dodging behind bookcases whenever she heard Priscilla's voice. After a few minutes of careful maneuvering, she managed to get through history and science fiction all the way to children's without being seen.

With her gaze fixed on the counter, she nearly collided with a young boy browsing the picture books. She swallowed her yelp and crouched down to his level, her voice a hushed conspiratorial whisper.

"Hey, little dude, can you do me a favor? Could you distract the pretty lady at the counter for just a minute?"

He blinked up at her, confusion furrowing his brow. "Huh?"

"Just ask her to show you where a book is. I don't know, Dickens or something?"

He eyed her for a moment before running for the register. Alaina watched as Priscilla stooped to hear him, expression shifting from eager to confused. Maybe Alaina should've told him to ask for something more age appropriate. Either way, it was the distraction she needed.

Alaina slipped past the counter, keeping to the shadows like a woman on a mission. She took the stairs two at a time and didn't breathe until she closed the apartment door behind her with a quiet click.

After hiding the evidence, Alaina plopped onto the couch and checked the time. Still a little bit before Priscilla would close the shop. She grabbed the remote and flicked on the TV, flipping through the channels until she landed on a rerun of *How I Met Your Mother.* It wasn't her favorite, but she did think Robin and Ted were cute together.

She curled deeper into the cushions and let one episode roll into the next until her phone buzzed.

Nico: you are SO teaching me to ice skate when you get back

The idea of trying to teach Nico the way Priscilla had taught her made her laugh. They would both end up flat on the ice while some kid skated circles around them on the rink.

Alaina: unfortunately that was all Priscilla, I can barely make it three feet without falling over
Nico: fine, she can come too
Nico: how is the not-at-all-hot bookstore owner?
Alaina: She's great. I think you'd really like her.
Nico:... is she gay
Alaina: What??
Nico: every time you say I'd like someone, it's because they're gay!!! not all gay people like each other lani
Alaina:... Maybe she is. But you'd definitely like her!!
Nico: suuuree

After she swiped away from putting her foot in her mouth, another unread message caught her attention. She must've missed it while she was at lunch with Clark.

Unknown number: If this is Alaina, could you give me a call?

She stared at Shauna's message, unsure what to do. The polite thing would be to call. But polite didn't feel like enough of a reason. Not when she had no idea what Shauna wanted—or what *she* wanted. Did she want her family back in her life? And even if she did . . . what would she say?

She'd already ignored Shauna for the past few days. A little longer wouldn't change anything.

Instead, she opened Instagram, tapping through her story notifications out of habit. Nico had liked them, naturally. A few co-workers too. That guy from college who still hearted everything she posted. Her eyes skimmed—and then stopped.

Cole.

Her breath caught. He'd watched both stories—the one of her skating and the one of the sunset.

That had to mean something. Her heart fluttered in her chest. An involuntary smile tugged at the corners of her mouth.

All hope wasn't lost. She could still make this work.

Just then, she heard the squeaky hinges of the apartment door opening and—

Wait. Was Priscilla humming? More than that, was she humming a Christmas song? Yes, that was definitely the melody to "Carol of the Bells."

Alaina didn't move, wanting to enjoy this moment for as long as it lasted. Priscilla walked by her on the couch without looking up or noticing Alaina's presence. It wasn't until Priscilla reached the other side of the room that Alaina decided to speak up.

"'Sup, boss?" Alaina asked, and Priscilla flinched, nearly sending her armful of books flying.

"Oh my—Alaina!" Priscilla whirled around, her free hand flattening against her chest. "You startled me."

Alaina cackled. "You should see your face."

"Yes, well." Priscilla took a deep breath. "How long have you been ho—" She paused midword, adjusting. "Back? How long have you been back, here, in my—"

"Since around four."

"That was two hours ago," Priscilla said, brows raised.

She crossed the distance to the dining room table and set down the books in her arms.

"Are those all for you?" Alaina asked, sitting up.

Priscilla looked up. "Yes. I like to read."

"Clearly."

Priscilla gave her a tired look, but it wasn't without affection. "What did you get up to today?"

Alaina recounted the beginning of her day to Priscilla, who listened with interest as she leaned against the table. She glossed over the silent showdown with Lola, though the cat's sudden willingness to sprawl across the couch instead of hiding under the bed seemed to indicate progress.

"And then I ran into Clark—we had lunch together at Patty's."

Priscilla's mouth flattened into a thin line, a subtle crease appearing between her brows. "Was that nice?"

The tone made Alaina pause. It wasn't jealousy—she'd let go of her Clark-as-romantic-lead theory the second Priscilla said she was a lesbian. Still, there was something . . . off.

Whatever it was, Alaina had the perfect way to lift that furrow from her brow.

"Very." Alaina stood, walking over to Priscilla with her hands behind her back, unable to hide the bounce in her step. "I also did a little something else."

She nodded toward the plastic bags on the counter.

Priscilla tilted her head. "Did you go grocery shopping?"

"Sort of." She grinned. "I may have gotten some stuff to make cookies."

"Cookies?" Priscilla sounded bewildered.

"Yeah, you know. Sugar cookies? We can cut them into shapes and frost them."

"I'm familiar." Priscilla's gaze flitted from the bags back to Alaina, a touch of panic in her eyes. "I'm not the best baker," she said, like it was classified information.

Alaina shrugged. "That's what makes it fun!"

"You find it fun to be bad at things?"

"Sometimes. When it doesn't involve bruising my ass, at least."

"Language." Priscilla paused, then raised an eyebrow. "And phrasing."

Alaina's jaw dropped. "Why, Priscilla, was that a dirty joke?"

"What? No, I—" Priscilla sighed, pinching the bridge of her nose between two fingers. "Let's just get on with it."

Chapter Eleven

Priscilla observed as Alaina carefully leveled a scoop of flour with a knife, mouth pinched in concentration like she was defusing a bomb.

"I didn't know you knew how to bake."

"I don't. Or at least, not really. I haven't done it in forever, not since . . ." Alaina paused. "My mom liked to bake. I used to do it with her a lot."

"My mother liked to practice the art of competitive horse dressage with me," Priscilla said. "Because, you know, nothing says 'proper upbringing' quite like making a horse dance ballet."

Alaina froze midscoop. "That cannot possibly be a real thing."

"It most certainly is."

She didn't believe it until Priscilla pulled up a YouTube video. Even then, she remained skeptical.

"But why?" she asked as the horse trotted to the beat.

Priscilla considered this. "You know, I actually have no idea."

"Wild."

Alaina finished sifting the flour, then pulled out her phone to check the recipe. The cheery headline promised "no chill" cookie dough, which, as it turned out, meant you didn't have to refrigerate the dough, not that the cookies knew how to party.

Bummer.

She followed the steps, creaming butter and sugar until fluffy, then cracked in two eggs, silently praying no shells made it in. Miraculously, they didn't.

"*'Next, add vanilla extract and beat until combined,'*" she read aloud. "*'Scrape the sides of the bowl to make sure—'*"

Alaina glanced up to find Priscilla's eyes fixed on her, an exacting gaze that made her thoughts skitter like startled mice.

"What? Do I have something on my face?" She was surprised by the unsteadiness of her own voice, her throat as dry as a saltine cracker left out in the desert sun. She'd gotten used to it for the most part, but sometimes Priscilla's intensity was still enough to knock her off her game.

Priscilla stepped closer. "Yes, right—here!"

A puff of flour hit Alaina square on the nose. She reared back with a squeak. "Priscilla!"

Laughter bubbled up from Priscilla, unrestrained and infectious. Alaina couldn't help but be swept up in it, her initial shock melting into a grin. This was a side of Priscilla that she hadn't seen before, and it was exactly what she needed after the roller coaster of a day she'd had.

"You'll pay for that," she said.

Alaina returned to the dough, rolling it out as Priscilla poured drinks. There wasn't enough eggnog for two, so the result leaned heavily on rum—not that Alaina was complaining.

She sipped slowly, eyes drifting to Priscilla, who was focused on cutting cookie shapes. After a few quiet minutes, Priscilla looked up, pausing when she saw Alaina's eyes on her.

"Why are you smiling?" Priscilla asked.

"Because I'm happy?"

Priscilla narrowed her eyes.

Alaina shrugged. "I just like watching you." She nodded toward the cookie cutter in Priscilla's hand. "You're being very careful."

"Well, you worked hard on this dough. I wouldn't want it to go to waste."

Alaina bit back a laugh. She didn't have the heart to tell her the dough could be rerolled a dozen times and still be fine.

When the cookies came out of the oven, golden and fragrant, Alaina moved them to the cooling rack while Priscilla dipped a finger into the bowl to taste-test the frosting. The face she made—nose scrunched, lips pursed like she'd licked a battery—sent Alaina into a laughing fit.

"I can leave a few plain for you," she said between snorts.

"No, no." Priscilla squared her shoulders like she was preparing for battle. "If we're doing Christmas cookies, we're doing them properly."

"That's the spirit."

Once the cookies cooled, they set up across from each other at the kitchen island: bowls of colored icing, spatulas, and piping bags with snipped corners lined up like an artist's tools. Alaina's hands were steadier than she expected, outlining and flooding snowflakes in smooth layers of white and blue.

Priscilla's efforts, however, were less artisan bakery and more kindergarten art class. Alaina set down her fourth cookie to dry—a perfectly striped candy cane—and stifled a laugh when she glanced at Priscilla. The green icing clung stubbornly to the spatula, refusing to spread evenly, leaving the poor tree she was attempting to decorate patchy and bare.

"Need a hand over there, Picasso?"

"These look like a toddler made them," Priscilla exclaimed.

Alaina shook her head. "You're underselling yourself. A six-year-old, at least."

"They're awful."

"They're abstract. And besides—" Alaina reached across the counter to snatch up Priscilla's half-decorated cookie and bit off the top. "They still taste delicious."

Priscilla looked at her, eyes lingering for a beat too long before she glanced away. She cleared her throat, reaching for a piping bag. "Show me how to use this."

If Alaina didn't know any better, she'd say Priscilla was embarrassed. But by what? Her cookie-decorating skills?

"Here." Alaina came around the counter to stand beside her, picking up the piping bag and a fresh cookie. "Start with the edges. Like this . . ."

As the evening wore on, Priscilla's technique improved. By the last few cookies, she'd mastered the art of smooth icing and even attempted a few decorative swirls. They worked in comfortable silence, broken only by the occasional question or instruction, until Alaina glanced up from her final snowflake.

"So," she said, watching Priscilla concentrate on a particularly intricate design, dragging a toothpick through the wet icing to blend two colors together. "Another successful new Christmas memory?"

"Definitely." Priscilla's answer came with a small, genuine smile.

"Think we'll have replaced all the bad ones soon?"

Priscilla paused. "I wouldn't say my memories are bad, per se. Just . . ." She rolled her lips together, considering her words. "My parents never cared much for the holiday. Too commercial, not religious enough, in their opinion. But my grandmother made it special. When she passed, the holiday spirit seemed to go with her."

"How old were you?"

"Fifteen. In my parents' eyes, I was too old for Christmas."

"What? Fifteen is still a kid," Alaina said.

It was the same age she'd been when she lost her mother. Besides, there was no such thing as too old for Christmas.

"That may be so. But for my parents, the celebration, the joy, it all just stopped when she was gone."

"So they, what—didn't buy you presents? Didn't celebrate at all?"

When Priscilla shook her head, Alaina felt a twinge in her chest, a sympathetic ache. Priscilla's story was so similar to her own.

"Fifteen is so young to lose someone like that," she murmured, her voice barely above a whisper. "And your parents, they didn't want to keep her traditions alive?"

"Apparently not." Her voice caught on a sigh. "And I haven't done a great job of that myself."

"That's not your fault. Don't make that face, Sil, it's—of course you don't want to celebrate, if the memories only hurt."

Priscilla nodded. "I know that. I do. But if I'm being honest, these past few days, I've felt closer to her than I have in years." She paused, a soft smile playing at her lips. "She used to teach me carols on the piano. The kind you'd hear at church, so my parents would approve, but she'd make them fun. She loved to sing. I thought she sounded like an opera singer. I always begged for 'Angels We Have Heard on High' because I loved how dramatically she'd belt out the high notes."

Alaina's heart ached as she pictured a young Priscilla at a piano bench, her grandmother guiding her through the melody. Then the image transformed: Priscilla at fifteen, alone at that same piano, fingers hovering over keys that would never sound quite right without her grandmother's voice accompanying them.

Would they have been friends back then, two girls with holes in their lives shaped like the people they'd lost?

"I'm glad you have those memories," Alaina said, arranging cookies on a plate so she wouldn't have to look up. "I have a few like that too. Little things. Like how my mom used to hum while she baked, or how she'd let me open one present on Christmas Eve. We didn't have much, but somehow she made it feel . . . magical."

"I'm sorry you don't have many memories of Christmas from—from before."

Alaina hesitated. She didn't want to overshare. But Priscilla had told her about her grandmother. About her grief. Maybe it was okay to do the same.

"After she died, those memories kind of faded. My therapist said that can happen sometimes, with trauma. Your brain just . . ." She made a vague gesture with her hand. "Files things away where you can't find them."

"Even the good memories?"

"Even those."

Being here in Brooks had started to unlock some of those buried memories. Like her brain had finally decided it was safe to remember again. Maybe the same thing was happening to Priscilla this Christmas—old joy surfacing after years of keeping it locked away.

Priscilla's hand found Alaina's, fingers intertwining briefly, steady and warm. "Before I forget—something came in earlier today that I wanted to show you. Do you mind coming downstairs with me?"

They left the apartment hand in hand, only letting go to navigate the spiral staircase. When they reached the bookstore floor, Priscilla reached for her again, guiding her through the dim aisles. The space had settled into its evening stillness, hushed and soft, their footsteps barely making a sound on the rugs as they walked toward the children's section.

Priscilla scanned the shelves, fingertips trailing lightly over the spines. "Here." Priscilla pulled a book from the shelf. "We'd sold out earlier this month, but I ordered more and it came in while you were out and I thought you'd like to . . . Does it look familiar?"

Alaina stared at the cover.

"Oh my god."

It wasn't just a book, it was *the* book—the one her mother had read to her as a child. Her hands trembled as she took it, flipping it open. And there he was—Peter in his red snow suit, the bright color cutting across pages of endless white. She traced a finger along the illustrations, breath catching as memories surged forward, clear and sharp, no longer foggy: her mother's voice dropping low to mimic the *crunch-crunch-crunch* of Peter's boots, rising with a laugh as snow fell from a tree onto his head.

She didn't notice the tears until one landed on the last page, blurring the ink.

The memory crystallized: She was four or five, jamming snow into her coat pockets just like Peter. The next morning, her mom had found the coat in a puddle by the door, snow long gone. Alaina had started to cry. Her plan to keep the snow forever had failed. But instead of scolding her for the mess, her mother laughed—full and joyful—until Alaina laughed too, her disappointment melting away like the snow in her pockets.

God, her mother's laugh. How had she forgotten it? That

unmistakable full-body sound. The kind of laugh you could pick out of a crowded room. The kind that made strangers laugh too, even if they hadn't heard the joke.

Alaina hurried to wipe the tearstain off the paper, but Priscilla reached out, her fingers landing on the back of Alaina's knuckles to still her hand.

"Don't worry. It's yours."

Alaina mustered a grateful smile, though it wobbled a bit. "Thank you."

She tucked the precious book under her arm and pulled Priscilla into a hug. The solid warmth of her, the steady thrum of her heartbeat against Alaina's chest—it felt like being anchored in a storm.

No one had ever done something like this for her before, seen straight through to her heart and handed her back a piece of herself she thought was lost forever. Cole had given her plenty of gifts—a box of heart-shaped truffles for their first Valentine's Day, a bouquet from the corner store before a Friday-night date. But nothing compared to this. Even the moonstone necklace he got for her birthday had the wrong birthstone set in the middle. The only person who ever really tried to understand her was Nico, but her best friend's well-meaning attempts at comfort usually involved tequila shots and terrible karaoke.

But here was Priscilla, who'd known her for a few days, finding ways to reach the parts of her heart she'd walled off years ago.

When they broke the hug, Priscilla's hands stayed rooted to Alaina's shoulders, her thumb idly tracing the seam on her shirt. "Let me leave a quick note for inventory tomorrow."

Alaina followed Priscilla back through the store. She paused at a door behind the counter that had a pane of stained glass on the upper half, casting a quick smile over her shoulder at Alaina. "Won't be a minute."

Priscilla opened the door, revealing another small glimpse into her world. A well-organized desk sat in the middle, with an ancient-looking computer and a vintage banker's lamp. Priscilla moved efficiently, flicking on the light, pulling open a drawer, and retrieving a pad of neon-pink Post-its.

Alaina leaned against the doorframe. What was Priscilla's handwriting like? It must be beautiful. Even the way she held the pen was fascinating, as if it were floating between her slender fingers.

Priscilla stuck the note to the corner of the computer screen, tucked the Post-its back into the drawer, then looked up. Her eyes softened when they met Alaina's. "You all right?"

Alaina blinked, completely forgetting she had been crying minutes before until she spoke, her voice still a hoarse whisper. "Yeah. Perfect."

Priscilla stepped toward her then looked up, her gaze catching on something hanging just beyond the other side of the doorframe.

Alaina followed her eyes and frowned. "What is that?"

Priscilla's eyes widened, but she didn't answer.

Alaina stood on her tiptoes for a better view. "Holy shit, is that—that's mistletoe, isn't it?" A grin broke across her face, tears forgotten. "Did you put this here?"

Priscilla scoffed, scandalized. "Me? No. It must've been Callie; she's always pulling pranks like this . . ."

But Alaina had stopped listening. Her gaze slid from the sprig overhead to Priscilla's face, her mind running ahead without permission—imagining Priscilla stepping into her space, pressing her gently against the doorframe, and—

Whoa. *What?*

Her pulse jumped. Where the hell did *that* come from?

Priscilla's voice cut in. "Alaina?"

"Hm?"

"Why are you looking at me like that?"

"Like . . . what?"

"Like you—like it's—" Priscilla faltered, glancing back up at the mistletoe. She exhaled, reaching up. "Maybe we should—"

Alaina caught her wrist, cutting her off midsentence.

"Don't," she said, a little too fast, the word springing from her lips before she could filter it. "I mean, you don't need to."

Would it be so ridiculous? They were alone in the store. They were both attractive people. Alaina *did* want to participate in more holiday traditions, and she'd never been kissed under the mistletoe before.

Priscilla's hand, still held captive by Alaina, fell back to her side. Was Alaina imagining things, or did Priscilla inch a bit closer?

Priscilla's head tilted to the side, almost imperceptibly. "I don't?"

"It's tradition." Alaina aimed for casual while her heart launched itself around her rib cage.

Why was she so nervous? It would just be a peck—a little chaste kiss between friends. Girls did stuff like this all the time, right?

Girls, maybe. Priscilla? She wasn't so sure. Besides, Priscilla was actually gay. Maybe she didn't want to kiss a straight girl.

Priscilla's tongue made a quick sweep over her lips. Alaina felt it like static. Her breath caught.

"Right," Priscilla said. "Tradition."

A wild thrill shot through Alaina. She had expected a laugh or a dismissal, maybe even a blush and averted eyes. But instead, Priscilla's gaze landed on her mouth, and before she had time to second-guess the invitation, Priscilla was leaning in.

Alaina's whole body stilled—except her heart, which was pounding so loud it drowned out her thoughts.

Priscilla's lips brushed against hers. Not rushed. Not dramatic. It lit Alaina up from the inside, like flipping a switch she didn't know was there. The kiss was gentle, tentative, but something in it crackled with heat, something that made Alaina want more. To reach up and cradle Priscilla's face, her neck, to pull her even closer. She felt the whisper of movement near the skin of her jaw, like Priscilla was feeling the same pull, that same barely restrained energy dancing just under the surface.

She didn't know how long they stayed like that—lips pressed together, sharing a single, suspended moment—but when they finally parted, Alaina kept her eyes closed. Her knees felt unreliable. The world had gone a little sideways.

Did that really just happen?

She opened her eyes slowly. Priscilla was watching her, expression unreadable. Of course. Had Priscilla ever played poker, or was this particularly frustrating skill something she'd mastered just for Alaina in the short time they'd known each other?

"Sil?" Alaina asked. Her voice was unexpectedly rough. "You okay?"

Priscilla blinked, swallowed, then gave a shallow, breathy laugh. "Yes. But I'm going to kill Callie."

And then she turned and walked toward the spiral staircase, leaving Alaina swaying where she stood, the book still clutched to her chest.

For a heartbeat, she didn't move. Her lips tingled. Her thoughts spun like snow in a blizzard, directionless and impossible to catch. Then her feet moved, almost by instinct, following Priscilla up the stairs like her body knew where to go even if her brain hadn't figured it out yet.

Alaina tried to keep pace, though the silence between them was so thick it was practically another step to navigate. The snug turn of the staircase mirrored the twist of uncertainty in Alaina's stomach. Was Priscilla angry? Had she done something wrong?

Once in the apartment, Priscilla didn't even look at her. Just crossed the room and said quietly, "I'm going to take a shower."

Before Alaina could say anything, the bathroom door clicked shut.

Alaina flopped onto the sofa. She couldn't form a single coherent thought with Priscilla in front of her. Now that she was alone, they ran wild.

She and Cole were on a break, yes, but they were still . . . something, right? She'd crossed a line when she'd kissed Priscilla. No, Priscilla had kissed her. And it had been . . . different. Not better or worse than kissing Cole, just different. Kissing Cole was like diving into the ocean—that rush of being swept up. But kissing Priscilla? It felt like standing in front of a bonfire. Gentle heat at first, then deeper, more consuming, something that sank into her bones and refused to leave.

She pressed her fingers lightly to her lips, still warm from the kiss. A thrill shivered down her spine, followed closely by a sharp pang of guilt.

It didn't have to mean anything. Did it?

As the seconds ticked by, Alaina sank deeper into the couch, a heavy anchor of guilt wrapping around her heart and tugging her down.

It had just been mistletoe. A silly tradition. People kissed under mistletoe all the time. It didn't have to mean anything.

So why did her stomach feel like it was tying itself into knots? And why did she want to do it again?

She pulled out her phone, opening her thread with Nico. If she could tell anyone about this, it would be her best friend. But her brain froze as her fingers went to type the word "kissed."

They'd *kissed*. She and Priscilla had kissed. Holy shit. And she'd liked it.

She let out a low, frustrated sigh and pushed herself off the couch, feeling the weight of her thoughts as she stood. She needed something—anything—to distract herself. Her gaze darted around the apartment, finally landing on the kettle sitting on the stove.

Perfect.

Tea was safe. Tea was routine. Tea didn't have feelings.

She threw herself into the simple ritual of filling the kettle and setting it on the stove. The mundane task offered a small buoy in the sea of her emotions, and she clung to it gratefully.

As she reached for a mug, the soft patter of paws drew her gaze. Lola hopped up onto the counter next to the stove and sat primly, her gold eyes fixed on Alaina with unnerving stillness.

"Don't you give me that look," Alaina said, pointing at her. "I already know I'm losing it."

Lola blinked slowly, unbothered.

Alaina narrowed her eyes and returned the gesture, deliberately closing and opening her eyes in a mimic of the cat's supposed sign of trust. Lola remained unmoved. She might as well have rolled her eyes.

"Even you think I'm a disaster, huh?"

The kettle's shrill whistle sounded right as the shower shut off. Alaina kept her back firmly turned as the bathroom door opened, as if refusing to look would somehow prevent her mind from conjuring images of Priscilla stepping out in just a towel, steam coming off her like something out of a dream.

And there it was again—that sharp, dangerous heat, curling low in her stomach.

What the hell was happening to her?

The bedroom door clicked shut behind Priscilla.

Alaina poured hot water into two mugs, watching the tea diffuse like ink in water, slow and deliberate. The amber deepened. Mesmerizing. She didn't even like tea—too bitter, usually—but if it helped steady her pulse or calm the flush still clinging to her cheeks, she'd drink a gallon.

Behind her, the bedroom door creaked open.

Alaina turned.

Priscilla stood there, hovering in the doorway. Flannel pants, thermal shirt. Her skin was pink from the shower. There was something so unguarded about her like this—something that broke Alaina open in ways she wasn't prepared for.

She looked away, fast, zeroing in on the mugs like they were the most fascinating objects in the world.

"Hello," Priscilla said stiffly.

"Hey." She held out the mugs, moving so fast that a tiny bit sloshed from one of them onto the counter. "I, um—I made us some tea."

Priscilla moved cautiously forward. "Thank you."

"Oh, don't thank me. It's probably terrible." She tried for a smile, but even she could feel how unnatural it must've looked, stretched tight and thin like a drawn bow.

They settled onto the couch, one at each end like cautious strangers in a waiting room. The aroma of fresh-baked cookies did nothing to mask the palpable tension thickening the air. Alaina wished for something, anything, to break the strained quiet.

Was Priscilla regretting the kiss? Wishing it hadn't happened? Or was she stuck in the same loop Alaina was?

The thought of Priscilla crafting some gentle speech to explain that it hadn't meant anything slid through her like ice. It made no sense—Alaina should want it to mean nothing. She shouldn't want it to matter. She wasn't interested in women, certainly wasn't trying to lead Priscilla on. But then why could she still feel the ghost of Priscilla's lips against her own?

The memory of their kiss played on a loop in her mind, a merry-go-round she couldn't get off, each rotation bringing a new wave of panic. She'd kissed someone other than Cole. She'd kissed a woman. She'd kissed Priscilla. She'd kissed Priscilla and liked it. She'd melted into that kiss like she belonged there. She'd wanted more. She still wanted more.

Her thoughts grew heavier with each tick of the clock, the only soundtrack in the quiet room.

Alaina sucked in a deep breath. She couldn't let this silence stretch on any longer. Right as she steeled herself to *just speak goddamnit,* Priscilla beat her to it.

"I think I'm going to go to bed."

Alaina glanced at the clock. It was barely past nine. She didn't blame her—what else were they supposed to do? Priscilla moved toward the sink, rinsing out their mugs with the kind of focus that said she wanted to keep her hands busy. Alaina leaned back against the couch. Suddenly, the cushions felt a lot more lumpy than they had the first three nights she'd slept there. She could probably look forward to an hour or two of fitful sleep tonight, and that's if she was lucky.

Priscilla paused in the doorway of her bedroom. "You don't have to sleep on the couch if . . . you know, if you . . . slept better with me—in my—in the room."

In any other situation, Alaina would've laughed at the clumsy way Priscilla stumbled through that sentence. But now the thought of sleeping beside Priscilla sent a fresh new batch of nerves tap-dancing straight across her heart. "Are you sure? You don't have to—"

"I'm sure." Priscilla still wouldn't quite look at her, but she nodded. Alaina's shoulders loosened, the knot in her stomach easing just a little. It couldn't be that weird between them if Priscilla was still offering to share the bed. Maybe in the dark it'd be easier to talk again. Like last night.

But no. Within minutes of lying down, Priscilla's breathing had settled into a slow, steady rhythm. Alaina leaned in slightly just to be sure.

Yep. She was asleep. Seriously?

Alaina let her head fall back onto the pillow with a heavy thump. How could Priscilla sleep at a time like this? Had the kiss not sent her world spinning off its axis?

Alaina rolled away to face the wall before her eyes got a chance to adjust. If she saw Priscilla now, she'd never stop looking. Time blurred. She had no idea how long she lay there, eyes open, mind racing. But the bed felt colder tonight—Priscilla too far away, the space between them yawning wide.

She shivered, bracing herself for a long, sleepless night.

And then Priscilla rolled over and pulled her close.

Alaina was a cuddler by nature. Cole liked to joke that she clung to him like a koala in its favorite eucalyptus tree. But this was different. This wasn't a comforting embrace she could melt into. Every nerve buzzed beneath her skin. Priscilla's arm tightened around her middle, warm and strong.

The light skim of fingers at her waist sent a shiver darting down her spine. Priscilla's legs tangled with hers, the full length of her body slotted against Alaina's back—and God, Priscilla's chest, soft and braless beneath that nightshirt, pressed against her.

Was this on purpose? Was she still asleep?

Priscilla hummed, nuzzling into Alaina's shoulder, and let out a soft puff of air that was half sigh, half snore.

Okay. Definitely asleep.

Alaina squeezed her eyes shut tight, desperate to keep her imagination in check, but she failed—miserably. Images of the brief kiss under the mistletoe replayed in her mind like a reel, except this was the director's cut. Instead of the chaste kiss they'd shared, this time the scant space between them disappeared, their lips meeting with a deeper, hungrier intent. Instead of pulling away, Priscilla backed her against the office desk. Priscilla's hands found purchase on the edge, trapping Alaina between her arms. Her fingers traced paths up Alaina's back, and—

Alaina's face burned. She was so grateful for the dark.

She shifted, desperate to create space, but the moment she moved, Priscilla pulled her closer, her fingers curling at Alaina's hip with a low, possessive tug.

She wouldn't be getting any sleep tonight.

Chapter Twelve

THREE DAYS UNTIL CHRISTMAS

Alaina's back pressed into the arm of the couch, the weight on top of her driving her deeper and deeper into the cushion. There were lips and hands everywhere—her neck, her jaw, her ribs, her hips—she couldn't keep track of it all. It felt good, very good, but the hard backing of the couch arm kept stabbing painfully into her shoulder blades.

She put her hands on broad shoulders. "Cole, wait."

He pulled back and looked down at her with his signature grin. "Yeah?"

Alaina slid her hands down his chest, pushing until he sat back so she could straddle his lap instead.

"Much better," she murmured, ducking her head to kiss that spot under his ear, the one he liked. Strong hands settled on her hips, grounding her. She ran her tongue over the thrum of his pulse point and paused.

The sound that followed—low, needy—wasn't his. She pulled back.

Priscilla was staring back at her, eyes dark and wide. Alaina blinked, disoriented. Her brain tried to recalibrate—knees tight against narrow hips, smaller hands gripping her waist, the wrong chest beneath her palms. Not Cole. Priscilla.

"Something wrong?"

Alaina shook her head. "No. This is perfect."

Wondering why she had ever stopped, Alaina dove in to kiss her.

Priscilla's mouth was warm and tasted like eggnog and rum and something sweet Alaina couldn't name. Her hands tunneled through dark hair, tilting Priscilla's head back. She rocked in Priscilla's lap, restless, greedy. A breathy laugh escaped against her lips—Alaina's impatience clearly noted—and it only made her press closer.

Fingers traced the waistband of Alaina's jeans, deliberate, steady. The button popped. A slow drag of the zipper.

"Is this what you want?" Priscilla asked, gaze locked on hers, hand hovering.

Alaina nodded fervently. "Please."

Half a smile appeared on Priscilla's mouth, there only for a second before her teeth caught on her bottom lip, her hand slipping beneath the fabric and—

Alaina woke with a sharp gasp.

The room was dark. Her heart was a hammer in her chest. She slapped a hand over her mouth, willing her breath to slow.

Jesus Christ. What was that?

Her cheeks burned. Her whole body burned. She felt the phantom press of hands, lips, heat. She rolled onto her back, dragging both hands over her face.

She glanced at the nightstand. 3:02 A.M.

She closed her eyes and tried to think of anything else. Snow. Cold water. Socks. Filing her taxes. But the feeling of Priscilla still lingered. That voice. That look.

Alaina groaned and rolled onto her side, away from Priscilla. "Please, universe," she whispered, "just let me sleep."

Alaina was groggy when she opened her eyes to an empty bedroom five hours later. Cruelly, her brain had pivoted from sex dreams to stress dreams about work—the last one featuring her boss, who had somehow made it all the way to Utah to fire her in the middle of the bookstore while she stood there in her underwear.

Why couldn't she have dreamed about puppies, or rainbows, or—preferably—nothing at all?

Needless to say, it had not been a restful night.

When she made her way into the living room, Priscilla was already there, leaning against the counter. She didn't look up when Alaina entered, though Alaina didn't miss the subtle shift in her posture—the way her spine snapped straight, her shoulders rolled back into their usual tight line of control.

"Good morning." The words came out thin, careful.

Priscilla's eyes darted to Alaina for a second before she turned away. "There's coffee."

"Fantastic." Alaina almost winced at how defeated she sounded.

She fixed herself a mug, disappointed when Priscilla moved to the dining room table as soon as Alaina stepped into the kitchen. Last night hadn't been this awkward. Quiet, sure. But this? This was something else entirely. Alaina felt like she was watching a door slowly shut in her face.

Maybe Priscilla had had time to think. To spiral. Alaina sure had. Her mind had been a nonstop reel of "what the hell does this mean" for hours.

She couldn't help but wonder just *what* Priscilla was spiraling over, though. Alaina's own brain kept tripping over the fact that

Priscilla was a woman. She'd long ago examined the thought that she might be bisexual, back when she first met Nico in college. She'd toyed with the idea. Wondered. But there had never been a spark. Never been anyone who'd made her wonder enough to want more.

Until now.

Not that she was ready to grab a flag and march in a parade, but—this had to mean *something,* right? God, she really needed to talk to Nico.

Still, this wasn't new for Priscilla. She'd known she was into women for years. So what was she spiraling about? Was she regretting it? Trying to figure out how to let Alaina down gently?

Alaina couldn't take it anymore.

She slid into the seat next to Priscilla, her fingers wrapping around the warm mug for comfort.

"So . . . are we going to talk about it?"

Priscilla didn't look up. "Talk about what?"

"You kissed me," Alaina blurted. Priscilla's jaw tensed. Her bottom lip caught between her teeth in that same unreadable, locked-up expression. "We kissed."

Alaina's mind, unfortunately, chose that moment to replay last night's dream in vivid detail. The feel of Priscilla's hair tangled in her fingers, her lips swollen and flushed, the way her body had moved beneath Alaina's hands—

"Oh, that," Priscilla said, voice clipped. "It was mistletoe. It doesn't have to be a big deal."

"Right. No big deal." Alaina repeated the words numbly. She wanted to believe it. She should believe it. She couldn't possibly be interested in Priscilla, could she? Sure, Priscilla was hot. She'd have to be crazy not to acknowledge that. Admitting it to herself finally snapped the past few days into focus.

This didn't have to change anything about her sexuality.

This was a momentary blip, something fleeting brought on by her longing for Cole.

She'd spent the night worrying for nothing. Everything could go back to normal now. So then why didn't the thought make her feel any better?

"Good." The tension faded from Priscilla's face as her gaze finally rose to meet Alaina's. There was an almost dangerous glint to Priscilla's eye as she leaned forward that had Alaina's mouth turning dry. "Because we have a big day ahead of us."

"We do?"

"We're getting you out on the mountain. Today you are going to learn to ski." Priscilla poked her finger playfully against Alaina's sternum. Her lips curved into a smile that bordered on a smirk. Alaina's breath hitched, and she struggled to steady herself as heat spread from Priscilla's touch. The way Priscilla's finger lingered ever so slightly on her skin made her pulse race uncontrollably.

Okay, maybe this changed *a little* about her sexuality.

❄

Alaina announced she needed to shower before they left, out of a need for both cleanliness and a break from Priscilla. The bathroom filled with steam fast, curling around her like a cocoon, but it couldn't touch the heat already building low in her body.

She trailed her fingers along the slick tiles, absently tracing circles in the water beading down. Yesterday, Priscilla had been a friend. Just a friend. A smart, stunning, generous friend who'd taken her in without hesitation.

And now? Alaina's thoughts swirled like the water at her feet, faster and faster.

"It's no big deal," she told herself, lathering shampoo into her hair. It smelled like Priscilla—sweet and spiced at the same time—and Alaina rushed to rinse the suds out. "No big deal at all."

But the more she tried to ignore it, the more vivid her thoughts became. Priscilla's neck. That long, elegant stretch of skin. Her strong arms, how effortlessly she lifted Alaina from the snow and caught her on the ice. She imagined Priscilla's smile—a slow, careful thing that took Alaina's heart and twisted it into something useless.

And last night. God, that dream.

She leaned forward, bracing one hand against the tile. Her other hand moved down her stomach, slow. She tried to think of anything but Priscilla. It didn't feel right to think of her friend while her hand was sliding closer and closer toward a line she couldn't uncross.

They were friends. Just friends.

She tried to conjure Cole's face. Cole, whom she loved. Cole, who kissed her in front of sunsets and posted it for all the world to see. Cole, whose image immediately blurred and slipped away.

She grasped for one of the Chrises. Pine. Evans. Someone safe. But their faces dissolved like mist.

She tried to clear her mind. Just focus on sensation. On her body.

But the second her fingers slipped lower, her hips jerked forward and her thoughts ran—no, sprinted straight back to Priscilla.

Just a friend, she told herself again, but it was hopeless. She imagined Priscilla's lips at her neck. Her shoulder. Her thighs.

A sigh escaped her, more like a whimper, her forehead thunking softly against the cool tile. Her breath came fast, her body tighter with every second, nerves sparking like kindling.

"Fuck," Alaina whispered into the steam. The hand on the

wall tightened into a fist, and every few seconds a small moan slipped out. She bit her lip, desperate to swallow the noise.

If she closed her eyes, she could imagine it all. Priscilla's hands on her hips, guiding her. Priscilla's teeth dragging against the spot where her neck met her shoulders. Priscilla's lips bruising hers. Priscilla's voice calling through the door.

Wait, what?

"Alaina? Are you nearly done?"

Alaina flinched away from her own body so hard she smacked her hand against the tile, her knuckles immediately singing with pain.

"Ow, fuck!"

The door creaked open. "Are you okay?"

She pressed her forehead to the tile, voice thready. "Yeah—yeah, all good!" Her words came too fast, too high-pitched. "Just—uh, dropped the shampoo on my foot."

Silence. Then: "We need to leave in about twenty minutes. Will you be ready?"

"Yup! For sure, yes." Alaina wished she could stop the nervous words from falling out of her mouth, but they kept on coming. "No problem. Out in a jiff."

There was a slight pause. "Right. Good."

The door clicked closed again and Alaina turned the faucet toward cold for the rest of her shower.

Afterward, she rushed to pull herself together, getting dressed and dragging a brush through damp hair with shaking hands. She stared at her reflection, eyes wide, cheeks still flushed.

"Get a grip," she scolded her reflection in the mirror. She really needed to get herself under control, which seemed impossible knowing Priscilla was waiting on the other side of that door.

When she left the bathroom, Alaina almost tripped over her own feet at the sight of Priscilla standing casually by the door to the stairwell. She felt the air thin, her breath catching in her throat as she took in the sight before her.

Priscilla looked up, her eyes softening when they met Alaina's. No idea, clearly, that her very existence was currently short-circuiting Alaina's brain.

"Ready?" Priscilla asked, tilting her head.

The blush hit her hard. She blinked, realizing she'd said absolutely nothing for a solid three seconds.

She was supposed to be focused on Cole. Getting back to her actual life. Not getting distracted by how nice Priscilla's voice sounded when she asked simple, logistical questions.

She couldn't let herself get swept away by a crush.

God, even just calling it a crush made her feel dizzy.

"Yep. Good to go," she squeaked, then cleared her throat and tried again. "You excited?"

Priscilla smiled. Alaina could practically feel the heat roll through her stomach like she'd swallowed the sun. Not helpful.

"Very." Priscilla nodded. "This is my favorite thing about living here. Well—one of my favorites, besides my friends. Who are, coincidentally, meeting us there."

Alaina's eyebrows flew up. "They are? A group ski trip?"

Priscilla hesitated, her expression unsure. "Is that okay?"

"Are you kidding? It's amazing!" Alaina was genuinely happy about the prospect of Priscilla reconnecting with her friends. A selfish part of her wanted to keep Priscilla all to herself, but the rest of her? Relieved. A group meant distraction. Distance. Boundaries.

If she didn't keep her head on straight, she'd end up skiing off a cliff.

Priscilla opened the door, and Alaina bounded down the stairs, grateful for the excuse to move, only to stop short when she spotted Clark behind the counter.

Right. Clark. The guy she'd sort of rejected yesterday.

Whoops.

"Good morning, Alaina," he said.

"Morning, Clark!"

Priscilla slipped past him into the back office, nodding a greeting.

"I brought you these." He lifted a wrapped plate from behind the counter, a pile of gingerbread men visible under the cellophane.

"They look amazing." Amazing was an understatement. They looked like they were made by a professional, and she was certain that his mother had something to do with it. "Thank you!"

He lowered his voice. "Listen, about yesterday—"

"Oh, don't worry about that." Alaina waved her hand to cut him off. She wasn't sure how long Priscilla would be in the office, and she really didn't want her to be here for this conversation.

The silence lasted a few seconds too long, Clark looking like he wanted to say something else until Priscilla emerged from the door behind him. He looked back at her, then nodded. "Good, good. I'm glad that's settled then. Water under the—well, hope you two have a good day doing whatever it is you're getting up to."

Alaina bounced on her toes in excitement. "We absolutely will, thanks. Are you going to be okay here alone?"

"Who said anything about being alone?" Clark said with a grin. "We have a new hire. My mom will be here any minute to help out."

Alaina blinked. Priscilla, voluntarily handing over the reins during one of the busiest weeks of the year to a woman she'd probably met only a handful of times. A week ago, she'd barely trusted Alaina to read names off a list, and now she was about to leave her store and spend the day on a mountain.

All for Alaina.

Priscilla came up next to her, their arms brushing. "Are you sure she's going to be okay? I could pay her more," she started to say, but Clark waved her off.

"She'll be great. She's a smart lady. And she'd spend the day here with me for free. Besides, she's excited to get a look into my life. It'll be a good chance to show her just what I love about this town."

"Okay. And if you run into any trouble—"

"I'll call. But don't worry. You won't be hearing from us."

"Okay. Then . . . I guess it's time to go," Priscilla said, her hand brushing Alaina's upper back.

A bolt of electricity shot down her spine. She went still, every nerve on high alert. Alaina's heartbeat catapulted into overdrive as her mind begged for an ounce of composure.

But her traitorous body didn't care. It remembered everything: the kiss, the dream, the interrupted shower. Her pulse rocketed, cheeks heating as she blinked fast, praying her face wasn't giving her away.

Alaina waved to Clark, her voice straining a half octave higher than usual. "Catch you later!"

Outside, Priscilla glanced back toward the store. "What was that about? 'Water under the bridge'?"

Alaina winced internally. She'd hoped Priscilla hadn't caught that. "He's probably just feeling a little awkward around me," she said, stalling.

If she could find a way to *not* tell Priscilla that Clark had invited her out on a date, that would be super awesome. She didn't need to add another layer of complication to whatever was going on here.

Priscilla halted as they reached the truck, her body tensing, not moving to get inside. "Why's that?"

Maybe those years doing improv for warm-up before theater in college would finally get a chance to shine. Too bad her brain gave her absolutely nothing to work with.

"He, um . . ." She coughed. "He kind of asked me out yesterday?"

She ducked into the passenger seat before Priscilla could respond, pulling the door shut like she could somehow trap her embarrassment outside. Through the window, she saw Priscilla's face contort in confusion.

Maybe she was jealous. The thought made her pulse quicken. Would that be a good thing? Alaina had never found jealousy attractive, but this morning she was having a hard time finding anything unattractive about Priscilla.

Priscilla climbed into the truck, starting the engine with a little more force than necessary.

"What did you say?" she asked, eyes fixed on the windshield. "To Clark's . . . invitation."

"No!" It came out a little too loud. Alaina cleared her throat. "I mean, I said no. I'm only going to be here a few more days, and besides, I have—" Her mind faltered, and the truth hit her like a ton of bricks. "I, um, have a boyfriend. Sort of."

Priscilla nodded, putting the truck in reverse. Was Alaina imagining the way Priscilla's grip tightened around the steering wheel?

"Right, of course."

"And even if I didn't . . ." She paused, waiting for Priscilla to look over at her. When she didn't, she kept going anyway. "He's not really my type."

Her type involved dark hair, deep brown eyes, and a soft, warm smile.

She just wasn't entirely sure who that was describing anymore.

The mountain was "just outside of town," according to Priscilla, which meant about a twenty-minute ride. They drove mainly in silence, nerves thrumming through Alaina for a multitude of reasons. Not the least of which was that she had no idea how to ski and the idea of barreling down a mountain with nothing but two sticks strapped to her feet was a little horrifying. Add in the identity crisis she was currently spiraling through, and the cause of said crisis sitting three feet away, and, well . . .

Alaina blew out a breath through puffed cheeks, trying to regulate her heartbeat.

Her phone buzzed and she pulled it out, breaking into a grin when she saw the message waiting from Nico.

Nico: i think i found THE RING
Nico: also, i miss you
Alaina: AHHHHH EXCITING
Alaina: Pictures????

The photo came in immediately. The ring was a warm gold, with what looked like branches or vines winding around each other to form a circle. Little ornamental leaves popped off the branches, each with a small green stone set inside. It looked like it belonged in a *Lord of the Rings* movie—or, at least, Alaina assumed that was true. She'd never actually seen them, much to Josie's disappointment.

Alaina: It's gorgeous. She's going to LOOOVE it!!!!

Alaina: And I miss you too.

Alaina: I reallllly wish you were here. I have so much to talk to you about

Nico: you can't just leave it there. now you have to tell me

Alaina glanced over at Priscilla. She'd put on sleek black snow pants while Alaina was in the shower, though she left off the matching jacket for the drive, opting to wear a dark thermal instead. Her hair was twisted up in that neat, no-nonsense bun that left her jawline exposed. Alaina tried very hard not to look at it. Or think about it.

Which she was failing at. Miserably.

Alaina: I think I might be bi. Or like...at least not as straight as I previously thought? Is that a thing?

Nico: YESSSSSS

Nico: finally

Nico: i told you your fascination with meryl streep in death becomes her wasn't straight, dude

Nico: wow, a few days with a hot lesbian has got you questioning your sexuality, huh

Alaina: Well...

Alaina: Actually...

Alaina: We kissed?

Nico: WHAT

Her ringtone—"Like It's Christmas" by the Jonas Brothers—started blaring. Alaina jumped, almost dropping her phone in her hurry to silence it.

"Sorry," she said, wincing.

Priscilla took her eyes off the road for a second to glance at her. "Do you need to get that?"

"Nope!"

A second after she sent it to voicemail, her phone started ringing again.

"Sorry," she repeated. "I'll just—"

She silenced it a second time, then immediately texted Nico.

Alaina: I'm in the car with her right now so I can't talk but I promise to catch you up later

Nico: THIS IS SO CRUEL

Nico: i can't wait to hear all about your little gay awakening

Nico: so

Nico: wait

Nico: what does this mean about cole

She stared at the last message, unsure of how to answer it. Her kiss with Priscilla had been eye-opening, to say the least. But that didn't change anything about her plans. It couldn't. Even if she accepted that she had a crush on Priscilla, she was in love with Cole.

And she would not give up on love.

"We're here."

Alaina looked up from her phone to find they'd pulled off into an already half-full parking lot in front of a beautiful old building with gigantic windows on every wall. Behind it, the mountain rose impossibly high into the sky. She forgot everything else for a second. The view stole the breath right out of her.

Priscilla put the truck in park and hopped out without a word. She lowered the front seat and reached into the back for the ski jacket she'd tossed back there. Alaina leaned forward in her seat, eyes locked on the towering mountain ahead.

Was she really about to do this?

Her door opened, and Priscilla appeared, tilting her head to look inside. "Everything okay?"

"Yes! Yeah, I'm—sorry, I'm coming." Alaina slid out of the cab, Priscilla shutting the door behind her.

"Are you nervous?"

"Kind of." Her eyes wandered back up to the slope. "It, um, looks a lot bigger in person."

It was a silly thing to say. Breaking news—mountains are big.

"Hey." Priscilla dipped her head to catch Alaina's gaze. "We don't have to do this if you're not comfortable."

The wave of relief that washed over her was short-lived. She didn't want to give up—not after Priscilla had been so excited to bring her. She could probably manage the bunny hill, at least. Maybe get a photo with just sky behind her so no one could tell she hadn't even made it up a slope.

"Nope. I came out here to ski, and ski I will." She thought back to how carefully Priscilla had taught her to skate. The patience she showed, only letting go of Alaina's hands once she was ready. "Besides—you wouldn't let me get hurt. I trust you."

Priscilla straightened, blinked, then smiled so softly that Alaina could tell she wasn't even trying to hold it back.

They started toward the lodge, and only then did Alaina notice just how out of place she looked compared to the crowd. Sleek jackets. Goggles. Helmets. She was super underprepared.

She tugged on Priscilla's sleeve. "So, where do I get one of these?"

"Callie brought one for you to borrow." Priscilla looked past her and smiled. "Speaking of—Callie! Ned!"

They crossed the lot toward the group—Callie, Ned, Grant,

and Lauren—all bundled up and laughing about something as they pulled gear from the back of the Jeep. They all exchanged hugs, and Callie handed Alaina a large duffel bag.

"Priscilla said you would need these."

"Wow, thank you so much. Seriously." Alaina took the bag with both hands. "You sure it's okay?"

Callie waved her off. "It's not like I'll be using it."

"Wait—you don't ski?"

Callie shook her head. "I'm more of a tubing girl. But you'll have fun, I promise!"

They headed into the lodge, the others breaking off in search of a locker room. Priscilla touched Alaina's arm, holding her back for a moment. "You might want to change in the bathroom," she said. "Callie brought you some—um, underlayers."

Priscilla's cheeks tinged adorably pink at this, her eyes darting away from Alaina's.

Alaina almost made a joke—something reckless about needing help getting dressed—but stopped herself. What if Priscilla said yes? One wrong move and she'd combust on the spot.

She ducked into the bathroom, unzipped the duffel, and froze.

Oh no.

Five minutes later, still hiding, she heard a gentle knock.

"Alaina? Are you okay?"

She took a final look at herself in the mirror, goggles sitting crooked on her forehead no matter how many times she adjusted them. "Yeah, I'm fine, I'm just—okay, I'm coming out, but you can't laugh at me."

"Why would I laugh at you?"

"Because." She opened the door, poking her head out of the bathroom. She held her arms out as she emerged in what had to be the world's puffiest jacket.

A flicker of a smile passed over Priscilla's face as she took her in, but she schooled it back into submission almost immediately.

"Because?" Priscilla asked, stepping closer.

"I look ridiculous."

Alaina looked like a giant teal marshmallow in her snow suit. As if mocking her, the goggles slid a little lower, covering her brows.

Priscilla reached to adjust them, and Alaina's heart leapt into her throat. Up close, Alaina could see the rings of gold in Priscilla's eyes, the delicate shadows cast by her lashes.

And then—her gaze dipped to Priscilla's lips. Soft. Pink from the cold. Lips that had kissed hers. Lips she'd dreamed of. Alaina swallowed hard, barely holding herself back from leaning in just a little closer.

Her breath caught as Priscilla's fingers brushed her temple, adjusting the strap with a gentle touch that lit her skin on fire.

"The point isn't how you look, Alaina," Priscilla murmured, a smile playing on her lips as she studied Alaina's face, like she had no idea she was single-handedly unraveling Alaina's sanity.

Maybe she didn't. God help her if she *did*.

Alaina nodded, dizzy, her heart thudding like it was trying to outrun her thoughts. When Priscilla finally stepped back, Alaina managed to speak. "It kind of is, though. For the photo?"

Priscilla's smile faltered.

The thought of Cole hit Alaina like stepping outside without a coat—sudden and cold and sobering. She had come to Utah to reclaim her love story, and here she was practically short-circuiting because Priscilla touched her face.

Priscilla blinked, her posture shifting ever so slightly, like she was tucking something away. "Right. Well—if Cole is the traveler you say he is, he'll appreciate how . . . well equipped you are."

"Yeah, right," Alaina grumbled. "Nothing says adventurous like being mistaken for a walking sleeping bag."

Alaina was thankful that Callie had lent her the clothes—she was much closer in size to Alaina than Priscilla was. But the puffy layers were hardly a flattering look. Even more infuriating was that Priscilla still managed to look amazing in her own black snow pants and matching jacket.

Priscilla gestured toward one of the windows, where Alaina could see skiers coming down the mountain. "We'll take a few photos in front of the mountain first. Learn the ropes on the bunny hill. Then I figured I'd bring you up the lift to the gentlest trail. I'll snap some action shots on the way down. You can pick whichever looks the most convincing."

Alaina groaned. "I should've just photoshopped myself onto a mountain and called it a day."

Priscilla shook her head, starting toward the ski rental line. "Come on. You'll do great."

Alaina followed, heart pounding, nerves jangling.

After the excruciating process of acquiring and then trying and failing to put on the skis—in the end, Priscilla did it for her—they were finally outside and ready to go.

Alaina waddled forward, legs already burning. Who knew something could make her clumsy attempts at ice skating feel like walking on a cloud? She lifted her goggles to get a better look at the others.

"Looking good," Grant said.

Ned elbowed him, then turned to her. "You excited?"

Alaina let out a shaky laugh. "Nervous, excited—same difference, right?"

Callie smiled. "You'll be fine. Priscilla will take good care of you."

The sentence twisted something deep in Alaina's stomach, flashes of her dream once more playing across the big screen of her imagination, and she let out an unnaturally high laugh. "Right."

Callie wrapped her arm around Lauren's shoulder. "Have fun. If you need me, I will be in the lodge, reading a cozy mystery and enjoying a hot drink while you all freeze your butts off."

Wait, that was an option?

Priscilla nudged Alaina's shoulder. "I'll get you a hot chocolate after, okay?"

Alaina briefly considered asking Priscilla to just snap a photo here, in front of the lodge—Cole wouldn't know the difference. But then she looked over at Priscilla.

Her cheeks were pink from the cold, her eyes bright, the corners of her mouth curled up in one of those rare unrestrained smiles that Alaina had been collecting like precious stones. Alaina couldn't bring herself to dim that.

Even if it meant spending the afternoon falling down a mountain.

"Ready?" Priscilla's head tilted to the side as if she were reading Alaina's mind.

Alaina, who was feeling less and less prepared by the second, plastered on a smile and nodded. "I was born ready."

Chapter Thirteen

Alaina stared up at the blue sky, admiring the fluffy clouds as they hurried past.

Priscilla appeared in front of one of them, looking down at Alaina's body. "Are you all right?"

"Oh yeah." Alaina held a hand up to block the sun. "It's very peaceful down here, actually. You should try it sometime."

"I'll consider it."

They were still on the little training hill next to the lodge and couldn't have been out more than fifteen minutes, but Alaina had already lost count of her wipeouts. She hadn't mastered stopping yet, and this time she'd flopped backward to avoid mowing down a group of inexplicably competent children.

Alaina wasn't bitter. Not at all.

She groaned as she let Priscilla haul her upright again by the elbows. "Aren't you getting bored of the bunny hill? The others are probably having the time of their lives on the actual slopes while you're stuck here watching me eat snow."

"It'll be worth it once you're able to hit the slopes with me."

The idea of Priscilla looking forward to doing anything with her was enough to keep Alaina going, especially after the rocky start to their morning.

On the next attempt, she made it all the way down the hill before she lost her balance. The time after that, she was even able to successfully stop without falling when a fearless tiny child planted himself directly in her path. Another thirty minutes later, she had turning down to a science.

"This is actually kind of fun!" she said as she came to a stop in front of Priscilla.

"Don't sound so surprised. I think you've mastered the basics." Priscilla's smile held more than a hint of pride. "All that's left is to get up there and try a run."

Maybe it was adrenaline. Or maybe it was the way Priscilla was looking at her like she'd just won gold in the Olympics. But Alaina pointed toward the sign for the longest of the easy trails and said, "Let's do that one."

Priscilla's eyebrows drew together. "That's a little over two miles long. Are you sure?"

"You know what I like to say: go big or go home."

Priscilla narrowed her eyes, giving a slight shake of her head. "I've never heard you say that."

Alaina scoffed. "You've only known me for, like, five days."

A strange look passed over Priscilla's face at that, but it vanished as quickly as it came. She nodded toward the lift. "Lead the way."

Alaina made it into the queue without knocking anyone over, which felt like a victory. But as they got closer to the constantly moving chairs, her nerves returned.

"So we just . . . sit?" she whispered.

"You'll be fine," Priscilla said calmly. "Follow my lead. When the chair comes—bend your knees—there you go!"

The chair scooped them up, and Alaina's stomach dropped

as they left the ground, her skis dangling. "Oh god oh god oh god."

It took her a few seconds to realize just how close Priscilla was sitting, their thighs pressed together through layers of snow pants. She forced herself to focus on anything but the parts of her body that were touching Priscilla's.

The view helped. The mountains stretched endlessly in every direction, their snow-covered peaks glittering under the sun. Even looking down at the ant-sized skiers below couldn't ruin it—though it did make her stomach lurch.

She had the sudden urge to take Priscilla's hand, remove their gloves, and lace their fingers together. Screw frostbite. It would be worth it to feel the comforting warmth of her skin. The thought made her cheeks flush. She pushed the feeling aside and settled for covering Priscilla's gloved hand where it rested in her lap and giving it a squeeze.

"You all right?" Priscilla asked. "Nervous?"

"A little." Maybe more than a little, and for more than one reason, but Priscilla didn't have to know about all that. Alaina wished she could pull out her phone and snap a picture of the two of them together with the mountain in the background, but she was afraid her frozen fingers would drop it straight into the snow below. She glanced down, following the imaginary path her phone might take. A wave of nausea rolled through her.

She couldn't seem to look away. The lift climbed higher and higher with no end in sight.

"Hey, um, how high is this thing bringing us?"

Priscilla's grip on her hand tightened, steady. Alaina dragged her eyes back up and met her gaze. "We're getting off soon, don't worry." Priscilla nodded toward the chairs ahead of them, where skiers were sliding off the lift.

"Uh, Sil?" Alaina asked, watching in horror. "Why isn't it stopping?"

Priscilla turned to her. "Have you really never seen how a ski lift works? Not even in movies?"

"No?" Her fingers tightened around the safety bar.

"All you have to do is get your skis flat on the ground. Gravity and momentum will take care of the rest." Priscilla's voice was steady and reassuring, but Alaina's heart still raced as they approached.

Alaina repeated the words in her head like a mantra as they rolled toward the landing. She braced for impact—but somehow, her skis touched down and she slid off the lift with surprising ease. She followed Priscilla, coasting to a wide, open stretch of snow near the edge of the trail.

Priscilla pushed her goggles up. "Not too bad, right?"

"Oh, it was great. In fact, I think I can say I've officially skied. Time to call it a day?"

The mountain lay before them, a grand canvas of white stretching over the landscape. Gorgeous, sure, but the height sent a frisson of fear through her.

Priscilla cracked a smile. "Sure. But the only way back is down." She must have heard the fear Alaina was trying desperately to hide because she leaned in, dropping her voice to a gentler tone. "Don't worry. I'll be with you the whole time, but in case we get separated, follow the signs for the easiest way down, okay? And slow down where trails come together—that's where the most collisions happen. And remember, if you start to lose control—"

"Do that pizza wedge thing until I stop. Got it, boss."

"Good." Priscilla nodded at her. "Ready?"

"Almost." Alaina turned and waved to a nearby group. "Excuse me? Can someone take our photo?"

"Alaina, I could've taken your picture," Priscilla said.

But Alaina barely heard her. She handed her phone to a kind stranger and bounced over, throwing a thumbs-up as she leaned in beside Priscilla, grinning like she was at a theme park.

When the phone was back in her hands, she stared down at the screen. "What do you think?" she asked, angling it so Priscilla could see.

A thin smile pulled at Priscilla's lips. "I think it'll impress him."

Right. *Cole.*

It should've felt like a win. The photo was perfect—Alaina looked windswept, rosy-cheeked, adventurous. Exactly the version of herself Cole had wanted. But the flutter in her chest wasn't about him. It was the way Priscilla's face tilted just slightly toward hers, the crinkle at the corners of her eyes, the way they fit together in the frame like they'd done it a hundred times before.

Alaina tucked that feeling away, smile fixed in place. Now was not the time.

Oblivious to Alaina's internal struggle, or maybe just mistaking it for a simple case of cold feet on the slopes, Priscilla nudged Alaina's shoulder. "Now come on. Before you lose your courage."

Out of excuses, Alaina followed her to the start of the slope.

"Ready?" Priscilla asked one final time.

Alaina nodded. "See you at the bottom."

Without stopping to second-guess herself, Alaina pushed forward and began the descent. Her skis cut through the powder as she coasted down the slope—tentative at first, then bolder with each curve. It was quiet, save for the rush of wind in her ears and the soft hiss of snow beneath her.

A laugh burst out of her—raw, breathless, joyful. The air stung her cheeks, but she welcomed it. The thrill was pure and new, unlike anything she'd ever felt. Priscilla was behind her the whole way, weaving back and forth in a steady rhythm.

After nearly ten minutes, the lodge came into view. By then, Alaina's legs were burning, her skin was wind-whipped, her heart was racing. As she neared the base, she repeated Priscilla's instructions—tips in, heels out—and skidded to a stop. Not graceful, but still standing.

"Oh my god." Alaina could have kissed the ground at the bottom of the hill. Her knees shook from the rush of adrenaline, threatening collapse.

Priscilla glided to a stop beside her, effortless, lifting her goggles to reveal eyes sparkling with pride.

"You did it!" She held out a gloved hand, and it took Alaina an embarrassing four to five seconds to process that she wanted a high five. Alaina would have preferred a hug, but she indulged Priscilla with a tap from her gloved hand. After all, friends gave friends high fives and *didn't* find every excuse to touch each other. And she and Priscilla were just friends.

Friends who had kissed.

"Guys!" Callie trudged over through the snow, her breath visible in the cold air, holding a steaming paper cup in one hand and her phone in the other. Grant, Ned, and Lauren were behind her. "I got a video!"

"We saw you coming from a mile away in that getup," Grant said with a grin.

The lodge had a large window near the base of the hill, offering a perfect vantage point for people watching. Sure enough, there was Alaina in her teal snow suit, navigating the slopes like a pro—or at least a pro in training.

Alaina was astounded. "I actually look . . . kind of cool?"

"I'll text it to you!" Callie said.

"You did fantastically," Priscilla said, eyes never leaving Alaina's. "Want to go again?"

Alaina hesitated. The rush of skiing was addictive. Priscilla's enthusiasm even more so. But her legs were trembling, and the siren call of hot chocolate was too enticing to resist.

"I think maybe that's it for me," she said.

Priscilla's smile faltered a bit, concern flickering in her eyes. "Are you okay? Did you not enjoy it?"

"No—Sil, it was incredible." Alaina stepped closer, trying to erase the faint crease between Priscilla's brows. "Never in a million years would I have thought I could do something like that. Thank you."

"You're welcome." Priscilla's voice was soft, but doubt lingered in her eyes. "Want me to come in with you?"

Alaina gave her a gentle nudge. "No, no. You should go have fun. I feel bad you were babysitting me all day."

"We'd be happy to take Sil off your hands." Ned clapped a hand on Priscilla's back.

Priscilla looked poised to protest, but Callie stepped up next to Alaina, linking their arms.

"You guys ski. I'll get this one some cocoa."

Alaina smiled. "Sounds perfect."

After wrestling off her skis and boots at the rack outside—a daunting task with her cold fingers—Alaina followed Callie through the glass doors into a soaring great room where massive windows looked out on the snow-covered slopes. Stone fireplaces stretched up toward the vaulted ceiling, their crackling flames drawing clusters of tired skiers who'd draped their damp gear over the furniture. The air was warm and the scent of pine from the firewood mingled with the rich aroma of coffee from the busy café counter.

Alaina peeled off her snow-crusted jacket and joined Callie in the line of rosy-cheeked people waiting for hot drinks.

Ten minutes later, she fell into a plush armchair in front of a fire. One sip of the cocoa had her grimacing—Priscilla's was definitely better—but the warmth seeping into her chilled hands was worth it. With a sigh, she melted into the cushions, letting the cozy lodge atmosphere relax her.

"Did you have fun?" Callie asked from the chair beside her.

Alaina couldn't help the grin that broke across her face. "A lot. I mean, I made a total fool out of myself, but I think I was kind of getting the hang of it at the end there. Sil's a great teacher."

Callie's smile softened at the nickname. "She is. She seems to really like having you around."

The words should've been comforting. But after the kiss, and everything that followed, Alaina couldn't shake the feeling that something between them had changed, no matter how normal Priscilla had tried to act.

She could ask her. Try to talk it through. But what if it made things worse? What if she wrecked the easy rhythm they'd finally fallen into?

"I really like *being* around." The words tumbled out of her before she could examine them too closely.

"Good." Callie's eyes sparkled. "How much longer do we have you for?"

Alaina did the math. Only three more days. A bigger part of her than she cared to admit didn't want this to end. But it had to. Her life was waiting for her out there, ready for her to go and take it back.

That didn't make it any less hard to imagine saying goodbye. "I'm leaving on Christmas Day."

Callie's smile dimmed. "That's a shame. We're going to miss you."

"I'll miss you too. You've all been so nice to me."

She'd felt like she belonged here more in the past few days than she had anywhere else in her entire life. After years of searching for that feeling, she couldn't believe she'd found it here, in rural Utah.

"It's just . . ." Callie's hands fidgeted in her lap. "I don't think I've ever seen Priscilla this happy before. She's not one to easily let people in, but with you, it's like she's come alive."

Alaina's heart gave another traitorous thump. "She's brought a lot of good out in me too." Mistletoe kiss and identity crises aside, Priscilla had awakened something in her—something she hadn't known she was missing. She felt more like herself here than she had in a decade. "I didn't know people could be as kind as she is, you know?"

"I do. It's one of the things I love most about her. She's hard to reach sometimes, but when you do, it's—" Callie stopped, sighing. "It's been great having her around more. Before this week, the last time we all hung out was—I guess it must have been at this weekend trip to a lake we take every summer. God, I can't believe it's been that long."

Alaina blanched. Priscilla had been avoiding her friends for nearly half the year?

"You haven't seen her since then?"

"Not really. Just around town. I've tried to ask her about it, but she always deflects. And Lauren's always telling me I can be . . . a bit persistent."

Alaina's heart sank at the revelation. She thought about what she knew of Priscilla's past, how being pushed too far, too fast had cost her everything once before. Maybe this is just what Priscilla did when people got too close—built walls, retreated to the safety of her bookstore. Was she going to do that to Alaina too?

"That must have been hard, not knowing why she pulled away."

"It was," Callie said. "But look at her now. She seems happy. Ever since you've been around, she's been more like the old Sil. Oh, that reminds me—we're throwing a little shindig on Christmas Eve at the inn. Something for the guests and locals. It would be really great if you could get her to come."

"Absolutely," Alaina said. Between Nico's endless house parties in college and working at a bar, she'd developed a healthy appreciation for any kind of gathering, though she imagined this would be a far cry from that scene—fewer rounds of shots, more charcuterie boards and passed hors d'oeuvres. Given how things had been going with Priscilla and her friends lately, she had a feeling she could get Priscilla to say yes.

"Thanks, Lani."

As the conversation died down, Callie pulled out a paperback and slouched down in her chair. Alaina wished she'd grabbed another romance novel from the bookstore. Instead, she fished out her phone and sank into the familiar scroll—perfectly plated food she'd never cook, hypnotic time lapses of artists weaving intricate designs, useless DIYs she'd never try.

Nearly an hour had passed when Alaina froze, a different kind of post catching her attention. Photos of a skyscraper, the Statue of Liberty, a slice of pizza, and—lastly—one of Cole with a charming grin and a cocked eyebrow, looking as handsome as ever as he held up an electric-blue can.

Her heart stuttered. He'd finally posted something. He *was* in New York. She scanned the caption—mostly sponsor-speak hyping a new Berry Blitz flavor. Nothing personal. But he looked good. Happy. Too happy?

Alaina's fingers moved without her brain's permission, typing out looks like a hell of a town :) in the comment box. She hovered over the post button. Hesitated. Then tapped it.

It popped up under his photo, and she stared, waiting.

Just three more days, she reminded herself. Three more days and then she'd fly to New York, pick up her life, and put everything back where it belonged.

But the longer her comment sat there unanswered, the more her doubt churned.

Fuck. Why had she done that? They hadn't spoken a word to each other since Cole left. What did she want him to say—*wish you were here*? He obviously didn't, otherwise he would have reached out, right? Was her entire plan to prove she was adventurous totally pointless? What if showing up unannounced wasn't the grand romantic gesture she thought it was? What if Cole just thought she'd lost it?

Her thumb hovered over the delete button when a notification popped up: colememaybe liked your comment.

Her heart jumped. She stared at the screen, waiting for more—a reply, a DM, something. But nothing came.

Deflated, she opened her photo library, determined to post something to her own story before he vanished again. Her thumb paused over the photo of her and Priscilla by the lake, their heads tilted toward each other, both smiling—hers wide and beaming, Priscilla's softer, gentler. Her freckles glowed in the sun.

Just a friend, she reminded herself. Just a gorgeous, funny, smart, sweet friend.

That kiss last night may have been eye-opening—life changing, even—but it was just one kiss. Cole was still the one she loved. So why did it feel like she was trying to convince herself?

She swallowed hard and swiped past the selfie, landing on a

close-up of her on the ice. Harmless. Appropriately adventurous. She added animated snow and hit post.

A few minutes later, another notification pinged at the top of the screen: colememaybe liked your story.

Her breath hitched. Cole saw the photo and chose to like it. This was step one. Get his attention. Remind him she could be spontaneous. Show him what he was missing. So why did her stomach knot with something closer to dread than triumph?

Two likes weren't exactly an olive branch. They weren't even an olive twig.

Alaina turned off her phone screen and let the device drop to her chest. Probably better to leave it alone, at least for now. She reached for her drink, and Callie looked up at her over the edge of her book.

"So . . . I've been meaning to ask—notice any interesting new decorations around the bookstore lately?"

Alaina paused with her cocoa halfway to her mouth. There was something too careful about the question, like Callie was trying very hard to sound casual. "What do you mean?"

"Oh, you know." Callie waved her hand vaguely, placing her book in her lap. She leaned forward, voice dropping into a whisper. "Mistletoe?"

The pieces clicked, and Alaina's eyes widened. "That was *you*?"

Callie shrugged, her smile impossible to contain. "Maybe it was, maybe it wasn't. You found it then?"

"We found it," Alaina said. Just how much detail should she give Callie here? Would Priscilla be comfortable with her sharing this particular bit of information?

"And?" Callie asked, her eyes boring into Alaina's.

She crumbled under the pressure immediately. "What do you mean, 'and'? And we *kissed*!" She whispered the last word like it was a secret, and maybe it was. But it was worth spilling it to see the way Callie's eyes lit up with glee.

"I knew it! Lauren didn't think it would work, but Ned and I—"

"Wait, wait—you're all in on this?"

Callie nodded. "Sil is our friend, Alaina. And she's been—well, lonely, as I'm sure you've noticed. We just wanted her to take a chance."

"Yeah, well." Alaina bit her lip, nervous fingers reaching for her necklace. She lowered her voice. "She doesn't want to talk about it. The kiss. She said it was no big deal."

"Was it?"

"I don't know. Kind of? I mean, she's—"

Callie's phone rang, cutting her off. Thank god. She didn't even know how that sentence was going to end.

Amazing. Frustrating. Gorgeous.

Confusing.

Callie brought the phone up to her ear, a wide smile on her face. "Hey, baby. Oh, yes! We'll be right there." She hung up and looked at Alaina. "Lauren says they're going on their last run now. Do you want to go look for them?"

"Yes, please." Anything to escape this conversation before she said something she couldn't take back.

The icy December air greeted Alaina as she stepped outside the cocoon of the lodge's warmth. She hugged herself against the chill, trailing after Callie with quick steps.

"There!" Callie pointed to the slope where four figures were weaving their way down.

Alaina squinted until her gaze found the one in all black—clean lines, steady rhythm, slicing through the snow. Priscilla. Her stomach flipped.

Callie jogged ahead to meet Lauren. Alaina followed at a

slower pace, her attention pinned to the figure pulling off her goggles.

Priscilla's cheeks were flushed, her eyes bright. She was breathtaking.

Alaina pushed the feeling aside. "Did you have fun?"

"Very much, yes." Priscilla was still slightly out of breath, voice raspy. "What did you get up to?"

"Nothing much. I missed you." Alaina's words slipped out without a second thought, and the surprise on Priscilla's face made her chest ache.

"You did?"

Alaina nodded, her cheeks burning despite the cold. "Of course."

"Sil, Lani!" They both turned at the sound of Ned's voice. "We're headed back to our place, gonna order some food. You two coming?"

Priscilla looked back at Alaina.

Alaina thought of what Callie had said—how happy Priscilla seemed lately. How much she'd withdrawn before. She couldn't stand the thought of Priscilla pulling away again, not from them. Not from her.

"I'm down," she said, smiling. "Sil?"

"Sounds lovely."

Chapter Fourteen

They rumbled down the road to Grant and Ned's house in comfortable, exhausted silence. The truck's worn seats cradled Alaina's weary body, yet her mind was a live wire, zipping through thoughts she tried to corral. She had finally earned a bit of Cole's attention, but it didn't make her heart sing the way she'd thought it would. Instead, it left her feeling more confused and conflicted than ever.

Getting back together with him was her goal, so why couldn't she stop thinking about someone else's broad shoulders, brown eyes, soft lips moving against hers, strong hands wrapping under her thighs and—

Nope, no, nuh-uh.

She shook her head, as if she could rattle the images loose. Her palms pressed against the rough denim of her jeans, an attempt to stay in the moment and not let her thoughts wander into fantasy territory.

Alaina risked a glance at Priscilla. Focused as ever, Priscilla gripped the wheel with both hands, her jaw taut with concentration as she navigated the snow-covered roads. Alaina's gaze traced the arch of Priscilla's neck, eyes catching on her pulse as it tapped a steady beat at her throat. She couldn't help but admire the way Priscilla handled the truck with ease, every movement calm and controlled.

Enough, her inner voice snapped. Priscilla was just driving. How could she find an action as simple as driving a truck this attractive?

Priscilla must have felt Alaina's unsubtle stare, because as they slowed to a stop at an intersection, she turned to her. "How are you doing?"

Alaina's heart skipped. There were too many ways she could answer that question.

She brushed it off with a breezy laugh. "Just enjoying the scenery. I'm almost glad I crashed my car. Having a chauffeur is kind of nice." She flashed Priscilla a grin, hoping her nervousness didn't show.

Priscilla didn't smile. Her brow pinched. "Are you sure you're okay? You seem a bit . . . quiet today."

"Yeah, I'm good," Alaina said, fidgeting with the hem of her jacket. "Just, um, lost in thought, I guess."

Priscilla looked at her a second longer. "If there's anything on your mind, you can talk to me, you know."

Something sharp pricked at Alaina's chest. Was Priscilla serious right now? Pretending she didn't know what might be on her mind? Did the kiss really mean that little to her?

A car horn blared behind them. They both jumped.

"Oh, honestly," Priscilla muttered, lifting her foot off the brake to roll past the stop sign.

Alaina was fine. Or, at least, she could be fine.

Just overthinking things again. If she could get out of her own head for five minutes, maybe everything would go back to normal.

Grant and Ned's house was a cozy one-story with a porch swing and twinkle lights strung along the roofline—just as charming as the rest of Brooks. Priscilla pulled into the driveway behind a Jeep and a black truck. The others were already gathered between the cars, middiscussion.

"It's a crowd-pleaser," Grant was saying as Alaina hopped out of the cab.

Ned shook his head. "If you're craving heartburn, sure."

"What're we arguing about?" Priscilla asked, stepping up next to Alaina.

"Dinner," Lauren said flatly. She was clearly so over this conversation. "Callie wants tacos, Grant wants burgers, and Ned wants—"

"Sushi, obviously," Ned said.

"I think Alaina should choose," Callie said. Everyone in the group turned to look at her.

Her mind stuttered. Cole's Instagram post floated to the surface.

"Pizza?" she said.

Callie perked up. "Romanesco's makes a mean Sicilian."

Grant was rolling his eyes before she even finished her sentence. "Are you kidding? Their sauce is terrible. No salt. Now, Mary's is where it's at."

"Their garlic knots are always stale," Lauren said. "And they don't have salad."

As the debate raged on, Alaina let her focus drift—right to the woman standing beside her.

Priscilla had changed out of her snow pants before they left the lodge and was now in soft wool flannel trousers and the black thermal she'd worn underneath her ski jacket. Her cheeks were still pink from the wind on the mountain.

Alaina couldn't stop staring. It wasn't just how Priscilla looked—though that alone was enough to short-circuit Alaina's brain—it was the way she carried herself. Even now, even after an exhausting day. Straight-backed and proper, at attention.

Grant sighed, and Alaina caught the tail end of his eye roll. "Come on, lovebirds. Let's go inside."

Alaina froze. Lovebirds? Oh no. Was she really that obvious? It shouldn't surprise her. Her face read like a damn billboard most of the time, sure—but was this weird little crush so clear that even people who barely knew her could see it? Could Priscilla?

Alaina couldn't bring herself to look over at her.

Priscilla cleared her throat. "That's not—we're not—"

Grant held up his hands as he turned to walk away. "Oh, sorry. I guess I just assumed. Silly me."

"Sorry about him," Priscilla said under her breath.

Alaina finally gathered the courage to look at Priscilla. Her voice was quiet, her eyes locked on the snow. She didn't seem flustered, exactly. More like . . . sad? Or maybe annoyed. Alaina wasn't sure which was worse. Either way, it was another reminder that Priscilla wasn't feeling the same way.

She needed to shift the mood, and fast.

"Watch this." Alaina winked at Priscilla—which she definitely shouldn't be doing, all things considered—and bent down to scoop up some snow. She packed it into a tight ball and lobbed it at Grant.

By some Christmas miracle, it hit him square in the back.

Grant spun around, eyes narrowing. "Oh, it's *on!*"

In one fluid motion, he scooped, patted, and hurled a snowball with terrifying precision. The snowball smacked against Alaina's shoulder before she had time to duck.

Lauren grinned as Grant dove for more. Without hesitation, she flung her own snowball at Priscilla, who dodged it just in time, laughing as it sailed past.

"You're going down, Lauren!" Priscilla shouted, firing back with a perfect shot that hit Lauren square in the chest.

From the porch, Callie and Ned exchanged a look.

"You kids have fun," Ned called as they slipped inside.

"Come on, Alaina." Priscilla's voice was low and determined as she packed another snowball. "Let's show them how it's done."

Alaina nodded, mouth too dry to form words. Confident Priscilla was hot. That is, even hotter than usual.

Snowballs flew from all directions as they ducked and weaved, laughing as they tried to avoid getting hit.

"Let's take cover," Priscilla said, gesturing toward the trees before bolting. Alaina scrambled after her, slowed by snow up to her shins. Before she could catch up, Lauren cut her off, and Grant came from behind.

Cornered. She raised her hands in surrender—then heard Priscilla's voice.

"Alaina, get down!"

Alaina dove to the side just as a snowball zipped past her ear. A shout rang out as it hit its target—Grant, definitely—and she bolted for the trees.

An arm caught her around the middle, pulling her behind a wide trunk. Her back pressed into the bark, and when she looked up, Priscilla was right in front of her, a wild look in her eyes as she smiled at Alaina. She was suddenly very grateful to have something sturdy to lean back against.

"You all right?" Priscilla was breathless, and the sound was totally doing something to Alaina's heart.

"I'm good. Great. Thank you for saving me—again," Alaina said through a laugh.

"Wait." Priscilla straightened. "Do you hear that? I think—"

A loud cry came from the other side of the tree, and suddenly they were being pelted by snow from both sides. In an instant, Priscilla was shielding Alaina with her body, arms planted on either side of her face as snow splattered against her back.

"Surrender!" Lauren shouted from somewhere nearby.

Priscilla's breath puffed warm between them, their noses nearly touching. Her hair had come loose, strands falling across her face. Alaina's breath caught—and then vanished entirely—when Priscilla opened her eyes and looked at her.

"We surrender!" Alaina called out, unsure if she would survive even another second of Priscilla this close to her without doing something about it. "We surrender."

The snowballs stopped, but Priscilla stayed in place, even after Lauren called out, "Good. Losers buy dinner!"

Footsteps crunched away. But Priscilla didn't move. Not right away.

Her arms still caged Alaina in. For a moment, neither of them said anything. Then Priscilla exhaled sharply and stepped back, her eyes dropping to the ground.

"I guess we should probably—"

"You have a little—" Alaina said at the same time. Her hand shot out, reaching up to gently dust the lingering snowflakes from Priscilla's dark hair, tucking one of the stray wisps behind her ear before she thought better of it. "There."

Priscilla shivered. Alaina hesitated, fingertips grazing the curve of Priscilla's ear, her thumb faintly skimming her cold cheekbone. Priscilla's eyes darted to Alaina's lips, and Alaina could hear the effort that went into her next breath.

And Alaina knew.

It wasn't just her.

Despite what Priscilla had said—that it was no big deal—it was clear that Alaina wasn't the only one feeling this.

Priscilla's eyes dragged up to Alaina's, heavy with a want that made Alaina's heart race.

But something in her held back. Maybe it was caution, maybe fear. Maybe it was the part of her still holding on to her plan, the one that said she'd be back with Cole in three days and everything would return to normal. Or maybe it was just this: She didn't want to mess up what she and Priscilla had, not if she wasn't sure what her heart wanted yet. Not if there was any chance it might hurt her.

She couldn't be another person who made Priscilla retreat behind her walls.

Alaina leaned up, pressing a chaste kiss to Priscilla's cold cheek. Priscilla exhaled, breath staccato against Alaina's ear, and a shiver coursed through her.

"C'mon." Alaina stepped away, hand outstretched as she waited for Priscilla to grab it. "We've got a pizza to buy."

❄

The front door opened directly into a living room that told Grant and Ned's story: mismatched furniture that somehow worked together, cozy clutter built piece by piece. Through an arched doorway, Alaina glimpsed the tiny kitchen, every inch of counter claimed by cooking equipment—a sturdy stand mixer, towers of mixing bowls, countless baking sheets.

Her heart did a funny little flip at the sight. It reminded her of her childhood kitchen, warm and well used, filled with the tools of someone who loved feeding the people they cared about. She could picture Ned here, teaching her Patty's secret pie crust recipe if she ever visited again. The thought that she might not—that this could all disappear when she left for New York—tightened her chest, and she dragged her eyes away.

The living room was small but inviting, dominated by a worn leather couch near a crackling wood-burning stove. Even after shedding her coat, Alaina felt too warm in her layers of clothing. Between the fire and what had just happened outside—Priscilla's eyes on her lips, her breath against her skin—the sweater felt suffocating.

"Do you have somewhere I can change?" she asked Ned. She needed to cool down, and stat.

"For sure," Ned said, nodding toward a hall. "Sil, you want to borrow something a little lighter?"

Priscilla nodded. "Please."

They followed Ned until he disappeared into the bedroom, leaving them standing alone. Alaina stole glances at Priscilla, at the flush still visible on her cheeks, at the way she suddenly found the framed photos fascinating. The narrow hall made it impossible not to notice every inch between them. It would be so easy to close that distance. She wanted to. God, she wanted to. But she'd made up her mind. Even though watching Priscilla's tense jaw made her chest ache, Alaina stayed rooted to the spot, letting the moment pass.

Ned emerged with two T-shirts. "Grabbed one for you too, Alaina. Bathroom's right there," he said, nodding to a door on the left.

Alaina examined herself in the bathroom mirror, tugging at the oversized shirt Ned had provided.

"This is certainly a look," she muttered to herself, fidgeting with the hem in a futile attempt to make it appear more fitted.

She'd never been this conscious of her appearance around Priscilla, except for maybe on that first night in another unfamiliar mirror. Now that Alaina knew that Priscilla was looking, she noticed every wrinkle, every unruly hair.

She twisted, searching for an angle where the shirt didn't make her look like she was a kid playing dress-up. It was fruitless. She sighed and added a French tuck to give the illusion of some shape to her waist.

Not bad.

Now for the hair. She attacked the snarls with her fingers, grimacing at each tug. Skiing had been fun, but her goggles had turned her hair into a bird's nest. Spotting a stray hair tie—thank god Ned had long hair—she pulled her hair back into a ponytail.

Taking a steadying breath, she stepped into the living room. Priscilla wasn't there yet. Good—she could use a moment to compose herself. Was Priscilla having the same trouble breathing normally?

Callie brightened from her spot on the couch, patting the cushion beside her. Alaina happily sank down as the couch springs protested.

"So!" Callie whispered eagerly. "We got cut off earlier."

Alaina glanced toward the kitchen, where Ned and Lauren chatted. Grant was nowhere in sight. He must've left for pizza.

"Did we?" She feigned ignorance.

"Yes," Callie said. "You were just telling me about how you and Sil—"

"Oh, right. That." Alaina bit her lip. "She doesn't seem to want to talk about it, but I think she might—I don't know, like me? I'm getting mixed signals."

"That sounds like Priscilla. She said it was no big deal?"

"Yeah."

"God, she's a dumbass."

Alaina laughed, startled. "I— Hey! That's not nice."

"Well, she is! I mean, she has this gorgeous girl drop into her life at, like, the most romantic time of year, and she's blowing it?"

"To be fair, it's kind of complicated."

Because to Priscilla, Alaina was straight. And in love with a man. And determined to get that man back. And leaving in three days. Not exactly ideal circumstances for figuring out what the hell they were doing.

Alaina sighed. "I thought I knew what I wanted, but this whole week has been—"

Callie's eyebrows shot up as her gaze slid past Alaina's shoulder. Alaina turned to see Priscilla and Ned entering the room.

Jesus.

Priscilla wore a T-shirt with cutoff sleeves—Grant's, Alaina assumed. Had Alaina ever seen Priscilla in sleeves this short? Because wow. Those arms. Lean and toned in a way that made perfect sense given how effortlessly strong Priscilla was, but still. Her imagination hadn't done any justice to reality. What would it feel like to run her hands down—

Callie laughed, and Alaina tore her gaze away.

Her cheeks ignited. "What?" she whispered. "I'm—I'm looking respectfully."

"I think we both know you aren't."

Priscilla glanced toward them, offering a hesitant smile before heading into the kitchen. Great. They were definitely back to awkward.

Thankfully, Callie dropped the subject now that Priscilla was within earshot, instead recounting how she'd inherited the inn from her parents and met Lauren when hiring her design firm.

Alaina listened with half an ear, her gaze repeatedly drifting to Priscilla as she helped Ned set the table. The tucked-in shirt highlighted her broad shoulders in a way Alaina couldn't ignore.

Stop staring. Stop staring. Stop—

"Who's hungry?" Grant called as he opened the front door holding a stack of pizza boxes. The smell of garlic and melted cheese made Alaina's stomach growl loud enough for everyone to hear.

Whoever picked Pagiano's Ristorante was an absolute genius. The pizza was next-level, and when Lauren uncorked an expensive-looking bottle of red wine, Alaina felt like she'd won the lottery.

As they all took seats at the table, Priscilla chose to sit across from Alaina, careful distance evident. Between the awkward morning, their playful afternoon, and whatever had happened in the snow, Alaina couldn't figure out where they stood.

But alcohol helped. Slowly, Priscilla relaxed into old rhythms with her friends, rolling her eyes at Callie's terrible puns, swapping book recommendations with Lauren, blushing at Ned's stories about her early days in Brooks, like when she'd slept on a camping mat in an empty apartment because she'd wildly underestimated shipping times from England.

It was like watching a flower unfurl in the sun, seeing Priscilla laughing openly, gesturing with her wineglass as she argued about the merits of different Jane Austen adaptations.

Alaina found herself pulled into the group's gravity too. Her worst customer stories had Ned gasping. She went toe-to-toe with Grant over the criminal act of putting pineapple on pizza. Bonded with Lauren when she learned she had seen *The Holiday* even more times than Alaina had, which was the surprise of the century.

But her attention kept drifting back to Priscilla. The soft light turning her eyes to honey. Fingers curved around her wine-glass. That rich, intoxicating laugh. With each sip Alaina took, pretending she wasn't memorizing every detail became impossible.

Sometimes Priscilla caught her staring, smiled briefly, then looked away. Each time it happened, Alaina felt more confused. Warm and open one minute—chuckling at Alaina's jokes about terrible customers—cold and distant the next. The push and pull left Alaina dizzy.

She was so focused on decoding every micro-expression, every slight shift in Priscilla's body language, that she didn't notice Callie watching her until she felt an elbow nudge against hers. When their eyes met, Callie winked at her.

Oh god. Her face heated, her cheeks probably turning the same shade as the wine. Subtlety was clearly not her strong suit tonight.

She coughed a little and took a hasty swig.

Clearly Priscilla's friends wanted something to happen between them—even hanging mistletoe to nudge things along. But as much as it felt like one, this wasn't a Hallmark movie. She couldn't abandon everything for this charming small town. No matter how much she wanted to lean in to this terrifying, exhilarating feeling, getting caught up in maybes and what-ifs meant letting everyone down when it all went sideways—including herself.

After dinner, Callie clapped her hands together as Grant cleared the table. "We have an even number of people," she exclaimed. "Let's do charades!"

Alaina wondered if it was hard for Priscilla, who had all but given up on finding a partner, to spend time with her friends who were all in relationships. Being a fifth wheel didn't sound very fun, especially on game night. Is that why Priscilla had distanced herself these last six months? But that didn't make sense—both couples had been with each other longer than that.

Ned rearranged chairs into a circle around the coffee table, crowding the small living room. Alaina was about to sit on one of the wooden chairs when Callie shooed her toward the couch. "You had a long day, you should get the best seat in the house. You too Priscilla—the two of you will be a team."

Alaina shot a look at Callie that she hoped said *Are you serious?* but plopped down onto the sofa anyway. Priscilla sat next to her, still not making eye contact.

"Pens and paper," Ned said, dropping them onto the coffee table. "Everyone write down three prompts. And nothing too esoteric—I'm talking to you, Lauren and Sil."

When Alaina reached for a pen at the same time as Priscilla, their fingers met over a blue ballpoint. The brief contact sent a spark through Alaina, and she glanced up, ready to stammer an apology, but found Priscilla's eyes already on her.

"Sorry," Priscilla murmured, letting go of the pen like it had burned her. But Alaina could see the flush creeping up her neck, the way her breath had caught. Had she always had this much of an effect on Priscilla? Would she have noticed?

Alaina forced herself to concentrate on picking her three prompts—Kermit the Frog, Rudolph the Red-Nosed Reindeer, and Ariana Grande—and not on the warmth radiating from Priscilla.

"I hope you all are ready." Alaina clapped her hands, rubbing them together. "I happen to be excellent at charades."

Alaina and Priscilla found their groove as a team quickly and easily. Maybe Priscilla had a competitive streak, or maybe just having something to focus on that wasn't the tension between them was a relief, but she seemed to finally defrost when the first round ended and they were ahead by one point, thanks to Alaina's spectacular imitation of a chipmunk.

There were only a few stumbles along the way—"Who doesn't know who Squidward is?" and "Honestly, Alaina, I couldn't have been more clear that I was Yuri Gagarin."

Alaina's finest moment was when she launched into an incredibly accurate impression of Jack Sparrow, stumbling as she held up an imaginary bottle of rum, and Priscilla shouted "*Pirates of the Caribbean*!" almost immediately.

"You two are cheating," Grant muttered. "Some kind of shared brain wave or something."

"Aw, babe, don't be jealous. We'll get the next one," Ned said.

"Okay, seriously, how did you get that so fast?" Alaina asked, breathless with laughter.

Priscilla gave a little shrug. "I had a thing for Keira Knightley. I may have watched those movies more than once."

Alaina's jaw dropped. "*You* had a crush on Keira Knightley?"

"Didn't everyone?"

The game came down to a tiebreaker between Alaina and Priscilla and Grant and Ned. Alaina stood facing Priscilla, trying not to glance at Grant desperately miming beside her.

"A high school principal?" Ned asked, and Alaina heard Grant groan in frustration. "I don't know, I just feel like I'm in trouble for some reason. What are you doing with that hand?"

Alaina reset, took a deep breath, and put her hands on her hips. She stared down at Priscilla and summoned her best unimpressed look. She nodded, as if listening to someone rattling off something, and pretended to write it down on an invisible pad. Then she flashed the smallest hint of a smile, and Priscilla's eyes widened.

"It can't be—*Patty*?"

"Yes!"

Alaina punched the air, her victory dance wobbly from the wine. In a heartbeat, Priscilla scooped her into an excited hug, spinning her slightly off the ground. Alaina's laughter bubbled up, breathless and dizzy, not entirely just from the spinning. Priscilla's arms tightened around her, sending Alaina's pulse racing.

When Priscilla put her down, Alaina ducked her flushed face, grinning shyly. "We make a good team."

Priscilla beamed. "We do."

Alaina caught Callie and Ned exchanging knowing looks, while Grant rolled his eyes, hiding a smile.

After a few more moments of celebration, Priscilla glanced at her watch. "We should probably get going," she said. "Big day tomorrow."

Tomorrow they'd cross off two items on The List: hike a mountain and camp under the stars.

As they gathered coats, Alaina hugged Callie and Ned, accepted Grant's awkward one-armed squeeze, and even received a small smile from Lauren—a major diplomatic win.

The night air hit them as they stepped out onto the stoop, the cold sobering after the warmth of wine. Callie leaned out the door behind them. "Good night! Hope to see you soon!"

Alaina waved back. "Good night!"

"Love you guys, get home safe!"

Callie's words caught Alaina off guard, and she nearly stumbled, the weight of those three simple words grabbing at her ankles and almost tugging her down.

Her smile froze, then faltered completely as they climbed into the truck. Her earlier glow faded into something heavier. Silence filled the vehicle, thickening with every passing minute as Alaina fidgeted with the hem of her borrowed shirt.

When nearly five minutes had passed on the ride back to the bookstore and Alaina hadn't spoken, Priscilla shot her a worried glance from the driver's seat. "Are you all right?"

"Yep!" Alaina replied automatically, eyes fixed on her lap. "Totally fine."

"Are you sure? You had a good time?"

Priscilla's voice was so laced with concern that Alaina felt like she couldn't lie. She sighed. "Your friends have been so welcoming. The way they've just accepted me into your circle . . . they're—I've never had that before."

Priscilla's knuckles tightened on the wheel, and she sat up a little straighter, seemingly ready to defend Alaina from any pain she might be feeling. "Were his friends not nice to you?"

Alaina tried not to read too much into the fact that Priscilla was drawing a very direct comparison between Cole's friends and her own, and therefore between Cole and herself.

"They were fine, I guess. It always felt like they were just putting up with me. Not a single one of them has reached out to me since we broke up, even though we were together for a year. I spent so much time with these people, and—for what?"

The moment the words left her mouth, Alaina realized how childish they sounded. Of course Cole's friends hadn't reached out to her—they were his friends first. They weren't obligated to maintain a relationship with someone their friend had apparently decided to break up with, even if he hadn't bothered to let *her* know it was a breakup. Her disappointment wasn't really about Cole's friends at all. It was about how easily she'd been erased from his life, like she'd never been there at all.

"I'm sorry," Priscilla said softly.

Alaina turned to look at Priscilla, whose profile was illuminated by passing streetlights as she drove. The light caught on her cheekbones, creating shadows beneath that made her look like something carved by a particularly talented sculptor. She was so pretty it made Alaina's chest ache. It would be easy right now to say it out loud, to set fire to all her reasoning about being careful and just tell Priscilla exactly what she thought of her profile in the half-light. The wine humming in her veins nudged her to do exactly that. But she shook her head, trying to clear it.

"Don't be. I guess if they were never really my friends, I don't need them. But it was never like that with your group. Even from the minute I first met Callie, before *you* even liked me, she was nothing but kind."

"She's got a way about her." Priscilla used the pause at a stop sign to look over at Alaina, reaching out and grabbing her hand. They settled together over the middle console. "And . . . for the record, I always liked you."

Alaina's chest tightened with a sudden rush of warmth so intense it brought tears to her eyes—happy ones that caught her by surprise. She sniffled, and Priscilla's head whipped toward her.

"Sorry, I didn't mean to—"

Alaina couldn't help but laugh at herself, wiping a tear from her cheek with her free hand. "No, it's not you. Wine just makes me sappy."

Priscilla didn't reply, but she didn't let go of Alaina's hand for the rest of the drive home.

Chapter Fifteen

Two Days Until Christmas

Golden morning light streamed through the window above the kitchen sink, haloing Priscilla as she washed something Alaina couldn't quite see. Alaina lingered in the bedroom doorway, edges of a sleepy smile pulling at her lips. Her days here were winding down and she wanted to hold on to this—quiet contentment, belonging in someone else's space, the simple joy of watching Priscilla move through her routine, unaware of being observed. She'd never had this easy domesticity with Cole.

Priscilla straightened as Alaina approached, her head tilting slightly, catching her from the corner of her eye. A soft smile spread across her face.

"Morning," Alaina mumbled through a yawn.

"Did you sleep okay?" Priscilla turned off the tap.

She'd slept fine—better than fine, with Priscilla warm beside her, dreams full of things not appropriate to share—until she'd woken up to an empty bed and cold feet. "Not bad. You been up long?"

"Just an hour or so," Priscilla replied, drying her hands. "I couldn't sleep."

"Everything okay?"

Priscilla nodded. "Perfect, actually. I'm excited for today—I love this mountain. I can't wait for you to see it. But I do hope I didn't wake you."

"No, it wasn't you." Alaina leaned against the counter, stretching her arms overhead. Nerves had woken her—the realization that tomorrow was Christmas Eve, her last full day in this cozy bubble before reality would come knocking.

Sure, she'd have to come back to Brooks for her car post–New York, but it could only be a pit stop on her way home. After all the effort she'd put into her plan—the plan she and Priscilla had been executing perfectly—her hopes were high that it would work. When she managed to convince Cole to give her another chance . . . what then? Would he fly back to Brooks with her to get her car? Cole, meeting Priscilla—the knot in her stomach tightened at the thought.

Alaina shoved that thought into a mental box marked LATER.

Priscilla stirred Alaina's coffee—three spoonfuls of sugar, a heavy splash of milk, just the way she liked it—and handed it to her. Instead of moving to the table as she usually did in the mornings, Priscilla settled onto the couch with a book. From what Alaina could gather by the cover, it seemed to be about an old king. She remembered Priscilla mentioning her father was a professor. Alaina followed, the warmth from the coffee seeping into her palms, mirroring the heat that seemed to gently pulse whenever Priscilla was near.

She sat on the opposite end of the couch—a safe distance to keep that heat at bay. She pulled out her phone, scrolling through photos from the ski trip, marking a few favorites for posting later.

Then she opened her text thread with Nico, looking at the unanswered message from yesterday.

Nico: what does this mean about cole

Alaina hesitated only a moment before typing a reply: the truth. It took several minutes to shape her feelings into a wall of text, condensing the past few days into words.

Alaina: I don't know. I'm so confused. I mean, I love Cole, but the more time I'm here, the more time I'm away from him, I'm not sure... I think that relationship wasn't good for me? Bi awakening or whatever this has been aside, I feel like I've grown more in this past week on my own than I have with him in a year. So even if I did convince him to take me back, things would have to be different. But I don't even know how? I can't really explain it.

Alaina: I want to be the kind of person who never gives up on love, like my mom would've wanted. Love is supposed to be hard. You have to work for it, right? But, I don't know if she would've wanted me to stay with someone who doesn't see how great I am. And Priscilla... I know you don't know her, but you'd really like her. She's smart, and kind, and she has this great dry sense of humor. But she lives in Utah. And I've only known her a week. And she doesn't exactly believe in love. I don't think she even wants... whatever it is I'm offering, which I don't even know what that would be or look like and it's all just such a mess and I wish you were here to tell me what to do

The typing dots immediately appeared, and she chewed her lip as she waited for Nico's response. What would it be? Ditch Cole and get the girl, probably.

What she hadn't expected was:

Nico: wow, babe, i'm sorry. this sounds really rough. when you get back we're so having a rom-com marathon, no matter how it goes. i'll buy the ice cream

Nico: i'm not going to tell you what to do, that's your decision, but... for what it's worth, love isn't supposed to be hard. i think that's just a thing people say to justify their shitty relationships.

Nico: life is hard, but love makes it easy

Alaina stared at that last sentence until her eyes started to burn.

It sounded like something her mom would have said.

Alaina: I love you so much. I don't tell you that enough huh

Nico: you don't

Nico: but i love you too :)

Guilt twisted in her chest, the feeling that she'd been a bad friend finally bubbling to the surface.

Alaina: I'm sorry I have been so focused on Cole for the past year. I feel like I haven't made nearly enough time for you. I promise I'll be better

Nico: oh, honey. you don't have to apologize. people grow in different directions, but it doesn't mean we grow apart

Nico: besides, look at us now—still here for each other's mental breakdowns like the good old days!

Despite everything, Alaina smiled. She reread the message a few times, relief easing the knot that had been slowly forming in her stomach over the past year. Nico was right. Growing with someone versus growing away from them—that was the way it should be, even if that wasn't the way it had always been for Alaina. When her mom had chosen her father over everyone else, cutting ties completely when her family disapproved, Alaina had felt that loss for years. By the time Alaina reconnected with her family, she'd grown so far apart from her aunt, uncle, and cousin that the chasm between them felt uncrossable.

But what if it didn't have to be so black and white? What if you could become a new version of yourself without losing the people who'd loved all your previous versions?

Alaina: When did you get so wise?
Nico: please, i've always been a genius

Alaina left a heart on that message, then shut off her screen. Sliding her phone back into her pocket, she returned her attention to Priscilla, tracking subtle shifts in her expression as she read—amusement tugging the right corner of her lips, confusion twisting the left, sadness softening her eyes.

Priscilla looked up, catching Alaina staring, and lowered her book. "What?"

Alaina exhaled, her emotions a little too big for her chest. So much for blaming her sappiness on wine. Maybe this was just who she was around Priscilla.

But she couldn't say that. Instead, she stood, mug empty. "Nothing. When do we leave? I want to run an errand."

Priscilla's brow pinched. "An errand?"

"Yeah, just a quick one," Alaina said, her smile attempting to mask her racing thoughts. "An hour, tops."

Priscilla nodded. "Okay. We can wait an hour. But I'd like to be on the road by noon."

"Perfect." Alaina leaned down, pressed a quick kiss to Priscilla's cheek, and pulled away before catching her reaction—

though if Priscilla's face mirrored how Alaina felt, she would be glowing.

❄

Priscilla was nowhere to be seen in the bookstore when Alaina returned after her errand with a small gift bag in one hand, a plastic bag from Patty's in the other. Clark stood at the counter, smiling warmly as she entered, yesterday's tension gone.

"Alaina! How were those cookies?"

"Great!" Truthfully, she'd forgotten them, abandoned on Priscilla's counter, but he didn't need to know that. "Have you seen Priscilla?"

"Out back, packing her truck. Mentioned something about a camping trip with you?"

Alaina nearly vibrated with excitement, rocking onto the balls of her feet. "Yes! I've never been before." But something snagged in the back of her mind, giving her pause. "But—wait, will you be okay here alone? Won't the store be busy today?"

It was just two days until Christmas. Surely Priscilla needed to be at her store.

But Clark waved away her concern. "Don't you worry about it. Mom did great yesterday, and she'll be here by noon when traffic picks up."

"That sounds so lovely. Tell your mom Merry Christmas for me."

"Will do." Clark glanced around the room, then dropped his voice. "I hope you don't mind me asking—it's really none of my business—but are you and Priscilla . . . do you two . . . have something going on?"

Alaina's pulse quickened. Had Clark noticed something? Had Priscilla said anything?

"I just didn't want to step on any toes," Clark said quickly, color rising in his cheeks. "Like, asking the boss's girl out. She's been acting off around me ever since our lunch the other day."

"No," Alaina said, shaking her head quickly. "Nothing like that."

Even if a part of her wished there was something "going on," she wasn't about to say that to Clark. Priscilla didn't believe in love, and Alaina was already in love with someone else. It was hardly a blueprint for a romance, no matter how many butterflies Priscilla set loose in her stomach or how many times she'd made Priscilla's breath catch. "That's just Priscilla. She can be a bit . . . odd sometimes, you know?"

"Sure." The frown on his face deepened, even as he nodded in agreement.

It didn't sound like he believed her, but it was true. There were no toes to step on here.

"All right then. You two have fun out there."

She wasn't sure if the smile she forced was meant to reassure Clark or herself.

Alaina hurried upstairs into Priscilla's apartment, clutching the gift tightly. Clark said Priscilla was packing the truck, but who knew how long that would take? She could be back any second.

Alaina racked her brain for the perfect hiding place. The closet? No, too obvious. Under the bed? No, what if Priscilla used that space for storage? She could go looking for an extra blanket and find the present, spoiling the surprise. She scanned the living room until her gaze landed on the couch. Perfect. The slight gap between the bottom of the sofa and the floor was just big enough.

She knelt and slid the gift bag beneath it, safer here than under the tree downstairs. If Priscilla saw the gift early, she might refuse it outright.

The door opened just as Alaina stood, quickly arranging her expression into casual innocence.

Priscilla, to her credit, didn't jump this time at the surprise. "Clark didn't mention you'd come back." She was slightly out of breath, like she'd been hauling something heavy. "Did you get what you needed?"

"I did. Did you bring everything down to the truck?"

Priscilla nodded. "Yes, we're all set."

"I could've helped, you know," Alaina said, faintly disappointed she'd missed watching Priscilla haul things around.

Priscilla waved her off. "Don't worry about it. Let's get you dressed and ready, okay?"

Dressed and ready, it turned out, meant getting more bundled up than Alaina had been on any of the other days she'd spent in Brooks. Priscilla had loaned her yet another thermal shirt, a flannel, and a parka that created a cocoon of heat around her by the time she emerged from the bathroom. Coupled with wool socks and, most important, Priscilla's trapper hat, which Alaina practically begged to wear, she was downright toasty.

Alaina drifted into the empty living room while Priscilla was still getting changed behind the closed bedroom door. She pulled out her phone, hoping to mindlessly scroll while she waited. But as she tapped the screen to life, a notification stopped her abruptly.

New voicemail, the banner read, but that wasn't what had her heart stuttering. It was the number the voicemail came from. She hadn't saved it to her phone, but she knew it anyway: Shauna.

Swallowing hard, she raised the phone to her ear and pressed play.

"Alaina? Hi! I'm hoping this is the right number. Mom wasn't sure, but I—anyway. I just wanted to call and see if you had any plans for the holiday. It's been a few years, and . . . well, I wanted to talk to you in person, but thought maybe you . . . Sorry, I'm getting off track."

Shauna's voice was older but unmistakable—still quick, a little breathless. Alaina stood straighter, the room suddenly too quiet. Her hand gripped the phone tighter.

"Okay, long story short, I got married last year! It was, like, an elopement or whatever, just my parents and his. We went to Vegas, actually. I don't know if you can imagine my mother taking a picture with a dollar-store version of Elvis, but . . . we did it! And we're pregnant! I'm due in March. I just thought . . . you know, what better time to reconnect family, right?"

Married. Pregnant. The words hit with a strange mix of joy and ache. Good for Shauna—she deserved happiness. Alaina blinked hard. Her early memories of Shauna weren't crisp anymore—just flashes of made-up games, secrets whispered beneath blankets, a bond that had once felt unbreakable. Until her mom packed up their life and moved them halfway across the country for a man who hadn't stuck around.

"Sorry, this is getting really long. Um, basically, just—I'm having Christmas dinner at my house, if you want to come. Let me know and I can text you the address. No pressure. Or if it's easier, let me know if you want to grab lunch or something sometime. I just . . . family is family, and I want my baby girl to have as much of it as possible."

Family is family.

The phrase lodged in Alaina's throat. Shauna wanted her baby to have as much family as possible—meanwhile, Alaina's own mother had burned every bridge while chasing love halfway across the country. She'd followed a man who'd left them both, severing ties with cousins, aunts, and the kind of roots Alaina could've clung to.

After a week of memory after memory surfacing—her mother's laugh, the smell of cinnamon rolls in a warm kitchen—the sudden flare of anger startled her. It broke through the haze of nostalgia like a crack in the ice, sharp and cold. Alaina didn't want to feel this way. Not after everything she'd been remembering. Not now.

"So, if you want, you can call me back," Shauna's voicemail was saying. "Or text me. Or, if this isn't Alaina, can you let me know so I can try to track her down? I'd really appreciate it. Either way, Merry Christmas."

Her chest felt packed with things she didn't know how to name—regret, hope, disbelief. All of it got stuck somewhere behind her ribs, thick and unmoving.

The bedroom door creaked open.

"Sorry, I couldn't find my—" Priscilla stopped short. "Alaina?"

Priscilla crossed the room in a few strides, then reached for Alaina's hands, brushing her thumb across the back of one. That simple touch threatened to undo her. "Talk to me. What happened?"

"My cousin called." Alaina held up the phone. "She's, um—she's pregnant."

Priscilla tilted her head. "Is that not good news?"

"No—it is. It's great. I just . . ." She exhaled. "My aunt and uncle were the ones who took me in after my mom died."

That explained nothing about her reaction. She could tell by the look on Priscilla's face.

"Were they . . . unkind to you?"

"No, nothing like that. Not really. They weren't bad people. We just didn't . . . click. I was fifteen when my mom died, and I hadn't seen them since I was maybe six? It was hard. I'm sure they were grieving too. And I was a mess."

Priscilla squeezed her fingers. "You had every right to be."

Alaina looked down at their joined hands. "I know, I know. I just—I didn't try. And they did, at least at the start. But that whole first year was a blur. And by the time I could think straight again, I think they'd given up. And I let them. Everything about them reminded me of—of *her*"—Alaina's voice started to crack—"of what I'd lost. And it was too much. So I kept them—even my cousin, who I'd been so close with as a kid—at a distance. And when I left for college and they stopped inviting me back for breaks, I just let it slide. I thought I didn't need them. But now Shauna is having a baby, and she wants that baby to know her family. She wants to plan a visit. Catch up."

She left out the part where Shauna invited her to Christmas this year. Impracticality of her making it back to Colorado aside—if that's even where her family still lived—she absolutely wasn't ready for that.

Priscilla nodded slowly, like she wasn't quite sure of what she was about to say and needed time to think it over. "Do you want to talk to her?"

"I don't know. I think so. I just don't know if I can."

"That's okay." Priscilla's fingers squeezed her own, and Alaina's eyes fell to look at their hands, clasped together. "You can take your time."

Alaina blinked back forming tears. How many times had she let her guard down in front of Priscilla over the past week?

"Thanks," she whispered. Priscilla didn't say anything more. She didn't have to. She just held her hands tighter.

Alaina cleared her throat. "We should probably get going before Clark thinks I chickened out."

She managed a smile—wobbly, but real. She was glad for the distraction of the camping trip, for something to focus on besides the mess in her head.

Priscilla hesitated. "If you're not feeling up to it, we can always—"

"Are you kidding?" Alaina said, a flash of feigned bravado in her voice. "I was born for camping. I may be a city girl, but deep down, my heart longs for the outdoors."

Priscilla's eyebrows arched skeptically. "We'll see about that."

❄

As they started the drive to the mountain, Priscilla reached into the glove compartment and pulled out an old, slightly worn CD case.

"The radio up here is pretty unreliable, so I brought along a bit of backup," she said as she fed the CD into the player. The speakers clicked on with harmonious refrains of strings playing Christmas tunes.

"Classical? What are you, like, eighty?"

Priscilla shrugged. "Not everyone can appreciate the finer things." She shot Alaina a quick glance. "This album belonged to my grandmother. It's one of the few things of hers I was able to keep, besides the crucifix she used to have hanging in her kitchen. I listen to it every December."

Alaina thought of the photograph on Priscilla's wall—tiny Priscilla in a tutu, beaming up at her grandmother like she'd hung the moon. Had little Priscilla twirled to these same violins? The image made something ache deep in her chest.

She wished they could have known each other when they were younger. How different would life have been? Maybe after her mom died, instead of crying alone in her bedroom for weeks, she would have had Priscilla to sit beside her. Maybe the hollow place inside her wouldn't have grown so fast.

"What's it called?" Alaina asked.

"*Bach's Christmas Oratorio.* She'd play it every year while decorating the tree."

The trumpets swelled suddenly, voices joining in a language

Alaina couldn't understand but somehow felt in her bones. Her playlist from their tree-decorating party now seemed embarrassingly basic. But then again, the Priscilla from six days ago wouldn't have even cracked open this particular door to her past. No, something had changed between them—something profound and terrifying and thrilling that made her heart race whenever she allowed herself to think about it too deeply.

Alaina reached over and turned the volume higher, letting the music fill every corner of the cab. "Thank you for sharing it with me."

Priscilla's shoulders relaxed visibly. Her fingers tapped in perfect time against the steering wheel, giving Alaina the opportunity to shift the conversation into something less heavy.

"Did you play an instrument?" Alaina asked.

"Flute, violin, piano," Priscilla said nonchalantly. "But I always really wanted to learn the drums."

There was something vulnerable in the way she said it, like a secret slipped out before she could stop it. That small, bashful smile wasn't one Alaina had seen before. It made something tender bloom in her chest.

"I could see you being great at that." She could imagine Priscilla letting go in a way she rarely seemed to allow herself. Not careful or quiet. Just free.

Priscilla ducked her head, like the thought was too indulgent to entertain for long. But her smile lingered.

About twenty minutes into the drive, Alaina reached behind her seat and tugged out the plastic bag from the café. "Sandwich time? Something to keep us from dying out there."

Priscilla glanced at her with a smile. "You came prepared."

"Don't act so surprised."

They were almost an hour into the CD when Priscilla turned down the volume, slowing as she put on her blinker.

"Here we are," she said as they pulled into a snow-covered parking lot—if you could even call it that. It was more of a clearing, with a single other pickup sitting parked. By the looks of the snow piled on it, the truck had been there for days.

Once they climbed out of the truck, Alaina's first clue that she might be in over her head came when Priscilla hauled a wooden sled off the bed with a heavy thunk.

Alaina looked down at it, then back at Priscilla. "What's that for?"

"Carrying our gear. It's a bit of a hike."

She barely had time to process that before Priscilla handed her a pair of snowshoes.

"Oh, so *this* is the moment you finally decide to kill me. I've been wondering what's taking you so long. Death by hike is an interesting method of choice, I've gotta say."

Priscilla shook her head with a smile. "Do you need help getting them on?"

"How hard can it be?"

For once, it actually wasn't all that hard. The shoes snapped on easily, and within minutes they were setting off, Priscilla pulling the wooden sled behind her with a rope slung over one shoulder. It glided smoothly over the packed snow, loaded with a tent and several bags.

The late-morning sun shone brightly in a cloudless sky, casting golden light that did little to warm the crisp air. Still, Alaina was plenty comfortable in her borrowed layers. Her breath plumed white in front of her face as they moved through a forest of towering pines and bare-limbed aspens. The trail was no manicured path, just the occasional orange ribbon tied to a branch. Had Priscilla placed them herself?

The higher they climbed, the more the forest opened up, revealing glimpses of the valley below, a patchwork of white fields and dark evergreens. The untouched snow suggested they were the first to come this way all day. Every sound felt amplified in the stillness: the crunch of their steps, the soft swish of the sled behind them, the distant cry of a bird.

As the incline grew steeper, Priscilla glanced back. "Need a break?"

It was the fifth time she'd asked, each one met with a stubborn shake of Alaina's head. But this time, her calves were burning, her breath coming in short bursts, and she gave in with a winded, "Let's just catch our breath for a moment."

"Here. You need to keep up your strength." Priscilla held out her hand, offering a pack of trail mix. Seeing Alaina's hesitant look, she added, "There's chocolate in it, promise."

Alaina took the packet and ate it eagerly. She didn't realize how hungry she'd gotten in the short time since she last ate.

"Where are we going?" This time, she resisted the joke about Priscilla being a murderer—though this *would* be the perfect place to hide a body.

"Not too much farther now. It's one of my favorite spots."

Alaina didn't press for more. She liked hearing the fondness in Priscilla's voice, soft and reverent, like she was guiding her to something sacred. The last stretch of the hike was quiet, their snowshoes crunching over snow, the trees thickening around them.

Then, just as Alaina was starting to wonder if maybe they'd gotten lost, Priscilla paused beside a tall spruce. She glanced back with the ghost of a smile, then reached up and pulled back a low-hanging branch.

"After you," she said.

Alaina ducked under the branch—and froze.

The trees fell away into a hidden clearing, wide and still blanketed in snow. In the distance, mountain peaks rose like white teeth against a sky so blue it looked unreal. The only sounds were the faint rush of wind and the soft creak of the forest settling.

Alaina didn't say anything at first. She just stood there, heart thudding in her ears, taking it in.

"You found this place?" she asked finally, her voice quiet.

Priscilla stepped beside her. "A few years ago. I'd gotten lost trying to follow a trail I thought I remembered. Ended up here instead." She looked out at the view. "Best wrong turn I ever made."

It was too perfect not to document. She pulled out her phone, snapped a photo, and then another—one of the clearing, one of the mountains, one with Priscilla off to the side, her profile framed by trees and sky.

"It's beautiful," she said softly.

Priscilla looked at her then, smiling slowly. "I thought you might like it," she said quietly.

Alaina leaned into her, her shoulder brushing Priscilla's. "That's a criminal understatement."

They stood like that for a long moment—just the two of them, wrapped in the hush of snow and sky.

"So what now, boss?" Alaina asked.

Priscilla nodded toward the edge of the clearing. "We've still got an hour or so of daylight. That'll give us time to pitch the tent and get a fire going."

Alaina followed her toward the trees, heart still thrumming. The idea of staying here overnight—of waking up to this view, to the quiet, to Priscilla—made her stomach flutter.

First, they chose an area for the tent. Working together, they packed down the snow with their snowshoes and a shovel Priscilla had brought. As Priscilla expertly assembled the tent, Alaina stumbled around, trying to help, but mostly just tripped over cords and fumbled with stakes, drawing a laugh from Priscilla.

Once the tent was secure, they crawled inside. The interior was snug—just large enough for two people, as long as they didn't mind the proximity. They unrolled the mats and sleeping bags Priscilla had packed, laying them side by side on the tent floor.

"Sorry if it's a bit tight," Priscilla said, cheeks pink. Whether it was from the cold or embarrassment, Alaina wasn't sure. The way she avoided Alaina's gaze made her think it might be the latter. "I'm usually out here by myself."

Alaina entertained the idea of flopping down onto the makeshift bed and asking Priscilla to curl up next to her. She could still feel the way Priscilla's body pressed against her own the night of the mistletoe incident, when she had spent hours memorizing every spot their bodies touched as she fought for sleep.

Her mind leapt ahead to tonight—lying side by side, inching closer for warmth, their bodies fitting like puzzle pieces.

She reeled herself back in, catching the reins of her imagination before it ran too far.

"It's no problem." Alaina offered a dismissive wave. And then, because she couldn't help herself, she said, "It'll be easier to stay warm this way."

Priscilla's blush deepened, turning her face an adorable shade of red, and Alaina basked in the thrill of getting that sort of reaction from her. After six days of gradually cracking through Priscilla's walls, there was something wildly satisfying about making her composure slip this easily.

Priscilla cleared her throat. "Yes, well—"

Alaina grinned. "What's next?"

Priscilla was visibly relieved as she took a deep breath—her first in about thirty seconds, Alaina was pretty sure. "We look for kindling, start a fire."

Alaina followed Priscilla back out into the snow. "You know, this trip seems less like relaxing and more like putting me to work."

"Relaxing comes later," Priscilla said. "You've got to earn it."

Alaina's footsteps faltered as the words hung in the air, a sudden warmth flooding her cheeks as her mind flirted with implications. She stood there, frozen for a moment, while Priscilla continued on her hunt for sticks, blissfully unaware of the double entendre.

By the time they'd gathered enough tinder, Alaina was freezing cold and ready to sit in front of a fire and defrost. While Priscilla unloaded the logs from the sled, Alaina dug out a circular pit in the snow under her direction, using a small hand shovel to clear down to the frozen earth below.

"Like this?" she asked once she'd finished.

Priscilla nodded. "Perfect."

They arranged the kindling, padding it with crumpled newspaper. Alaina handed over wood as requested, watching Priscilla's face as she worked—focused, lips pursed in concentration, explaining things softly as she went.

"Are you going to do that thing where you rub two sticks together, then—" Alaina mimicked a burst of flames with her hands, blowing a loud puff of air out of her lips.

Priscilla reached into her pocket and pulled out a lighter.

Alaina laughed. "That works too."

Priscilla knelt beside their carefully constructed pile of tinder, flicked the lighter, and held it up to a piece of crumpled paper. It caught immediately, crackling as small flames licked up toward the kindling.

The fire roared to life, and Alaina, nestled on a woolen blanket Priscilla had spread out, let the fire's embrace thaw her chill. She watched as Priscilla unpacked a compact metal contraption with its tiny dials and fuel canister. "What is that?"

"A gas stove," Priscilla answered.

"My fire not good enough for you?" Alaina said, hugging her knees to her chest, still a little cold despite the growing flames.

Priscilla's lips quirked upward. "In case it rains—it's always good to have a backup so we can melt down some water." She glanced up, eyes catching in the firelight. "Right now I was thinking I'd use it to make you some hot cocoa."

At the thought, Alaina lit up. Proper warmth—both inside and out—sounded like heaven right now. "Can I help?"

"Fill these with snow." Priscilla handed her two metal pots, handles folded flat against the sides. "Pack it in tight—it'll melt down considerably."

Alaina packed snow into the pots, firming it with cold fingers. When the first batch melted to barely an inch of water, she filled them again, watching the level slowly rise.

"How'd you learn all this stuff?" she asked. She took off her gloves, holding out her hands to warm them over the fire while Priscilla emptied a packet of cocoa into one pot and dropped a tea bag into the other.

"Grant, mostly." Priscilla stirred the cocoa with a tiny collapsible spoon. "He's been coming out less the past few years, so it's just been me."

"Why's that?" Alaina tucked her legs underneath her, shifting to find a more comfortable position on the frozen ground beneath the blanket.

Priscilla's hands stilled. "I haven't really asked. I just assumed he wanted to spend more time with Ned."

She carefully poured the steaming cocoa into a mug and passed it to Alaina.

"It's hot," Priscilla said, settling beside her on the blanket, close enough that their shoulders almost touched. She cradled her own tea between her palms, steam rising.

Alaina stuck the mug in the snow to help it cool down faster. "How often do you come out here?"

"I used to try to come at least once a month and stay for a few days, but . . . I don't know. I just haven't been in the right headspace, I suppose. Being alone out here with my thoughts hasn't been as appealing. I think the last time I was here was probably sometime last spring."

"That's a long time." Alaina bit her lip, concern creeping into her voice. "You need to make more time for yourself, you know? And not just to rescue damsels in distress when they come crashing into your life."

"Technically, you crashed into a snowbank, not my life." Priscilla stirred the fire with a stick. "I know. Everyone tells me that. But the bookstore . . . sometimes it feels like it's all I have. I forget there's so much more out there for me."

Their eyes met, and a rush of air left Alaina's lungs under the weight of Priscilla's intense look.

The space between them felt charged with a spark that threatened to ignite something Alaina wasn't sure she was ready for. Not because she didn't want Priscilla—god, that wasn't the problem at all—but because wanting her meant admitting that this entire plan to win Cole back had been a lie she'd been telling herself. What if the future she'd imagined for herself wasn't what she actually wanted anymore?

She snatched a new topic from the tangle of her thoughts like a lifeline.

"So, about this party tomorrow. I'd really like to go and see everyone one more time before I leave."

Priscilla's eyebrows knitted together, her head tilting just a fraction to the side. "What party?"

"At the inn?" Alaina's words tumbled out in a rush. "Tomorrow night. Callie wanted to know if we'd come."

Priscilla's response was a series of rapid blinks, then she turned her head toward the fire with a jittery, humorless laugh.

"Priscilla?" Alaina's heart clenched at the clear display of sadness on Priscilla's face. Her emotions were usually guarded, but she must have forgotten to put up her walls this time, and Alaina could see right through to Priscilla's hurt.

"Sorry, sorry, I'm—" Priscilla's voice frayed, dissolving into the thick air. She stared down at her hands, the gears in her mind seemingly turning. Her jaw worked for a moment before she sucked in a deep breath, exhaling it with a gust. "I didn't know about the party. They probably assumed I wouldn't come." She rubbed at her temple. "And honestly, they're not wrong. I've said no to so many things it makes sense they'd stop asking but . . ." She shook her head gently, lips pressing into a tight, contemplative line. "It stings."

Alaina reached out to draw Priscilla's hand toward her. Their eyes locked. "Why do you push away the people you obviously care about?"

"It's complicated."

"We've got time," Alaina replied softly.

"Yes, I suppose we do." Priscilla trained her eyes on the tree line, peaks silhouetted by the setting sun as she spoke. "I met Callie first when I moved here. We clicked instantly. It was like I'd known her forever, and—well, you've met Callie. You know how she is."

Alaina hummed in agreement. It was impossible not to like Callie.

"We would get coffee together once a week. She's the one who introduced me to Grant and Ned. I'd seen Ned before at Patty's, but I didn't really get to know him until Callie had us all over for dinner. Ned is so much like her I think the two of them might have been separated at birth or something. He's an amazing baker, so he and Callie made us dinner and dessert, and Grant and I just got to talking. At first I wasn't sure that we'd have anything to talk about, but he's an old soul. He loves jazz and history, and he had this collection of first editions he'd inherited from his grandfather that he showed me. After that night, the four of us were inseparable. We'd all do everything together. We'd take trips, and have game nights, go skiing, and . . . it felt like the family I'd never had."

Alaina nodded. She'd had a taste of that herself the past few days.

"But then Lauren and Callie started dating. And I like Lauren, I really do—she's probably the most similar to me out of all of them—but when she and Callie got together, it was just . . . I was just . . ."

Priscilla hesitated, and Alaina waited for her to continue.

"It was like I didn't fit anymore." Priscilla picked a stick up off the ground, using it to shift a log back over the flame. "Five is a crowd, it turns out."

Alaina's mind rewound to the other night, remembering Callie's enthusiastic remark about having an even number for game night. Being the perpetual fifth wheel among two pairs of happy couples was bound to be draining.

"I even went on these pity dates Callie and Ned set up just to appease them. But none of those women really fit in with the group, not the way you'd need to if you were going to stick around. Some tried too hard, others barely tried at all. But there was always this . . . tension. Like I knew they were all trying to make whoever I brought around comfortable, but we could all feel it wasn't working."

"That's hard to imagine. They've all been so welcoming to me."

"That's true." Priscilla's expression softened as she glanced back at Alaina. "It's different with you. You just walked in and it all clicked. Even Grant and Lauren warmed up, and they're not—" She stopped herself. "They weren't like that with anyone else I brought around. After so many failed attempts, I started to think that maybe I was just better off alone."

Alaina forced herself to focus on what Priscilla was saying, and not the fact that she was drawing a clear and obvious line between Alaina and women she'd dated in the past.

"So, you distanced yourself."

"I did." Priscilla's gaze dropped, her lip caught between her teeth in contemplation. "And now I'm not sure I can ever go back. We used to be so close. Now I'm just . . . watching from the sidelines."

"Maybe you can't go back to the way things were," Alaina said. "But maybe there's something better." Their eyes locked, and she added, "Sometimes when you let go of what was, you make room for what could be."

Alaina felt her own words reverberate through her chest with uncomfortable clarity. Who was she to give Priscilla advice when she was the one chasing the past?

She tucked a loose strand of hair back into her hat and cleared her throat. "Step one is going to tomorrow's party."

"Are you sure?"

"I am. They really want you to come. That's why Callie asked me to ask you. She probably just didn't want you to feel pressured, but she wants you there."

Priscilla's mouth twisted to the side in thought. "She *has* been trying to get in touch with me."

"Right."

"And she—you're sure she wants—"

"She told me very specifically that I should try to get you to go." She chose her words carefully, not wanting there to be a trace of doubt left behind on Priscilla's face.

"Okay." Priscilla straightened a little, the tension easing from her expression. "We should go then. If you want to, that is."

"I really would like to. I'm going to miss them almost as much as I'll miss you."

A lie. A transparent one, probably. Yes, she'd miss the others. But that was a ripple next to the tidal wave of how she felt about the woman next to her.

Alaina had never met anyone like Priscilla—kind, smart, funny, caring, beautiful. She thought back to the kiss under the mistletoe, to the look in Priscilla's eyes last night under the tree when she'd so clearly wanted to kiss Alaina again.

She would be happy to have Priscilla in her life in any way she could, but the need to have her in *that* way rose above all the others, a buoy in the storm-tossed sea of her emotions.

Priscilla's voice was a gentle tug back to the present, laced with an honesty that made Alaina's heart swell. "I'll miss you too, you know."

"I'll just have to come back then, won't I?"

"I'd like that very much."

Something on Priscilla's face—her eyes, and the sadness there—gave Alaina the impression Priscilla didn't believe her. But she was telling the truth. She'd come back, and not just for her car. She couldn't let this be the only week of her life that included Priscilla.

At this point, Alaina wasn't sure she wanted to leave at all.

Chapter Sixteen

As the sun dipped lower, Priscilla cracked open a few soup cans and set them over the stove to heat.

"Can I help?" Alaina asked.

"There are bowls and spoons in the tub on the sled," Priscilla said. "And an extra blanket in the blue duffel, if you're cold."

Alaina groaned as she stood, joints stiff. At the sled, she quickly found two metal bowls and spoons in the tote. In the blue duffel was a familiar herringbone blanket—the same one Priscilla had tucked over her that first night after pulling her from the snowbank.

She returned to the fire, spreading the blanket across her lap. Pink and orange streaked the sky. Across from her, Priscilla stirred the soup, face lit by firelight and concentration. The sight filled Alaina with a warmth the flames couldn't touch.

With the last of the daylight, Alaina pulled out the now worn and crumpled piece of paper from her pocket, using a pen to cross out number four: hike a mountain. The next item—camping under the stars—she'd save to mark off tomorrow morning, wanting to experience it in full, to savor it before striking it through.

Less than forty-eight hours until she'd be on a plane to New York.

The thought caused a lump to form in her throat. Tomorrow was her last full day here. Her last full day with Priscilla. They could stay friends. No, they *would* stay friends. She would make sure of that. She could send Priscilla postcards and silly videos of cats—whatever it took to stay connected. Maybe she could even visit again in the summer, or maybe Priscilla would come to San Francisco.

But even as she imagined it, the idea felt like a consolation prize. The real thing—this time, this connection—was slipping through her fingers.

"Here you go." Priscilla slid under the blanket beside her, handing over a steaming bowl. The familiar aroma of canned chicken noodle wafted upward, warm and comforting. Alaina quickly tucked The List away.

Priscilla's gaze followed it. "We've almost made it to the end of your list. Besides—"

"—the big movie moment," Alaina said, finishing her sentence. She sipped the soup. "Still haven't thought of what I'm going to do for that."

"It'll come to you."

"What if it doesn't?"

What if I don't want it to?

The thought socked Alaina square in the gut, leaving her breathless.

After a moment, Priscilla said, "It's like you said. It's about taking the risk. It's not about what you say, it's what you're willing to do, right?"

What *was* she willing to do for Cole? Sure, she had started this whole adventure with the goal of winning him back, but with each passing day it felt as if she was taking one step forward for herself and two steps away from him.

And this moment? Knees touching Priscilla's under the blanket, sharing warm soup under a sky full of emerging stars? She didn't want it to involve Cole at all. She wanted to erase this night from The List completely, tuck it away somewhere safe where it wouldn't be tainted.

Priscilla nudged her. "You'll figure it out. Don't worry."

Alaina forced a weak grin. "Look at you, believing in love."

Alaina had expected Priscilla to brush her off, to roll her eyes, to shake her head.

Instead, she let out a breathless laugh. "What can I say? You're a bad influence."

Alaina's pulse stuttered. Sometime over the past week, something in Priscilla had shifted. The cynic who'd sworn off love was sitting here, admitting that something in her had changed—and that Alaina had been the one to change it. Alaina wasn't the only one who had learned something new about herself over the past six days.

Just Priscilla's hand grazing Alaina's was enough to spark a full-body reaction. Had Cole's skin against hers ever made her need to forcibly restart her heartbeat?

It almost felt like—

No.

She was being silly. She couldn't fall in love with someone in under a week.

Could she?

The question hung heavily in her chest, like a secret she wasn't sure she wanted to keep. If she could just hit pause, even for a second, maybe she could untangle the web inside her.

Priscilla sat with her empty bowl in her lap, gaze locked on the flames, hands clasped tightly in front of her. Her face was unreadable—blank in a way that made Alaina ache.

"Earth to Priscilla." Alaina nudged her. "You okay?"

Priscilla's face softened as she turned to Alaina, her smile a little too small, a little too forced. "Yes, sorry. Just lost in my head."

"Care to share?" Alaina set her own bowl down in the snow and took Priscilla's hand, moving it into her lap. She tugged off Priscilla's gloves, letting her fingers brush over the skin of Priscilla's knuckles.

Priscilla tilted her head back, eyes on the stars. "I've missed this place. It grounds me. I know you're not religious, but this is where I feel . . . connected. Not to God the way I was raised to understand it, but to something deeper. To myself."

Alaina said nothing, watching her.

"When everything fell apart with my parents—when they told me I wasn't their daughter anymore, that who I was was *unholy*—I lost my faith. They'd turned our beliefs into a weapon to use against me. But the first time I came here, looking up at the stars, I felt it again. For the first time in years, I felt that connection—not to a church or a doctrine. Just me, God, and the stars."

Her voice barely carried above the crackling fire. Alaina squeezed her hand, heart tight.

"Thank you for sharing that with me," she said softly. "I think I know what you mean. Not about faith, exactly, but . . . After my mom died, I used to sneak into my aunt's yard at night and lie on the lawn. Stare up at the stars. They made my problems seem smaller. Not in a way that diminished them. It was more like . . . they were being held by something bigger."

She paused, searching for the right words, feeling the familiar ache in her chest sharpen into a sudden, surprising flash of anger toward her mom—for leaving her alone, for forcing her to find comfort in something as distant and cold as stars. She pushed it down.

"When my grief felt too big for me to hold, I'd imagine I was storing pieces of it in different stars, scattering it across the universe so I didn't have to carry it all alone." She laughed, shaking her head. "It sounds silly now, of course, but—"

"It doesn't."

Alaina swallowed around the lump forming in her throat. "I'm glad you found that connection again, despite everything they tried to take from you."

Priscilla's hand squeezed back. "Me too." She ducked her head, a hint of embarrassment crossing her features. "Sorry for unloading all of that on you."

"Don't be." Alaina shook her head. "I think I could listen to you talk forever."

Alaina's grip on Priscilla tightened. She knew these hands now—knew the shape of each knuckle, the creases along her palm like they were her own. When had that happened?

Priscilla looked over, the fire casting light through her lashes, flames dancing in her eyes.

"You don't mean that." Her gaze dropped to their hands. "You'd get sick of me, eventually."

Something sharp and protective flared in Alaina's chest. How many people had failed this woman? Her parents, her ex—Alaina would never be one of them.

"Not a chance."

Her eyes dipped to Priscilla's mouth. Two days since the mistletoe kiss, and the want hadn't faded. It had only sharpened. Why was she holding back?

"Sil?" The name left her lips before she could stop it.

"Yes?"

Their eyes met, and suddenly they were close. Too close. Not nearly close enough.

There was a raw look of longing in Priscilla's expression—the same yearning Alaina had caught glimpses of before, but now stripped of all its careful guards and hesitations. Intoxicating.

When Priscilla's tongue darted out to wet her lips, Alaina's focus snapped back to that mouth like a rubber band. Something pulled her forward until her breath mingled with Priscilla's.

Was she really about to risk everything they'd built in the last week? Maybe. But Priscilla wanted this too—Alaina could feel it in the tight grip of her hand, the rapid rise of her chest, the way her gaze darkened like spilled ink.

All Alaina had to do was take the plunge.

She leaned in, eyes fluttering shut, heart racing as she crossed the final breath of space. Even blind, she could feel Priscilla—her warmth, her scent, the hitch in her breath.

Then their lips met.

Soft, uncertain. A tentative brush that turned ravenous in an instant. God, why had she waited this long? Priscilla's mouth moved urgently against hers, hands slipping beneath Alaina's layers to find the bare skin at the back of her neck, fingers icy, touch electric.

The kiss was a match struck in a dry forest. Alaina went up in flames.

Her hands rose to cup Priscilla's face, marveling at the softness of her skin and the warmth of her cheeks. She fumbled for Priscilla's hat, frustrated she couldn't thread her fingers through that thick, dark hair. Then Priscilla tilted her jaw, deepening the kiss, and the frustration disappeared.

Gone was the woman who kept her hands to herself, who measured every word. Now Priscilla moved without thinking, her hands everywhere—Alaina's neck, her waist—gripping, guiding, pressing her back onto the blanket. Her usual quiet had vanished, making way for breathy noises that had Alaina's head spinning.

Priscilla's thigh slid between her legs, and thought became impossible. Alaina arched into the pressure, fingers greedy at the strip of skin she'd found at the base of Priscilla's neck. It only stoked the fire. She needed more. She needed Priscilla's coat off, her clothes gone, her skin under Alaina's hands.

"Priscilla." Her voice was hoarse, wrecked. She pressed a hand to Priscilla's chest. The other woman stilled instantly, pulling back. But Alaina's fingers curled in Priscilla's coat. "No, no—just—the tent."

"You're sure?" Priscilla's eyes were nearly black in the warm glow of the fireside.

Alaina leaned in, kissed the corner of her mouth. "Please."

Never in Alaina's life had anyone kissed her the way Priscilla did as they tumbled into the tent. Not her middle-school boyfriend who still had Cheeto dust on his fingers, or the guys at parties, rushed and graceless and forgettable.

Not even Cole.

None of them could have, even if they tried, because none of them were Priscilla. They didn't have Priscilla's lips, opening heatedly against Alaina's mouth, or her delicate poise, crumbling deliciously at Alaina's resulting moan, or her lithe fingers, grabbing Alaina's chin and tilting her head back, convincing Alaina to part her lips like an offering.

Then it hit her—a neon-lit, billboard-sized epiphany. For the past week, she'd been chasing a shadow, seeking warmth from a distant star, when the sun was right in front of her.

Blankets cushioned her back. Priscilla kissed her mouth, her cheeks, her jaw, her neck—each press lighting her nerves like a fuse. Priscilla's tongue traced the pulse point beneath Alaina's ear, and Alaina gasped through her teeth, heart pounding. Could Priscilla feel it? The wild rhythm beneath her skin?

Alaina's hips lifted instinctively. Priscilla groaned and pinned them down, that firm grip only feeding the fire.

"Sil." The name slipped out on a breathy exhale, loud in the quiet tent. Alaina flushed with embarrassment—until Priscilla's hips stuttered at the sound, a pleasant reminder that maybe it wasn't just her world that was being dismantled piece by piece.

Alaina searched for Priscilla's hands, pinned to her hips, and dragged them upward to the zipper of her coat. "Off—take it off." She needed both of them to be wearing less clothes, like, immediately.

"Impatient, are we?" Priscilla's voice was low, husky. Alaina shivered.

"Very."

Alaina rolled her hips to prove her point, and Priscilla dropped her forehead to Alaina's temple.

When their lips met again, there was no holding back. Alaina's fingers grasped the fabric around Priscilla's collarbone, holding her close. Priscilla's legs tightened around hers, hips canting with barely contained restraint. Alaina's mind lost any semblance of a train of thought beyond Priscilla, Priscilla, *Priscilla*.

Priscilla's hands found her coat, undoing one button at a time. When it slipped open, Priscilla paused, gaze searching Alaina's face.

"Better?"

Alaina's body beat out her brain, nodding before she'd even formed a single thought. "Yes, but not enough. I want—"

She didn't finish. Priscilla pulled her close, kissed her again. Alaina groaned as Priscilla's hands slid under her shirt and pulled it over her head in one smooth motion. The cold air hit her skin and she shivered—then gasped as Priscilla's lips found her shoulder. Her own hands scrabbled at her pants, the urgency near frantic. They caught at her ankles, and Priscilla laughed into her neck, low and fond.

"Let me."

She leaned back, hands dragging down Alaina's thighs, freeing her from the fabric. The firelight cast shadows across the tent, flickering over Priscilla's face as her eyes dragged over Alaina's body—her bra, her hips, her bare skin. The intensity of it made Alaina's legs press together involuntarily.

When Priscilla took off her coat and reached for her own shirt, Alaina's breath caught. The slow reveal—one inch at a time—settled something in her. She wanted to remember this. Every inch of skin, every glance. Every moment Priscilla let herself be seen.

God, she was beautiful.

Priscilla's eyes found hers, pupils blown, cheeks flushed. Alaina reached for her. "Come here."

Priscilla kissed her again as their bodies slotted together. Alaina lasted maybe thirty seconds before shoving at Priscilla's pants with impatient hands. She needed to feel her. Skin to skin. Once they were gone, Alaina moved against her, needy and wet, riding the pressure of Priscilla's thigh. It wasn't graceful, or slow, just desperate friction that made her groan. She would've been embarrassed, but Priscilla clearly loved it, hands slipping under Alaina to pull her closer, to urge her on.

The tension built fast. Too fast. Every movement was a wave that broke before it could fully crash. No matter how she moved—angled her hips, arched into each press of Priscilla's mouth at her neck—it wasn't enough.

And Priscilla knew. Every time Alaina got close, she pulled back, slowed down, kept her dangling just out of reach.

It was torture. It was bliss. Alaina let her have it—until she couldn't.

She cupped Priscilla's jaw and kissed her deep. "I think I'll die if you don't touch me in the next thirty seconds."

Priscilla's nose brushed hers. A slow grin spread across her lips. "Always so dramatic."

But even as she said it, Priscilla's fingers traced delicately over Alaina's skin, leaving a trail of goosebumps rising in the cool air that surrounded them. They dragged over her neck, past the bump of her collarbone, skirted her ribs, and finally, finally settled near the waistband of her underwear.

"Fuck." Alaina couldn't stand it. "*Please.*"

It was a hot pant against Priscilla's mouth, one Priscilla wouldn't make her repeat.

"Sil," Alaina moaned when her fingers finally dipped lower. "Priscilla, god."

Priscilla didn't chide her, didn't lecture her on language, just covered Alaina's mouth with her own and silenced her in Alaina's new favorite way.

This had to be what heaven was like. She couldn't imagine there could ever be anything more divine than this.

Priscilla's touch was reverent. Certain. Like she already knew her—what made Alaina shiver, what made her break. Priscilla's fingers moved with aching precision, and Alaina arched into her, a sound catching in her throat as everything inside her began to unravel.

She couldn't hold back—not with Priscilla kissing her like

that, not with the firelight diffusing through the tent wall turning them both to gold, not with the way Priscilla held her like she was something rare. Something cherished.

Alaina came apart like a tide rolling in, slow at first, then swallowing her whole. She gripped Priscilla tight, trembling as the wave swept through her. Her face buried in the curve of Priscilla's shoulder, her name spilled from Alaina's lips again and again, muffled against bare skin.

Priscilla held her through it, her hands firm where they needed to be, gentle where they didn't. She kissed Alaina's temple, her hair, the hinge of her jaw. She murmured something Alaina couldn't catch—just breath and warmth and the quiet echo of her name.

When the world stilled, Alaina blinked up at the ceiling of the tent, heart pounding wildly off tempo. Priscilla was watching her, soft-eyed, lips parted.

Alaina didn't give her a chance to second-guess what just happened. She reached for her, pulled her close, and kissed her.

They lay tangled beneath blankets and sleeping bags, the fire outside dying to embers. Alaina rested her head on Priscilla's chest, listening to the steady rise and fall of her breath. Her fingers traced lazy shapes along her stomach. Neither of them spoke.

Alaina didn't know what tomorrow held—or next week, or next year. But lying there in the dark, she was certain. This didn't feel like the end of something.

It was the beginning.

Chapter Seventeen

One Day Until Christmas

Alaina woke to cold. The space beside her was empty, the sleeping bag cool where Priscilla should have been. Before falling asleep, they'd reluctantly dressed again—the mountain nights too frigid for anything else—and Priscilla had slipped outside to extinguish the last embers of their campfire. She'd returned with flushed cheeks, sliding into Alaina's sleeping bag, her chilled body seeking Alaina's warmth as they drifted off, wrapped around each other.

Now, the tent was too quiet. She expected the sound of Priscilla outside—zipping a bag, boiling water, something—but all she heard were morning birds. She propped herself up on her elbows, then startled.

Priscilla was huddled at the far end of the tent, knees drawn close, face creased in a tight frown, staring down at something in her hands.

"Sil?"

Priscilla's head snapped up.

"Sorry, I was just—" Priscilla's voice faltered, and she held up a phone—Alaina's phone—as if in confession. Alaina could just make out the gallery of memories on the screen—their photos from the past few days. "I couldn't sleep. I thought looking at the pictures from this week might help clear my mind."

"It's okay." Alaina felt a strange flutter in her chest—not anger at the invasion, but something tender at finding Priscilla studying their memories together in the quiet of the morning.

Alaina crawled out of the sleeping bag to join Priscilla. On the screen glowed their lakeside selfie—Priscilla radiant, her hair windswept, eyes catching the sparkle of the surrounding snow.

Alaina shifted her focus to the real Priscilla beside her, all mussed hair and kiss-swollen lips. On impulse, she leaned over and planted a quick, soft kiss on Priscilla's shoulder.

"You look beautiful in that one."

"So do you," Priscilla murmured, brushing a thumb near Alaina's face on the screen. Then she swiped the photo away, closed the app, and handed the phone back. "I'm sure they'll work."

Work?

Reality crashed over her like an icy wave.

The photos. The plan. Cole.

The List felt like something from another life now, like a faded Polaroid from someone else's vacation. For the first time since their breakup, Alaina saw the truth with perfect clarity: she didn't want Cole back. What she wanted was sitting right next to her, sleep rumpled and uncertain, living states away and somehow closer than anyone had ever been.

One week of knowing Priscilla had eased a lifetime of heartache. The timeline made her dizzy, but it was suddenly, blindingly obvious. The only thing that felt real was last night—the warmth of their breath mingling in the cool air, the gentle touch of Priscilla's fingers on her skin, the way they knew how to find just the right spot to—

Priscilla stood, ducking to avoid the tent ceiling.

"I'm going to start packing."

She snatched her coat and vanished through the flap.

Alaina scrambled to follow, finding her boots but not her coat. Where had they thrown the damn thing last night? Screw it. Some conversations outranked frostbite. She shoved her feet into unlaced boots and burst out into the biting cold.

Priscilla stood a few feet away, hands buried in her coat pockets, staring into the misty quiet. Goosebumps erupted across Alaina's skin as she stepped beside her, heart hammering against her ribs.

"What if I don't want them to work anymore?"

Priscilla narrowed her eyes. "What if you don't want *what* to work anymore?"

"The photos, the grand plan. Cole?"

Priscilla's face hardened. "You don't mean that. You did all this to get him back."

"Maybe I did. But I've never felt more like myself than I have this week." The confession poured out, unstoppable. "I've been chasing someone who wanted me to be different, when you make me feel like enough exactly as I am." Her voice cracked. "What if I want more of this? More of . . . us?"

Priscilla turned back to the trees. Her posture stiffened, gaze locked on somewhere distant.

"I don't think that's a good idea."

Alaina's heart twisted. "I— Why— Why not?" Her voice faltered. She hugged herself against the sudden chill in her chest.

"We're different people, Alaina." Priscilla sounded tired. "We want different things, and I don't—I can't give you what you want."

Alaina blinked. "How do you know what I want?" Her voice was ragged. "I'm still figuring that out myself."

Priscilla didn't answer.

Maybe the problem wasn't what Alaina wanted. Maybe the problem was that Priscilla didn't want *her.* It didn't add up perfectly—the woman who'd been caught memorizing their photos at dawn had to feel something for her. But rejection followed Alaina like a persistent ghost, materializing at every threshold she dared to cross. Here it was again, right on schedule.

"Tell me you didn't feel it too." Alaina's voice cracked as she stepped toward Priscilla, tears already blurring the edges of Priscilla's face. "Last night—this whole *week*—tell me it was all just in my head and I'll never mention it again."

The silence between them stretched thin.

This week had felt like a dream. Priscilla's friends adopting her without question. Warm nights spent under Priscilla's blankets. Fresh-brewed coffee waiting for her in the mornings. Last night . . .

But fairy tales always ended, didn't they? The clock struck midnight, the carriage turned back into a pumpkin, and Alaina turned back into unwanted baggage.

When Priscilla finally looked at her, her eyes shimmered with unshed tears. For a second, Alaina thought maybe—maybe—

"It doesn't matter." Priscilla's words fell between them like stones. "Last night shouldn't have happened."

And then Alaina understood.

It wasn't that Priscilla didn't want her.

It was that she'd already decided wanting her wasn't enough.

The fight drained from Alaina as quickly as it had surged. She hugged herself, a cross between a shiver and a sob wracking her body as a tear slipped down her cheek. "Right. Of course." She studied a pine needle by her boot. "Consider it forgotten."

"Alaina," Priscilla said, then paused, her words dying on her lips. Finally she murmured, "I'm sorry."

Of course she didn't feel the same. She'd told Alaina right from the start she didn't believe in love. At the time, Alaina had worried that Priscilla thought she was stupid for wanting love, and maybe she'd been right.

Somewhere far away, Alaina's rational brain knew that she wasn't unlovable, that there were people who wanted her around—she knew it in the way that Nico always made sure to buy her favorite cereal, or in how Priscilla's friends welcomed her in so easily. She felt it in the memories of her mother that she'd finally dug out from under a decade of grief.

But rejection had always spoken louder.

Her family, ceasing to text her even so much as a "happy birthday" the past few years. Cole, buying the wrong gemstone in the necklace he'd given her. And now Priscilla, looking at her with that soft expression Alaina recognized all too well—not love, but pity.

Nico would say she was catastrophizing again. That not everyone left. That someone would stay.

Something hot bloomed in Alaina's chest—anger, sharp and clean. Why was she always the one left behind? Why did she keep offering pieces of herself to people who didn't want them?

"Nothing to be sorry for." Alaina's voice was clipped and precise. "We're both adults. It's fine." She rolled her lips together, acutely aware of the unconvincing edge to her voice. "I'm going to go for a walk, clear my head a little."

She hesitated—just long enough to give Priscilla the chance to stop her, to say wait, to say anything. But Priscilla just turned away. "Don't go too far."

Alaina ducked back into the tent, fumbling for her coat under the sleeping bag that still smelled like both of them. Her fingers shook too hard to work the buttons. She blinked, and more tears spilled.

Alaina stumbled away from the campsite, wiping furiously at her face. The surrounding forest seemed to close in on her, the shadows of its towering pine trees stretching like accusing fingers in the morning light.

She leaned back against a tree, letting the bark bite into her spine. Tomorrow she'd fly to New York. Toward Cole. Toward the version of herself she'd built this entire trip around, the version that didn't fit anymore.

But what was her alternative? Stay in Utah with someone who didn't want her? Drive back to California with nothing but rejection riding shotgun?

She pressed her palms against her eyes. She'd go to New York because it was the only direction left. Because motion felt better than standing still. Because having a destination—any destination—meant she wasn't completely lost, even as the map of her heart had been redrawn overnight.

A fresh wave of anger swept through Alaina, fierce and hot. Her mother's voice—*you don't give up on love*—echoed bitterly in her ears. What a stupid mantra. If her mother hadn't chased that fantasy of love halfway across the country, if she hadn't uprooted them from everything safe, Alaina wouldn't have spent the last few years of her childhood untethered and alone. She wouldn't have had to grieve her mother's death with distant relatives who barely knew her.

How dare she teach Alaina to believe love was worth sacrificing everything for, when she knew better than anyone how much it hurt to be the one left behind?

Alaina drew in a shuddering breath, chest aching with a pain far older than this morning. Maybe love wasn't always worth it. Maybe sometimes the cost was too high.

When she returned, Priscilla offered her a granola bar. Alaina took it but couldn't stomach more than a few bites. They packed in silence. Alaina retreated inside the tent to roll up the sleeping bags, grateful for the wall between her and Priscilla, even if it was made of nylon. Tears burned behind her eyes, but she refused to let them fall again.

One thought replayed mercilessly in her head: she should have known better.

The walk back down the mountain was quiet. On occasion, Priscilla would wordlessly offer food, or allow Alaina to wander off by herself for a break without saying anything. Once or twice Priscilla would point something out—"Watch your footing," "It's a bit tricky," or, "There's some ice here, be careful"—but beyond that, their journey was marked by a resounding silence.

As the truck finally came into view, nestled between the trees at the foot of the mountain, a wave of relief washed over Alaina. She let out a sigh as she sank into the worn leather seat, glad to have a break from the wind.

Priscilla didn't start the truck. Her hands sat still in her lap. The silence inside was colder than the air outside. Alaina waited, staring at a small stain on the fabric of the glove box, an imperfection she'd never noticed in the otherwise immaculately kept truck.

"Alaina?" Priscilla's voice was hesitant. "Will you look at me? Please?"

Biting the inside of her cheek, Alaina reluctantly turned her head, willing her eyes to stay dry as they found Priscilla studying her with an intensity that made no sense coming from someone who'd dismissed her so completely just an hour ago.

"I'm sorry. I shouldn't have—"

Alaina didn't let her finish her sentence. "We don't have to do this."

Priscilla blinked, confused. "We don't?"

"I'm leaving tomorrow. What's the point?" The words came out sharper than she intended, and when Priscilla flinched, a small part of Alaina felt satisfied—then immediately awful.

Priscilla swallowed, her voice rough. "Right."

It felt like a year before Priscilla reached for her keys. As they pulled out of the parking lot, Alaina turned to stare out the passenger window, watching pine branches sway in the wind rather than facing that searching gaze boring into her profile. Even with Priscilla's eyes now mostly on the road, Alaina could feel her occasional glances like lightning on her skin.

She felt ridiculous for snapping at Priscilla like that, like her emotions were too big for her body, spilling over in ways she couldn't control. But it wasn't Priscilla she was angry with—it was herself.

For letting her heart open so easily, like some perpetually hopeful flower that never learned its lesson. For mistaking kindness for something deeper. For watching just about every person she'd ever loved vanish in the rearview mirror, and somehow still believing that this woman—this beautiful, impossible woman—might be the one who stayed.

Her phone buzzed with notifications the second they reached the road and signal returned.

The first was a text from Callie, probably sent sometime yesterday after they'd left the bookstore.

enjoy camping! can't wait to hear all about it!!!!

Then there were the Instagram notifications. A handful of likes from yesterday on the ice-skating photo she'd posted to her story, and a spam message asking her if she'd like to grow her Instagram account with 100 percent guaranteed followers for the low, low price of ten dollars. Nothing from Cole, and no more voicemails or texts from Shauna.

Alaina turned off her screen and leaned her head against the window. She didn't want to have to tell Callie what happened, or think about Cole or her family. She didn't even have the energy to block the spammer. Right now, all she wanted to do was cry, and she wasn't about to do that in front of Priscilla.

The tires crunched over the snow in the alley behind Brooks Books. Before Priscilla could even kill the engine, Alaina had her seatbelt off and door open, desperate to escape the suffocating silence that had accompanied them the entire drive back.

She paused just before reaching the entrance. Through the window, she saw the store packed with Christmas Eve shoppers. The checkout line stretched all the way to the back wall, Monica standing at the register.

Priscilla caught up, keys jingling in her hand. "I should help with this madness. You go on up."

Alaina hesitated. She could stay. Help with the rush. Distract herself. But the thought of standing next to Priscilla, pretending nothing had happened? Her stomach turned.

She nodded mutely and pushed the door open, navigating through the crowded maze of bookshelves, mind fixed on the promise of scalding water to wash away everything—pine needles, woodsmoke, and the ghost sensation of Priscilla's lips on her skin.

Under the spray of the shower, Alaina cranked up the heat until her skin bloomed angry red. Desperate, she tried counting the tiles on the wall to escape thoughts of Priscilla, but she was unable to stave them off for more than a moment, especially not with the smell of her shampoo filling the air. The scent was so distinctively Priscilla—that blend of bergamot and cinnamon. It enveloped Alaina, making her heart ache all the more.

She closed her eyes, the water cascading down her face, indistinguishable from the tears that had started to flow. She tried to focus on the physical sensations—the heat of the water, the steam surrounding her, the tiles cool and hard under her fingertips—in an attempt to ground herself.

She shut her eyes.

What am I doing?

Alaina knew she could be mad at Priscilla. She had every right, the rejection still stinging like antiseptic on an open wound. But anger took energy she couldn't spare, not with less than twenty-four hours left before her flight to New York.

The math was brutally simple: hold on to pride and lose Priscilla completely, or swallow the hurt and salvage what she could. Even if it was just friendship. Even if it was only a shadow of what they'd almost had.

She squashed the rising tide of hurt in her chest. This wasn't the kind of problem they could sort out over text once Alaina was back in her apartment in California. She needed to buck up before it was too late, before these precious final hours slipped through her fingers like sand. At this point, she'd take Priscilla in her life in any way she could get.

And then there was the Cole factor. She could revert to her original game plan: try to win him back. Maybe once she was back with him, she'd realize this was all a fluke—a temporary crush that would fade with distance, a projection of her feelings for Cole onto the nearest person.

The idea sat like a brick in her stomach as she washed the suds out of her hair, watching as they swirled down the drain.

Forty minutes later, unable to stand the silence of Priscilla's apartment, Alaina descended the stairs to the bookstore, pausing halfway down. With Priscilla there, the Christmas Eve crowd had thinned to a manageable trickle, just a few people left in line. Clark stood mid-aisle, arms full of books for an older woman who kept plucking more from the shelves. Monica was handling the pickup line. Behind the counter, Priscilla chatted with a customer, smile in place but not quite reaching her eyes.

Alaina positioned herself at a nearby display table, pretending to be intensely fascinated with a celebrity cookbook while sneaking glances at the register. Even after the last customer left the line, Priscilla didn't look up. She busied herself with straightening pens and adjusting a receipt roll, eyes skipping over every corner of the store but Alaina's.

So she'd have to make the first move.

Alaina approached the counter, heartbeat keeping time with her footsteps. She could do this. She could drag them back to something resembling normal. Her fingers tapped an anxious rhythm on the polished wood of the counter as she cleared her throat.

"Hey!" The word emerged too bright. She dialed it back. "I was thinking I'd go grab us some food."

Priscilla's head snapped up, surprise temporarily replacing her careful blank expression. "You were?"

She could understand Priscilla's confusion, with Alaina acting as if nothing had changed between them. It must have seemed like a drastic about-face, but Alaina was determined to keep the mood light.

"Anything in particular you want? I'm kind of starving after that hike."

They'd skipped breakfast, and she'd only had the few packets of trail mix Priscilla had offered as they descended.

Priscilla hesitated, her reply coming slowly. "No, I—anything you pick is fine."

"Cool, cool." Alaina nodded, rubbing her hands together. "So, can I borrow your truck? I promise not to crash it into any snowbanks."

"Oh, um—"

"I'm messing with you, Sil. I'll walk."

Priscilla breathed out a laugh, a small, uncertain smile working its way onto her lips. "All right."

Alaina glanced at the clock, seeing it was nearing two. "I'll be back in, like, a half hour? Forty-five?"

She was just guessing—she had no idea where she was going to go, just that she needed time to reset.

"Okay." Priscilla still sounded baffled. "Alaina, are you—are we—"

"We're good." It didn't feel true yet, but it could be, if she just tried hard enough. She backed away with a forced bounce in her step and a wave. "See you soon!"

She could do this. She could be normal. Everything was going to be fine.

❄

Alaina wandered aimlessly until the smell of coffee lured her into a corner café. The line moved slowly, giving her time to eye the chalkboard menu. She needed to bring back something more substantial than pastries, no matter how delicious the Danishes on the counter looked.

"Next!" the teenage barista called, pierced eyebrow rising as Alaina's eyes frantically looked for something to choose.

"Um—two ham-and-Swiss paninis, please. Oh, and a small black coffee, and . . . a bee sting?" She had no idea what that drink was, but it sounded like it would be sweet as honey. She gave the barista her name and drifted toward the back of the line to wait.

"Alaina?" a voice called from behind her.

She turned around to find—

"Lauren! Hi." Alaina froze, a smile stretching stiffly across her face. Was Lauren a hugger?

"Hello," Lauren said, not moving to close the distance between them. Definitely not a hugger. "How was your camping trip?"

Alaina wasn't sure how to answer that. She decided to aim for as close to the truth as she could manage without getting into the details. "It was beautiful up there."

"That's nice."

God, Lauren really wasn't giving her much to work with here. She had thought Lauren was finally starting to warm up to her the other night at Grant and Ned's house, but trying to have a conversation just the two of them was a whole different ball game.

Alaina clasped her hands behind her back, mirroring Lauren's straight posture. "How are you doing?"

"I'm well, thank you. And yourself?"

"Great! Very good. Just getting some lunch, coffee, you know the drill."

Lauren hummed in agreement. Alaina glanced back to the counter. How long did it take to heat up a fucking panini?

She turned back to Lauren. "So, um, are you guys ready for the party?"

"As ready as we can be. Callie looks forward to it every year. And I . . ."

"Enjoy making Callie happy?"

Lauren's mouth turned up in a smile. "You get it."

She did. Because Priscilla was the same way, happily indulging Alaina all week.

"I'm sure she appreciates it. I know I do, at least—with

Priscilla, I mean. Not that we're—we're not—" Alaina's face flushed. She hadn't meant to compare them to a real couple like Callie and Lauren, especially not after what had happened this morning. "Anyway, that's very sweet."

"Order for Alaina?"

Thank god.

Alaina reached for the bag and cup holder. When she turned around, Lauren was looking at her with a strange expression, eyes narrowed on the necklace Cole had given her, before flitting back up to her face.

Was it hot in here? Alaina was sweating.

"I'd better get these back to the store." Alaina held up the bag for emphasis. "Enjoy your lunch!"

"You too. Alaina?" Lauren said her name just as Alaina went to move past her, and she stopped maybe a bit too far into Lauren's personal bubble. "Callie is really happy you've gotten Priscilla to come around." Alaina took that to mean that Lauren was happy about it too. "We'll see you tonight?"

Alaina nodded. "Looking forward to it."

Chapter Eighteen

Brooks Books was chaos. Alaina stepped inside to find a second wave of Christmas Eve panic in full swing.

For a moment, Alaina just watched Priscilla behind the counter—the focused line between her brows, the way she tucked her hair behind her ear between customers, how her smile remained genuine despite the rush. Something snagged in Alaina's throat. This woman who'd rejected her hours ago still made her heart stutter like a scratched record.

She swallowed hard, shoved the feeling down, and slipped behind the counter, stashing their food in a safe corner.

She stepped up beside Priscilla, bouncing on her toes. "Hey, Sil. Put me to work."

Priscilla's head jerked, so focused on the task at hand that she hadn't noticed Alaina come up behind her. "You don't have to—"

"Tell me what you need, boss."

Priscilla hesitated, eyeing the growing line, then the pile of books customers had left at the register after deciding not to purchase them, then Alaina. A quick calculation played across her face.

"Have you ever worked a register before?" she asked, already reaching for the next customer's stack.

"Just the one at the restaurant. How different could it be?"

Priscilla made room for Alaina to slide in next to her. "Watch me do a few. Our system is a bit outdated, but it gets the job done."

Alaina observed as Priscilla rang up three customers, narrating steps in quiet asides. Scan the books, verify the price, apply any discounts, take the payment.

"Ready to try?" Priscilla asked as another customer stepped up, a teenage boy clutching a fantasy novel.

"Born ready," Alaina replied automatically.

A smile flickered across Priscilla's face before she rolled her lips together and stepped to the side.

Alaina ran the first transaction slowly, then a second, then a third. By the fourth, Priscilla let out a breath. "I think you've got this," she said, backing away. "I'll get to reshelving. If you need me . . ."

Her sentence trailed off. She reached for the books and darted away.

With Priscilla gone, oxygen returned to Alaina's lungs. She hadn't realized how much energy it took to pretend everything was fine, to stand next to her like her heart wasn't torn to bits.

The customers were friendly despite the long line. Christmas Eve brought out either the absolute best or the worst in people, with little middle ground. A few frosty tones were thrown her way by customers who hadn't found what they were looking for, or were unhappy with the wait time, but Alaina melted them with the same disarming smile she'd perfected over years of working for tips.

"Did you find everything okay?" she asked a particularly harried-looking woman who approached wearing a deep frown.

"No!" She said it so sharply it was almost as if she was insulted that Alaina had dared to ask. She held up a copy of *The Night Before Christmas*. "You only had this one in paperback. I need the hardcover."

Alaina glanced up, catching Priscilla's eye across the store. She held the book up, mouthing, "Hardcover?" Priscilla nodded once, already gliding toward a holiday display at the front of the store.

"We'll check on that for you," Alaina told the woman, ringing up the other items she'd brought to the counter until Priscilla appeared with the book.

The woman's entire demeanor changed when Priscilla handed it to her. "Oh, you're an angel!"

For the next twenty minutes, Alaina navigated the register solo until—

"You're running low on gift bags," she called out to Priscilla as she darted by. Alaina had just handed the last medium-sized one to a grateful man dressed in a blazer and tie who was on the way to his fiancée's family Christmas party. Clark had helped him find the perfect book about golf for his soon-to-be father-in-law.

"Behind the counter, second drawer," Priscilla answered without missing a beat.

"You're an angel!" Alaina said, parroting the woman earlier.

By the time the rush had died down, Alaina was sure their food was ice-cold. It was worth it to know that despite everything, they still clicked—two hands on a clock, working in sync.

After closing, Alaina retreated upstairs to get ready for the party. She pulled her black dress from her suitcase, the one she'd packed for New York, imagining a night out on the town.

How quickly things had changed.

In the bathroom, she checked her reflection—hair a little frizzy, circles under her eyes from the restless night. She turned to fix her necklace and froze.

Oh my god.

Just beneath the chain, on the slope of her neck, was a mark. Red. Faint, but obvious. A constellation of bruised blood vessels, clear evidence of last night.

Her hand flew to cover it. That's what Lauren had seen at the café.

Normally, Alaina wasn't the type of person to be embarrassed by these sorts of things. Sex wasn't something to be ashamed of. But after everything that had happened, the idea of Priscilla's friends knowing what they'd done put an uncomfortable knot in her stomach. She shook it off, hoping Lauren wouldn't say anything.

At the very least, there was no use worrying about it now.

Alaina slipped on the dress and fastened her earrings. She did her makeup carefully, dabbing concealer over the red mark on her neck without letting herself dwell on what had caused it. Her fingers hesitated at her necklace clasp. One last glance in the mirror, then she unhooked it, setting it on the counter. For the first time in months, her collarbone was bare.

Just for tonight, she told herself. She wanted to be in this moment, in this town, with Priscilla—without the weight of the past or the pressure of the future hanging around her neck.

Tomorrow she'd go back to Cole.

When Alaina stepped out of the bathroom, she felt like a whole new person—on the outside, at least. Inside, her nerves were still fluttering.

Priscilla stood in the kitchen, hands in her pockets. She wore a dark gray sweater with a red collared shirt underneath, her hair down in loose waves. Alaina's fingers itched to reach for it, to bury her hands in it. Instead, she curled them into fists.

Priscilla's eyes widened when they landed on her.

"You look . . ." Priscilla trailed off, and it was difficult to tell just which part of Alaina she was focusing on from this distance. "You look really nice."

"Thanks. You do too."

The silence stretched. Priscilla looked away. The space between them felt unbearable. If they were going to survive the night without falling apart, someone had to speak.

"I need to say—" Alaina said.

"We should probably—" Priscilla said simultaneously.

They both stopped. Alaina laughed nervously. Priscilla shook her head.

"I'm sorry," Alaina said.

"You go first," Priscilla said.

Alaina took a step closer. "This isn't how I want to spend our last night together."

Priscilla's face turned toward hers, her expression subtly shifting to one of concern. "Going to the party? We don't have to if you'd rather not."

"No. Not that."

"Oh." One word, soft and full of implication.

Alaina's heart climbed into her throat. She stepped close, just shy of touching her. She needed this to feel normal again—to pull them back to where they'd been before everything crashed and burned.

"I shouldn't have taken what you said this morning so personally." Alaina paused to inhale a deep breath, then sighed it away. "I knew how you felt before we—you told me yourself. You don't believe in love."

Priscilla flinched at the word, her shoulders tensing. Alaina realized what she'd inadvertently implied—*love.* Heat rushed to her face as she hurried to course correct.

"Not that I—I mean—" she stammered, waving her hands as if she could physically erase the word from the air. "I just meant that you were clear about your boundaries from the start, and I should respect that. I think we should enjoy the time we have left, yeah?"

Priscilla nodded once. "The time we have left. Just tonight then?"

"Yeah. We'll just . . . enjoy tonight."

And then she'd be gone.

Alaina had expected a small, intimate gathering. Instead, at least fifty people milled through the inn's festively lit lobby. The tree in the corner was at least twelve feet—Alaina was sure of it this time—and draped in so many twinkling fairy lights that it threatened to short-circuit the entire town's power grid. Garlands dripped from every available surface. Doorways, banisters, even picture frames had a small bit of greenery wrapped around them. The front desk had an army of nutcrackers standing at attention guarding a giant bowl of candy canes.

"Sil! Lani!" Callie appeared in a blur of red and green, arms wide. "I'm so glad you made it."

Grant was behind her. He wrapped Priscilla in a quick, one-armed hug before offering Alaina a handshake. "Good to see you again."

"You too." Alaina swept her gaze over the throng. "You know, when you said 'a little shindig,' I pictured . . . well, fewer people."

Callie laughed, bright and easy. "We throw it every year and invite practically the whole town. The more the merrier, right?"

The crush of bodies, the clinking glasses, the overwhelming scent of pine—it all pressed in on her.

"Where can a girl get a drink around here?"

Callie grinned and grabbed her hand. "Follow me."

Alaina let herself be dragged into the crowd, catching one last glimpse of Priscilla as Grant leaned in to speak to her.

When they reached the refreshment table—sugar cookies, peppermint bark, a punch bowl glowing an unnatural shade of red—Callie turned to her, eyes sparkling.

"I can't believe you actually got her to come. I feel like I've seen Priscilla more this week than I have in the past six months. Thank you!"

Alaina's smile felt heavy on her lips. "It wasn't hard. She really loves you guys. You should hear the way she talks about you all."

Callie softened. "I could say the same about you."

Alaina's hand hovered over the ladle. Priscilla had talked about her? When? What had she said?

She swallowed the follow-up questions burning on her tongue. A room crowded with strangers on Christmas Eve wasn't the place or time.

She busied herself pouring punch into two cups, praying it had enough alcohol to take the edge off the night.

"Lauren said she saw you earlier."

Alaina's face flushed, and she reached her hand toward her neck, fingers grazing the bruised skin.

She let her hand drop to pick up their cups. "Yeah, uh, we had just gotten back from our camping trip. I was grabbing lunch."

"That's right! How was camping?" Callie asked.

Alaina could tell Callie was digging for details about more than the camping logistics. "It was . . . nice."

Callie raised her brows, clearly unconvinced. When Alaina didn't elaborate, her expression softened. "Oh no. What happened? You look sad."

"I guess I am." Alaina's gaze found Priscilla immediately. Still near the door, still talking to Grant, looking calm, composed, like she hadn't ripped Alaina's heart out twelve hours ago.

"Priscilla and I, um—it's not going to work."

"What?" Callie sounded genuinely shocked. "Why? You two seem so—"

"It's complicated."

Callie nodded like she knew exactly what that meant. "She's being stubborn, huh?" She squeezed Alaina's arm. "I'm not going to tell you what to do, but . . . don't give up on her, okay?"

"I won't," Alaina said. Even if she wanted to, the hope in her heart wouldn't let her. No matter what happened next—if Cole took her back, or told her to get lost—she knew she'd still be thinking of Priscilla and all the ways this could've gone so much differently. The plan had morphed somewhere along the way, from a mission to win back her ex into something more desperate: a search for proof. That love could last. That it was worth it. That someone might choose to stay.

Callie's attention darted to the front of the room. "Oh! The Hendersons just arrived." She squeezed Alaina's arm, already backpedaling. Lauren was greeting the man who'd just walked in—Franklin, the guy who had sold Priscilla those beautiful ice skates. Alaina's heart twinged at the memory.

"Mingle! Have fun!" Callie called over her shoulder.

Alaina clutched both glasses of punch and took a deep breath. Right. Fun. She could do fun. Or at least fake it until the night was over.

She let her gaze sweep the room, cataloging familiar faces.

Clark stood near the back with Monica, laughing at something she'd said. Patty from the diner waved at someone across the buffet table. There was the guy Clark had pointed out as the owner of the hardware store, and the post office clerk she and Priscilla had made a delivery to that first day. She even recognized a few of the tourists who'd come through the bookstore that week.

For a moment, Alaina just stood there, absorbing it all—the town, the people, this life she'd stumbled into. A few weeks ago, her life had been so predictable. She was lounging in her tiny apartment, binge watching some forgettable reality show. The most complicated thing in her life had been deciding between buying groceries or saving up for rent, and debating whether to pick up an extra shift at work or finally indulge in a rare day off.

Then the breakup had knocked her completely off course. Crashing her car into that snowbank felt at first like a disaster, then a blessing, and now? Now she wasn't sure if it was either, and—

Her thoughts stilled as her eyes found Priscilla across the room. She and Grant stood tucked into a quieter corner. Priscilla glanced up, catching Alaina's gaze. The second their eyes locked, everything else dropped away. The noise faded, the crowd blurred—it was just her and Priscilla and the breath that caught sharp in her throat.

With Cole, Alaina was always chasing the feeling of being understood. She'd felt wanted, sure—she knew he found her pretty enough to show her off to his followers, or funny enough to bring to parties—but never seen. Never this bone-deep recognition that made every cell in her body simultaneously relax and stand at attention.

Priscilla's mouth turned up in a smile, small and subtle and unquestionably for her, and just like that, Alaina was drawn back in. Alaina moved toward her like the decision wasn't hers to make. As if the gravity between them decided for her.

By the time Alaina reached them, Grant and Priscilla were speaking more intently. Alaina slowed when she caught the tail end of a sentence, Priscilla's voice clipped and tense. When she looked up and saw Alaina approaching, something shuttered in her expression. She turned away from Grant with a terse "Just—forget it."

Alaina sidled up next to Priscilla, handing her the cup of bright-red punch. Priscilla took it wordlessly and knocked back half in a single sip.

Maybe Alaina wasn't the only one hoping to drown some feelings tonight.

"Everything okay?" Alaina asked quietly.

Grant gave a nod. "Yeah. Perfect. Your car is fixed."

She blinked. Priscilla's jaw tightened just enough to betray her discontent. Had she been hoping the repairs would take longer? That Alaina might have to stay after she got back? That they'd have more time?

"Oh," she said. "That's convenient timing, I guess."

"Yes." Priscilla's voice was sharp enough to sting. "You can pick it up when you get back from New York."

Back from New York—with or without Cole. Would Priscilla still want to be in her life if she got back together with him? Would Alaina still want Priscilla in hers? After all, it was undeniable that her feelings for Priscilla went far beyond friendship. That wasn't exactly setting the stage for rekindling her romance with Cole—if that was still what she wanted.

The thought left a hollow ache behind her ribs.

"Great," she said. She cleared her throat, turning to Grant. "How much do I owe you?"

"It's on the house."

Alaina's eyes widened. "What? No, I can't let you—"

"It's fine, Alaina," Priscilla said, her eyes locked on to Grant's.

Something simmered under the surface, but Alaina wasn't about to dig. Not here. Not now. "Thank you," she said instead. "That's really kind."

Priscilla scoffed and looked the other way until Grant disappeared into the crowd.

Alaina leaned in, lowering her voice. "Are you okay?"

Priscilla chewed her lip for a moment before answering. "Yes. I'm sorry. I'm being unpleasant."

"You could never, not to me."

Priscilla drained the rest of her punch in a long sip. Alaina's eyes followed the motion of her throat, lingering too long before darting away, her face feeling flushed. She knew exactly what that skin tasted like. What sounds Priscilla made when Alaina's teeth grazed it.

She swallowed the thought. "Will you dance with me?"

Priscilla looked unsure. "I'm not much of a dancer."

"Come on—you can't tell me your parents didn't have you in, like, prenatal ballroom dance classes or something."

"This is hardly a ballroom, Alaina," Priscilla said, but she cracked a smile, and the vise around Alaina's heart loosened, if only a little.

Priscilla took her hand, and the contact sent a jolt through her. After everything—last night, this morning—just that simple touch lit her nerves on fire.

The music that filtered through the speakers was a slow song, a deep-voiced crooner singing about snowfall, or jingle bells, or something else Alaina couldn't focus on. She stepped into Priscilla's space, her arms around her neck, breath catching when Priscilla's hands found her waist.

They moved without talking. One song, then another. Priscilla had been wrong—she was clearly comfortable on the dance floor, leading with a gentle confidence.

When the third song started up, Alaina couldn't keep her thoughts to herself any longer.

"Your hair looks pretty down," Alaina murmured, brushing a loose strand back from Priscilla's face. Her hand hovered, then settled on Priscilla's cheek.

Priscilla leaned into the touch. The contact sent a shiver through Alaina. She ran her tongue between her lips, her mouth suddenly dry. "Sil?"

Their eyes met, and for a moment Alaina let herself drown in memories—the feeling of Priscilla's lips on hers, the intoxicating blend of desire and confusion. The room around them, the party, all their problems, dissolved, leaving only the desperate need to have Priscilla's lips on hers once more. She was drawn in, the gap between them narrowing until—

Her lips pressed against Priscilla's cheek. Priscilla had turned her head. Alaina froze there, her mouth against Priscilla's skin, her heart thundering in a sudden panic. She rocked back on her heels, her arms quickly dropping to her side as she propelled herself backward.

"Alaina, I—" Priscilla's head shook side to side, almost imperceptibly, like rejection was a blow she couldn't quite bear to deal to Alaina yet another time. "We shouldn't."

Alaina wanted to be swallowed by a hole. Shame, sharp and immediate, burned through her. The room spun. Her vision tunneled.

"I'm sorry, I need some air." She didn't wait for a response. Just turned and pushed through the crowd.

Outside on the porch, the heaters blasted warmth, but Alaina barely felt them, her body shaking. She pressed her hands to her burning cheeks and tried to breathe.

God, why had she done that? Priscilla had been clear this morning—she didn't want anything more. And still, Alaina had leaned in, practically begging for heartbreak.

"Alaina?" Priscilla called from behind her.

She dropped her clenched fists to her sides, eyes fixed on the snow beyond the covered porch. She didn't turn.

Priscilla's hand landed gently on her shoulder. "Please. Look at me."

Alaina did, but she wasn't sure what to say. She could apologize for her behavior, for pushing. She could get mad at Priscilla for letting it get this far if she didn't feel the same way. Instead, her voice cracked like thin ice under too much weight.

"Why can't we just *try*?"

Priscilla blinked. "Try what?"

Alaina bit back a sharp laugh. For someone who devoured complex literature daily, Priscilla was playing deliberately obtuse.

"This. Us. Making it work." Her pulse thudded in her ears. "People do long distance all the time. Or I could—I could move here. Not right away, but—"

"Alaina." Priscilla rubbed a hand over her face, and something in Alaina shut down. She'd said too much, handed Priscilla her whole heart, and Priscilla couldn't even look at it.

"I told you. There wouldn't be a point. I'm not . . . I can't be what you need."

Something hot flared behind Alaina's ribs. "And what exactly do you think I need?"

Priscilla looked away, stepping toward the railing like distance could spare them both. Alaina followed.

"Priscilla—"

Priscilla spun to face her, frustration flashing in her voice. "You're leaving tomorrow, Alaina."

"I don't have to. I could stay."

"For how long? A week? Two?" The words were said without any warmth, reminding Alaina of the Priscilla she first met—bristling and cold. Then she sighed, the storm passing as quickly as it came. "We live different lives. You want adventure. Spontaneity. Cole. Not to be stuck in some small town with—"

She clamped her mouth shut so fast Alaina almost heard the click.

The unfinished sentence hung in the air: *with me.*

After a beat, Priscilla scoffed, a short, bitter sound. "—with nothing to do."

Alaina shook her head. "There's more to it than that. There's something you're not saying."

"There isn't."

Alaina took another step closer, grateful when Priscilla didn't retreat this time. "I know you, Priscilla. You might not think so, but I do."

"You've known me for a week. You don't—"

"I do." The certainty in her voice surprised even herself. "I just want to know why. I know you feel this too. You can't tell me you don't."

Priscilla didn't hesitate. "I do. Of course I do."

The admission should have been a victory. Instead, it lacerated something vital in Alaina's chest. "Then why? Why can't we—"

Priscilla's jaw tightened visibly. "Because it wouldn't last. It might seem good at first, when it's all shiny and new. But there'll come a time when that wears off, and it would all come crashing down, and—"

"It might. You're right, it might. But it might not." Alaina stepped closer. Priscilla didn't move. "I'm willing to take that risk."

She knew Priscilla had been hurt before—by her parents, by her ex. Alaina could see those old wounds reflected in Priscilla's eyes, familiar enough to recognize because she had matching ones of her own. But that was the difference between them—Alaina still believed those scars could heal. She believed in love. And she knew Priscilla could too. All Alaina needed was a chance.

A sudden cheer erupted inside. Through the window, they could see Callie standing on a chair, raising her glass.

Priscilla took a step back. "We should go in."

Alaina's fingers curled around Priscilla's wrist. "Priscilla—"

"Lani. Stop." The nickname sliced straight through her. When Priscilla spoke next, her voice was resigned. "We said we'd enjoy the night."

Her eyes were pleading, and it broke something in Alaina. Priscilla had made her choice.

Alaina wasn't a risk worth taking.

"You're right." Alaina let go, the loss of contact immediate and brutal. "Let's go."

Callie's voice echoed across the lobby as they reentered the party.

"—for coming here every year and sharing this night with us. We know Christmas is a time we like to share with family, and that's what all of you are. So to our friends—old and new—" Callie spotted Alaina in the crowd and raised her glass. "Happy holidays!"

Chapter Nineteen

For the rest of the night, Alaina drifted through the party like a specter: the Ghost of Christmas Faux Pas. She caught Callie casting worried glances her way, brows drawn together in concern. Alaina felt the weight of them but couldn't summon the energy to pretend everything was okay.

Eventually, it was time to say goodbye.

Grant was first, offering her another firm handshake. "Take care, Alaina. It was good to meet you."

Then came Callie and Ned, each pulling her into warm, sincere hugs. Callie lingered. "I hope we see you again."

Lauren came next, surprising her by stepping forward with her arms out. "If you ever find yourself back this way, you know where to find us. You could even stay at the inn next time—*if* you have a reservation."

As they pulled away, Alaina was left with a bittersweet taste in her mouth. She had found something special here, a connection she hadn't expected. But now that it was time to say goodbye, she felt more alone than ever.

Alaina's throat tightened. She looked between them—Callie,

Lauren, Grant, Ned—and smiled sadly. "I know it sounds ridiculous after a week, but . . . you guys feel like real friends. I haven't felt this comfortable with new people in . . ." She trailed off, then added quietly, "I don't want this to be goodbye. Maybe we could keep in touch?"

"Oh my god, yes!" Ned lit up. "I'm adding you to our group chat. It's mostly me and Callie talking to ourselves while everyone else lurks, so you'll be a welcome addition."

Callie pulled her into one last hug before they stepped out into the night.

Five minutes later, the truck's engine hummed softly as they made their way down the winding roads, the world outside bathed in the soft glow of the truck's headlights. The silence inside the vehicle was almost tangible, heavy and awkward. Every so often, she could feel Priscilla glance over.

"Thank you for coming tonight," Priscilla said finally.

Alaina turned her head to look at Priscilla. She tried to smile, but it felt forced. "Yeah, it was . . . nice."

There wasn't much else she could say without dragging the conversation back to the one neither of them wanted to have.

Priscilla's hands tightened on the steering wheel. Desperate to fill the void, Alaina reached for the radio dial. The familiar strains of Priscilla's grandmother's Christmas collection filled the truck, the same CD they had listened to on their drive up the mountain. She cranked up the volume, hoping to drown out her thoughts with the swell of violins.

❄

The apartment felt eerily silent as they entered. Alaina normally would feel a need to smooth things over, but she'd embarrassed herself enough for one night. She knew when something was a lost cause.

"I'm going to change," she mumbled, heading for the bathroom.

The cool tiles beneath her feet sent a shiver up her spine as Alaina shut the bathroom door. She leaned against it, chest tight, fists clenched at her sides. Her breath caught. With a slow exhale, she tried to steady her heartbeat, but it was useless. She braced her hands on the sink and breathed out, slow and shaking. She turned on both taps, hoping a few minutes alone would be enough to pull herself together.

When she reemerged, the living room was empty, the door to the bedroom closed. Alaina eyed the small stack of bedding perched on top of the couch, unused since her third night here. Was that really the last time she hadn't slept at Priscilla's side? She moved forward, ready to transform the couch into a bed for the evening, knowing she wouldn't do anywhere close to as good a job as Priscilla had. She couldn't bring herself to care.

"Alaina?"

Priscilla stood in the bedroom doorway.

"You don't have to sleep out here."

Alaina hesitated. "Do you really think that's a good idea?"

It took a few seconds for Priscilla to answer. "I'm not sure."

Neither of them moved. Logic told Alaina to decline. That it would be smarter, safer, less painful. But time was running out. She didn't want to spend their final night apart.

She stepped forward, and Priscilla's breath released audibly. She turned, retreating into the bedroom, and Alaina followed.

Alaina slipped under the sheets, the cool cotton raising goosebumps along her skin. Priscilla joined her a beat later, careful to keep space between them.

They lay still for what felt like hours. Alaina watched the ceiling, every breath too loud, her heartbeat too sharp. The ache behind her ribs refused to settle, and she kept shifting, unable to get comfortable.

Eventually, the sheets rustled.

Priscilla didn't ask if Alaina was still awake—she didn't need to. Her restlessness was answer enough.

"Are we still okay?" Priscilla asked.

Were they still *okay*? What did that even mean?

Obviously they weren't okay—Alaina's heart was broken. She'd put herself out there, and Priscilla had shot her down. Like, all the way down. But still, she couldn't find it in her to be angry.

She was just sad.

Sad that Priscilla had been burned so many times that she couldn't trust something good when it was right in front of her. Sad that Alaina had let herself believe, just for a second, that this could be different. That she might be different.

Sad that she wasn't worth the risk.

Alaina thought of the promise she'd made to herself just last night beneath a sky full of stars—how she never wanted to hurt Priscilla. How she wanted to stay. Now, she could feel Priscilla already bracing to add her to the list of people who left.

She reached out in the dark until her fingers found Priscilla's.

"We're okay," she said. Her voice was steadier than she felt. "Or . . . we will be."

Priscilla's breath shook on an inhale and lodged somewhere deep in her chest before she spoke in a whisper. "I'm sorry. I wish I could—I wish that things were different."

"Me too."

Alaina thought back to their first night in this bed, when Priscilla had said love took courage. At the time, Alaina hadn't believed her. Now, she knew better.

That night, as she fell asleep, she wished Priscilla would be brave too.

❄

For the first time, when Alaina woke, Priscilla was still beside her.

She'd never gotten to really look at Priscilla while she slept, until now. Sure, she'd woken up in the middle of the night once or twice—but it was dark, and Priscilla's face was nothing but a shadow. Here, in the soft morning light, Alaina could appreciate her.

The soft curve of Priscilla's cheek. Her lashes, dark and delicate against her skin. The faint mark where Alaina's teeth had pressed just under her jaw. It felt like a miracle and a punishment all at once. A final glimpse before the lights came back on and the dream ended.

They'd stay friends. They could do that, couldn't they?

When Priscilla stirred, Alaina didn't look away. Their faces were only inches apart. For a moment, all they did was breathe. A subtle shift played across Priscilla's lips once she opened her eyes, a hint of a smile that made Alaina's heart dance.

"How long have you been awake?"

Alaina's own smile grew at the drowsiness in Priscilla's voice. "I lost track. But, hey—Merry Christmas."

"Happy Christmas to you too."

"Or that, sure." Priscilla laughed, and Alaina cherished the sound. "Do you mind if we just stay here for a while?"

Priscilla didn't ask why. She didn't say anything at all, just nodded, her eyes never leaving Alaina's as she reached for her hand.

❄

When they finally climbed out of bed, Alaina pulled back the curtain and gasped. "Oh, wow." She leaned in closer. "It's snowing."

She felt Priscilla move up beside her, close but not quite touching. Alaina wished she'd reach out—wrap her arms around her, press close the way she had before—but instead, she focused on the view.

"It's pretty magical, isn't it?" Alaina said. "A white Christmas."

Something warm brushed against her ankles. She glanced down to see Lola winding around her legs, tail flicking as she purred and nudged her shin.

Alaina laughed and crouched to pet her. "Of all the times to warm up to me, huh?"

"Cats are funny like that." Alaina raised her eyes to find Priscilla watching them with a smile. "What would you like for breakfast?"

"Oh—I don't know, cereal?" She didn't want to make more work for Priscilla, not when she was going to spend her Christmas driving Alaina to the airport.

"No." Priscilla shook her head. "It's Christmas. We have to make something special."

That made Alaina smile. A week ago, Priscilla wouldn't have said that.

"Do you know how to make French toast?"

In the kitchen, Priscilla broke out an old copy of *Joy of Cooking*. "Seems manageable."

Alaina brewed some coffee, then added a dash of cinnamon to each cup—a hint of festive cheer, even if her heart refused to get into the spirit. She turned her phone volume up as loud as it could possibly go and selected her Christmas playlist. Priscilla didn't try to hide her smile.

The music couldn't drown out the thought that was playing on repeat in Alaina's head, over and over and over—*I'm going to miss this.* She thought it when Priscilla tapped her foot to the music—barely perceptible, like she didn't even know she was doing it. She thought it again when Priscilla bent to check the French toast, frowning when one corner stuck to the pan. And she felt it in full force when Priscilla turned, offered her a syrup-drenched test bite on a fork, and waited for her to take it.

I'm going to miss this.

I'm going to miss her.

After breakfast, Priscilla told Alaina to wait on the couch while she grabbed something. When she reappeared, she was holding a small package wrapped in plain brown paper, a red ribbon tied neatly around the center.

"Priscilla, you shouldn't have—"

"I wanted to. It's a small thing, don't worry."

Alaina peeled back the edges, careful not to tear the wrapping. Inside was a white box. She glanced up at Priscilla before lifting the lid.

When Alaina opened the box, she couldn't help the smile taking over her face as she pulled a black trapper hat out of the tissue paper. "Oh my god."

It was just like Priscilla's, and Alaina's heart swelled. She put it on immediately, tugging the flaps tight over her ears, the same way she had the first night they met. "How does it look?"

Priscilla's smile spread slowly. "Great."

"I've always wanted one of these." Alaina wanted to run to the bathroom to look at herself in the mirror, but that would mean losing this moment with Priscilla. "Thank you. It's perfect."

"I thought you could use it on your adventures," Priscilla said. She reached out to straighten it on Alaina's head. "I wouldn't want you freezing to death in a snowdrift."

Alaina's laughter was a reflex, but it faltered.

Christmas at Aunt Doreen and Uncle Craig's had been careful exchanges of gift cards and practical items—sweaters with patterns she'd never choose, flower-scented bath sets that made her sneeze. They'd tried, she knew that now, but the gifts always felt like obligations wrapped in festive paper. Safe choices that required no real knowledge of who she was or what she loved.

Nico didn't believe in presents—they preferred to "share experiences" for birthdays and holidays—and Cole had only bought her one real present during their relationship that wasn't chocolate or flowers, and that was the necklace—beautiful, expensive, but wrong.

But this? She didn't know how to handle this level of thoughtfulness.

"Thank you." She leaned in and wrapped her arms around Priscilla, careful not to hold on too long even though every part of her wanted to. When they pulled apart, Priscilla's hand lingered in hers. Alaina squeezed it once before letting go.

"I got you something too."

"Alaina, you didn't have to—"

"I really did, though. Hold on."

Letting go of Priscilla's hand and dropping to her knees, she reached beneath the couch, rummaged around, and then triumphantly held up the small, shiny bag.

Handing it over, Alaina felt her pulse quicken, her experiences with gift giving—or the lack thereof—suddenly at the forefront of her thoughts. It wasn't that she didn't *want* to find the perfect present for friends or loved ones, but rather that she simply hadn't gotten much practice.

Alaina's fingers twisted together in her lap, the rhythm of her heart an erratic drumbeat as Priscilla reached into the bag. The tissue paper crinkled softly as she pushed it aside. Her fingers found something solid, rectangular.

She pulled out a matte black frame.

Priscilla's breath caught. Inside the glass was the photo of her, Alaina, and her four friends in front of the Christmas tree they'd decorated down in the store. All of them laughing, faces bright with joy.

Alaina watched Priscilla stare down at it, her nerves building up in silent suspense until she couldn't stand it any longer. "I was thinking you could hang it on your wall with the others. If you wanted, of course."

When Priscilla looked up, there were tears gathered in her eyes and her lip was quivering. She bit into it to stop its tremble. Alaina's hand moved without thought, cupping her cheek. Priscilla closed her eyes, breathing through the moment, and when she opened them again, her tears were gone.

"Thank you," she whispered.

Alaina nodded, letting her hand drop. "Something to remember me by."

It was the wrong thing to say, Alaina knew instantly. Priscilla's face cracked open in the smallest, saddest way.

Priscilla's gaze dropped. "Right."

"Priscilla." Alaina squeezed her hand. "Sil, look at me. I didn't mean it like that, okay? I just meant—it's a keepsake. I'll be back."

Priscilla nodded once. "For your car."

"And for you."

The words were a tightrope stretched between them. Neither was willing to cross it.

Priscilla broke first, clearing her throat as she dropped her gaze. "We should get ready to go."

Alaina only nodded.

Her heart was heavy as she packed her bag. It didn't take long—half the week, she'd been living in borrowed clothes. She tucked the children's book Priscilla had given her and her new hat into the suitcase with care, each item a small piece of the life she'd stumbled into. When she zipped it closed, the sound was louder than it should have been. Final.

Priscilla busied herself with the dishes, avoiding eye contact. When Alaina stepped out of the bathroom, showered and ready, Priscilla was just standing there—hands buried in her pockets, staring at the floorboards.

"Ready?" Alaina's voice didn't seem to draw Priscilla out of her thoughts. She moved closer. "Sil?"

This time, Priscilla slowly looked up at Alaina, her eyes coming into focus as she registered her presence. "Yes. Let's go."

She grabbed Alaina's suitcase, and Alaina followed, suddenly aware that every step pulled her farther from what they could have been.

At the door, Priscilla paused, her hand lingering on the knob for a beat too long.

"Hey." Alaina reached forward, placing her hand over Priscilla's. She didn't have any words planned—she just needed this moment to last a second longer. "I'm really glad I met you."

Priscilla sucked in a breath, one half of her mouth turning upward in an attempt at a smile, doomed from the start by the sadness in her eyes. "Come on. You're going to miss your flight."

Priscilla was right there in front of her, and Alaina couldn't do anything but let her go.

❄

The truck was cold, Alaina's skin never warming even with the heat blasting from the vents. As Priscilla drove them to the airport, the tension between them was palpable, like a thick fog clouding the cab. They both knew what was coming. The goodbye neither wanted—at least, Alaina didn't. Maybe Priscilla would be relieved, finally able to return to her quiet life.

That's just your broken heart talking, Alaina reminded herself. Priscilla wanted to be friends. She'd said so.

As they pulled into the short-term lot, dread sank into Alaina's bones.

She sat there, staring at the dashboard, until Priscilla's soft "hey" drew her gaze. She looked up to find Priscilla, already out of the truck, peering through the open door at Alaina.

"You ready?"

"As I'll ever be."

The airport was quiet for Christmas Day. Priscilla carried Alaina's bag to the security line, silent at her side. A sign at the front of the line read: ONLY TICKETED PASSENGERS PAST THIS POINT.

This was it. The end of the road.

"Here we are." Priscilla's words echoed her own thoughts. "I guess this is—"

"Don't—don't say it." Alaina's throat constricted. She couldn't hear Priscilla say goodbye.

"O—kay?" Priscilla said, her voice soft with uncertainty. Her face shifted, vulnerable in a way Alaina rarely saw. "Alaina . . ."

Alaina's heart leapt, foolishly hopeful.

Instead, Priscilla exhaled, steadying herself. "Safe travels."

Alaina's hope splintered. She ducked her head to hide her

disappointment. "Yeah, yeah. Don't talk to strangers, be aware of my surroundings, I know."

"Do you really?" When Alaina looked up, Priscilla's eyebrows were raised in playful challenge. "Because I recall you talking to at least one stranger."

A smile tugged at Alaina's lips despite everything. "Well, that turned out pretty okay, didn't it?"

"Yeah, it did." Priscilla's gaze held a warmth that made Alaina's chest clench.

Alaina tried for levity. "Well, this is your last chance." Priscilla's eyes widened, and Alaina realized how that sounded. She just *had* to seize her one final opportunity to stick her foot into her mouth, she supposed. "To, uh—kill me. You know, since you're an ax murderer and all."

Priscilla's laugh was forced. "Right. Of course."

Alaina took a step forward. There were only a few people left in line in front of her. They were out of time. "Thank you again."

Alaina stepped up on her toes, and Priscilla dropped the handle of Alaina's suitcase to meet her. The hug was lacking in so many ways—their bodies didn't press together like she wanted them to, Priscilla's grip was not tight enough, all comfort missing from the embrace—but Alaina nonetheless had to peel herself away from it.

"I'll let you know when I land, okay?"

Priscilla nodded, taking a step away from the line, then another. The distance grew, and with it so did Alaina's need to cry. She'd save that for when she was alone—right now, she wanted to use every bit of her energy to memorize the sight of Priscilla standing there.

"Next," the TSA agent called, and Alaina turned and walked away.

Well, sort of.

She made it all of four steps before she spun around. Priscilla's eyes were still on her, and she watched as Priscilla's chest rose with a sharp inhale. She shot forward, throwing her arms back around Priscilla in a tight squeeze.

Alaina buried her face in the curve of Priscilla's neck, gripping the fabric of her coat, already damp with melting snow. "I'm really going to miss you." The words came out muffled. This whole week had felt like a dream—one she was afraid would vanish the second she stepped back into her old life.

Get it together.

"You'll be back after the New Year." Priscilla's voice was soft against Alaina's ear. "Maybe we could get dinner."

"Maybe?" Alaina pulled back to look at her. "Like you could keep me away. I know where you live, you know."

That earned a smile—soft, real. Priscilla lifted her hand to brush Alaina's cheek, her thumb just grazing the damp skin below her lashes. If she noticed the tears, she didn't mention them. Just held Alaina's gaze, her own throat working. "I'll hold you to that."

"Miss!" The TSA agent's voice snapped from behind her, sharp with impatience.

Alaina didn't flinch. She didn't even look away. Instead, she waved vaguely to let the next person go around her.

"Happy Christmas." Priscilla leaned in. Alaina's heart launched itself against her ribs. But Priscilla's lips only landed softly on her cheek, and somehow that small, steady kiss undid her more than anything else could have.

Alaina squeezed her eyes shut, trying to hold on to the moment for just a little longer.

Then Priscilla stepped back. The cold hit her immediately.

Alaina opened her eyes. The distance between them felt insurmountable now.

"Merry Christmas," she whispered.

Priscilla gave a tight nod, her smile small and brittle.

Then she turned and walked away.

Chapter Twenty

"Ma'am!"

The shout jolted Alaina from her daze. Priscilla had disappeared from view, and she was now face-to-face with an unimpressed TSA agent.

"Either you get up here or get in the back of the line."

Under normal circumstances, Alaina would have apologized profusely. Right now, the lump in her throat was too large to try to speak around, so she just nodded and moved forward.

After passing through security, she made her way through the terminal and over to her gate, dragging her luggage behind her glumly, feeling much like a character out of Charlie Brown with her head hung low.

She slumped into a chair near the window, her gaze locking on to the plane that would take her to New York. She reached for the comfort of her necklace—only to touch her shirt.

Her heart stuttered. Where—?

Then she remembered. The bathroom counter. Back at Priscilla's.

Her hand fell uselessly into her lap, her mind racing.

What was she going to do when she arrived in New York? The obvious answer was to look for Cole. She could send him a text once she was on the ground. It wasn't exactly the big movie moment she'd had in mind at the beginning of the week, but she was out of time to make a better plan, and she wasn't even sure she wanted one anymore. She'd loved him once, but now the feeling was distant. Maybe it would rush back in when she saw him.

Needing distraction, she picked up her phone and scrolled through her photo gallery. It wasn't until she saw all the pictures Priscilla had taken—candids between posed smiles, shots where she looked truly happy—that her throat tightened.

She'd left more than her necklace behind. She'd left a piece of herself with Priscilla.

Alaina quickly selected two photos she hadn't posted yet—a shot Priscilla had taken of her careening down the hill on her skis, and the video Callie had taken from the lodge—and sent them to her story.

Then she came to the group photo. The one from in front of the tree, the one she'd printed and framed for Priscilla. Her thumb paused over it. She zoomed in on her and Priscilla—smiling, laughing, her head on Priscilla's shoulder, Priscilla's hand gently on her back.

She carefully framed their joy-filled faces, the tree twinkling softly in the background, added a tiny heart to the corner, and posted it.

Sure, she might not have a lot of followers compared to her influencer ex, but there was still something nice about posting a photo of the two of them. It made the past week feel like less of a fever dream and something more real.

The ache behind her ribs spread like wildfire. Her head

tipped back against the wall, eyes squeezed shut as if she could hold back the tears that way. It didn't work.

How had she gone from the best Christmas she'd ever had to the worst in twenty-four hours?

An intercom crackled to life above her. "Now calling all passengers in boarding group A."

Alaina glanced at her boarding pass displayed on her screen. A glaring C7 stared back at her. Her phone buzzed. An Instagram notification slid across the top of the screen.

colememaybe liked your story.

Alaina stared at the notification, unmoving.

Another one popped up a second later: colememaybe sent you a message.

Cole: hey
Cole: where have you been? looks awesome
Cole: do u think we can talk

Alaina's finger hovered, then clicked on the image that brought up Cole's profile. A new highlight reel labeled NEW YORK caught her eye, framed by fireworks emojis. She clicked.

Clips flickered by—cocktails in dim bars, rooftop selfies, a panorama of Times Square. All from the past week. None of which had shown up on her feed when she was checking for signs of life. Cole had shown her once how to hide your stories from people without blocking them, so they wouldn't know they were missing anything.

Now he'd done that to her.

Most of the photos and videos were shots of him holding out a can of PowerPunch, so it wasn't like she'd missed all that much, but that wasn't the point.

The point was: he'd chosen to shut her out. And now, suddenly, he was back—liking her stories, sliding into her DMs.

Her plan had worked.

Alaina exited the app. Hit the power button. Stashed her phone in her pocket like it burned.

Then she stood.

She grabbed her suitcase and walked away from the gate, each step sharper than the last. Her heart thudded hard and fast, not with nerves—with clarity.

It had taken her the entire week to realize, but she hadn't done anything wrong the day Cole had sprung the New York trip on her. He knew how much this holiday meant to her—she'd been unable to keep her excitement at bay for weeks before. He shouldn't have expected her to give it up at the snap of PowerPunch's fingers.

He didn't care about what she wanted. The first time she'd said no to him, the moment she didn't fold herself into the shape of his expectations, he walked. And somehow, she'd convinced herself she was the one who needed to change.

But after just a week with Priscilla, she knew better.

Better was mugs of hot chocolate with piles of whipped cream, pancakes and French toast and coffee sweetened to perfection. Better was an arm to hold when her feet were unsteady, a hand in hers, a friend by her side. Better was spontaneous snowball fights, sugar cookies, secrets shared under the stars.

Better was Priscilla.

And even if Priscilla wasn't an option, Alaina didn't want Cole. Just a week ago, she'd thought she wasn't good enough for him. That she had to prove herself worthy of his love. But that was all wrong. He was the one who wasn't good enough for her.

So no, Alaina didn't want Cole.

She wanted love. The kind her mother had told her about when she was young—the kind you fight for. Her mother had believed in it. Alaina believed in it. And now, more than anything, she wanted Priscilla to believe in it too.

Bursting out of the airport's front doors, Alaina waved down a cab.

She couldn't leave. Not yet.

Not without keeping her promise not to give up on love.

The taxi jerked to a stop in front of Priscilla's shop, two traffic-choked, anxiety-riddled hours after Alaina had climbed in. Christmas Day gridlock had nearly unraveled her.

Now her fingers trembled as she shoved cash at the driver and bolted for the curb, her pulse pounding louder than the slamming taxi door. Hope fluttered stubbornly in her chest, fragile and impossible to ignore. She wasn't ready to let it go.

The shop was as silent as the snow-covered streets, and her breath formed little clouds of anxiety as she peered through the glass, searching for a sign of life behind the locked doors. Nothing. Even the lights were off upstairs, no glow around the door that led into Priscilla's apartment.

Alaina glanced at her watch, then looked up at the softening sky, a gradient of pink and orange hues.

She knew where Priscilla was.

The Christmas tree in the town square was stunning, even unlit—a towering spruce that looked at least a hundred feet tall to Alaina, though Priscilla would probably claim it was closer to thirty. Its thick, snow-dusted branches stretched proudly toward the sky, and for a fleeting moment Alaina could almost see how magical it must look when lit up.

But she didn't have time to think about that now. Her lungs

burned from the sprint, her suitcase wheels catching on ice more than once. Her fingers ached from gripping the handle. But none of it mattered.

She scanned the faces with growing urgency, heart pounding with every second she didn't see Priscilla's.

Please be here. Please be here.

"Alaina?"

She turned so fast her balance almost tipped. Callie and Lauren stood nearby, bundled up and blinking in surprise.

"Priscilla—have you seen her?"

Lauren shook her head. "She was here, but she left. You just missed her."

"Which way?" Alaina stood on her toes, trying to see over the crowd.

Callie pointed back down Main Street, and Alaina spun in that direction. The crowd was dense and she'd be moving against the current, but she could push her way through.

"Alaina, wait!" She stopped to turn around, finding Lauren had followed her a few steps into the throng. She wasn't sure what she was expecting Lauren to say, but it certainly wasn't, "Let me hold your bag."

"What?"

"We'll watch your bag. Go get your girl!" Lauren's grin lit up her entire face, and Alaina could finally see how she and Callie made sense together.

"Thank you, thank you, thank you." Alaina gave Lauren a quick squeeze around the shoulders that made the other woman squeak in surprise. And then she was off—shoving through the crowd, pushing past elbows and strollers and puffy coats.

Her eyes searched the crowd as she moved forward. Alaina was almost positive Priscilla would be headed back to the bookstore, but she couldn't wait another minute—she needed to see her here and now.

Come on, come on—yes!

There. She spotted Priscilla's familiar coat on the edge of the crowd. Her shoulders hunched against the cold, her gait slower than usual, like she didn't want to be going wherever she was headed.

Alaina's lungs burned from exertion, but she found her voice anyway. "Priscilla!"

Priscilla froze. Alaina said her name again, and this time, she turned.

"Alaina?" The look on Priscilla's face was nothing short of bewilderment. "You're not in New York."

"No." Alaina came to a stop in front of Priscilla. Her heart slammed against her ribs. "I'm not."

"But—why?"

"I couldn't leave." The words rushed out, breathless and unpolished. God, she wished she had something planned, knew all the perfect words to make Priscilla see how much she wanted this. "Not without telling you how I feel."

Priscilla's expression was unreadable. She looked like she'd stopped breathing. Alaina stepped closer anyway, the air between them thin and charged.

"I know we've only known each other a week—and maybe that's not long enough for this to make sense to anyone else. But it's enough for me. It's been the most incredible week of my life. I can't go back to not knowing you, Sil. I don't want to."

Priscilla's chest rose and fell with quick, shallow breaths that fogged in the cold.

"My whole life I've felt like I was looking for something—like I was always on the outside of everything. Even when I tried my best to be what someone else wanted, it would never work. They would always leave, and I'd be alone."

Her throat closed around the word.

"But not this week. Not with you. I never had to try to be someone else with you. To be honest, at first it didn't even occur to me *to* try. From the very start, you didn't get some version of me that I thought you'd like. You just got me. The real me. And for once, that was enough. You let me in. Your life, your home, your friends. And now I know what I've been missing. What I want."

Her throat tightened. "It's you, Sil. Just you."

This was it. Now or never. Alaina reached for Priscilla's hands and hoped her own weren't shaking too badly.

"I know you're scared. You think I'll leave, or lose interest, and it's safer to be the one to walk away. But I can't let this go without telling you—"

She inhaled, heart balanced on the edge.

"I'm falling in love with you, Sil. And I really, really don't want to stop."

The words lingered, suspended in the cold air. Alaina searched Priscilla's eyes for any hint of what she was thinking, her own heart thudding in her chest. Either the crowd around them had fallen silent, or Alaina was just too focused on Priscilla to notice anything else.

Then, all at once, everything started to glow.

For one wild second, she thought her mind was casting Priscilla in some cinematic illumination. But the crowd erupted into cheers and Alaina turned, stunned, to see the Christmas tree bursting to life, every branch glimmering with soft yellow light as snow began to fall.

A laugh escaped Priscilla, low and startled.

Alaina whipped around. "What?"

Priscilla shook her head, her hands finally gripping Alaina's back. "You just gave me a big romantic, end-of-the-movie speech."

Alaina's breath hitched. "I did, didn't I?" Her lips curved despite the nerves still buzzing in her chest. "Did you like it?"

"It was perfect."

Alaina's heart cracked wide open at those words. A laugh escaped her, unsteady with emotion. "Too perfect?"

Priscilla shook her head. "Just perfect enough." She took a step forward, their hands still joined in front of them. Her voice dropped, brow pinching as she studied Alaina's face. "Are you sure?"

"Sure of what?" Alaina's voice was still breathless.

"Of everything. Of me. That I'm—that I'll be enough. Just me."

Alaina's heart squeezed. For years, she'd begged the world to make her worthy—of family, of Cole. Now here was Priscilla—brilliant, beautiful, kind—asking the same thing. They were both walking around with the same wound, the same fear that they weren't worth staying for.

"You won't be just enough," Alaina said, voice trembling. "You are so much more than enough."

She leaned in, closing the last breath of space between them, and kissed her.

It started soft, tentative. Then Priscilla's arms wrapped around her waist. She pulled her in with a hum, deepening the kiss like she'd been holding back for too long. Alaina melted into it, every nerve singing, the cold forgotten.

When they finally broke apart, foreheads pressed together, breath mingling, Priscilla's thumb brushed a happy tear from Alaina's cheek.

Behind them, a cheer erupted.

Alaina and Priscilla turned to see the smiling faces of the four other people who had come to mean so much to Alaina in such a short time.

Callie let out a giddy squeal as she ran forward and threw her arms around both of them. "Oh, I'm so happy!"

"Me too," Priscilla said. Alaina could hear the smile in Priscilla's voice, and it made her melt.

"Finally!" Grant said. "I was beginning to think the two of you were going to dance around each other forever."

"Lesbians *love* to pine, babe," Ned said.

"I think I'm bi, actually," Alaina said. It was the first time she'd said that out loud, and even though this was probably the safest possible space to come out, it still made her heart race.

He winked at Alaina. "Either way, we've been rooting for you since day one."

"It's only been a week," Lauren said, but even she wore a small smile as she rolled her eyes.

Callie pulled back to look at Alaina. "Does this mean you're going to stay?"

Alaina wasn't sure how to answer. She couldn't just never return to San Francisco—she had a few months left on her lease with Nico, and somehow she didn't think that step one in being a better friend was saddling them with a lease on a two-bedroom apartment.

Priscilla stepped in. "We still need to talk it through."

"This calls for a celebration." Ned stepped up behind Callie. "We're having these two over for Christmas dinner, and we made way too much food. Why don't you guys come along?"

They looked at each other, sharing a smile, and Priscilla was the one to answer.

"We'd love to."

The Christmas tree gleamed through the window of Grant and Ned's house, its lights a comforting, festive sight against the winter's evening chill.

Priscilla's hand found Alaina's, giving it a reassuring squeeze as they sat in the driveway, the truck still warm from the ride over. "Ready to go in?"

"Yeah, just—one thing."

Alaina unbuckled her seatbelt and turned, heart already racing. The quiet street, the dark houses, the way they were totally alone—it was all the convincing Alaina needed that this was a good idea.

"Wha—"

She leaned in, kissing Priscilla hard enough to steal the words right out of her mouth. Gratitude, relief, affection—she poured it all into the kiss. Into the way her hands curved around Priscilla's jaw. Into the way she sighed against her lips like she'd been waiting all day to breathe again.

"Alaina?" Priscilla gasped when they broke apart.

"Mhm?" Alaina pressed a kiss to the corner of Priscilla's mouth, her fingers tracing the hairs at the back of her neck.

Whatever Priscilla was about to say, she must've decided it wasn't important. Her hand wound into Alaina's hair, pulling her back in.

The center console was in the way, but Alaina barely noticed it. She shifted until she was straddling Priscilla's lap, one hand braced against the back of the seat, the other buried in her hair.

Alaina rocked against her, chasing the sharp inhale it earned, the warm press of Priscilla's mouth against her skin. She kissed her way down her jaw, open-mouthed, barely restrained. She didn't care if she left a mark. Priscilla had left one. It was only fair.

But the second her teeth grazed Priscilla's throat, Priscilla caught her wrists and held her still.

"If you keep doing that," she said, voice rough, "we're never going to make it inside."

Alaina stilled. Swallowed. Nodded.

She took a moment to look at Priscilla, admiring her own handiwork—her shirt wrinkled around the collar from Alaina's grip, her hair falling out of its neat bun so strands of it framed her face. She looked like a mess. A very, very hot mess.

Good.

Alaina smiled, swiped her thumb across Priscilla's bottom lip, and kissed her softly once more. Then she grabbed the door handle and stepped out into the cold.

"C'mon," she said, bouncing on her toes like nothing just happened. "It's Christmas!"

❄

After dinner—which was spectacular, thanks to Ned—they all sat in the living room around the lit fireplace. There weren't enough seats for everyone without dragging over some chairs, a problem Alaina was more than happy to solve by draping herself across Priscilla's lap.

She nuzzled in without apology, her fingers idly trailing over the spot on Priscilla's neck she'd kissed earlier.

"Okay, lovebirds. You get one night of PDA, then we're giving you shit," Grant said, but he was smiling.

Lauren looked less amused. "A whole night?"

"I think it's cute," Callie said. She raised her glass. "To Alaina. And her absolutely horrendous driving."

Alaina lifted her glass with a laugh, her heart full. "I'm really glad I got stuck here with all of you."

Grant cleared his throat. "About that."

Alaina turned toward him. "About what?"

"There was never anything wrong with your oil pan."

"Huh?"

"You could've left a week ago," Grant said, shrugging. "But I saw the two of you that first day, and—I don't know. You looked like exactly what Priscilla needed. So I stalled."

Alaina blinked. "You lied?"

Grant's expression didn't shift. "You're welcome."

Ned reached over and took his hand, smiling like this was the most romantic thing he'd ever heard. All this time, and Grant was a secret romantic?

Alaina's mouth dropped open as she connected the dots. "Is that what you and Priscilla were fighting about at the party?"

Grant's shrug didn't deny it. "Maybe."

Alaina felt Priscilla tense underneath her but couldn't find it in herself to be mad. She just felt . . . grateful. Overwhelmed and grateful.

Alaina slid off Priscilla's lap and flung her arms around Grant before he could duck out of reach.

"Thank you."

Grant's hand patted her on the back, and he couldn't hide the fondness in his voice. "Yeah, yeah."

❄

As the evening wound down, Alaina curled beside Priscilla on the couch, content as the others exchanged presents. Priscilla, of course, had nailed every gift. A cookbook for Ned by a chef Alaina had never heard of. An autobiography of Miles Davis for Grant. Callie unwrapped a cozy mystery about a cat detective and squealed with delight. Then Lauren tore into hers—and out came a contemporary romance.

Alaina really had Lauren pegged all wrong.

Callie leaned across the couch to hug Priscilla, then turned to Alaina with a sheepish look. "I feel bad we didn't get you anything. We didn't know you'd still be here."

"Neither did I," Alaina said. "But just being here is gift enough. Besides, I don't exactly have anything for you guys either."

"Next year?"

"Next year," Alaina said. She turned to press a kiss to Priscilla's cheek, soft and certain. "Be right back—I've got something I need to do."

Priscilla's brows creased, the concern in her eyes immediate. But Alaina just smiled, steadier than she felt. Her pulse was racing, but her gut told her this was right.

In the kitchen, she stood at the window and watched snowflakes fall in the moonlight, letting the quiet wrap around her. A familiar ache sat heavy in her chest—grief, once sharp and unbearable, now softer but still present. For years, she'd had so few memories of her mother to cling to, just fragments that felt too precious to examine too closely.

But this week had changed that. Being here in Brooks had unlocked something—memories flooding back in vivid detail, her mother's voice and laughter suddenly as clear as if she were in the next room. And with them came the full picture, not just the golden moments Alaina had treasured. Her mother wasn't only laughter on cozy nights watching rom-coms, or the devastating emptiness left by her absence—she was also the reason Alaina had grown up isolated, far from family, all in the name of chasing love.

For so long, admitting that felt like betrayal. Like she was being ungrateful for the one person who'd loved her unconditionally. When you only had scraps of someone left, criticizing them felt dangerous. What if acknowledging the flaws meant losing what little remained?

But she could see her mother clearly now. The woman who loved fiercely but imperfectly, who had left wounds Alaina was only now letting herself acknowledge, while also teaching her that love was worth fighting for. If her mom could be flawed and still deserving of love, maybe Alaina could be too—messy and uncertain and human, without having to earn her place in the world by being perfect.

She pulled out her phone and pressed a few buttons.

There was a single ring, and then, "Alaina?"

Alaina's voice froze in her throat, years of uncertainty holding her back.

Then, her mother's voice: *You don't give up on love.*

Maybe that counted for this kind of love too.

She took a deep breath, nerves settling. "It's me. Merry Christmas, Shauna."

After the call, Alaina found Priscilla standing alone, staring into the fire. The others were in the dining room, divvying up slices of a pie Ned had brought home from Patty's.

Alaina stepped beside her, close enough their shoulders brushed. The simple contact sent warmth skimming down her spine.

Would she ever get used to that? Probably not.

She nudged Priscilla. "Penny for your thoughts?"

She'd told Priscilla everything she was feeling, but she was still in the dark when it came to where Priscilla was at.

"It's what you said, back at the tree lighting—that you're falling in love with me."

Heat flushed Alaina's cheeks. "Oh. That." She tried for a smile. "I know, I got carried away."

Priscilla's eyebrows shot up. "Did you?"

The question stopped her short. She could make a joke. Deflect. Backpedal.

But this was Priscilla.

"Not really." Then, because vulnerability made her babble, she said, "I probably could've waxed poetic about you for at least another three to four minutes."

Priscilla didn't laugh. Her tongue darted out to wet her lips—a gesture Alaina was learning meant she was working up to something important. "You know I'm falling for you too, right?"

The relief that flooded her body was so immediate, so intense, it was dizzying. Her muscles unwound all at once, like her heart had been holding her hostage all day and finally let go.

"Confirmation is always nice," she murmured, grinning like an idiot.

Priscilla's fingers found hers, interlacing. "It's been a wonderful Christmas, Lani. The best, really. Thanks to you."

"It's my best Christmas too." Alaina beamed, tugging Priscilla closer until her head rested comfortably against her. She took a deep breath, her heart full. "So far, anyway."

Priscilla raised an eyebrow. "Is that a challenge?"

"Maybe. You up for it?"

In the warm glow of the fire, with Priscilla's hand in hers, Alaina knew this was only the beginning.

"Definitely."

One Year Later

Ten Hours Until the New Year

"Should old acquaintance be forgot . . ."

The melody drifted faintly through the walls as Priscilla cracked the door open. There was Alaina, swaying at the stove in her canary-yellow apron—the one Priscilla had wrapped in tissue paper just a week ago. A wooden spoon in hand, her voice soft and uncertain.

"And never . . . ? Shit." Alaina faltered, switching to a hum to fill in the missing words.

Priscilla eased the door shut behind her. "—and never brought to mind."

"Jesus!" Alaina whirled around, brandishing the spoon like she meant to duel.

Priscilla's lips twitched. "Is that your weapon of choice?"

Alaina sighed, dropping the spoon to her side. "How do you always sneak up on me?"

"The better question is why you're so easy to sneak up on."

"I was . . . preoccupied." Alaina turned back to stir the pot a little more aggressively than necessary.

The kitchen was rich with the scent of onions and garlic

sizzling in oil, plus something sweet wafting from the oven. Although Alaina's baking skills far outshone her cooking—especially now that Patty had taken her under her wing at the diner, teaching her the secrets behind those legendary pies—Priscilla always found Alaina's culinary attempts, however experimental, to be a delightful adventure. What she lacked in skill, she made up for in heart.

Priscilla moved behind her, looping her arms around Alaina's waist and resting her cheek against her head. "I like your singing."

"Really?" Alaina chuckled, a playful note in her voice. "Thank you. You know, for a long time, I didn't even realize this was a New Year's song. I just thought it was from *When Harry Met Sally.*"

Priscilla pressed a kiss to her temple. "Of course you did."

"What's that supposed to mean?"

"Just that I know how much you love that movie."

"You liked it too!" Alaina insisted. She was right. Alaina had made a list of holiday movies Priscilla hadn't seen, one for each night in December, and that one had landed near the top. "Oh! Nico called today. They say hi."

"I'm sorry I missed them."

Priscilla really liked Nico. They had visited over the summer to help Alaina move, and had only given Priscilla a little bit of a hard time about stealing their best friend away from California. Alaina had waited until their lease was up to move, and Josie—Nico's newly minted fiancée—was more than happy to take over Alaina's half of the rent and turn the extra bedroom into a craft studio. Now, Nico and Alaina made sure to call at least once a week to catch up. Sometimes Alaina would be on the phone for hours—others, just a few minutes. But she was always smiling after she hung up.

"They want to visit, by the way—both of them. I already talked to Callie and she said she'd give them the friends-and-family rate."

"They're always welcome." Priscilla kissed her cheek, then nuzzled her nose into Alaina's hair. She peered over her shoulder. "How much longer until you're ready?"

"Everything's prepped. Once we're back, it all goes in the oven. Chicken takes an hour and a half to cook and then it needs to rest for another thirty minutes, so we just need to be home by . . . six?"

"I could go by myself, you know."

"No way." Alaina turned in her arms. "I need to leave the house. I crave human interaction."

"You'll have four humans here later. Five, if you count me."

Alaina tipped her head up, planting a sweet kiss on Priscilla's cheek. "You absolutely count. But still, there are a few more things I need to grab from the market. And you promised me a scone."

"Did I now?"

Alaina confirmed with a nod. "You did. And I'm holding you to it."

Priscilla had, in fact, promised Alaina a scone in exchange for all the cooking she'd done to prepare for tonight. In truth, her main goal was to keep Alaina pleasantly distracted as the hours dwindled down to the New Year. Her heart fluttered at the thought of the impending countdown.

"Okay." Reluctantly, Priscilla extricated herself from Alaina's embrace. "I'll just pop into the shower, and then we'll go, all right?"

"I could join you? Save water, you know," Alaina said. "Just give me ten minutes."

"Tempting," Priscilla said, amused. "But if you come in, we'll never leave. I'll be quick. You won't even miss me."

"Impossible," Alaina called out as Priscilla left the room.

The bathroom still held traces of Alaina's morning rush. Her makeup bag was open on the counter, one sock left abandoned on the tile. Priscilla smiled as she went about tidying up, tucking everything back into its designated spot—a habit of hers she'd yet to successfully instill in Alaina.

She reached for one of the towels Alaina loved—plush ones she'd insisted on buying because "every day deserves a little luxury"—and hung it next to the shower before turning the faucet.

The water warmed beneath her hand. She stripped down and stepped into the stream, letting it ease the nerves that had quietly built all day. She wished she had longer to shower, but their friends would be there in a few short hours, and Priscilla was intent on making sure the night would go off without a hitch.

❄

Priscilla had just pulled on her underwear when the bedroom door creaked open. She didn't turn. If Alaina wanted to sneak up on her, she'd let her. Fair was fair.

Even knowing she was there, Priscilla couldn't suppress a shiver as Alaina's arms encircled her waist. Alaina's lips brushed her spine, featherlight at first, then firmer, more purposeful. A line of kisses trailed up to the nape of her neck, each one sending a ripple through her.

"Alaina, we really shouldn't—"

Her protest broke off in a gasp as Alaina's mouth found her ear. "We've got hours," Alaina whispered. "Everything's ready. I swear."

Priscilla sighed, already leaning back into her. Alaina's fingers traced along her sides, up past her breasts, flattening over her sternum as Alaina pulled her close. Heat bloomed low in her stomach.

"We have to go to the store." It sounded weak, even to her own ears. Priscilla's resolve was fading fast.

"We will." Another kiss, right behind her ear. "But first, let me help you relax."

Alaina took a step back, and Priscilla instinctively turned to face her. She found Alaina looking at her with an all-too-familiar grin, the one she wore when she knew Priscilla was incapable of telling her no. Hands on Priscilla's shoulders, Alaina guided her to sit on the edge of the bed, then straddled her lap.

Priscilla's palms slid instinctively to Alaina's hips. "What's got you so worked up?"

"You left me alone for too long. You know how my mind wanders." Alaina's hands reached for Priscilla's, dragging them around and lower until they were cupping her from behind.

"So this is my fault?"

"Entirely." Alaina moved against her, teeth digging into her lip as she smiled. "But you can make it up to me."

Priscilla was ready to respond—with something clever, certainly—but Alaina kissed her before she could speak, hands framing her jaw, mouth insistent and hungry.

They toppled back together, Alaina's hair framing both of their faces as they lay against the bed. Priscilla used one hand to push it away, fingers curling to hold it in place, while her other hand gripped Alaina's hip, guiding her into a slow grind.

Priscilla realized quickly how unevenly matched they were—her nearly naked, fresh from the shower, while Alaina was still dressed. Alaina must've had the same thought; she tugged her shirt up, both of them laughing when it snagged around her shoulders.

Priscilla pulled it off and rolled them, savoring the startled exhale from Alaina as her back hit the bed. She dipped her head to Alaina's throat and sucked gently, smiling at the sharp intake of breath it earned her.

"Thought—*ah*—thought you were in a rush." Alaina's head lolled to the side, giving her more access.

Priscilla didn't respond, just scraped her teeth against the bared skin beneath her lips, enjoying the way Alaina's pulse picked up a few extra beats. If Alaina had to wear a little extra makeup later, then so be it. Priscilla wasn't the one who started this.

She took her time. She always did. Her hips rolled lazily, keeping just enough distance to make Alaina chase after her, the tension mounting with every near contact. Her fingers hooked in the waistband of Alaina's pants, lingered—then changed course, trailing up her ribs, nails scraping lightly over skin.

Alaina squirmed, trying to kick her pants off without breaking the moment. Priscilla smiled against her chest, lips finding a nipple, tongue flicking, teeth grazing. When Alaina's hips jerked upward, she slid a hand down.

"Impatient." She marked the word with a teasing bite against Alaina's chest. It wasn't hard enough to leave a bruise, but Alaina let out a breathless whine at the pull of her teeth anyway.

Alaina's hand covered hers, guided it lower, fingers pressing hers against soaked fabric. "Please."

Normally, Priscilla would've gone slowly. Drawn things out. Made Alaina beg a little.

Maybe that's why Alaina's breath hitched in surprise when Priscilla slid her underwear aside and pushed in without warning, her fingers finding that exact spot like they were made for it. The sound Alaina made—half gasp, half moan—bordered on obscene.

Not that she was ever shy about letting Priscilla know what she liked.

"Fuck, Sil, you—" Alaina's voice cracked as her hips jerked, desperate for more. Priscilla watched for a moment, enjoying the show—Alaina's head tilted back, her eyes slammed shut, her lip trapped between her teeth as she exhaled heavy breath after heavy breath. "*Fuck.*"

Only then did she start to move. Just her fingers at first, slow and steady, until Alaina began to meet her rhythm, hips rising in sync with each thrust. Nails dug into Priscilla's shoulders, anchoring her, urging her closer.

"More," Alaina panted. "Please. More."

Priscilla shuddered. That voice—needy, wrecked—tore straight through her. She gave in easily, eagerly, until Alaina's hand suddenly shot beneath her body. "Wait, wait—you too."

Priscilla barely had time to process before Alaina's fingers slid between her legs. Her breath stuttered out, sharp, and Alaina's smile turned wicked with satisfaction. Her touch was slow, maddening and deliberate.

A groan clawed its way up Priscilla's throat, and Alaina arched into her in response.

"Baby, I need—yes, just like—oh *god,* Sil."

Suddenly, Alaina's hand pulled away. Priscilla would've protested the loss if she hadn't been so focused on the look on Alaina's face—eyes shut tight, lips parted, cheeks flushed. Slick fingers caught Priscilla's wrist, tugging her closer until her palm was flat against Alaina again.

Priscilla leaned down so their foreheads were touching. "Take what you need."

Alaina nodded, the motion jerky and desperate, and then she was grinding against Priscilla's hand like she was chasing the edge with everything she had.

She could never get tired of this. Sex, before Alaina, had been perfunctory—fine, physical, but never like this. Never like discovering something new every single time.

It had been over a year since that first night, but it didn't feel routine. If anything, it felt cumulative. Every touch layered with memory. Every kiss charged with something deeper. She knew now how Alaina lost her ability to speak when Priscilla curled her fingers just right. How she whispered Priscilla's name like it was a prayer. How she always wanted to be kissed as she came.

So Priscilla kissed her.

Alaina's lips were cool from her ragged breathing, her mouth slack and soft. It wasn't a real kiss—Alaina was too far gone for that—but Priscilla stole what she could, suckling gently on Alaina's bottom lip to catch the sounds she made as her thighs clamped tight around Priscilla's hand and her back curved off the mattress.

Minutes later, Alaina blinked at her, hair plastered to her forehead, breath uneven, chest flushed. Priscilla couldn't look away.

"This was supposed to be about you." Alaina's cheeks were pink with something between embarrassment and bliss.

Priscilla dropped a kiss against Alaina's shoulder. "This was very much about me, trust me. I'm great."

Alaina huffed a breath of laughter. "Could you be better?"

That smile—lopsided, smug, soft around the edges—was all the convincing Priscilla needed. She kissed her swollen lip, and when Alaina deepened it, she didn't bother pretending to resist.

Eight Hours Until the New Year

Alaina insisted on going to the café first—*I worked up an appetite, Sil!*—before they tackled the rest of their errands. By the time they arrived, the lunch rush had faded, and the space had settled into a quiet lull.

Still, Priscilla turned to Alaina as soon as they got inside. "Why don't you find us a seat? I'll handle our order."

"Sounds like a plan," Alaina said with a peck on Priscilla's cheek.

Priscilla joined the short queue, skimming the café's menu on the board overhead although she already knew what she wanted.

"May I have a croissant, a flat white, and also—"

"A bee sting and an orange scone for Alaina?" Matt, the barista, said with a smile, his eyes drifting past her.

Priscilla turned to see Alaina grinning back at them.

"Yes, that's right." She couldn't help but smile, appreciating the small touch of familiarity in their routine. "Thank you, Matt."

He put in the order before returning to the register. "That'll be nine dollars and fifty-four cents." Priscilla raised her eyebrows. She'd already done the math—it should be closer to thirteen.

Matt shrugged. "The scone is on the house. Customer loyalty program."

Priscilla had been coming here for years and had never heard of a loyalty program. She didn't press. She knew why. Alaina had that effect on people. Even Lauren had admitted that she had "a soft spot" for Priscilla's girlfriend. It had taken months, and nearly a full bottle of wine, for her to own up to it, but it had happened nonetheless.

"Thank you," she said.

"I'll bring it over when it's ready."

"Oh, you don't have to—"

"I insist." He flashed her a warm smile. "You go, be with her."

Priscilla did her best to return it just as brightly. "Thank you."

Alaina was waiting at a window table, glowing in the soft afternoon sun. The natural light played beautifully across her features—the slant of her smile, the glint in her eye, the tip of her nose still pink from the cold.

"What are you looking at?" Alaina asked, catching her mid-stare.

Priscilla slipped into the seat across from her, still smiling. "You."

Alaina lit up, her hand reaching automatically for Priscilla's across the table.

Seven Hours Until the New Year

The grocery run was taking longer than Priscilla had planned.

Alaina kept tossing last-minute items into their cart: oranges, for the old-fashioneds she planned on making; rosemary garnish for the chicken; an unnecessary amount of ice cream to go on top of the pie.

By the time they made it to the liquor store, Priscilla could practically feel her nerves fraying, ready to snap like an overstretched elastic band. A glance at her watch confirmed it: they were running out of time before their friends descended on their apartment. She'd wanted to do a final sweep before they arrived.

Alaina brushed her elbow gently. "Everything all right?"

Priscilla nodded. "Yes, everything's absolutely fine. It's just . . . they seem to be out of your preferred pinot noir."

Alaina looked at the bottle in Priscilla's hand. "Oh, but I like this one just as much." Priscilla knew this wasn't true, but was grateful to Alaina for trying to make her feel better.

"We could make a quick stop at the other liquor store. It's on the way—"

"This one is great." Alaina took the bottle from her hands and set it in the cart. "Let's grab this, a white, and a bottle of that bourbon Grant likes. Then we can get back so you can at least be adorably stressed in the comfort of our own home."

"Thank you." Priscilla planted a swift kiss on Alaina's lips.

"Sil, baby." Alaina laced their fingers together. "You know tonight doesn't have to be perfect. Our friends are going to have a great time, no matter what wine we have."

Priscilla let out a deep breath, though it did little to release the tension in her shoulders. "I know, I know."

It was a lie. Tonight, she needed everything to be perfect.

Five Hours Until the New Year

Priscilla swung open the door to Brooks Books to find Grant and Ned on the other side.

"Long time no see," Grant said with a grin.

They had just celebrated Christmas at the couple's house with a delightful dinner that seemed destined to become an annual tradition. Alaina had immediately offered to return the favor for New Year's.

Priscilla led them up the stairs, making easy conversation about what they'd been up to since Christmas. Grant had spent most of that time playing video games on the new system Ned had gotten for him, and Ned had managed to read two out of the three books Priscilla had gifted him.

"It's a miracle I'm able to read at all, what with the constant shooting and all—"

Grant held up his hands. "I told you I would use headphones.

You can't pretend like you're not interested when you're asking me questions about it every two seconds."

At the sound of their voices, Alaina burst from the bedroom, practically skidding to a halt in her socks. "Hey! You're early."

Grant checked his watch. "By five minutes."

Alaina grinned. "Which means, since I'm always ten minutes late, you're basically fifteen minutes early."

Priscilla shook her head with a smile. "That's not how that works, darling."

Alaina momentarily adopted a playful pout before eagerly embracing each of their friends. "Give me your coats, I'll toss them on the bed."

Priscilla mixed the drinks, combining the bourbon, sugar, and bitters before topping them with a twist of orange peel. Beside her, Alaina was adding the final touches to the meal. She had planned most of the dishes to require minimal attention once their guests had arrived, though the food wouldn't be ready for another hour.

It was just after seven when Priscilla's phone buzzed with a text from Callie that they were waiting outside. Priscilla headed down to greet them.

Callie threw her arms around Alaina as soon as she entered the apartment. "Oh, I missed you!"

Priscilla smiled at the sight. Callie and Lauren had spent just over a week visiting Callie's family in Canada for the holidays. It was strange not seeing them for that long—a stark contrast to before Alaina's arrival when Priscilla often wouldn't see her friends for weeks at a time. Another one of the many, many reasons she was grateful to have Alaina in her life.

"I missed you! And you, Lauren." Alaina flashed a cheeky grin over Callie's shoulder. "Don't worry, you don't have to say it. I know you missed me too."

Lauren rolled her eyes, but there was no bite to it.

Callie grabbed Alaina's hand, leading her away. "Come on, I want to show you the pictures! And where's Miss Lola?"

Four Hours Until the New Year

As the night wore on, Priscilla's nerves didn't vanish so much as fade into the background—a low, persistent hum under her skin. By the time dinner was served, she almost managed to ignore them.

Their table was small for six people, but they made it work by having Alaina squeeze in next to Priscilla, Callie doing the same with Lauren on the opposite side. They left the serving dishes on the kitchen counter, buffet style.

It was probably the best meal Alaina had made yet: decadent squash soup, wine-braised chicken with crème fraîche, fresh pasta, roasted sprouts, stuffed mushrooms, bacon-wrapped dates—it was enough food for twelve, and then some.

Priscilla couldn't stop watching Alaina as she beamed at each first bite, scanning every face for a reaction. When Grant gave a satisfied sigh, Alaina lit up. Priscilla reached for her hand, squeezing it gently. Alaina turned to her, grinning, before finally digging in herself.

After dinner, Callie and Lauren insisted on being the ones to clear the table. Alaina couldn't stand idly by, so she was leaning against the counter near the stove, directing them where to put things. Lola sat next to her, overseeing the whole ordeal.

Priscilla made her way into the living room, where Grant and Ned had already claimed the couch. She knew chatting with them would help settle the nerves she could feel rising again now that the meal was over.

Grant looked up as she approached. "Hey, Sil."

"You two having a nice time?"

"Perfect." Ned's smile was wide and knowing. "How are you feeling?"

"Good."

Grant nodded toward the kitchen. "Your girl can really cook."

"She'd be delighted to hear you say that."

"I'll be sure not to tell her then."

Grant's gaze drifted to the wall of framed photos, and Priscilla's followed it. New additions dotted the collection—the photo Alaina had given her last Christmas, a shot of the whole group when they'd driven to California to surprise Alaina for her birthday, the one Ned had sent of Alaina grinning in Patty's kitchen on her first day, a snapshot of them dancing at Ned and Grant's wedding that summer. And, of course, Alaina's favorite—their faces pressed together, smiling out on the lake last winter—was in the middle.

Ned broke the silence. "I can't believe it's been a year already. It feels like just last month the two of you were ordering dessert at an ungodly hour at Patty's."

Priscilla nodded. "And at the same time, it feels so much longer."

"Yeah. Time is funny like that." Grant leaned in a little closer, dropping his voice so only Priscilla could hear. "So, you more excited, or nervous?"

She kept her eyes on Alaina, who was laughing now, hands gesturing wildly as she spoke with Callie. The nerves that had dulled during dinner came surging back.

"Very much both."

Grant raised an eyebrow. "You know she's going to say yes."

It was true; Priscilla and Alaina had discussed their future extensively. Alaina had been clear from the start that she wanted Priscilla in her life forever, that she couldn't imagine her life with anyone else, that she loved her. But still.

"I know. Or at least, I think I do. It's just . . . I want everything to be perfect. I'm not exactly adept at conveying my feelings." Priscilla gestured vaguely, as if trying to physically grasp the right words.

"You? Not good with words?" Ned raised an eyebrow incredulously. "You're one of the most articulate people I've ever met. I find that hard to believe."

"I'm not—at least not like Alaina. She has this way of expressing how she feels so effortlessly, so beautifully. I often find myself feeling inadequate. Like I can't quite capture the depth of my feelings for her in words."

Grant placed a comforting hand on her shoulder, giving it a reassuring squeeze. "You're going to do great. Just be yourself and speak from the heart. She's going to love whatever you say."

That's what scared her the most. Her heart still tended to stutter around Alaina, even after a year together. The last thing she wanted was to be a flustered mess.

Noticing her lingering hesitation, Grant leaned in closer, lowering his voice to a whisper. "So, are you going to show us the ring?"

It was a whisper, but Priscilla's pulse immediately began to race at the words being spoken out loud, like even mentioning it might jinx something. She glanced over—Alaina was still happily chatting with Callie and Lauren, oblivious.

Priscilla was grateful for the distraction their friends provided. She knew that if she were left alone with Alaina for the entirety of the night, her nerves might just betray her intentions.

Priscilla angled her body away, then slipped her hand into her pocket, retrieving the small black velvet box she had been nervously fidgeting with all evening.

Grant's eyes widened when she opened it. "Wow."

The ring she had chosen was delicate—a thin gold band, adorned with a modest yet sparkling emerald at its center. She had stumbled upon it months ago, well before she had even considered making the purchase.

Ned leaned in, admiring it. "It's perfect. Just like her."

"Babe?" Alaina's voice broke through the moment.

Priscilla startled, the ring box snapping shut in her hands. She tucked it out of sight before turning, her heart hammering in her chest.

"Can you help me get ready for dessert?"

As Priscilla rinsed off the dessert plates, dusty from disuse in their cabinet, Alaina stood beside her, towel in hand, ensuring the dish rack never overflowed.

Afterward, Priscilla shut off the tap, briskly shaking her hands to flick away the water droplets.

Alaina bumped her shoulder lightly. "So, how did I do?"

Priscilla's eyebrows knit together in confusion. "With what?"

"I mean, I know tonight was important to you. You seemed really on edge. Was the food okay?"

"It was incredible. Grant even went back for seconds."

"You think so?" Alaina's eyes sparkled, her smile blooming.

Priscilla nodded, then kissed her temple.

"I don't know if I tell you enough, but I'm really happy here." Alaina sounded choked up, and when Priscilla pulled back slightly, she found Alaina's eyes glossy. Alaina sniffled. "Sorry."

Priscilla cupped her cheek. "It's the wine," she said softly.

"It makes me sappy," Alaina said, finishing with a laugh. She leaned into the touch, her voice a whisper. "I love you."

The oven timer interrupted them. Alaina reluctantly broke away to attend to the dessert. Priscilla watched as she plated slices of the homemade apple pie, topping each with melting scoops of vanilla ice cream. Observing Alaina in this simple moment, Priscilla couldn't help but marvel at just how lucky she was.

Two Hours Until the New Year

Priscilla glanced at her watch for what felt like the hundredth time that evening. Just past ten. She was torn between wanting time to speed up and wishing it would slow down.

Across the room, Callie caught her eye. "You okay?" she mouthed.

Priscilla nodded, probably too fast, judging by the way Callie bit back a smile.

She'd confided in Callie about her plans during a phone call while Callie was in Canada. Priscilla had barely finished the sentence before Callie shrieked loud enough to blow her eardrum. Lauren took the phone away from her to offer congratulations, which Priscilla insisted she hold off on until Alaina had answered the question.

"How about we play a game?" Callie's suggestion broke through Priscilla's thoughts, and she felt a wave of gratitude for the distraction. Sitting still and waiting for the next couple of hours felt like an impossible task at the moment.

"Charades?" Alaina said, her eyes seeking Priscilla's for agreement.

"Only if we mix up the teams this time," Grant groaned. "I'm tired of being demolished by you two."

"I think it's cute how well they work together." Callie looked over at Priscilla, barely able to contain her grin. Behind Alaina's back, Priscilla widened her eyes at Callie, silently begging her to keep her excitement under wraps. "But yeah, let's switch it up. I call Alaina!"

One Hour Until the New Year

Priscilla busied herself mixing another round of drinks for everyone. She had abstained from drinking throughout the night, wanting a clear head, but if Alaina had picked up on it, she hadn't mentioned anything.

Returning to the group, Priscilla overheard Alaina exclaiming, "We have to watch *New Year's Rockin' Eve*!"

Grant was frowning at her, the remote in his hand. "But isn't New York two hours ahead of us? The ball already dropped there."

"I recorded it!" Alaina held her hand out for the remote. "If we press play in exactly—forty-three seconds now—we'll be perfectly synced."

Priscilla shot Grant a look that begged him not to push.

He caught it immediately. "All right," he said, holding the remote out. "*New Year's Rockin' Eve* it is."

Thirty Minutes Until the New Year

"I'll be right back!" Alaina said, disappearing into the bathroom.

The door clicked shut. All eyes turned to Priscilla.

"Stop it." Priscilla sank deep into the couch, uncomfortable with the sudden attention.

Grant chuckled. "Look at that, she's blushing."

"I am not."

"Don't be nervous," Callie whispered softly, leaning in.

"I'm fine," Priscilla said, though her voice betrayed a tiny wobble.

"Thank you for letting us be a part of this." Callie's voice remained soft, but her smile was radiant. "This is, like, the highlight of my life."

"Hey!" Lauren said, frowning at Callie. "I thought you didn't 'believe in the institution of marriage.'"

"I don't!" Callie exclaimed. Priscilla held a finger up to her lips, her eyes flying over to the bathroom door. Callie lowered her voice to a whisper when she continued. "But this is love, and I am *all in* for love!"

Ned reached over, giving Priscilla's knee a reassuring squeeze. "You've got this. She's going to say yes."

Priscilla nodded faintly, swallowing against the tightness in her throat. She knew Alaina loved her. That wasn't the question. But Alaina had made so many moments magical for her—Priscilla just wanted to return the favor. To make this one unforgettable.

The sound of the faucet cut off.

When Alaina stepped into the room, all eyes turned toward her. She paused, blinking at the unexpected attention. "What?" she asked, eyes narrowing. "Do I have something on my face?"

"No!" Priscilla said quickly, bolting upright. She hesitated for half a second, then reached for Alaina's hand. "We were just—"

"Waiting for you. You're the life of the party, kid," Grant said, his tone surprisingly genuine. Maybe Alaina wasn't the only sappy drunk.

"Right." Priscilla extended her hand to Alaina. "Come on, you're missing the show."

One Minute Until the New Year

Everyone stood, drinks forgotten, the energy in the room palpable. Alaina, oblivious to the buzz of nerves, tugged Priscilla forward as the countdown began.

"Ten, nine, eight, seven . . ."

Priscilla's fingers curled tight around the velvet box in her pocket.

"Six, five, four . . ."

She shifted her weight, heart pounding, and dropped to one knee.

Some couples waited much longer before taking this next step. Grant and Ned had spent nearly six years together before finally deciding to get engaged. For Alaina and Priscilla, it had only been a year, but those almost four hundred days already felt like an eternity in the best way.

Priscilla was ready for countless more lifetimes together. The box came out smooth and steady—just like she'd practiced.

"Three . . ."

Alaina still hadn't noticed.

"Two . . ."

Priscilla opened the box.

"One—happy New Year!"

The room erupted—cheers, clinking glasses, laughter—and then Alaina turned, grinning, looking for Priscilla. It took a moment, but her eyes eventually found her kneeling and waiting, and Alaina's expression transformed.

"Sil?"

"Auld Lang Syne" played in the background, Times Square a distant blur.

Alaina's eyes brightened, joy spreading across her features. And just like that, the last of Priscilla's nerves dissolved.

The smile on Alaina's face told her all she needed to know.

Acknowledgments

Writing a book, it turns out, is not something you do alone. Physically, sure, I wrote most of this book at five in the morning while everyone I know was (understandably) asleep. But I have never once felt lonely during this process, and that is because of the people on these pages.

Thank you first to my editor, Katy, who saw exactly what this story could be and helped me get it there. Your notes made me laugh out loud more times than I can count. Working with you has been an absolute joy!

To my agent, Patrice, whose love of cheesy holiday romance made all of this possible. I will be forever grateful that you took a chance on me.

Thank you also to JP, Whitney, Avideh, Donna, and everyone at the Dial Press who worked to bring this book into the world, and to all at the Caldwell Agency for their dedication and support behind the scenes.

Now for the people who had to live with me while I wrote and edited this thing.

To Katina, my partner, my best friend, and my confidant:

Thank you for listening to endless tangents, for having the patience of a saint, and for knowing exactly when to tell me I'm stretching myself too thin. I am, and will always be, your biggest fan. Also, thank you for marrying me! That was pretty cool of you.

Katie, my sister and partner in crime. You are a brilliant writer, and you're going to write a book whether you like it or not. There are so many things I wouldn't be able to do without you, and publishing this book is near the top of that list.

To my mom, whose inspirational drive and determination as a dedicated journalist shaped who I am. You were my first teacher, and you made sure I loved to read from the very start. Thank you for reading my book even though you rarely read fiction, and for telling me you thought happily-ever-afters were silly but loved mine anyway.

To my dad, who read every draft and then asked for more. I don't know what else to say except thank you. Thank you for teaching me to be goofy, to have fun, and to not take things so seriously. You've made me a better writer and a better person.

Hannah and James, my dearest friends. Being creative alongside you both inspires me to keep chasing ridiculous dreams.

To my bookstore family at Barnes & Noble, who have made me love books even more than I thought possible (and who make me blush every time my book comes up): thank you.

Amber, thank you for the stunning cover and all the promo art. You are incredibly talented and somehow manage to bring even my blurriest visions to life.

This story started its life as fanfic, and I wouldn't be here without the community that encouraged me from the beginning. Silas, thank you for your editing when this book was just a baby. Ashley, Erin, Haley, Smalls, Fiddle, Ang, Goey, Maddie, Halley, Al, Alex (and Alex!), Mercedes, and so many more: A shared love of characters brought us together, and even though it's been years and we've scattered to different corners of the fandom world, I'm still so grateful for each of you. You came from across the world to be at my wedding. I love you all!

And to everyone I'm inevitably forgetting: Thank you. My book exists because of you.

A Very Merry Detour

Court Behr

Dial Delights

Love Stories for the Open-Hearted

PATTY'S FAMOUS CINNAMON ROLLS

Makes 9–12 rolls

DOUGH

1½ cups whole milk
3 tablespoons butter
⅔ cup granulated sugar
1 tablespoon salt
2 packages active dry yeast (¼-ounce package)
5 to 6 cups all-purpose flour

FILLING

Patty refused to give exact measurements and told me to "measure with my heart" but my heart likes it a lot sweeter than Sil! Half cup sugar if just for me, a third if sharing with Priscilla.

Butter, melted
Granulated sugar
Cinnamon

ICING

Mom's had some sort of citrus. Patty suggested trying orange zest! Maybe OJ in dough?? Have to experiment!

4 ounces cream cheese, softened
2 tablespoons butter, softened
1 teaspoon vanilla extract
⅔ cup powdered sugar

UPDATE: OJ IS DELISH!!! You have to reduce amount of milk, though, about half milk/half OJ (now I sound like Patty).

DIRECTIONS

1. Preheat the oven to 350°F. Grease a 9 by 13 by 2-inch pan.

2. In a medium saucepan, heat the milk and butter until the butter melts. DO NOT BOIL!!! Let cool.

3. In a large bowl, place the milk and butter mixture.

4. In a separate bowl, whisk together the granulated sugar, salt, yeast, and five cups of the flour.

5. Gradually add the dry ingredients to the wet ingredients, mixing until just combined. Add more flour if dough seems too wet. Cover with a dish towel. Let rise until dough doubles in size.

6. Punch down the dough. Turn out onto a floured board. With a rolling pin, shape dough into a rectangle about ⅓ inch thick.

7. Spread melted butter over the dough. Sprinkle with sugar and cinnamon.

Instagram says to use floss to cut. NOT MINT!!!!

8. Roll up the dough like a jelly roll. Cut into ½-inch slices. Place in greased pan.

9. Bake in the preheated oven for 30 minutes.

10. To make the icing: in a medium bowl, beat the cream cheese, butter, vanilla extract, and powdered sugar until smooth and fluffy.

11. Spread the icing over the warm rolls.

© SAM LESSER PHOTOGRAPHY

Court Behr is a journalist turned graphic artist living on Long Island, New York. She writes heartwarming queer romance and shares a cozy home with her spouse, Katina, and their three cats. Believing that queer people deserve to see themselves in all the love stories, Court focuses on writing the happy endings for sapphic relationships. When she's not writing, you can find her hanging out in her local bookstore, experimenting with new recipes, or attempting to finish puzzles before her cats can dismantle them.

@courtbehrauthor